Glasscock, Sarah,
1952-

Anna Lmno

$17.45   g

DATE			

ANNA   L · M · N · O

Sarah Glasscock

ANNA
L·M·N·O

RANDOM HOUSE

NEW YORK

Library of Congress Cataloging-in-Publication Data
Glasscock, Sarah, 1952-
Anna Lmno.
I. Title.
PS3557.L346A8   1988   813'.54   87-43223
ISBN 0-394-55930-4

Manufactured in the United States of America
Typography and binding design by J. K. Lambert
98765432
First Edition

In memory of my father,

JAMES WILSON GLASSCOCK,

who wanted to go to Mexico and write short stories,

and for my mother,

JEAN EPPERSON GLASSCOCK

ANNA   L·M·N·O

hen the telephone woke Anna, she saw Grace Nettinger standing beside the bed, holding a pair of hair-cutting scissors. She was irritated that Grace had gotten into the house and found her good scissors. Reaching up to take the scissors away, Anna remembered that Grace was dead. She had committed suicide the day before by dissolving a bottle of Percodan in a bottle of bourbon.

Anna took a sip of warm beer from a bottle on the floor and waited for the phone to stop ringing. It was bound to be bad news or an obscene caller. Nobody else would call at two in the morning and let the phone ring and ring and ring. She hit her chest hard as if that would slow her heart. She didn't believe in omens or ghosts, but it was a bad sign that the call had dragged Grace Nettinger out of some dream to stand beside the bed.

The phone rang five more times before Anna got out of bed and walked into the hall. "Hang up. Quick," she said before she picked up the receiver.

Giving the caller a last chance to hang up, she pressed her palm against the earpiece to warm it.

"Her hair's not right," a girl's voice said, speaking very fast as if she were rehearsing what to say. "It's all wrong. The part. Everything. You have to come fix it."

"Who is this?"

"It's Delia Nettinger," the girl said impatiently. "I remembered you did her hair. I don't know how to fix it. The funeral's not till eleven. You have to come. Please," she pleaded.

"Jo Anderson always handles the clients at the funeral home—"

"You did her hair for ten years. You *know* her hair. You can make it do what it's supposed to. Jo doesn't know her hair, not like you do. . . ."

Anna shivered and was almost grateful for the breaks in the girl's voice. The conversation couldn't last much longer. All she wanted to do was go back to bed. "Okay, okay. I'll be there at eight-thirty." She hung up and ran to the bedroom.

The sheets were still warm. Hoping that Delia Nettinger would reconsider and call Jo, Anna reset the alarm for eight. If Grace Nettinger had waited one more day, she would have had her hair done. The world might have looked different then. Her daughter could be sleeping now instead of making desperate phone calls. Grace's husband wouldn't have had to call the shop to cancel her weekly appointment. At least Grace Nettinger would have gone out looking like herself.

The sound of the clock ticked its way through the covers. Anna pulled a pillow over her ears and found herself straining to hear the clock. She wished Bryan were home to distract her.

There was no sense in staring wide-eyed at the underside of a quilt. Anna sat up and turned on the lamp. Her bankbook was in the nightstand along with a notebook containing the shop's quarterly inventories for the last five years. By three-thirty she had triple-checked the figures and assured herself that in a year she would have enough money to buy the shop, fixtures and inventory.

Spring had the upper hand on the day of Grace's funeral. After almost a week of bowling tumbleweeds down streets, the March wind had squandered its energy. Every now and then a maverick gust slung dust particles into Anna's legs. The hard, radiating blueness of the West Texas sky made her fight to keep her eyes open. She welcomed the burning in her legs and her eyes. She was alive. Another wind ambushed her and whipped her along. Look what Grace Nettinger had already missed.

Crossing the bridge by the newest satellite dish company, Anna wondered if the creek would ever flow again. The town of Alpine had four bridges spanning the dry bed, and there were six other low-water crossings where a motorist took a chance if there was any rain in the mountains. The bridges hadn't been built to transport anybody over water; they were there, where the banks were too steep, to take people from one side to the other. Anna leaned against a concrete abutment and studied the creek. It was hard to believe that water had ever run slowly and graciously through this town. She didn't know where the water had gone.

Last summer a flash flood had come out of the mountains northwest of town. Anna had seen the first wave of brown water charge around the bend in front of Mary Frances's shop. The beauty shop sat on the creek's high side. At first Anna had watched from an upstairs window as the water rose higher and higher. Lawn chairs stolen out of backyards tumbled along the current. Moving to the ground floor to stand in the front door, she had wanted to jump into the wild and childish rush of it, to join in and be swept away. It hadn't mattered that young trees had been uprooted and forced downstream to the last bridge north of town, where they formed a natural barrier. Anna believed that she could fight the water and could go where she wanted to go.

For a whole day people had gathered on the banks to watch the water. They sat on their car hoods, and Anna could almost hear the ranchers urging the water to slow down, to stay. But by midafternoon the streams in the mountains had dried up, and by nightfall the creek was dry again. Flood or no flood, Brewster County was still the largest county in the United States, and still one of the driest.

Catcalls and whistles from the red-brick jail that squatted cater-cornered took Anna's attention away from the creek. Resurrected by the noise, a hangover headache spiked her right eye. The white stucco funeral home waited on the east corner. Anna wondered why she had agreed to repair Grace's hair. For points, she told herself. For points.

The pearl gray fin of a Cadillac hearse protruded from the funeral home's garage. Richard Pullock answered when Anna rang the bell. He escorted her down the hall, squeezing her elbow, judging the amount of life still left in her. The cold touch of his manicured hands accentuated her hangover. Anna hated to think where his hands had been. She didn't know how Jo could stand to give him a manicure every Thursday.

Delia jumped up when they entered. Her pink lids retracted as if she hoped the air would keep her silver-plated eyes dry. The girl's wild straw hair needed more help than her mother's did.

"Thanks for coming, Anna. Really. Thank you." Delia stopped and looked at Richard Pullock until he bowed himself out of the room. "I couldn't think who else to call. I had to call. You can see—you can see that what they've done to her is all wrong. Anybody can see that."

Stands of flowers guarding the opened bronze coffin brushed against Anna's bare arms. Grace's body looked more relaxed in death. All the tension had taken refuge in her hair. Electrified brown strands of hair clung to the satin pillow. Anna held her breath and bent over the casket. Not wanting to release any of the unhappiness that had settled in Grace's hair, she kept her touch lighter than usual.

The waves that Anna had manipulated for ten years failed to respond. Hair threaded itself around her fingers. There was no telling what Richard Pullock had used on Grace's hair, but Anna wasn't about to start from scratch with shampoo and conditioner. Delia's expectations and a belief in her own abilities kept her over the casket for another ten minutes. She hated being unprepared and trapped. Finally she leaned on the casket and asked Delia, "What about flowers in her hair?"

Delia maintained her distance. "You can't do anything, can you? It's no use, is it?" The admission seemed to give her impetus and she took charge. "If you'll hand me some of those irises and baby's breath, and a couple of those daffodils, I'll make a wreath."

Fighting an urge to flip the cards on the arrangements and read them, Anna separated flowers from their sprays. The cream-colored room was too warm. Floor-length curtains covered two of the windowless walls. Hypnotized by the rhythm of Delia's childlike fingers and overpowered by the fragrance they released, Anna felt as if she were competing with the flowers for the same air and losing. She didn't see why they couldn't fill the creek for a day and just let Grace float downstream.

"I learned this at camp," Delia said conversationally. "Who'd ever think it would come in handy? It's a good thing I'm in college. Who knows what I'll come up against next?" The flowers trembled as the girl suddenly shielded her eyes with the wreath.

"It's pretty." Anna wanted to say more, to explain to Delia that she had a hangover, that she was sorry but she didn't understand why the three of them were in this fake pint-size living room, that Grace had been one of her few customers who had never skimmed the mirror with those furtive looks of hope and fear. Grace had always met the mirror head on. Until now Anna had admired her for that. "It's pretty," she repeated, touching the smooth petals and bringing the wreath back to Delia's lap.

"Do you think so?" Delia asked and twisted the wreath critically. "It's not bad, I guess. With what I had to work with." She eased a balky iris out of the wreath and asked, "Why do you think she did it?"

Anna felt as if she'd been conned, surprised first by the phone call and now by the sudden question coming from somebody who should already have the answer. "I don't know," she said crossly and immediately regretted her tone. "I'm sorry. I really don't know."

"It's okay." Delia shrugged. "I don't know either. Why should you?" She handed the wreath to Anna. "I keep thinking, though,

that probably in about ten years some guy'll be sacking my groceries and he'll say, when he realizes who I am, that it was too bad
about my mother and he'll come out with the real reason, like all
the world knew, or maybe a teller at the bank." She paused to fluff
the petals of a miniature rose. "Or maybe the woman who did her
hair for all those years." She laughed and choked. "Ten years from
now, just when I've beaten it all down. I can't wait."

The smell of Richard Pullock's after-shave knifed through the
scent of flowers, and Anna's stomach pitched. The undertaker's
face was pink and smooth. He tried several facial expressions of
sympathy before one locked into place. Lightly clasping his hands
so that the diamond lodge ring wouldn't cut into his soft flesh,
Richard Pullock paused beside the casket. A straggling tulip
snagged his restless eyes. Delia scratched at the striped silk pillow
in her lap and watched the undertaker nip the yellow head off the
tulip and stick it into his lapel. Anna and Delia stared Richard
Pullock away from the guest book and out the door.

"Fucking little gravedigger," Delia said bitterly. She tore the
fragile lavender skin of the leftover iris. "Couldn't even remember
how she parted her hair."

———

Anna finished at the funeral home by nine-thirty. Sprinkling water
on the satin pillow had helped cut down on the static. Grace's hair
looked as good as it ever would. When Delia went to help her
father bring in more flowers, Anna slipped out the back door and
walked to the shop.

She stood outside Mary Frances's and watched Claude plug
bottles of root beer into the empty sockets of the soda machine.
He relayed the bottles from hand to hand without looking; his
attention was focused on the middle styling room. Protected by
the long bill of his baseball cap, his eyes ranged across the legs of
the women whose faces were hidden under the dryer hoods.

The front door had never hung right. Anna let it slam back into
the frame. The gold letters scrolling Mary Frances's name across
the glass shook. Claude's eyes shifted to Anna's ankles. "Hi,
Anna."

"It's a good thing you're a leg man and not an ass man, Claude," Anna snapped. "You'd be around here forever, waiting for some woman to stand up."

"You and Josephine and Liz stand up most of the time, Anna," he pointed out mildly. "Go see who that is getting a shampoo back there. At first I thought it was Grace Nettinger—same kind of high kneecaps—but then I remembered." He spit tobacco juice into a plastic cup. "Why would a woman with such nice legs kill herself?"

"Maybe she didn't like the rest of herself. Maybe she needed somebody to tell her she had great legs. Maybe somebody did tell her. Maybe it was the wrong person. Maybe she was tired. Maybe she couldn't—"

"Nice legs, Anna," Claude corrected, "not great legs. And I used to tell her all the time. You know me, there's always hope." He shook his narrow head. "No note or anything. You know who's got great legs—that navy blue dress under the third dryer. Go see who it is and tell her I love her. She'll never want for strawberry soda."

Jo shouted from the styling room, "Don't you give her a free strawberry soda, Claude, I'm warning you! Liz is hosing down your ten o'clock, Anna, there's no time to weasel a free drink out of him." Smoke from Jo's cigarette drifted to surround the tower of black curls constructed on her head. The ash was volcanizing various shades of hair lying underneath Jo's chair into one powdery tint. She used her long red nails to separate strands of hair from her customer's scalp. Jo's presence hurt Anna's eyes and made her headache worse.

Claude ran his fingers around the brim of his baseball cap. "You know, Anna," he said appreciatively, "I didn't know what they meant by a ripe woman until I set eyes on you."

Anna imagined herself fallen off the tree tomorrow, lying bloated and black in the shadows. "You know, Claude," she said, "I never knew the meaning of the word 'shrimp' till I saw you."

"Anna!" Claude's hurt was almost drowned out by the sound of dimes and quarters chiming to the floor. The empty coin box, held between index finger and thumb, gently battered his knee.

He stared sightlessly at the nervous shining dance of the money. When all the coins were quiet against the dark green linoleum, Claude squatted on his heels and swept his fingers around a foil-wrapped rubber plant. Its thick oblong leaves, the same color and texture as the floor, shivered and springboarded dust into the air.

"Claude. I'm sorry. I'm sorry," Anna repeated. "I didn't mean it." She watched in irritation while he methodically moved Mary Francces's small jungle of plants away from the baseboard. He rose slowly, as if he were calling her a liar and proving it by growing right in front of her eyes. This is it, she thought. This is what hell must be like. You think you're lighting a fire under somebody else and getting away with it, but the flames are under your feet the whole time. Great. I burn and Claude finds his dignity.

He rammed the coin box into the machine. There was no rattle of Claude's lone dime, the dime he always shot back into the box —"just to get you girls going again."

"I don't expect anything better from a fatherless child," Claude said instead.

His attempt at retaliation made Anna laugh. "Oh, Claude. Is that the worst thing you can think of? My mother *had* a man. At least once. Just because I've never set eyes on him—"

The upper and lower lids of Claude's narrow eyes almost met. He had the thickest eyelashes Anna had ever seen on a man. "It's not the same thing, Anna, having a man once."

"Well, I know that—"

"Or even twice, in your case," Claude interrupted. "It's one thing to leave a man who's a hitter, it's another thing to take a man in and make him love you and then kick him out after he's got his green card." The door rattled behind him.

"What did you do to him?" Jo demanded. She lounged in the doorway and tapped the tail of a comb against her big yellow teeth. "He's going to short us on strawberry soda now for about a month."

"Don't worry about him. He gave as good as he got." The glint of a dime caught Anna's eye. She worked it out from behind the machine with her foot. The coin box sprung open when she pounded the lock where Claude always did. After depositing his dime, she pushed the box shut.

———

At three o'clock Anna checked the appointment book. Grace's name, written in Jo's heavy back slant, had been erased but was still legible. No one was scheduled to come in for forty-five minutes. All Anna wanted to do was lean back in her chair and sleep, but that would make her a target for questions about how Grace had really looked and how Delia and Ed were really taking it.

She began straightening her section of pink Formica counter. Bobby pins and roller picks spun into each other. Lilac and gray plastic curlers bumped across combs and hand-held mirrors. Two rattail combs clattered to the floor. A can of hair spray disguised as a pink tulle poodle rolled off the counter. Years of dust had dyed its pink netting a mottled tan. Anna kicked the can to the far wall. "I hate this thing! I don't see why we have to keep hiding hair spray in this stupid little poodle outfit. Like nobody knows. Like this is all hocus-pocus."

Jo stepped back from her chair and tightened her lips until ash dropped from her cigarette. "It's only a piece of net, Anna; dye it red or throw it away. Paint a mustache on it, anything. But don't let it get to you, all it is is a piece of dirty pink net."

"Well, that won't change anything, will it?" Anna challenged. "This place'll still have a rack full of ten-year-old *Photoplays* and pink spool curlers." She kicked the can to the wall again. "I can't *wait* to get my hands on it."

"Now you listen to me," Jo said, pointing the tail of her comb at Anna. "Grace Nettinger was always wound tighter than a cheap perm. She *always* was. I started first grade with her, and that's just the way she was. I never thought she'd kill herself, but then I don't expect that from anybody. Besides, I thought we went all through this last night."

Anna restored the hair spray to its rightful place on the counter. "I don't understand it, that's all. I just don't."

"Whether you understand a thing or not isn't going to change it. I don't imagine Grace Nettinger had you in mind when she started swallowing."

Jo's customer, a woman who left Mary Frances's every three months and then came back with stories of how much cheaper haircuts across the tracks were, interrupted. "How could she shut herself in a meat locker like that, with a side of beef and half a dozen rabbits, and then pull the trigger like that? You'd think she thought she'd keep better in there in case they didn't find her for a while."

With the half twist of a roller, Jo chastised the woman. "If I told you little green men from Mars stole Grace away, you'd add on to that and pass it on. Don't you be so quick. You know how she did it." She stashed the woman under a dryer and turned back to Anna, who was using metal clips to bite at the hair spray's pink netting. "What I remember about Grace Nettinger is this—she never did anything she didn't want to. Nobody fed her those pills and poured that liquor down her throat."

Jo's house sat on a rise across the highway from the trailer court. The city limits sign was fifty feet to the east. There were pockmarks in the sign where Jo's sons, Bevo and Marvin, had shot their BB guns at the numbers in POPULATION: 5,465.

By six o'clock in the afternoon the sun was balanced above Twin Peaks. Anna shaded her eyes with a beer can and tried to make out the sun's true shape before it slid into the craters of the extinct volcanoes, which were joined at their upper slopes like Siamese twins. Jo alternately raked gravel through her cactus garden and leaned over to tamp cigarette ash into a potted ivy that snaked up the iron porch supports and across the overhanging roof.

"That can't be any better for that poor plant than it is for you," Anna said.

"People pay good money for potash. It's the same thing." Jo ground her cigarette into the pea gravel and smoothed over the hole with the back of her rake. "Besides, how many times do I have to tell you to wear sunglasses, especially if you're going to sit around and stare at the sun?" Using the rake for support, she vaulted onto the porch. The rake clattered backwards as she went inside.

Anna heard the aluminum and glass door slide open again. "Why do you think she did it?" she asked Jo. "If she never did anything she didn't want to do—that doesn't make any sense. If she always had her own way, then why did she kill herself?"

"Here." Jo tossed a pair of black-framed sunglasses into Anna's lap. "We'll trade. You tell me about you and Bryan, and I'll tell you about Grace Nettinger." Waiting for a response, she trickled the last of her first beer into the ivy. "Now, don't rush to this poor plant's defense, Anna. Plants need relaxing too."

"It's not the plant I'm worried about. Who's going to defend me against you and Bryan?"

"I should make you go first, but as a sign of my trust in you, and since I'm your very best friend, and I'm older, I'll go first. Now, just because you wind up not doing what you don't want to do doesn't mean that you've got it made. You're making the mistake of thinking Grace Nettinger did what she wanted to. Grace Nettinger didn't ever know what she wanted, she just knew what she didn't want."

Anna blinked and missed the last sliver of sun. Long, ropy jet trails flamed across the sky. There was a rippling distortion in the thick green lenses of the sunglasses and they were too big. She had to clamp the earpieces to her head. "I think these things are prescription."

Jo took the glasses and squinted through them. "Probably are. I can't tell. All I know's Burgess found them in a '76 Firebird along with a smashed stick of Dentyne gum. You know how he is, he always thinks some old owner's going to show up twenty years from now looking for that bobby pin his wife left in the car before they traded it in."

"It sounds more like something he'd do for you. You've got him so wrapped around your finger. So what didn't Grace Nettinger want?"

"Where's your wedding ring?" Jo asked.

The indirect reference to Bryan annoyed Anna. He didn't belong in their conversation and Jo knew it. "It's somewhere. At Mary Frances's. In one of my pockets. I don't know. Stuck behind the seat of a 1980 Subaru. Somewhere. You're not finished. What didn't Grace Nettinger want?"

"You know what I'd like to know," Jo mused. "I'd like to know why you've been so hard on her these last couple of weeks. I remember you coming in and swearing you'd never work on her anymore. Maybe that's why she decided to kill herself."

"She insulted me," Anna flashed. "She threw five dollars in my face. Ten years with a half-dollar tip every week and all of a sudden she throws me five dollars."

"Now I'm not the star you are," Jo acknowledged, "but still, I could take insults like that and keep right on smiling."

"That's not the point. How could she not wait one more day? If she had held out one more day, she could have gotten her hair done—"

Jo laughed. "The great cure-all, a day at the beauty parlor. You think if she sat in your chair, you could have saved her? Anna, you're good, but you're not that good. Nobody's that good."

"Then tell me what she didn't want."

"That ranch, for one thing. Any more children, for another, maybe *any* children for all I know. Happiness—I don't know, Anna, it's anybody's guess."

Anna wanted answers, not guesses. After leaving the funeral home, she had stopped to watch Delia and Ed Nettinger unload more flowers. There was a physical resemblance between father and daughter; there was also a distance between them that looked as if it had only recently been introduced. "If you'd seen them today. Grace Nettinger did a shitty thing and she's getting away with it."

"*Got* away with it, Anna. She's gone. Now, you don't know what you saw in them today. You don't know what's gone on behind closed doors."

Fine. Delia Nettinger didn't know. Jo didn't know. Maybe Grace had asked herself the same thing as she washed down the pills. Then why hadn't she stopped? Because sometimes once you started something it was easier to keep going?

"Hold out your hand," Jo commanded and dropped a wedding ring into Anna's waiting palm. "My turn, you and Bryan."

"What did you do? Sneak into my house and swipe it off the nightstand?"

"You left it in the shampoo room. I've had it for a week."

"Some friend you are."

"Did you not ever miss it, or do you just not care?"

"That's not fair. You witnessed our agreement. Do I have to go to the bank and get it out of the safe-deposit box and read it to you?"

"Oh, I remember what it says, Anna, but I don't know what that piece of paper means to you. I don't know what Bryan really means to you. I don't know, after two years, what you're walking out of that marriage with. I know what he wanted, what he started out wanting—"

"And I've kept my part of the bargain, haven't I? He's got his green card. He's not deported. He's not in jail. Yet."

"I've seen the way Bryan looks at you—"

"He's got you fooled," Anna said. "You, of all people, should know better. You and Burgess know more about Bryan than I'll ever know."

"He loves you, he needs a home."

It suddenly dawned on Anna. This was Burgess's idea. Jo would do anything her husband asked. "You're testing me. Burgess thinks I'm going to break at the last minute. He thinks I'm going to call the INS and the Border Patrol and turn Bryan in."

"Now, I love my Burgess," Jo said, "I do, and I wish you two got along, but this is between you and me. Let's leave him out of this."

"I don't know what you and Bryan see in him to love."

Jo raised her eyebrows. A big smile brought her cheekbones into prominence. "That's my secret. Maybe that's why I want you and Bryan to stay together, so you can have what Burgess and I have."

"Drop it!" Anna said sharply. "We aren't a love story. We

aren't you and Burgess. We have *agreed* to pretend. Every two weeks, when he's in town, we pretend. Every once in a while I forget that we're pretending, and every once in a while he does.

"Bryan is in the present. I deal with him when I see him. The most important thing to me is getting that shop away from Mary Frances. I don't want any distractions. I don't know what he's involved in. I don't want to know. And I don't want to see you get sucked into his dealings."

Jo stood and pulled the collar of her starched shirt taut. "I'm a big girl myself. I can decide what's a good cause and what's not." She patted the top of Anna's head lightly. "Mary Frances asked me the other day what you used to get those red highlights."

"What did you tell her? That it was a trade secret?"

"I told her the truth. I told her it was one hundred percent Anna. She didn't believe me. 'Georgia's head doesn't have one factual strand of red hair on it,' she said. I had to remind her that your mother might not have red hair, but the Phantom Mechanic might."

"We'll never know," Anna said.

Jo let loose a jaw-cracking yawn. "Come help me get Burgess's supper." She stopped suddenly before the front door. "You know what I think it is? You've never pulled duty at a funeral home, have you? That's what all this is. It's seeing behind the scenes is what it is."

————

Three days after Grace Nettinger's funeral her daughter made an appointment with Anna. By six-thirty they were the only ones left in the shop. Delia Nettinger watched in the mirror as Anna got the feel of her hair. "I'm leaving early tomorrow. My dad's driving me to Midland to catch a nine o'clock plane." When there was no answer, she twisted her head to look up at Anna.

"Keep your head still," Anna advised, "or you may lose part of that ear."

"I don't know when I'll be back," Delia warned.

Customer patter had never been Anna's priority, but all the other chairs were empty. There was nobody else around to play

the girl off of. She'd sink to small talk if that's what it took to keep
Delia's visit professional. "Dallas must seem like a big place after
Alpine—"

"Fort Worth," Delia corrected. "Fort Worth is where TCU is.
I'm thinking of changing my major. Psychology."

Anna gathered Delia's hair and bunched it on top of her head.
Dissatisfied, she freed the mass. "You're lucky it's so thick. But
a couple of inches off would make a big difference. It'll hang a lot
better."

"My major was math. It's got no guts. I can relate to psychology. Trying to figure out why certain people do certain things. I
bet standing behind that chair for as long as you have, I bet you
probably have as much experience as lots of psychiatrists."

"People think that," Anna said carefully. She wasn't hung over
today. Thinking about why Grace Nettinger committed suicide
only made her feel like a dog chasing its tail. What would knowing
the answer prove? "It's too high a price to pay. Having people
think you can solve their problems for them. What I do is style
hair, and I do it better than anybody in six counties. Period." She
met Delia's defiant eyes in the mirror. "Either two inches off the
bottom or layered. It's your money."

"I'm leaving today, and I don't know if I'll ever come back to
this stinking little place again, so if you have anything to tell me
about my mother, you'd better do it now."

Anna gave up on Delia's hair and sat in the next chair. She
searched through Jo's drawer and retrieved a pair of her scissors
and a tube of styling gel. "What do you want me to say?"

"I want you to tell me that she gave you a videotape to hand
over to me on my thirtieth birthday. I want you to pull a note from
her out of that drawer. I want the reason."

"I don't have it."

"Who does then?" Delia slid her palms up and down the
slippery black arms of the chair. "You mean you looked at her face
in that mirror every week for years and years and you didn't see
it coming on?"

Anna concentrated on squeezing a perfect coil of gel onto her
palm. "You mean *you* looked at her in the face every day for years

and years and you didn't see it coming on? I'm sorry. You've come
to the wrong person. I just fix hair."

"How am I supposed to know anything?" Delia demanded. "I
wasn't here. I was at school. How was I supposed to know?"

———————

Jo pointed to the front door. "Uh-oh, here comes Daddy Nettinger. Mama's not even in the ground a good month, daughter's
on the phone every week, and here comes Daddy." Ed Nettinger
stood outside the shop, hat in hand, straightening the green Astroturf welcome mat with his boot. "How long do you suppose he
can keep that up?"

"Leave him alone, Josephine," Anna said. "How many men
besides Claude come in here? Your beloved Burgess hasn't even
been in here."

"Claude! Oh Lord, I thought you said men. If you need me,
I'll be in the shampoo room tightening the caps on the cream
rinse. Just holler if you need my help."

Anna rarely smoked, but watching Ed Nettinger deliberate
outside the door sent her searching through Jo's drawers for a stray
cigarette. What's it going to be? she thought. Tell me why my
wife did it or tell me why my daughter calls you once a week
instead of me. Knowing he couldn't see her because of the sunlight on the glass, she paced back and forth, impatient with his
indecision. None of the Nettingers seemed interested in keeping
their lives private.

"He still out there?" Jo yelled. "He better hurry, I'm working
on the shampoo tops now."

"Hush! His hand's on the door." Anna quickly stubbed out her
cigarette and turned to look in the mirror. When she pushed the
hair off her wide forehead, it cascaded down again. She ran a hand
against the grain of her short neck hair.

A cowbell nailed to the top of the door rang mournfully, and
Ed Nettinger was in. Anna stepped into the reception area and
tried to look surprised. "Don't tell me you've got an appointment," she said.

Ed smiled. "I thought I'd drop by and take my chances."

Anna relaxed a little. She had expected him to be embarrassed. Most men were uncomfortable in beauty shops. They poked their heads in the door and yelled where the car was parked. She couldn't ever remember Ed picking up Grace. "We don't exactly have a full house this afternoon with the parade going on. We threw everybody back into the world."

"That's what I figured," he said. "I could always stand a haircut."

"I don't take walk-ins. Sorry." This was one Nettinger who was staying out of her chair.

He kept reshaping the crown of his sweat-stained Stetson as if he had all the time in the world. "I wasn't sure if you operated the same as a barbershop or not."

"I don't know how barbershops operate," Anna said. "How about a cold drink?" Without bothering to wait for his answer, she went to the machine and pulled a root beer bottle against the faulty locking mechanism.

"Here, my treat." Ed shot two dimes into the slot before Anna could stop him.

"You just lost two dimes."

"It won't break me."

Anna watched while Ed looked freely around the shop. The sun had worked the skin on his arms until it was grainy like sausage. She was surprised that the Stetson hadn't left a white band across his forehead.

His gray eyes watered, and he lifted his almost empty bottle. "It burns going down," he said.

"Drink it slower," she suggested.

He smiled. "It smells good in here. I always kind of wondered, you know, what it would be like in here. It's real . . . womany. It's nice."

"Womany?" Anna looked around. Jo's dusty English ivy covered the picture window and reduced the sunlight. Wasps were building a mud nest under the outside eaves; all the magazines were curled from being rolled into weapons. "You're lucky we haven't given many perms today."

"I like finished products," he said, "but I like to see how things are done. As long as I know I'm on my way to something, it doesn't take away anything for me to see how things operate. Delia thinks you like what you do."

"I'm good at what I do," Anna said. "Which is fixing hair. Period."

Ed looked at her. "But every once in a while, you get more than you bargained for."

Anna rolled the bottle across her lips. "Every once in a while." She still didn't know why he was sitting beside her on the couch that his wife had sat on; she wasn't sure she wanted to know. "I've got to get ready for a four o'clock."

Ed rose and held out his hand. "Thank you for coming to the funeral home, and for watching after my daughter. She thinks a lot of you. I appreciate it." He took Anna's empty and slid it with his into the wooden rack beside the machine. The skin at the corner of his eyes twisted when he smiled. "Tell Jo she can come out now," he said.

Anna stayed on the couch and remembered the last time she'd shared the couch with a Nettinger. It had been the day of Jo's birthday, and Burgess had had the package store deliver champagne. Grace had dawdled, brushing the hair off her clothes, retouching her lipstick, studying the spectrum of nail polishes that Jo carefully lined up on the manicure table. Anna had never socialized with Grace outside the shop. Champagne and side-by-side placement on the green vinyl couch in the front reception area seemed like a good way to break the barrier. Respect for privacy ranked high with Anna; Grace's self-containment was admirable, but once the comb was out of Anna's hand, she was as curious as anybody else. Grace clearly had a purpose for staying behind. But Anna had been wrong about the reason. The absence of a comb and a little champagne hadn't equalized their relationship.

Grace pounced quickly. "You're not wearing your wedding ring. I heard you were getting a divorce."

"I usually don't wear it to work. Hair gets tangled in it."

"What about the first one? Did you wear his ring?"

"We were only seventeen. We used our high school rings. But

a nest of diamonds wouldn't have changed that one. It didn't take. Some don't." Anna caught the slight wrinkling of Grace's eyebrows. Over the years her actions had indirectly caused Grace pain —short neck hairs caught in rollers, unregulated blasts of hot water, the sting of curling solution—but those actions had never reshaped Grace's face the way her words just had.

"You're bitter," Grace said triumphantly. She sounded as if she'd been waiting a long time to say it.

Anna considered any bitterness over her eighteen months with Ronnie Mauss a waste of time. "Maybe that's what you want to hear. More champagne?"

Tension seemed to enliven Grace. She leaned toward Anna. "Are you saying that I'm bitter? What have I got to be bitter about?"

Throwing up her hands, Anna said, "You tell me."

Grace sank back on the couch. She tapped the plastic glass with an unpainted fingernail and shook her small, freshly set head. "You don't want to know. Not really. All you can think is, why is that woman so ungrateful with all she has? What does she think she's missing?"

She hunched her shoulders suddenly. "I miss being able to love those mountains out there. That are out there twenty-four hours of every blessed day. They are always out there, standing in my way. I miss being able to cross over those mountains and come back with something, a belief in something. You know what's behind them? More mountains. But if you keep going long enough, then you hit the plains, and then the ocean, and then you miss the mountains because they aren't there to protect you, and then you realize you're on the wrong side of them again." She sank back again. "I'm tired. I am so tired of them."

Grace's words made the shop seem empty and cold. Anna found it hard to believe that there had been a celebration only an hour ago. "You have to keep moving and wait it out, that's all."

"That's all." Grace's laugh sounded dry and dusty. "Moving and waiting, all at the same time. That's a tidy little philosophy. No wonder, Anna. No wonder you had to crawl out a window to escape your first husband. The one that just didn't take."

"It's served me," Anna said tightly. Why was she taking the trouble to explain? Grace negated the words with a motion of her head, but Anna refused to be dismissed. "You keep moving while you're waiting. You never let the water close over your head. Never."

Grace turned to separate the ivy. "There's not much water out there, Anna. Believe me, I know. My husband's catfish could be in terrible trouble. They could smother in the mud." She stared through the window as if she could measure the encroachment of the brown velveteen hills.

A car's headlights took momentary possession of the far wall. There was silence as they realized that the champagne was gone and they were sitting in the dark. Anna reached for the lamp reluctantly, wishing that the night, which seemed so tangible, would carry her home so she would be spared the futility of trying to level Grace's mountains. But when she switched on the lamp, there was no appeal in Grace's eyes. Anna reached out to touch Grace's arm with her own appeal. She wanted to know why Grace had confided in her. She wanted to know what Grace had meant about the mountains, but Grace outmaneuvered by reaching in her purse and pulling out a five-dollar bill.

"What's this for?" Anna demanded. "Nobody pays me to listen to them."

Grace threw the money down on the coffee table. "Consider it a gift from one lucky woman to another." She walked to her car and got in without once looking toward the mountains that surrounded Alpine.

Grace Nettinger had singled her out for an attack and considered the mission a success. Anna had never allowed herself to feel she was a casualty; she had had no intention of letting Grace label her a victim and get away with it.

She had crumpled the five-dollar bill and dropped it in an ashtray. A dousing of hair spray encouraged the bill to catch fire. The edges of the flame were tinged with green and pink.

And now, with the green vinyl couch still warm from Ed Nettinger's body, with Grace Nettinger buried, it seemed that the dead woman was still present, maneuvering the people who had loved her and the people who had barely known her into accounting for their past actions.

Grace Nettinger had gotten away with it.

———

Jo twisted the hair out of her brush. "Well?"

"Well what?" Anna asked.

"What did Daddy Nettinger want?"

"He thinks it smells womany in here. No wonder she killed herself."

Mary Frances swished down the stairs. The rustle of petticoats supporting her plump skirt washed out their conversation. She tapped Anna's shoulder. "I thought I heard a man's voice down here earlier. I'm running a beauty salon, not an escort service—" Her breath caught as Jo inserted a long red nail into the tangle of her hair and scratched. "I never know what you're going to pull out of that mess. You're the world's worst advertisement for a beauty salon."

Jo flicked her fingernail. "It was the newly widowed Ed Nettinger."

Mary Frances went to the picture window and peered through a hole in the ivy. "That's when they need you the most. What did he want?"

"Ask Anna," Jo answered. "She's the one he came to see."

"He wanted a trim. I've told you, Mary Frances, we could charge double what the barbershop does and get away with it. Six to eight in the evening. Two days a week." Anna escaped into the styling room before Mary Frances could remember what her original question had been.

"One man in twenty years comes in to get a trim, and she's ready to unisex this place." Mary Frances raised her voice and said, "Don't forget you owe me for that call to Forth Worth." She swiveled toward Jo and whispered in a voice loud enough for Anna to hear, "Who does she know in Fort Worth?"

"Grace Nettinger's daughter," Jo answered.

"Grace's daughter?" Mary Frances's eyebrows lifted. "What's she calling her for? Don't tell me they didn't pay her for that house call at the funeral home."

"If you'd ever come down here and help us out, you'd know that Delia Nettinger's been calling Anna every Tuesday at three-fifteen for a month now. She didn't call one Tuesday, so Anna got worried and called."

Mary Frances wet a fingertip and smoothed her right eyebrow. She flexed the wings of her honey blond, Paris Mist #3, bangs and squeezed more hair spray on them from a soft, round-bellied container. "The daughter calling all the time, the father wanting a trim. You don't think Anna had anything to do with Grace's death, do you?"

Jo grabbed the hair spray and directed the spray at Mary Frances's bare neck. "Go to your room."

ll the dryers were occupied. Mary Frances was giving herself a manicure. Liz had one woman under a dryer and one perming in the shampoo room. Jo had two women waiting to be unrolled and styled, so Anna took one of them into her chair.

Jo worked the silver clips that hung out of her mouth like walrus teeth. "I've got my eye on you, Anna, don't think I don't. Elsie, you watch out she doesn't talk you into putting in green highlights."

"I can always give her to Liz," Anna warned.

Liz was sitting in the chair to Anna's left and shaking end papers out of their pack. The thin tissues floated to the floor. Liz looked as if she were still in high school. Her straight brown hair was thick and fine and blunt-cut. The whites of her eyes were as white as her even teeth, and her gums were the color of pink bubble gum. She had a beauty mark under one eye and no pores.

"Oh, Lord!" Jo said. She snapped the long clips

open. "Stay where you are, Elsie. Better a green head than half an eyebrow accidentally shaved off."

Mary Frances rose as far as she could from the manicurist's chair while still keeping her fingers curled in the bowl filled with softening lotion. "Elizabeth, dear, you know how I hate charging supplies against your check. See if you can fit those little things back in their little box." She modeled her manicured right hand close to the hand of the woman sitting under the closest dryer. "If I keep deducting from your paycheck, how will you pay for Leo's school? He'll never finish."

Liz crumpled the end papers against her mouth and started crying. "I don't care, I hate him!" She ran into the bathroom and locked the door.

Mary Frances wheeled the manicure table over to the bathroom door. "Elizabeth. Dear. We've discussed this before. What if one of my ladies has to powder her nose?"

"Leo should be along any minute now," Jo said. "We'll just send him in there with the Ivory Girl."

The bathroom door vibrated. "You better not tell him where I am!" Liz shouted.

Mary Frances inserted a nail file into the lock. "Dear. This is the first place he'll look. This is the first place we all look—" A look of horror came over her face. "Elizabeth, you're not pregnant, are you? You promised me—"

"Leave me alone!" Liz wailed. "I'm never, never, never, *never* going to have a baby!"

"She'll be gone by next semester, I know it," Mary Frances prophesied. "No more college husbands. They graduate and snap their fingers, and I lose a girl. Change is upsetting to my clientele. I cannot have it."

"Clientele, hell." Jo laughed. She aimed a red fingernail at Mary Frances. "It's upsetting to you. Besides, it's the only way to get new blood pumping through here, M.F."

Mary Frances grabbed Jo's finger. "Josephine. There are several things a lady does not do. She does not point. She does not use initials in the naming of. *Besides,*" she released Jo's finger to approached Mary Frances at the manicure table. "Mrs. Forrest, do you have my money from last week yet?"

Mary Frances rolled the manicure table closer to herself. "You're dripping, dear. Go towel yourself off, and ask the girls if they can chip in and tide you over until next week."

Anna and Jo came out of the shampoo room and led Sandra back to Mary Frances. "M.F.F., pull ten dollars out of that stocking top of yours for this girl," Jo said. "If I have to shampoo on Saturdays and I wind up breaking a nail, it's going to cost you more than that. And we all know Anna's attitude toward giving shampoos. Roll that garter down."

"I used to shampoo," Mary Frances said, holding up her hands. "There were times when these cuticles were in shreds. In shreds. They looked like macaroons. Two dollars a week for Sandra from each of you seems reasonable to me." The cowbell on the front door clunked. "Stations, girls!" she commanded. "A client!"

Leo framed himself in the window cut out between the reception and styling areas. His eyes tightly closed, he reached through the open space in the direction of Liz's chair and swiped at the air. "I've come for my baby. Where's my Lizzie? Where, oh, where's my baby?"

"Just hold still, we'll bring her to you," Jo assured him. She took the scissors Anna handed her and they both advanced.

"Who's here?" Leo asked. "Is Sandra still here? I promised to help her with her term paper. I've got a load of books in the car for her to look over. She's going to have the best bibliography Alpine High School has ever seen—"

Jo snipped at Leo's mustache. He picked the hair out of his mouth the same way she picked tobacco out of hers and kept talking. Anna stretched his free-ranging curls but didn't use her scissors. Leo needed more than pruning. He needed an hour, minimum. "A trim, Leo," she pleaded. "That's all. The things I could do."

"When I graduate," Leo promised. "Where's my Lizzie? Everyone decent? Can I open my eyes? You know, some places have hug Anna, "we have Anna here as an unencumbered example. O'Bryan notwithstanding."

"That was ten years ago when Anna cruised into our little harbor here," Jo pointed out. "*Besides,* you have to count Thomas O period, capital B Bryan whether you want to or not."

"Oh, he doesn't count. He's got his green card. He's already out of the picture," Mary Frances said. "Anyway, it doesn't matter how many Annas are out there as long as this one's still *here.*" She rested her head on Anna's shoulder. "Not that I think there are that many Annas out there."

Anna eased Mary Frances's head off her shoulder. "If Liz doesn't watch out, she'll be an Anna before long."

"Oh, I think Leo loves her, I don't think he would hit her or try to make a farce out of the matrimonial state," Mary Frances protested. "He looks more like a two-timer to me. Oh, if only they would award the degree and the divorce on the same piece of paper, I could keep my girls." She sighed. "But no, they have to go someplace else to split up."

"I can hear you!" Liz shouted. "I'm not going to be done in by the Beauty Operator's Syndrome. Nobody's leaving me because they think I'm too stupid! If I wanted to go to college, it wouldn't take me any eight years to get a degree."

Mary Frances carefully pressed hands together. "Wouldn't it be wonderful if he decided to change majors again? He hasn't tried the range animal science program yet, has he? It's one of the best in the—"

"I'm never coming out!" Liz swore.

"Just comb out Elsie the way she was rolled, Anna," Jo said.

Despite the pincurl pattern that was mapped out on Elsie's head, Anna had discovered a natural wave formation fighting to assert itself. "Does your daughter have a hand-held dryer?" she asked Elsie.

———

At the end of the day Liz was still in the bathroom. The high school girl, Sandra, who shampooed on Thursdays and Saturdays, robes instead of those plastic cape things. It looks very nice. It elevates the establishment—"

"Would you go to a barbershop and put on a T-shirt other men, who knows how many, have worn before you?" Mary Frances asked. "Do you think they wash those things every day? Besides, women feel more comfortable with their own clothes on underneath."

Leo beamed. "I *like* women. I like talking to women." He came into the styling room and parked himself at the appointment desk. "Coming here, watching the ebb and flow, hearing your concerns—"

"We're not taking part in any more studies," Jo warned. "I about lost three customers with your harping on hot rollers and curling irons and their masculine significance."

"Phallic symbols, she still can't say it." Leo mourned. "I really think there's a connection between the amount of hair spray a woman uses and her sexual attitudes."

Mary Frances patted his cheek. "Sometimes, dear, you are so far off the money."

The phone rang. Leo whipped a pen out of his shirt pocket, centered the appointment book and picked up the pink receiver. "Mary Frances's. Anna? Let me see if she's available. And this is? Georgia? Georgia! It's me, Leo! Did you get the article I sent you on mothers raising daughters alone? I know we've never met, but I—"

Georgia, Anna's mother, called only on Sundays, when rates were the cheapest. She'd never called Mary Frances's shop before. Anna was beginning to hate telephones. Let the man who liked talking to women find out what Georgia had to say.

Leo brought the phone over to her station and Anna had no choice but to answer. "What's wrong?"

"Ronnie Mauss just got off an oil rig in the North Sea. He wants your location, baby," Georgia said.

"If he found you, he can find me." The superstitious feeling that saying something caused it to happen hit Anna. She told herself that she wasn't six years old anymore and that her first husband wasn't that smart.

"Of course he can," her mother agreed. "He's a sharp boy. But don't you see, though, he's going through proper channels, testing your waters. He's changed."

Anna had hoped her mother would say that Ronnie Mauss might as well look for spit in the North Sea as try to find her in the vast landscape of West Texas. "He told you he's changed and you believed him."

"You were married to him, after all. He told me, voluntarily, that he doesn't hit women anymore. Nobody's perfect, Anna. He says he isn't hungry anymore."

"I can't believe you're sticking up for him!"

"He respects you for leaving him."

"Oh, please! He never hit you, now did he?"

"I don't have to stick my hand in a fire to know what a burn feels like. I can sympathize."

"If you tell him where I am, I'll disappear as fast and for as long as the Phantom Mechanic did, which is forever. At least you finally found another man, but getting another daughter to replace me—at your age—that might be a little tough."

"I just want what's best for you." The reproach in Georgia's voice picked up strength as it sped across the four hundred miles of wire from the Panhandle.

Anna snapped the curls out of the telephone cord. Georgia was lingering over her s's. She was hiding something. "Then don't talk to him. Look. I want what's best for me even more than you do, so just let me take care of my own business."

"You never write, and when you do, you don't mention him. How was I supposed to know you didn't want to see him?"

"I don't mention his name because I don't want to see him. He's out of my life. What exactly did you say to him?"

"Only that you were in a town somewhere out in West Texas. He guessed Odessa. I had to tell him, again, that it was a town. He may never even find you out there. There's one other thing—"

"You *told* him? Why didn't you just drive him down here

yourself?" Anna hung up the phone before Georgia could defend herself.

"I'm calling Bryan," Jo said.

Anna hid the receiver behind her back. "No. Ronnie Mauss won't follow through. That's why he called my mother. He doesn't need her to find me. He knows she's a soft touch." There was a shaky edge to her anger that she didn't like. It's the surprise, she told herself. It's not fear. It won't happen again. I won't ever run away from him again.

"There's a terrific self-defense course for women the phys ed department offers," Leo said. "It couldn't hurt."

Mary Frances pushed Leo out of the way. "What she needs is a gun."

————

Anna unplugged the phone but stayed in the front room, a combination living room and dining room whose boundaries only she knew. The wooden floor was cool under her bare feet. Staring out the screen door with half her mind trying to remember exactly what Ronnie Mauss looked like, Anna felt as if she were waiting on the edge of a clearing, undecided whether or not to make a run for it. Mary Frances and Alfred honked as they drove by in their Delta 88, targeting her house and destroying the spell of Sunday afternoon.

She made herself consider the possibility that Ronnie Mauss might actually turn up on her front porch, his compact body blocking her escape. Always, when Anna thought of Ronnie, she rubbed her right upper arm. The first time he had hit her, a glorious bruise had blossomed there, deep purple and blue with a border of green. She had sported the bruise proudly like a badge that first time because she had had a bad day, too, and her anger had stood up to his and defeated it. Until the bruise started to fade, she poked its yellowing edges to revive the elation she had felt in defending herself. The heart of the bruise stayed shaded like the center of a pansy for a long time. Touching that sensitive center sent a corresponding pain twitching in her stomach and she felt sick, unable finally to justify her pride. The abandon and then the self-righteousness of the anger scared her. If he raised his hand again, she wouldn't be able to protect herself in the same way. The second blow had fallen a few months later on a rainy September evening. A cold had kept her inside all day. She felt clogged and slow-moving. It was an off Friday at Anita's Style Shop, where she did the shampooing. Ronnie scraped his car against the side of the garage. Anna shuffled into the kitchen, picking at her lips that were as dry and flaky as her frayed terry-cloth robe. Ronnie tore off his wet shirt and threw it in her direction.

"You called in sick today, didn't you?" he accused. "I'm out there busting my butt in the rain and the cold, and you're in here, nice and dry, toasting your fat ass."

Anna's ears were buzzing, and the kitchen light was mining its way to the very back of her skull. Not up to a fight, she nevertheless made a face and flapped her hand. Ronnie took the kitchen floor in two steps and laid one across her face. Though Anna had seen the blow coming for weeks, she froze at the upswing of his hand as if the absence of action on her part would counteract the motion. But it was too late. Nothing could have stopped his hand.

As she nursed her cheek, Ronnie cradled his hand, and Anna had seen that his hurt was the only thing he understood. He had hit her and hurt himself. The injustice further aggravated him. He unbuckled the championship belt he had found at a flea market, held on to the buckle and wrapped the strap once around his fist. The leather tail hit her across the back before she made it to the safety of their bedroom. She pushed the chest of drawers against the door, grabbed her purse and a dress and climbed out the window. She changed her clothes under a neighbor's grape arbor. Holding the terry-cloth robe over her head, she took backyards and alleys to the bus station.

A converted private garage had served as the bus depot in Levelland, where Georgia and Frank lived then. At two in the morning her only company was the moths that dashed themselves against the unshaded yellow light. Shivers still went down Anna's back whenever she recalled the cold touch of the outdoor bench, a seat torn from an old school bus, she had sat on while waiting for her mother and Frank.

That was the past. Anna had no intention of reliving it. She roamed the three rooms of the house as if she could herd all her old memories together, all the cheap shots rising unbidden from the past, and drive them out. An unwillingness to drop the past was her mother's problem, and Ronnie Mauss's, not hers. Tomorrow was more important than yesterday.

Crossing the threshold into the sun, Anna congratulated herself on the housecleaning that someone like her mother would never finish or someone like Grace Nettinger would never have attempted. She bent over the pepper plants. The sun warmed her back, the pepper leaves were thin and smooth, the smell of damp earth rose to moisturize her skin, but it was difficult for her to lock onto the present.

A vehicle pulled into the driveway behind her and the certainty that it was Ronnie made her stomach freeze. Georgia hadn't said what he was driving. Anna had a good idea of makes and models, but she didn't have her mother's dead-certain ability to identify a car or a truck by the pings and whirs of its engine's rotation.

"Anna." It was Ed Nettinger's voice. He got out of his truck and stood by her. "I have some catfish here I wanted to leave off with the Russells, but it looks like they're not home. You'd be doing me a favor taking some. Caught fresh not more than an hour ago. I've had to harvest them a little early this year."

Anna stood up and shielded her eyes against the sun and against Ed's drought-ridden face. "I can run them over to the Russell's when they get back."

"That's all right," Ed said easily. "They've probably still got a freezerful from the last seining. Take these, you won't taste a better catfish."

She delayed accepting. There was the question of what Ed Nettinger wanted from her. Was this a bribe or payment of a debt?

"There's some beautiful fish in here, Anna, channel catfish, some of the biggest I've raised yet. It'd be a shame to let them go to waste."

She considered Ed awhile longer, smiling into the sun because of the way the inside of a beauty shop and the catfish struck him. "Sure," she said. She let him hold the back door open for her since he seemed to want to so much, and then she led the way into her kitchen. How else would she find out what he wanted?

He stood over the sink to clean the fish. "I guess Delia's probably in Barcelona by now. It's Catalan she's studying over there, you know, not Spanish."

Anna watched his back, thinking that something had been reversed. She felt like a pampered guest while Ed Nettinger ran his hands under her kitchen faucet as if he were at home. There was no reason for him to feel so comfortable, unless making himself at home was one of his talents.

Ed wedged half the catfish into Anna's small freezer compartment and the other half in the refrigerator below. "This is ready to go, by the way, all cleaned. Grace never liked to clean catfish."

Anna hadn't invited Grace Nettinger into her kitchen. Hoping to keep Ed quiet, she draped a kitchen towel over his dripping hands. They were the kind of hands she liked in a man, long-fingered with the nails clipped, not bitten. Nothing preying on his mind.

"I couldn't see why Delia shouldn't go," he said. "She'd been planning that trip for a long time. A summer here wouldn't do her any good."

"What about you?" Anna asked. "What does a summer here hold in store for you?"

"The harvesting might go through July. I'm digging a new pond, for bass, half a surface acre bigger than the one now. I'd like to get it done by the fall so I can start stocking sunfish for forage." Ed folded the towel slowly as if he knew how much she appreciated the play of his hands. "I've been alone for a long time, Anna." He looked into the sink and held up a limp catfish. "Hungry? Looks like I forgot a couple."

Anna didn't think he forgot much, but she nodded and began

to allow herself to enjoy the sight of him working in her kitchen. For someone whose outward shape and texture seemed to have been stripped and sanded by the sun and the wind, he flowed with life. His cracked and colorless lips blended into the general topography of his face. Anna wanted to kiss wetness into them. She knew the inside of his mouth would be cool and satisfying, like drinking from a well.

————

Anna called her mother later in the week, on a Thursday when the day rates still applied and Georgia wouldn't be able to bring herself to talk long. "What have you told him this week?" she asked when Georgia answered.

"You don't believe a man can change. I'm still waiting for the jury to come in on Ronnie Mauss."

"The jury came in on him ten years ago at six forty-three P.M. on Friday, September the seventeenth, 1976. You saw what he did to me. I can't believe you're on his side."

"All I know is this," Georgia said. "He's searching for you. After all these years, he's looking for you. That's worth something."

"To you maybe. To a woman who probably still stands by the kitchen door before supper, waiting for Michael Leandros to back his 1951 Plymouth into the garage. What's it going to take? How do you think Frank feels knowing that every time he walks in the door you were hoping it would be that two-bit mechanic you spent a couple of nights with and have the nerve to call my father? Do you still think I don't know what the truth is? I can face it. Frank can face it. You're the only one who can't. I don't know why you just didn't kill him off in the Korean War."

"I just want you to be aware, Anna, that Ronnie Mauss is still in the game, and as long as he thinks that, then you're in it, too. He's real. They both are."

"You're the only one who thinks so. They're not in my lineup. Neither of them. So stop playing hot and cold with Ronnie."

"I can't, baby. He's looking for you. Ronnie's looking for you. One of these days he's going to pull up at your front door in a new silver Volvo with Louisiana license plates. I just want you to be prepared."

Anna lowered the blinds halfway and relaxed in her attempt to identify the driver of every passing car. Georgia had been working in the parts department of a big auto repair shop on the outskirts of Houston when she'd met Michael Leandros.

"You should know," Georgia continued, "that last week I got a postcard from Ronnie with a Monahans postmark and a picture of the Sand Hills on front. Do you want me to read it to you? Or do you want me to read the one I got in the mail yesterday from Odessa? Did you know the place where you went to beauty college has their own postcard now?"

"Is this what you're doing with him? Dropping hints all over the place? I don't want to see him. Don't you understand? This is not romance. This is not thwarted love. This is not your Michael Leandros returning. He could have killed me."

"That's a little dramatic, Anna," her mother objected. "He's changed. He's got such a sweet face. Give him a chance."

"No!"

"You're overreacting. My advice is to just see him, finish it out." Georgia's voice softened. "Honey, you can't go into anything else with this account outstanding. I know—"

"You're forgetting that I'm married to Bryan now," Anna reminded her. "I've already gone on. You haven't. That's your problem. Ronnie Mauss is not Michael Leandros. I am not you."

"You're as unforgiving as your maternal grandmother was." Georgia sighed.

"No you don't," Anna warned. "Your mother never thought there was anything that needed forgiving. I finish one thing and then move on to the next thing. At least I finish. So maybe I do take after the Phantom Mechanic. Or my paternal grandmother. Whoever she might be."

Georgia's voice grew fainter as if she were walking away from the receiver. "I'll give your love to Frank."

Anna throttled the buzzing receiver. The sunlight was withdrawing. She hadn't thought their conversation would last so long. Dusk made Georgia restless. The particular rhythm of certain car engines always stopped her conversation. She timed supper so that the rolls had to brown or the cheese on top of a casserole had to melt or the potatoes in their aluminum coats had to be turned over. In those fifteen or twenty free minutes she would stand by the kitchen door or look out the window.

Anna had learned early on not to present the day's events then, but she would pester and pester to know what it was that they were waiting for. "I don't know, baby," her mother would say vaguely, "I don't know." Nothing could drag Georgia away from that window or door. Until she was eight, Anna was convinced that every evening her mother left her body and sent out an all-seeing mind to search the world.

When the sound of a certain car made Georgia jump, Anna had known she would find all the cabinets and drawers opened and emptied the next morning and her mother dressed in her moving dress with its abrasive navy blue pleats. They would dig up the gardenia bush, wrap the roots in a wet sheet and place it in the loaded back seat like an extra passenger, a brother or a sister. Other people grew gardenias, other women wore the scent, but only her mother could make the green, shiny leaves thrive in alkaline caliche; only her mother could wear the flower for a full day without the cream petals going brown.

After she had turned twelve, Anna figured out that the emptiness in her stomach at seven-thirty meant hunger. The hollowness had nothing to do with waiting for a father to come home. She'd put away the extra place setting if she hadn't brought a friend home for dinner. There was always enough; Georgia cooked for three.

At seventeen she had seen that Georgia was concentrating all her energies on trying to construct a lover and a father out of a man she had spent one or two nights with eighteen years before. Marrying Ronnie Mauss had seemed like one way to free her mother from the burden of the lies.

A car slowed and then gunned past before Anna had a chance to get to the window. The kick of fear reminded her of how little protection the past offered. Understanding the small moments wasn't enough. Her mother had spent all those years pretending to search for Michael Leandros when what she was doing was running away from him.

Anna wanted to find the heart of her house and hide there until Ronnie Mauss fell into the North Sea, until Michael Leandros no longer stood between her and her mother. Instead, she plunged into the dusk and, turning her back on the street, began to thin the pansies.

———

Ronnie Mauss, in a fisherman's knit sweater despite the dry heat of the June night, sat on Anna's front porch. Thanks to the full moon, Anna saw his curly hair and sweet face two blocks away and began measuring her steps in an effort to build an edge on him. Half a block away she had wrapped herself in hostility. She stopped at the sidewalk that ran in front of the house and with her hands on her hips stood staring at Ronnie.

He rose from the porch and held out a tissue-wrapped package. "Hey, Anna," he appealed. "Come on—don't be that way. I've got something here for you."

Anna continued to straddle her two squares of concrete. "I don't want it. I want you off my property."

He waved the package as an enticement. "You don't even know what it is."

"I don't care what it is. I want you off my property."

"It's for you, Anna." Ronnie continued to wave the package slowly. "Only for you." When that failed, he came down the steps and tried to join her on the sidewalk.

Arms crossed, Anna downshifted her hips to declare the territory her own. His hands dropped, and from his position in front of her on the grass, Ronnie looked at the surrounding concrete in hope of finding safe passage past her. "Ten years, Anna. Come on," he pleaded softly. "Let me out of this. You're the only one that can."

Anna didn't trust the break in his voice. His vulnerability, true or false, hardened her resistance against him. The weight of the moonlight pushed his shoulders down. Her contempt suddenly seemed out of proportion. Celebrating his defeat was a violence no better than his. She felt her hips unlocking and remembered their pattern. Her strength, his weakness, her weakness, his strength.

"You're as much to blame as me, Anna. You're the only woman I've ever really hit. That's why I had to find you. You're the litmus test. Either it's you or it's me. If it's you, then it doesn't matter how much work I put in on myself. Teresa's right. It's out of my control."

"You're crazy." Anna tried to move past him. Ronnie grabbed her arm, and she knew she had tipped the scales. Her doubt had again cost her her strength. She struggled against herself more than she struggled against his arm. Ronnie's hand, at least, was solid. She could grab it and reckon with it, but the past had flooded her mind and she panicked. She fought to fuse her body and mind to the present. There's a way out of this, she thought. Stop the action. Give me back fifteen minutes. Let me start over. I can handle it better this time.

Ronnie tightened his grip. He brandished her arm like a trophy and said triumphantly, "You see. You see. It's you, Anna. You're the source. It's not me. It's you."

"That's so easy for you! No matter who you hit or when, you're going to blame me. You think you won't ever have to answer for it—"

"You're in this just as deep as me. Who threw that first punch?" Ronnie asked. His voice was reasonable. Her struggle seemed to soothe him.

"You did!"

With a hard grip on her arm, Ronnie turned as if consulting a blackboard. "No. Now, whoever—whoever hits back—whoever hits back starts the fight. If you don't hit back, there's no fight."

She tried to pull away, but he hadn't relaxed his grip. "What is this then? Look at what you've done to my arm. You tell me what that is. And don't tell me—do *not* tell me—that I'm doing that to myself."

Ronnie unfastened his fingers slowly as if they were stiff and examined the evidence on her arm. "I couldn't have done it without you, Anna. You're the thing that sets it off."

The long wail of one of the Russell children next door and the distorted patches of bedroom light thrown suddenly across the yard broke their deadlock. Anna recovered first and ran into the house. Pressing herself against the locked door, she was more terrified by his version of logic than the possibility of his anger. There was no sign of lukewarm remorse, the next step. The pattern had changed.

He scratched at the screen over an open living room window. "I could get in, Anna. If I wanted to. You know that. You want me to come in. But I won't do it. I won't give in to you. Teresa was right. It's you. It's been you all the time." '

The reasonableness in his voice was almost seductive. Anna had to keep her fingers clamped down on the screen door's hooked lock so she wouldn't be tempted to open the door. A calm Ronnie Mauss wasn't what she'd been expecting. Her mother had been right; he had changed, and the change was frightening. The feelings of fear that Ronnie aroused made her angry. She had no intention of reliving his past or of accepting responsibility for his violence. "Get off my property. I'm calling the police."

Ronnie brought his face to the screen. "Good-bye, Anna. I'm leaving the blame on your front porch. I've visualized it. It's there. I'm a changed man now. It's up to you to decide what to do with it. I can forgive you. I'm a changed man now." His eyes recorded the details of the interior and then rested briefly on her face. The sight of her pressed against the inner door made him smile. "I wish you could see yourself now. That's how you made me feel."

Whistling through his front teeth, Ronnie skipped down the porch steps and stopped when he hit the sidewalk. "This isn't even your property, Anna. You rent." He was beside his car in three long steps.

Anna rubbed her forehead on the screen. A smell that was purely Ronnie's lingered. She quickly pulled away from the screen. It was a pleasant smell that brought a brief flash of memory that remained unclear. Disturbed at wanting that essence of him to remain, she ran her fingers across the screen and found herself straining to recapture what she had just lost. The sudden yearning might have been the desire to understand or the simple response of her senses. Before she could call out to Ronnie, to make him come back to collect the renegade Annas he had loosed inside her, the silver Volvo zoomed away from the curb.

His departure didn't settle Anna. She felt trapped. In her heart of hearts she knew that he hadn't left anything except a package on the front porch, but she couldn't make herself unlatch the door and walk outside.

This was where she lived. She didn't have to climb out of a window to get away from him. Tonight Ronnie was the one on the outside. She didn't have to go running into the night again to escape. Straight into his arms.

Anna bolted the front door and turned off all the lights. To monitor all sound and movement around the house, she went to the center of the living room-dining room and walked in a tight circle.

The beam of headlights hit the far wall as a car pulled into the driveway. Anna dropped to the floor. A car door slammed, and leather-soled footsteps sounded on the sidewalk. Ronnie had been wearing running shoes; his feet hadn't made a sound. She rolled over to the front window, where one of Bryan's golf clubs was jammed into the frame to keep the window open. The sash slammed into the sill when she jerked the club free.

Whoever was outside leaped onto the porch and pounded on the front door. "Mrs. Bryan!" a male voice yelled. "Mrs. Bryan, are you all right in there?"

Nobody called her Mrs. Bryan. Pressing her full weight against the door again, Anna turned the lock as quietly as she could. The golf club was in her left hand, ready to bar anybody's entry. She counted to five and then threw open the door.

K. O. Browne, Jr., gun drawn, stood on the sidewalk. His tan car, unmarked by the official Border Patrol seal, sat in the driveway. The car door was open; Anna could hear the static of the police band. "What are you doing here?" she asked.

"Don't come out on the front porch," K.O. said. "Your visitor left a package there under the nandinas. Come out the back door."

"What do you want?" Anna asked. None of this should be

happening. Ronnie Mauss was supposed to have stayed in the past. K. O. Browne, Jr., shouldn't be here either; he was Bryan's nemesis, not hers. He wouldn't have shown up unless he had the house under surveillance and thought Ronnie Mauss was a friend or an enemy of Bryan's.

"With your permission, I'd like to check out that package. I'd like to call the bomb squad in from El Paso," K.O. said. He waved both arms as if Anna were an airplane he had to direct to a hangar. "What I'd like for you to do is go to your back door and come out that way."

The border patrolman's inflated sense of caution made Anna impatient. Ronnie Mauss wouldn't leave a bomb on her doorstep; that would be too quick. What K. O. Browne wanted was evidence against Bryan. Moving to the right, she was able to see a corner of the package.

"Half the town would be blown to bits by the time anybody got here from El Paso." She unlatched the screen door and, before K.O. could stop her, bashed the package with the golf club. Nothing happened. The package didn't explode; a nest of snakes didn't activate their rattles and take aim at her ankles.

K.O. had drawn his gun and centered it on the bobbing white bow. "You took a big, big chance," he said. "You don't know what was in that package."

"I know the man who left it."

"I'd like to get in touch with your husband, Mrs. Bryan, and wait with you until he gets back."

Anna watched him sheathe the gun. He probably had a better idea where Bryan was than she did. "What I'd like you to do is drive me to Mary Frances's shop," she said and locked the front door. "And maybe find out where that man in the silver Volvo went." Let the officer think Ronnie was part of Bryan's dealings gone wrong. While the authorities were sniffing the wrong tracks, she could find out what damage Ronnie had done to other women.

K. O. Browne beat Anna to the passenger door and held it open. He smiled and dimples sank in both cheeks. That made the border patrolman look like a teenager and Anna feel as if he were taking her to the high school prom. He destroyed the image by transmitting Anna's address and the address of Mary Frances's shop over the radio.

"What are you doing?" Anna asked. She wondered if everybody in town had to know her business.

"Keeping in touch. You never know what's liable to happen out here in the field." He drove down the street, slowing every twenty feet to shine a high-beam light into cars parked along the curb.

As they approached the end of the block, Anna recognized Jo's car. K.O.'s light picked up two figures huddled in the front seat. Like a black hole, Jo's hair absorbed most of the light. When the border patrolman honked, Jo and Burgess reluctantly came out of a long, deep kiss.

It was after one o'clock in the morning. Jo and Burgess weren't teenagers; they had been married for close to thirty years. There was no reason for them to be making out in the front seat of a car. Anna had suspected that Burgess was watching the house, but she had never thought Jo would spy on her.

The patrolman smiled and waved. "They never stop, do they? Makes me miss my wife. It's hard, isn't it, being separated from someone you love?" He was a handsome, earnest man. Elongated, those dimples must measure two inches.

"It's the next left, two blocks up."

"It doesn't seem right, does it," K.O. continued, "that you have to deal with this all by yourself?"

"I'm sure your wife's saying the same thing," Anna said. "Doesn't she live in El Paso? Where the bomb squad is?"

"My wife and I believe in the same things. She believes in what I do. She knows it's right."

Which is more than I can say, which is what you want me to say, thought Anna. Here she was, sitting beside the man who probably knew more about Bryan than anyone did. All she had to do was ask. A fat lot of good her marital agreement with Bryan was doing. That piece of paper, designed to guarantee her ignorance of Bryan's activities, was protected by the heavy bars and steel door of the bank, but what was it doing to safeguard her own privacy?

Ronnie Mauss's name and vital statistics came over the radio. K. O. Brown spoke into the transmitter. "Has he ever been arrested?" Anna asked.

"Negative. You don't have high report figures on domestic violence. What I can tell you is that it looks like your ex-husband's on his way back to Baton Rouge. Looks like it was lucky I happened to be driving by."

Anna couldn't believe that K.O. had her history down, too. There had been too many collisions tonight for her to put any faith in luck or coincidence. It had been inevitable that she and K. O. Browne, Jr., would somehow cross paths because of Bryan, but she'd thought her private life would remain her own. Anna got out of the car at the next intersection.

The border patrolman let Anna go, but he concentrated the high beam on her back. "I'll be keeping an eye out for you, Mrs. Bryan, with your husband gone so much of the time."

Since the light was intended to pinpoint and not to guide, Anna let her immense shadow lead the way to the shop. She unlocked the shop's front door and stepped inside. The spotlight from the patrol car searched the Astroturf welcome mat for something else to track until K.O. extinguished it. He would have to take it on faith that nobody had grabbed her because there was no way she was turning on the light. Finally, in an end to the standoff, the border patrolman drove slowly past the shop and beamed the spotlight through the front door. Framing herself in the front door, Anna let the light prowl her body and the shop beyond. K.O. honked and backed up to the intersection.

There was no need for lights. Anna knew the shop better than she knew any other place. Usually the horrible aging of the pink trappings made her crave change. The translucent pink hoods of the dryer were turning orange; a layer of haze had settled in between the wall-length mirror's glass and silvering; packets of tissue-wrapped hairnets were now brittle. She didn't need light to see that these things had already happened.

A wave of relief that bordered on love washed over Anna. This was her world. Ronnie's visit hadn't altered it. There was no need for her to waste any energy in defending herself against his charges. She had plenty of work to do right here. The future, not the past, was important. Before going into the styling area, Anna pulled the shade on the front door halfway down so Jo would know everything was all right if she and Burgess drove by. There would be time later on to get angry at Bryan for letting his troubles spill into everybody's lives when he'd contracted not to let that happen. And at Burgess for getting his wife involved. And at Jo for going along with it.

"Later," Anna said. To ward off thinking about what kind of danger Bryan was in—because she had contracted to remain deaf, dumb and blind to his dealings along the Mexican border —or thinking about the current whereabouts of Ronnie Mauss, she stepped off the length of the styling room. It still measured forty feet. Not long enough. Mary Frances's baseboard jungle took up four feet in the waiting area. But once the shop was Anna's and Mary Frances had packed everything in the apartment upstairs except for the chaise lounge, the wall between the waiting area and the styling room was coming down. Each stylist would have his or her own L-shaped island of counterspace.

As Anna was in the process of mentally dismembering dryer hoods from the banquette, the phone rang. She decided the shop needed an answering machine. If there wasn't one in town, she would drive to El Paso and get one.

The ringing stopped for a few seconds but then started again. Anna picked up the receiver and held it to her ear without saying anything. She heard the ding of a car pulling into a gas station and someone coughing in the background.

"Anna?" Jo's voice sounded hollow. "Are you all right? I know that's you."

"Where *are* you? Don't tell me you and Burgess got so excited you decided to check into a motel."

"Now you know we do that only on the second Saturday of every month. Speaking of spending the night, do you want to come stay with us?"

"Burgess would love that. No way." He would keep her awake all night trying to find out what she'd told K. O. Browne, Jr. She had some grilling of her own to do. "What were you two doing out so late? Parked in my neighborhood?"

"I was worried about that Ronnie Mauss character, and when I worry, Burgess worries—you know that."

"Burgess has enough to worry about on his own," Anna said. Suddenly she had had enough. Ronnie Mauss had become a smoke screen. Burgess had been watching her house for Bryan's sake, but Jo wouldn't say that on the telephone, even on a pay phone. She was tired of the exaggerated secrecy. "If Burgess was there, then why didn't he try to stop what was going on? Solidarity with another wife beater?"

"Anna. Thin ice, very, very thin ice. I know you're upset—"

"Just tell me if Bryan's going to come busting through the door. He doesn't need to. I told K. O. Browne the same thing. Bryan doesn't need to come here. There's no reason for him to come here. Everything's all right." Where was Jo? Why wasn't she home in bed with Burgess? Were they following K. O. Browne, Jr., or had they switched to tailing Ronnie Mauss? Was there a danger that the shop phone was bugged? Infected by paranoia, Anna found herself wanting to say something that Jo should already know—that she hadn't told on Bryan, that even if she knew anything, she wouldn't tell—and unable to say the words because they sounded so incriminating.

"I don't want Bryan to find out about Ronnie Mauss. If anybody tells him, it'll be me. Burgess can tell him anything else he wants to. But not that. Leave Ronnie Mauss out of it. That's my business. It's separate."

"That boy didn't look a thing like I thought he would," Jo said. "I can't picture you two together at all."

"That was ten years ago. I was only seventeen. Promise me you won't let Burgess tell. Promise me."

"I've got my hand over his mouth right now, but I think you should call Bryan tonight and tell him your ex-husband dropped in for a little visit."

"I don't care what you think so long as you keep your hand over his mouth."

"Are you sure you don't want to come stay with us?"

"Positive." Anna was exactly where she wanted to be.

"All right, but don't you touch my ivy—I know you've been itching to pull it down. That shop's not yours yet."

After Jo hung up, Anna listened for clicks on the line or the static interference of a border patrol radio. There was nothing besides the usual buzz, and that sound was getting on her nerves. She wedged a brush handle into the telephone's cradle. The handle kept the buttons pushed down while she unscrewed the receiver at its speaking end. A round metal piece with eight holes fell into her hand. Examining the metal piece under the lamp at Jo's station, Anna thought it looked harmless, but she had nothing in her memory to compare it with. Surely, as a child, she must have unscrewed the telephones at one of her friends' houses to find out about sound. They didn't have a phone until Anna was fifteen. She had had to pay for the installation herself and convince Georgia to go halves on the monthly bill.

The idea of remaining out of touch was appealing now. Anna considered leaving the phone in pieces. Her mother might have had the right idea. Any customer who called at two in the morning needed more help than any stylist could give. There was probably a whole line of cars parked in the lot on the opposite side of the creek, and every driver probably had a pair of binoculars trained on the shop. If something happened, she wouldn't need to make an outgoing call. Everybody watching would see it happen before she did; one of them was bound to take action.

Anna tried to rotate the tension out of her shoulders. The loss of privacy was the worst thing. When the shop was hers, the upstairs apartment would also be hers. Mary Frances lived four blocks away and used the apartment for her daytime trysts, but Anna planned to make it her permanent residence. Living high in the air and being surrounded by trees would buffer her from any surprises.

T he next morning, at six forty-five, the attack of Mary Frances's high heels on the back stairs woke Anna. Her legs were numb from being crumpled in the well of the shampoo couch all night. Stretching carefully, Anna let her eyes follow the overhead trail of footsteps as Mary Frances went into the kitchenette, the bathroom, to one side of the bed, to the other side of the bed to use the phone, until she kicked off her shoes when the call went through. Mary Frances's lover's wife must have left the house.

Liz wandered in at seven forty-five. She took her coffee into the bathroom and locked the door. In the hope that the bathroom would be free before the first customer arrived and there would be time to wash her face, Anna went to the supply cabinet under the stairs for a towel.

Mary Frances dropped her shoes off the second-floor landing and almost hit Anna. "Thank goodness, *somebody's* here! Josephine called me at home. She won't be in this morning, probably a little romance *du jour* with Burgess. I've called the high school and gotten Sandra out of civics—I told them I was her grandmother and she had to come home quick. You take Jo's appointments, and I'll keep Liz out of the bathroom. And no arguments with my clientele, Anna. Just do what they want you to do, not what you think they need, or I'll have to dock you again."

"If you have to dock me again, then consider it part of my down payment on the shop." For once Anna hoped Mary Frances had overbooked so the time would pass quickly. Ronnie Mauss would go deep into the past again and K. O. Browne, Jr., would continue to orbit Bryan's world, not hers.

———

Jo arrived at one. Anna was doing a henna rinse in the shampoo room. Although Jo's voice had to travel the length of two noisy rooms before reaching Anna's ears, her general greeting sounded forced. Energy ordinarily upped Jo's volume, but this voice was loud and false. Anna hurriedly capped Esther, her customer. A look would tell her whether an argument with Burgess or romance had kept Jo at home.

But Esther held Anna at the black basin. "My head feels cold. Is it supposed to feel this cold? Nesta, my sister from Akron—the one you fought with over her part—for three hours, told me about henna, but she never said anything about it being so cold. I hope it doesn't get into my ear. It's not going into my ear, is it? I have trouble with my ears."

"Your ears are fine," Anna said automatically. With their heads wrapped in plastic and their scalps growing cold or hot depending on the treatment, the women had plenty of time to think about the drastic transformation they were undergoing. Anna had a stockpile of assurances ready; this client particularly needed them. She was also prepared to withdraw them if Esther kept harping on her sister. "That's why I looped all that cotton around them. The cap should keep them dry—"

"Should!" Esther's thick legs kicked in alarm, but the flying U shape of the pink shampoo couch had a firm hold on her behind.

"*Will* keep your ears dry. *Is* keeping your ears dry. Here I am.

Right here with a towel. Ready for any drip. You're safe. Relax."
Anna wiped a phantom dribble of henna from Esther's temple.

"Relax! I wish I could! It's not that easy. I don't have somebody
standing around all the time with a towel in their hands, just
waiting to wipe away all the drips, you know."

"I know," Anna said as she maneuvered around the couch to
get a better angle into the styling room. Jo was managing to keep
her back to the shampoo room.

Esther's ice cube blue eyes slid farther out of her lids, and her
body tried to struggle out of the couch's grip again. "Where are
you going?"

"To check on somebody under the dryer. I'll be back before a
drip even has a chance to think about doing anything." As Anna
reached under a dryer and felt her client's back curlers, she tried
unsuccessfully to catch a glimpse of Jo in the mirror.

Stepping back from her chair to light a cigarette, Jo kept her
back to the dryers and said, "Don't stare, Anna. It's rude."

Then turn around, Anna thought. Let me take a look at you and
see that everything's all right. She had come to rely on Jo as a
touchstone, and that reassurance was being tainted by Jo's knowledge of Bryan's activities along the border.

"Anna! I'm *dripping!*" Esther shouted.

The cotton was doing its job. No henna was creeping down
Esther's forehead, but Anna wiped the woman's face anyway.
Wedging herself in a corner an arm's length away, she soaked up
Esther's laments. When the timer rang fifteen minutes later and
the henna could be washed out, Anna felt twenty pounds heavier.

If taking on the problems of somebody she barely knew was so
tiring, how could she load Jo's thinner frame with her own troubles? It looked as if Jo already felt the weight. Usually a change
in customers wouldn't punctuate her speech; she could have con-
versations going with everyone within hearing distance. Jo could
have a line of women under the dryers, one at the manicure table,
one rinsed out and waiting for a conditioner and two in the middle
of a blowout and not lose her rhythm. But today the pinning of
a roller was enough to stop her in the middle of a sentence. Several
times she rested one wrist on her chair back and absentmindedly

finished a cigarette instead of a comb-out. Anna monitored the relationship between Jo's Bic lighter and the cans of hair spray all afternoon.

———

By the end of the day Anna had dropped most of the weight of her customers' lives. She tried to clip her own bangs while she waited for Jo to finish in the shampoo room, but the scissors felt heavy and awkward. Her eyes strayed from the mirror and she would become mesmerized by a clump of hair on the floor. Sitting seemed to sap energy from her body, so Anna got up and started cleaning the counter.

Jo had turned the deep cap of her hair spray into a silent butler. Anna spritzed the ashes and stubs with water before emptying the cap. A haze of smoke seemed to cover Jo's station; all the postcards taped to her mirror were covered with a film. The crowd of framed photographs that took up half of Jo's counter space got a thorough cleaning at the close of every day.

Anna breathed on the photo of Burgess and Jo and their two sons, Marvin and Bevo. At least three years old, the photograph was the last one to show them together. Marvin, blond and grinning sideways at the rest of his family, had joined the marines a few months after the photo was taken. Burgess was in the middle, dwarfed by Marvin but evenly matched with Bevo. Anna bet that Burgess had been standing on his tiptoes when the shutter clicked. Because of Burgess's uptilted chin the sweep of his pompadour rose a fraction above Bevo's head. As always, Bevo smiled directly into the camera, knowing that if he got to the photographer, then he would reach anybody who looked at the picture. Bevo wanted to seduce the world, but he had decided to start with the men first. For almost two years after finding out about his son's preferences Burgess hadn't spoken to Bevo. Only when Jo had intervened, telling Burgess that if there had to be a choice she would choose Bevo, did he consent to meetings with his son in public places. With her hair looking like a faraway funnel cloud, Jo hovered in the background of the family photo as if she were physically holding them together.

The loss of Bevo had coincided with the arrival of Bryan, and Anna believed that Burgess thought of Bryan as his third son. They had met in the Chihuahua Desert when Burgess and his tow truck had happened upon Bryan and his steaming car. She didn't understand what had forged their friendship so fast. "Male bonding," Burgess always said. "You don't understand, Anna, because you don't understand anything about men, or about bonding." A blurred picture of Burgess and Bryan riding burros across a shallow Rio Grande also graced the counter. Both of them had white smudges across their faces from smiling so hugely. Like they believed they were getting away with something, Anna thought. Riding into Mexico like that.

The centerpiece of Jo's collection was an eight-by-ten frame. A likeness of Bevo, outfitted in a royal blue robe for his graduation from beauty school in San Antonio, sat in the upper-left-hand corner. Streaks in his naturally black hair had been blanched prematurely white for his senior project. Marvin, in his marine dress uniform, sat across from his brother. He was trying so hard not to smile that his features were distorted. Taking up the bottom half of the frame was a photo from Jo and Burgess's thirtieth wedding anniversary. Anna and Bryan sat across from them.

Jo surprised Anna by coming in wearing a cape and a towel twisted around her head. "I should have known you couldn't keep your hands off my men."

"I thought you had a customer," Anna said.

"I did. My favorite customer." Jo lit a cigarette and squinted into the mirror. "Me."

"You should have told me. I would have shampooed you." Anna paused as Jo leaned back and shut her eyes. "You wouldn't be so tired if you hadn't stayed up all night spying on me."

"I was watching out for you, not spying on you, the same way Burgess watches out for Bryan—"

"Please! Are you telling me that if there had never been a Ronnie Mauss, you wouldn't have been out there keeping Burgess company? You're getting in too deep with Bryan."

"I don't want to talk about it anymore—you'll just have to trust me." Jo clicked her long red nails together. "Lord! Look at those gorgeous men in these pictures."

Anna knew she wouldn't get anything out of Jo. There was no sense in pursuing the discussion, but frustration and fatigue were making her temper short. Ronnie Mauss was heading back to Louisiana with a clear conscience. Why should she feel compelled to carry on the debate when she knew she had never offered the resiliency of her body to bait him? Where was Bryan while everyone else was assuming responsibility for his protection? Why didn't Claude stock a row of beer bottles in the soda machine for days like these?

"Help me here, Anna," Jo said. She was using both hands to position three postcards on the mirror and couldn't get to the tape dispenser.

"M.F.'s going to dock you when she finds out you're using the tape for personal business. I don't think it's in the best interest of the shop to help you." Anna snapped a piece of tape to prevent it from sticking to itself. "Where do you want it? Along the tops or across the corners?"

"Along the tops. I don't want the corners to tear. Have you heard from Charles?" Jo asked. She continued to press the post-cards against the mirror after they were firmly secured.

"You might as well call him Bevo like everybody else does."

"I would have named him that instead of Charles if I wanted to call him that," Jo said.

"I got a postcard from Las Vegas a couple of weeks ago," Anna said. "He didn't say anything about needing a place to stay soon so he must not be on his way here."

"Well, he's in Santa Fe this week." Jo smoothed lint from the photograph of her husband and sons. "If you and Bryan can't make a go of it, how about you and Charles?"

"No, thanks. Two marriages of convenience are enough."

"You could do worse," Jo said wistfully.

Anna wished there weren't so much seriousness in Jo's voice. "I have done worse. That's not the point."

"Now, I was worried at one time, when he was sixteen, that

time he ran off to Mexico and then he went back to your house.
. . . I really didn't know what might happen between you
two—"

"All I was teaching him about was hair. Not sex. He could have
done worse."

"Even Burgess would agree with you on that. He'd take even
you over one of Charles's boyfriends any day. Lord! The time I'd
have keeping you from tearing into each other—" The thought
made Jo laugh. It was a deep, phlegmatic laugh that sounded more
like a cough.

The sound bothered Anna. She patted Jo on the back, not to
comfort her, but hard, to knock the noise out of the lungs.

"I'm all right," Jo insisted. "Stop hitting me and let me sit
down."

Anna waited until Jo was settled and quiet. "Teach me how you
do your hair."

"Now that's one thing I'll never share. A woman needs to keep
one mystery in her life." With a smoker's sense, Jo opened her
eyes to follow the half inch of ash down to the pile of hair matted
on the floor. "You know Mary F. uses this mess to stuff pillows
with. I thought sure she wouldn't if I ashed in it, but she does.
I wonder how many people who buy those pillows at that church
bazaar of hers know what they're leaning up against."

She ground out her cigarette in a deliberate downward swirl.
"Get ready," she said and began to unwind the towel.

Anna was one of the few people who had seen Jo's hair undone;
she was prepared. The tower was a marvel of illusion. Jo used a
dye that uniformly coated every strand a dull black; light was
captured by her hair instead of being reflected by it so the mass
seemed more dense than it was. Jo's hair wasn't that thick or long;
if you looked hard enough, you could see through the teased hair.

But when Jo whisked away the towel, Anna was stunned. Veins
of silver coursed through her hair. There had never been a hint
of gray at the roots. Anna had always supposed Jo touched them
up every morning with a cotton ball dipped in dye.

"I'm fine," Jo said and reached over to pat Anna's hand. "This
is me. It's been so long I wanted to see what I really looked like.

I started to put it up this morning and saw the roots coming out and my arms were getting tired from all the teasing and I wondered why I even bothered. I just woke up and I felt like I was all covered over with frost. This cold touch."

Anna took the comb out of Jo's hand. She rested her hand on Jo's crown before making a deep side part. The silver slid so easily between the teeth of the comb that she wanted to cry. "It looks fine like this. Very dramatic. Very striking."

It was a lie. She wanted Jo's hair to be its own unnatural color again. "If you teach me how to do your hair, I can fix it when you don't feel like it. I'll keep your secret. You know how good I am at keeping my mouth shut."

———

That afternoon Anna walked home the long way. She cut through the backyard of the old four-bedroom house that had become the public library and peeked into the empty den where the mysteries were shelved. There was nobody in the room to spy on, so she sat down on the low stone wall that ran along the creek to sun herself. An identical wall banded the other side. Both walls of rock and mortar were sheared off at an unpaved crossing farther south as if a car had busted through. Since there was already a bridge two blocks away that shouldered a highway, the road careered in and out of the creek. The town couldn't afford to throw a bridge across every sharp drop.

Anna wished she was in her car. Whenever she felt restless, she would back the Valiant out of the garage and drive away from town for a hundred miles. The direction wasn't important. When the hundredth mile was clocked on the odometer, she would turn around. What was important was taking the unpaved crossing to the highway. The crossing challenged her driving skills. If she couldn't negotiate herself out of the creek, then she couldn't leave town.

The GM dealership was two blocks away. There was a small chance that Burgess would lend her one of the used cars from the lot. Anna dismissed the thought. She wanted to get away but not bad enough to ask Burgess for a favor.

Since the crossing behind the library was too steep to take on foot, Anna walked to the highway bridge and continued west for another four blocks before reluctantly turning toward her house. The street was quiet and the yards were empty. There was no evidence of Burgess's stakeout, or the border patrol's, no smoking Coleman stoves or lawn chairs hidden in the shrubs. She positioned herself across the street from her own house. The lawn she had chosen to lie on was soft with thin-bladed grass. Sweet white blossoms from a Chinese locust sprinkled the yard.

Linda Russell, Anna's next-door neighbor, rounded the corner. Three children were strung out behind her on a length of clothesline. Each of them carried a large can of orange drink. Linda had a sack of groceries in one arm and her two-year-old in the other. Sleepily counting her fingers, the little girl bumped against her mother's cushiony hip. Linda twitched the clothesline and they all struggled up the front porch steps. The last child in line threw his can down the steps. Linda aimed a wail at the sky. The little girl's concentration broke. She puckered her soft forehead and began to cry at losing count. Trying to follow their mother down the steps, the children went different directions and got tangled in the line.

Anna had to laugh. She could see everything that happened, and sound carried easily as if distance strengthened the waves. Involved in her own crises, Linda had no idea she was being watched. She didn't know that they all lived in shoeboxes and that the top to her box had been taken off. Privacy fences separated the houses from each other, but next-door neighbors weren't the danger. The danger came from the other lives they led or had led —marked and unmarked cars watching out for Bryan, Ronnie Mauss watching out for her.

Ed Nettinger came out of Anna's backyard. She couldn't stop laughing. Yesterday morning she'd believed she could keep the uninvited out of her yard. Ed skirted the hedge between the two houses. He righted an overturned tricycle whose wheels were still spinning. Linda Russell clasped her hands together as if she'd seen a vision of Jesus. Ed bobbed the small heads in and out until the clothesline was untangled. The children rushed his long legs and almost got themselves snared again.

Anna rolled over and rubbed her face in the grass. She should leave. Leave everything behind and let them keep watching the house and waiting for her. Someone sat down beside her and she couldn't think of a person she wanted it to be.

"You're quite a nature girl," Ed Nettinger said. He picked locust blossoms out of her hair. "I had no idea."

Anna shook her head out of his reach. "Are you *always* there when somebody needs help?"

"Not always. What's so funny?"

Ed's admission didn't make Grace materialize, but Anna moved a body's width away from him anyway. Everybody else was showing up. There was nothing in Ed's face that indicated any sense of grief or anger. His body didn't generate the heaviness of guilt. Failure hadn't eroded the set of his shoulders. Anna didn't see how he could escape Grace's death so easily. The absence of pain bothered her. It was too easy to believe that he had no past.

"I hear you had a visitor last night," he said.

"Are you sure you weren't over here in the bleachers watching the whole thing?" She felt his fingers circling the bruises Ronnie Mauss had left on her arm. His touch was gentle without being tentative as if he knew where the pain would begin.

"Did you call the police?" he asked.

"No. He's gone. He got what he came for. He left a satisfied man." The lack of sleep suddenly told. Anna felt her bones sinking into the grass. A freshwater smell came from Ed as he moved closer. She thought of his catfish and started laughing again.

A tennis ball bounded into Ed's chest. The Russell children, clumped on the corner, shouted across to him. "Don't go into the street," he warned. "Stay there, I'll throw it to you." The ball hit the front door, and the children scattered.

Linda flew out of the house. "I've had it!"

"Now you've done it," Anna said. She crossed the street to Linda. "It was Ed Nettinger." Her fingers itched to get hold of Linda's hair, which was always in the process of growing out. It fell brown and straight for two inches from her part and then dangled another six inches like yellow and orange crepe paper left in the rain. She kept her mouth shut since Linda had never been shy about asking for free styling.

"He's the nicest man," Linda said. "I think it's wonderful what he's doing to your backyard. I think people should help each other out—"

"My backyard?" Anna headed for a break in the hedge. Ronnie Mauss had taken possession of her front yard, and now Ed Nettinger thought he had a claim on the back.

Linda grabbed Anna's arm. "Listen! What do you think about that frosting kit with the two women on the front?"

"Don't do it. I'm not bailing you out of this one."

"I was just *wondering,*" Linda protested. She backed away, but her left rubber thong with a piece bitten off the heel remained in the mud. "I mean, I would come to Mary Frances's if I could afford it."

"You'd come to Mary Frances's if I didn't live next door."

Ed Nettinger ambled across the street. He picked up a pile of uprooted plants he'd left on the sidewalk. "Let me show you what I brought in from the ranch."

Anna followed him to Bryan's herb garden. A ring sprinkler sitting on the patch of bare ground in the backyard sent fountains of water into the air. She sat on the kitchen steps. The coolness that came from deep within the concrete was comforting. A pile of mint that Ed had thinned lay on the steps. Their exposed roots reminded her of baby birds' feet.

Ed brushed his hands against a basil plant. "I brought this in today. I think it'll take. The mint goes like wildfire, you want to watch out that it doesn't take over."

"That's pretty good coming from you." Anna rolled a grainy leaf of the sage between her fingers. The scent remained after she threw it away. Wiping her hands on the hem of her dress only transferred the smell. "What about the roof? Any loose shingles up there? I bet you'd be over here bright and early tomorrow morning to fix it. Why even leave? Why don't you and Delia just move right in?"

"There's the fish. Who'd take care of them?" Ed examined the lacy cilantro with the same gentleness he had given Anna's arm. "There's some yellowing starting here. You might want to thin it some." He reached down and carefully uprooted one plant.

Anna could hear the tearing of the tender roots. A chill went up her back. "I hate that sound."

"It's done." He laid the cilantro close to the mint and said, "Delia's coming home day after tomorrow."

"Is that why you're here? Trying to get the latest scoop on your daughter?"

Ed stood up to brush off his khaki pants. "I'm not here because of my daughter or my wife. I know them. I'm here because I had some extra basil and I thought you might like some. I remembered you were growing tomatoes."

"If anything, I'm Greek, not Italian." The easiness of his denials must have been like needles in Grace's skin. Anna started to tell him she was tired and he should go home, but she was unwilling to offer any explanations to him. "Forget it."

He reached out for her. "What, Anna? What?"

Rewarded by his frustration, she leaned back. "Nothing. Forget it."

"Maybe I've misjudged the situation between you and Bryan."

Anna shook her head and made room for him on the steps. Ed captured her face in his hands. "You don't trust me, do you?"

Her sharp chin broke the V of his palms. "No. I don't."

————

A squeal of tires woke Anna. The sprinkler had been turned off and Ed's car was gone from the driveway. Shadows from the pyracantha were still projected against the far wall; she couldn't have been asleep for more than an hour. Anna reached under the bed for a beer bottle to use as a weapon. Lulled by Ed Nettinger's presence, she hadn't remembered to lock the kitchen door. Last night, lulled by Ronnie's leaving and the thought that he wouldn't be back, she hadn't remembered to listen to the sounds his silver

Volvo made. She had fucked up. She should have gotten into the Valiant immediately and attacked the crossing. Ronnie Mauss's visit was making her feel too vulnerable.

Anna locked the house and went out to the garage. There was half a tank of gas in the Valiant; if traffic was light on Avenue C, she wouldn't have to stop for anything.

The intersection of Avenue C and Kramer Lane was clear. In the next block Kramer Lane, stripped of its blacktop, disappeared into the creek. Before its sudden descent, the road swerved as if even the engineers had lost their nerve. Anna parked behind the stop sign on Kramer Lane and walked across Avenue C. She wanted to see if the deep ruts embedded in the dirt had changed course. The true test of skill was steering out of the gravel skid and into the ruts. When the front wheels started to drop, she would have to turn the wheel sharply to the left and then to the right so the car would stay centered on the road. An overcompensation in either direction would send her traveling along the creek wall parallel to the bottom. Satisfied that the ruts hadn't changed and her approach to the creek would be the same as the last one had been, she returned to the Valiant.

The intersection was still clear. Anna gunned the accelerator, and the Valiant hurtled across the avenue. As the back end fishtailed on the gravel, she rocked the steering wheel to ease the tires into the ruts. Exhilaration shot through her body when the wheels fit into place. The front end hung for a moment and then dropped. Anna locked her arms against the first downward jolt. Letting her elbows hinge and cushion the shock, she urged the car left and then almost too much to the right. The rapid ascent drove her shoulders into the seat back. She floorboarded the gas pedal and struggled to regain the center of the road. The Valiant made it to the top and sped toward a stop sign. Heel on the floor, Anna let the ball of her foot steadily press the brake until the car stopped just short of the intersection.

It hadn't been one of her better crossings, but she felt the sense of invincibility that landing on the other side always brought. Ronnie Mauss's visit hadn't destroyed that. Nothing would.

Delia set her pictures of Spain on the front seat. "You drive like
an old lady. If this were Barcelona, you'd be dead now." She rolled
her window down and adjusted the outside mirror, tilting it back
and forth so many times that Anna was almost convinced that she
was an *avisadora,* one of the message senders along the border
who used mirrors to flash important news Finally satisfied by the
angle, Delia rolled up her window halfway and twisted to stare out
the back window. A last look at the scenery didn't seem to be on
her mind.

The tension of the girl's posture made Anna tap the loose
rearview mirror. She expected the new perspective to reveal a
convoy of eighteen-wheel trucks bearing down on them. The
mirror dangled like a loose tooth and in its swings reflected an
empty two-lane highway.

"This is a great car, Anna. Are you sure we'll make it to Hallie's
in this thing?" Delia reached behind the mirror. "There's not
even a screw or a bolt back here. God, Anna, what is this?"
Leaning over the split dashboard, she forced the mirror toward
her.

Anna doubled-checked the receding purple background caught
in her outside mirror. "There's a bobby pin in the glove compartment. Rewire it with that."

Between twists of the pin, Delia kept ducking down to peer
through the front windshield. "There." She rested her chin briefly
on the dash before sliding back. Her right leg stretched and flexed
against an imaginary accelerator. "You ought to get my father to
buy you another car. Grace's insurance money finally came in."

The car picked up speed. Delia folded her arms and smiled. "I
knew that would get you moving. You know, when I was in Spain,
almost all I could think about was"—she cranked her window
down and followed a flash of scenery with her hair streaming in
the wind—"all I could think about was some of Hallie's quail. She
puts a shitload of pepper on it, on purpose, and then she squeezes
lime all over it. I just wish you didn't have to come back here to
get it."

"If you don't watch your mouth and keep still, we may never get there." Anna took her foot off the accelerator.

Delia threw one loud laugh at the windshield and said, "Anna, you're a hoot. A real hoot." She arched her back as if she could give the car more momentum. "Let's get through this next pass, okay? Let's just get through this pass, and then you can go as slow as you want. Okay?"

Anna had traveled the road many times, but the rocking of Delia's body coupled with the anxiety in her voice made the road cut ahead seem menacing. The section of slope hadn't been plowed with the excess earth pushed ahead or mounded to the side; it had been sliced like a piece of cake and lifted. As the car sped through the strait, Anna wondered where the slices had been taken. The ages of the exposed rock were delineated by thin rust-colored lines the color of dried blood.

When the car began to follow the land's natural contours again, Delia slumped back in her seat. "Grace—my mother, used to take me driving with her when I was a little girl. We'd drive and drive, but we'd never stop anywhere. I could never understand that. And then my dad wouldn't let me ride with her anymore, not even out to the ranch."

Delia looked back. "That one place back there, when we drove on this road, she'd always say that it was real important for her to get past that one spot. And she went so fast there . . . I was so scared those two pieces of land would slam together," she clapped her hands, "and we'd be crushed. I couldn't understand why the road had to go through there. It's not that high, why couldn't it roll over the top? I still can't. And we have to go back that way."

Anna's resentment toward Grace rekindled. She'd left her daughter some legacy. Delia didn't need to hear any criticism of her mother, so Anna concentrated on the road, pretending that images of Grace popped up in the road and had to be knocked down.

They wheeled into Hallie's weedy parking lot. Delia hurried out of the car but waited with tapping feet at the café door for Anna. "I can't believe you lock your car out here, Anna. Really."

Hallie stood in front of a blackened stove, bullying pieces of frying chicken with crusted tongs. When two slices of her home-made bread shuddered up out of a rummage sale toaster, she speared them onto a plastic plate with a nasty-looking two-tined fork. She threw the toast onto the jaundiced Formica counter and clicked her teeth in satisfaction as the plate sideswiped a glass of water. To discourage any complaints, she untwined a pencil from her beaded hairnet, wrote out a check and slapped it on the wet counter. A man, red-faced and sweating his hair into spikes, thanked her and rustled a ten-dollar bill apologetically.

Hallie turned up the gas briefly to let the blue flame lap at the sides of the cast-iron skillet and snapped, "I got no time to be making change for everybody. Put it in the register yourself, and you, fella, by the jukebox, you come over here and see he doesn't rob me."

Under cover of the change transaction, Anna and Delia almost made it to a booth that was bandaged with silver duct tape, but Hallie, her back to them and still prodding the chicken, raised her voice. "You two sneaking in, what do you want?" Delia froze, and Anna bumped into her.

"I got to get rid of this chicken," Hallie threatened.

"That's what I came for," Anna said. "Chicken."

"Vegetables, vegetables, come on." Hallie tried to snap her fingers, but grease made contact and friction impossible.

"Whatever you've got," Anna said quickly. Sure that she had done well, she sat down and tried to avoid looking at Delia.

"It's a free country," Hallie reminded her irritably. "I got no time to be deciding vegetables for a grown woman. Okra or carrots or both."

"Both, both."

"You only need to say it once. Two chickens, two okras, two carrots."

Delia sobered up and said, "No! I want quail! Please."

Hallie appealed to the vent over her head and worked the jaws of the tongs. "Quail! What hat did you pull that one out of? Two chickens, two—"

Drawing back as if Hallie had slapped her hard, Delia insisted,

"No! I want quail!" The shaky intensity of her voice surprised Anna. She wanted to squeeze the tears out of the girl's voice and smooth her forehead with them. "I've been dreaming of your quail for three months. Over in Spain—"

"I don't have time for a travelogue. And I sure don't want to hear about other people's good fortune." She covered the chicken and yanked the refrigerator door open. A man and his son sitting at the end of the counter had to move their plates as Hallie unloaded the contents of her refrigerator. A head of iceberg lettuce rolled over a piece of coconut custard pie and crushed it.

Fascinated by Hallie's production, Anna rested her elbows on the table and watched the buildup of food and the rapid evacuation of the counter. She had worked on Hallie once at the beauty college in Odessa. Hallie had waited more than two hours for the free shampoo and haircut that were offered on Tuesday nights. She'd waited with flat-footed patience, holding her handbag in an iron grip. The red leather bag had been cured maroon by long, shiny streaks of grease. Anna had had to shampoo her three times. Hallie had let herself be swiveled around, she had taken the mirror that Anna had offered and examined the back, she had let herself be sprayed and brushed off and then she'd promptly encased her hair in a beaded net.

"I did her hair once. I don't think she's had it done since."

"My father must know a lot more about you than Grace ever knew. Or than I'll ever know."

Anna was getting tired of Delia's sneak attacks. She wished she had let the phone ring the night before Grace's funeral. Dealing with one Nettinger at a time was difficult enough; she hadn't asked for a package deal. She was beginning to think Grace had willed father and daughter to her. "Look. To me he's Ed Nettinger. Not your father, not Grace Nettinger's husband. I don't see him that way any more than I see you as anybody's daughter."

"Well, I am their daughter. There's nothing you can do that'll change that."

"In a lot of ways they don't have that much to do with what you end up doing with your life. You have to cut loose. Their problems are not yours. Grace's craziness—"

"I can't cut loose! I'm their daughter. I'm somebody's daughter. Just because my mother killed herself doesn't mean I'm not her daughter anymore. And now"—the color rose in her face— "I think of him with you—and what you do—and he's Ed Nettinger to me, too—a real, separate person who does . . . all these things that I never really thought about before. Everything's all screwed up."

"You have enough to think about without taking that on," Anna said.

"But I'm the one who found you," Delia said with intensity. "You were *my* friend."

"You're dragging me where I don't belong."

"What if I said, 'Dump my father or else I'll never speak to you again'?"

"It's none of your business what I do or don't do with him."

"*Quail!*" Hallie shouted.

Delia considered the spiral of Tabasco sauce she had squirted on a heel of white bread. "Not ever knowing your own father, don't you ever think you might have a time bomb inside you? You don't know what his father died of, you don't know—"

"No. I don't sit around wondering what somebody's passed on to me. It only matters if you let it. Go pick up your quail."

Richard and Sharon Pullock entered the café while Delia was at the counter negotiating for the release of her dinner. Anna hoped she wouldn't spot the couple. The undertaker and his wife brought a clammy humidity to the dry surroundings. They both had long, horsy jaws. Short but substantial legs held up their overlong torsos. A layer of perspiration was pooled under their skin.

Sharon threw up her hands and headed toward Anna. "*Just* the person I needed to see," she said. "You saved me a phone call." She sent Richard to hold down a booth and slid into Delia's place. "I have to cancel for tomorrow. Summer Haslip gave up the fight. I knew it was all over when Dr. Laurence couldn't help her. They're shipping her body back here from that clinic in Mexico tonight. We've got our work cut out for us on this one. How's Wednesday for you?"

"I have a few more customers passing through my hands than you do," Anna pointed out. "Here's my card. You'll have to call me at the shop tomorrow."

"When you think about it, though, we're both trying to make somebody look good. You get more than one crack at them, is all." Sharon studied the card. "Just 'Anna' and a phone number? No Mary Frances? No last name? We were thinking of getting some printed up, but we're the only funeral directors in town, so there didn't seem to be any point."

Anna remembered Grace's hair. Looking across the table at Sharon's fleshy face made her ill. "Last names don't matter in my business." She set her face and neutralized her voice. "Here comes Delia."

Sharon didn't budge. "There's Vidal Sassoon . . . and—"

"Alberto VO Five," Anna said.

Some of Hallie's technique seemed to have rubbed off on Delia. She dropped her plate on the table. Quail drippings spun into the okra and carrots and splattered the table. Sharon used the back of a wrist to push back her bangs lightly. There it is, Anna thought. She can't even stand the touch of her own hand.

Sighing, Sharon fluttered her fingers at them and said, "It's going to be such a job. Do you know how many rolls of cotton it's going to take to fill up those wasted cheeks? Toodle!"

Delia pushed her plate away and covered her eyes.

"Do you want to leave?" Anna asked. "I'll get Hallie to wrap it up."

After several attempts, Delia tucked her chin down. "Why should I leave?" she asked defiantly. "Why should I be the one to leave? No way. Fuck, fuck, fuck. *Fuck!* You can't get away from anything out here. You know he used to sell vacuum cleaners."

"So?" Anna asked, feeling that somewhere in Delia's mind selling vacuum cleaners and curling hair were the same.

"Are you kidding—a vacuum cleaner salesman? Door to door?"

"I don't think you understand that some people have to do certain things, or want to do certain things—"

"Draining bodies? God, Anna—that's a real calling. Really. A lot of sacrifice went into making that fucking little gravedigger."

"Forget it," Anna said. "We're not talking about the same thing."

"You think I'm spoiled."

There were echoes of the mother in the daughter after all. "I didn't say that."

"You wanted to."

"No. It's what *you* wanted me to say. Look. I'm on your side. You're still young. You don't understand that some people have more choices in their lives, and that other people haven't had the same choices. So when there aren't that many choices, you make sure what you really want and you go after it."

"Like you're after my father?"

"Don't you listen? If he's anything, he's the icing on the cake."

Delia squirted air out of the plastic mustard bottle. "I'm sure that makes him happy."

"It's none of your business."

"Good." Delia looked sadly at the bones she had picked cleaned. "I can't believe that I ate that little bird."

"Let's go," Anna said.

Delia followed her out to the car, eating peach pie out of a napkin.

"I thought we would go back through Fort Davis," Anna said.

"You would do that for me?" Delia put her hand to her chest. "You would drive twenty miles out of the way? Really? You would do that for me?"

"It looks like it."

Delia reeled out her seat belt and fastened it. "Alpine to Marfa is pretty bad. Marfa to Fort Davis isn't too bad. But Fort Davis to Alpine is even worse than Alpine to Marfa. All those curves and all those rocks waiting to fall on the car. That was her favorite. You know that big boulder right outside of Fort Davis? Where all those wrecks have been? You know how many times Grace scraped it? There's a streak of blue paint from her car on it. Marfa to Alpine's better."

Anna backed up and waited for the highway to clear. A diesel truck roaring past made the Valiant's antenna whip from side to side. Its load of moonstruck white-faced cattle blinked as they passed under Hallie's sign. The animals were crowded together, their long-lashed and big-eyed faces were bewildered. They tried to lift their necks to get more air and a better view.

"Anna? Thank you, though." Delia looked out the window as they pulled onto the highway. "You don't have to choose between me and Dad. That's just the Grace in me coming out."

"Don't say that," Anna commanded. She hoped Delia didn't believe that. Why hadn't Grace stopped to consider what the next day would be like? She'd removed herself and now had more power than ever. Look at the dominance she'd achieved over her daughter. Wherever Grace was, Anna hoped there were still high mountains in her way.

S mall Businesses from A to Z," an adult extension course offered by the college, met in the main building's east annex. Anna chose a seat at the end of the back row close to the large window that overlooked town. A chorus line of junipers stepped downhill to a rock wall surrounding the campus. Shrubs of dusty purple sage bordered the two-tiered parking lots; bursts of short-bladed Spanish daggers and long, thorny whips of ocotillo separated the upper and lower parking lots.

About fifteen people wandered into the high-ceilinged classroom. Anna recognized a man from the lumber company, a woman who did the books at one of the drugstores and an LVN from the nursing home. There were five teenagers with good postures grouped in the first and second rows. None of them looked old enough to be enrolled in an adult extension course. The two girls wore dresses, and the boys wore dress pants and white shirts. The rest of the class was scattered singly among the rows.

A blond woman established herself in the middle of the front row. She had the pert profile of a Barbie doll and wore large gold hoop earrings. Anna couldn't pin the woman's hairstyle to any hand in a three-county area.

The teacher came in, wearing a suit and tie in the un-air-conditioned building. He threw his coat over a chair, loosened his tie and began to roll up his shirt sleeves. When he grasped the outside edge of his desk and hunched his shoulders, it looked as if the Baptists were starting their summer encampment. The blonde in the first row had a notebook neatly aligned with the edges of her desk and held a pen expectantly, but as the teacher introduced himself as Alan Lehrmann and leaned into an explanation of the course, she frowned at the pen and lofted a purse into her lap.

Alan Lehrmann paused as the woman rummaged through the purse, rejecting first one pen, then another. Finally, he pushed gold wire-rimmed glasses into his receding hairline and rubbed his eyes. "Let me know when you're finished in there."

The woman's face was lost in her purse. "Do you have a pen I can borrow?" The mouth of the purse stayed clamped to her head. Everyone looked around to see who she was asking. One of the young, well-dressed boys started taking up a collection of pens from his group. "Do you have a pen I could borrow?" she repeated, bringing up her head to address the teacher.

Alan Lehrmann blushed and fumbled in his coat. Handing the woman his pen, he began his speech. "For most of you, this is not an academic course. For most of you—"

"Thank you," the woman interrupted after she had tested his pen.

He blushed again and eyed her until he seemed certain of the woman's silence. "For most of you, this is a precursor to establishing your own businesses or to more effectively managing the businesses which you already own or in which you are already involved. The goal here is one of practical application over theoretical approach—I think you'll find that the two, however, are not mutually exclusive and are, in fact, interdependent. The goal here is to set up the books for a business—one of your own choosing, whether it be a new start-up or the acquisition of an existing concern—and to carry the business through one year of establishing location, inventory, personnel, reputation. Quarterly taxes have to be met, licensing requirements, payroll, all specifically designed—"

The licensed vocational nurse raised her hand. "Will there be a term paper?"

Alan Lehrmann's shoulders slumped. Anna couldn't believe he was wearing a T-shirt under his shirt in June. "No. No, there is no term paper. There is a twelve-week project that consists of setting up your own small business and picking through the minefield of vendor discounts and tax regulations. Labor negotiations, et cetera. If that doesn't appeal to you, if that's not what your expectation of this course is, then, please, by all means leave." His outswept arms included the entire class, but he looked hopefully at the woman in the first row. The woman smiled in understanding. A fiftyish woman in the third row hugged her purse and sped out the door.

In the breeze of her departure Alan Lehrmann began to call roll from the class cards they'd handed him. "Cheryl Long." The woman in the front row raised a tanned arm. He scribbled a note on the card and slipped it to the bottom

Anna recognized the woman's name. She knew, in fact, many details of the woman's life. Cheryl Long's mother wrote a column for the newspaper called "Latitudes and Longitudes" which regularly featured news of her daughter. She'd turned down a scholarship at SMU to spend one semester at the University of Texas at El Paso. She managed Labrette's, the older and more conservative of the two women's clothing stores in town. The Longs' share in Labrette's had been a silent partnership until one Sunday afternoon when the manager of fifteen years was ousted and Cheryl was in place on Monday morning.

Every Thursday Anna and Jo turned to "Latitudes and Longitudes" to see what Cheryl Long had been up to the week before —what dress she'd worn to the Bluebonnet Ball in San Antonio or what Gulf Coast resort she'd descended upon for two weeks and, in what amounted to free advertising for Labrette's, what she'd picked up in Dallas at market and who would look marvelous wearing it. "Latitudes and Longitudes" had neglected to mention Cheryl's brief infatuation with a Mexican Mafia chieftain headquartered across the river in San Antonio del Bravo. Bryan had been their source on that item. Anna wanted to sneak out and call Jo to come sit in on the class.

"Is something funny? By the window, is something funny?" Alan Lehrmann aimed his class cards at Anna.

She wanted to say, "Cheryl Long," but Cheryl had turned around and was looking back with a sympathetic smile.

"Sorry," she said calmly, remembering that the course cost $215 and none of the money was coming out of Mary Frances's cashbox.

"James Bailey," Alan Lehrmann called. The man from the lumber company raised his hand.

"Anna—"

"Here." The LVN jumped on Anna's answer.

"Gomez," finished the teacher. "Anna Gomez?"

"That's me," the LVN said. She looked as if she were ready to fight for the name.

"Sorry," Anna said. "I jumped the gun."

"Bill Cutler . . . Jan Weir . . . Holland Sanborn . . . Gregory Lujan. Good. Anna Bryan." He tapped away ten seconds of silence with a pencil. "Anna Bryan. Last call."

Satisfied that nobody else in the room was going to claim the name, Anna raised her hand. She couldn't remember which last name she'd put down on the card. Bryan could have been one of them.

"You're sure?" Alan Lehrmann asked. "Vickie Davis."

Cheryl Long had turned around again and was smiling in solidarity. Anna ignored her, but the Miss America smile stayed put. Cheryl turned around to gather her things and moved to the chair beside Anna's. The teacher sank down in an old wooden swivel chair until Cheryl had resituated herself. "Is this a sister act?" he asked.

"So you're Mary Frances's Anna," Cheryl whispered. "I've been waiting and *waiting* for you to come into the store. I've got things put away for you."

Anna threw a small shrug to Alan Lehrmann to disassociate herself from Cheryl Long.

"I'm sorry," Cheryl Long apologized to the class. "I'm ready whenever you are, Professor."

The class lasted the full two hours without touching upon what Anna wanted to know: how to take over Mary Frances's shop before she was ready to give it up. She left Cheryl Long behind, returning the teacher's pen.

Sunset fired the western horizon. Walking across the parking lot, Anna traced the peaks and valleys of the skyline with her finger.

"Where are you parked?" Cheryl Long had slipped beside her so silently that Anna jumped.

Anna veered to the left. "I walked."

"You *walked?* Get in this car this instant," Cheryl Long commanded. She patted the hatch of a navy blue Datsun.

"I like to walk."

"Are you *nuts?*" Cheryl skipped down the steps to the second lot with Anna. "Wait, we can get a Coke or something and I'll drive you home. The worst that can happen is you'll be in my mother's column next week."

"That's A-N-N-A. I have a chair at Mary Frances's. That's F-R-A-N—"

"There. That's better," Cheryl Long said. She maneuvered Anna up the steps toward the Datsun. Are you and Bryan really going through with the divorce?" She unlocked the passenger door and walked through Anna's silent gaze. "Wait—don't start talking yet."

Anna couldn't help knowing things about Cheryl Long; anybody who bought the *Alpine Avalanche* was updated weekly. But who could have passed on the information about the divorce? Just how well did Bryan know Cheryl Long? Anna refused to believe that what she was experiencing was jealousy. It was impossible.

They had sworn to be faithful to their agreement, not to each other. "Don't worry. I'm not saying a word."

"I don't blame you, I wouldn't want to talk about it either. Divorce can be so . . . *depressing.*" Cheryl methodically locked the doors, fastened her seat belt and waited for the red generator light to go out.

"You don't happen to belong to the Chisholm Club, do you?" Anna asked.

"I don't blame you, I'd drink, too—worrying about what was going to happen to my soon-to-be ex-husband. If you promise to come into Labrette's and buy something delicious, I'll tell you where there's a bottle of bourbon hidden in this car."

"Next paycheck I'll come in," Anna lied. Cheryl Long was completely untrustworthy. "Who does your hair?"

"Do you like it? Guess!"

"It's no one here—"

"I do it! Don't tell—but I make my own clothes, too. I'm sneaking them onto the racks little by little."

"You cut it yourself, too?" Anna didn't like the idea of mousse and portable hair dryers making women think they were professionals. It killed her that she couldn't find fault with Cheryl's cut.

"I've *wanted* to come to you, though. Maybe we could trade out."

"I don't do trades."

"I don't blame you. I probably shouldn't either."

There were empty spaces at the Lobo Drive-In, but Cheryl circled the parking lot and returned to the highway. "It's a little ritual I've had since high school," she explained. "I never stop there, I *know* they use dog meat in their hamburgers, but I always have to drag the parking lot. I always have to eat at Hank's because his wife always buys her Easter outfit at the store, but we have to drag the parking lot four times before we can stop."

On the fourth go-round a pickup truck pulled out and they slipped into the space. "There. See how everything works out?"

They ordered Cokes with a side of french fries and cream gravy. Cheryl hid their cups by the brake pedal and poured bourbon into them.

"Seen at Hank's last night," Anna spread the headlines across the air, "C.L. and A.L. hyphen M. hyphen B. What was in those cups, girls, question mark, exclamation point, exclamation point, question mark."

"Don't laugh, my mother ghostwrote 'Teen Trails' one summer, and you wouldn't *believe* how many times I made the paper that summer."

"Oh yes, I would," said Anna, touching her cup to Cheryl's. Forty-seven. She and Jo had kept count.

Bryan lounged against the headboard, the yellow top sheet girded low around his waist, reading the newspaper. The newspaper was angled away from his broad chest to catch the late-afternoon light. Anna stopped on her way to the kitchen to raise one of the shades that shielded the bedroom from the backyard. Pieces of sunlight cut by the far-flung branches of a pyracantha bush landed on Bryan's chest. Ed Nettinger had offered to trim the pyracantha's harried branches, but Anna had told him she liked her privacy.

"Thanks, love," Bryan said. He patted the bed. "You must not have made an outstanding impression on our Cheryl Long. Three weeks of class together and you haven't made Adrienne's column yet."

Anna maneuvered past his reaching arms. "Our Cheryl Long? You're the one she wants to know about. Do you want a beer or tea?"

"I want you and only you." Bryan clutched a pillow and bit into one end. Red hair the color of Saltillo tiles shingled across his forehead.

"You've had me," Anna said. "It's time to broaden your horizons. Cheryl Long's out there. Waiting for you."

"Time!" he roared. "What is time to a homeless man like me?"

Anna went into the kitchen to give herself a chance to recharge. The closer the date of their divorce drew, the more energy it required to keep Bryan from feeling sorry for himself. She hadn't seen him since early March. There had been postcards from Los Angeles and Chicago with despondent messages that were fair

game for anybody's eyes. In April and May she had arrived home
to find the dust-stained trial car Bryan drove across four states to
test the endurance of batteries and tires sitting in the driveway,
but no sign of him. She hoped the extended absences were for
show, an entering into of a separation phase in preparation for the
divorce, and not because Bryan was getting himself deeper into
trouble.

Fifteen minutes after they'd first met at Jo's, Bryan had offered
Anna two thousand dollars to marry him. The money would have
brought her that much closer to putting a down payment on Mary
Frances's shop, but she'd walked out the door. Bryan had followed
her to the car. "Two thousand dollars for two years. I'm very neat;
I'm gone most of the time; I can be very charming around almost
everybody. All I really need is a closet for my clothes and a place
to get my mail. We'd have to convince the INS that we were in
love; but I think I do love you, and I'm not so bad."

Anna had been sure that Jo's husband, Burgess, had put Bryan
up to the whole thing. "Burgess may think I don't have any
morals, but I do," she'd said and driven off. Bryan had persisted,
Jo had intervened on his behalf, and Anna had begun negotiating
with him. She wanted Mary Frances's shop; she didn't want to
be sidetracked financially or emotionally by anybody, but the idea
of having somebody around for a week or two at a time was
appealing.

"You're not responsible for the things I do while I'm away from
you," Bryan had emphasized. "As long as you agree not to ask me
anything and as long as you promise not to try to find out anything, all will be well. I've had a document drawn up."

"Fine," Anna had said. Legislating a relationship had seemed
like the perfect thing to do. There would be no misunderstandings
because the boundaries and the duration would be clearly spelled
out.

Anna had thought that Bryan's devotion was for public display
until the first night they slept together and he began to speak a
little too eloquently about fatherhood. "You don't have to try to
fool me," she had reminded him. "I'm in on this. I'll enjoy you

while you're here and I won't wonder about you when you're gone. We'll say so long in two years." The next day she insisted they go back to the lawyer's and insert a clause about mutually assuming responsibility for birth control.

All things considered, Anna thought it had worked out well between them. He was a citizen. He could stay in the country indefinitely. She was happy to see Bryan when he was in town, and she didn't miss him when he wasn't there. There was affection but not love. Despite periods of hot curiosity, she'd kept her part of the bargain.

Shoots of long thin grass from seed scattered by Ed Nettinger's hand were beginning to glorify a bare spot in the backyard. Bryan shouted his question again in a voice that made the windows rattle. "Time! What is time to a homeless man like me?"

"Wait five weeks and three more days till I throw you out on your ear," she called. "It won't be five minutes before you've got somebody else lined up to take you in."

A clear plastic water gun sat on the windowsill beside a rubber-banded bunch of drying thyme. All the Russell toys from next door eventually landed in Anna's yard. Every two weeks or so she searched under bushes and in trees for the fallout from next door that had to be returned.

Anna filled the water gun and tiptoed down the hall. Bryan's freckled back made a perfect target. She stood behind the door and squirted through the crack. The anticipation of Bryan's retaliation made her giddy, and she skipped into the bathroom. There was no sound of the sheet being thrown back or of footsteps hurrying down the hall. He was trying to trick her into coming back. She ran into the bedroom and emptied the water gun on Bryan's head and back. Water trickled onto the sheets. Still expecting a trap, Anna edged closer to the bed.

The calendar with the picture of the Fighting Bucks, the high school football team, dangled between his knees. "It is thirty-eight days. Exactly. You have it precisely marked. How many hours, Anna?"

"Of course, I have it marked," she teased. "It's not every day a girl gets divorced." Bryan's stillness set a different kind of trap. Hoping to head him off, she licked his eyebrows into peaks and then twisted the hair into tiny horns.

His clear water blue eyes were half closed in hurt. "It's not every girl who so looks forward to her divorce," he finally said.

Anna tried to nudge him into a smile and repeated the words he had used upon giving her the calendar with all the cocky, grinning boys. "Just something to help pass the time while you're gone. I think you *like* looking at that calendar."

Bryan rested his large hands on his thighs and looked at Anna. The red hair of his legs entwined the lighter golden hair on the backs of his hands. "You've never accepted the fact that I'm here with you. You've been counting down from the start. It may only be for two weeks at a time, but I am at home here."

"We have an agreement," she reminded him. "You wanted to spell things out as much as I did."

"In thirty-eight days I'll be a homeless man again, a man without a family—"

The melancholy didn't fool Anna. Bryan could call himself homeless, but he homesteaded every place he traveled through. She moved to the closet where his things were stored and threw open the doors to display all the white boxes he'd bought at the dime store and neatly labeled. "You're a citizen now. You can live wherever you want to. What about Anadarko, OK? You made lots of friends there. Remember Bossier City, LA? Home of the Louisiana Hayride Country Music Show and the Kickapoo Motel." She upended the Bossier City box and a newspaper, postcards, swizzle sticks and matches fell onto the bed.

"A man without a helpmate," Bryan continued. "A man getting older, wasting his seed, booted out of his homeland, disowned by his father, a mortal disappointment to his mother—"

"Wrap it up, Shakespeare. Jo and Burgess'll be here soon."

"You're a hardhearted woman."

"A woman has to harden her heart against you," Anna said, but he was already browsing through the Bossier City newspaper.

She went into the bathroom to make sure Bryan hadn't tampered with her birth control pills. He'd argued for a clause in the agreement that read the "possibility of issue from the two-year union," but Anna had held out for "there will be no issue from the two-year union." That hadn't stopped Bryan from punching out a pill on their first anniversary and replacing it with a saccharin tablet.

Anna held up the pack to a light and looked for the telltale mark of a crescent moon shining through the foil back. She kept her real supply at the shop. Whenever a mistrust of science and Bryan seized her, she'd make him use a condom she'd bought.

Bryan's main fault was his meddling. Short-term reality never got in the way of his long-term objectives. According to Jo, Bryan was an honorable man in his own way, true to his principles and convinced of their righteousness. Anna worried about his being caught at the border, doing whatever it was that he was doing, but her greatest fear was for the people who got seduced into serving his cause.

The telephone rang. Bryan wrapped the sheet around his hips and walked down the hall to answer it. Anna thought that half the people in his four-state territory must have her phone number with strict instructions of when to call. His wallet was nested with scraps of paper bearing names, addresses and numbers. The only long-distance calls on the bill were Anna's to her mother. Bryan made his calls from a portable telephone in his car.

Anna turned on the bathtub taps so she wouldn't be able to hear the conversation. She hoped it was Cheryl Long calling, ready to take him on, offering him another oasis.

Bryan knocked at the bathroom door. "It's for you. Your friend, and more recently mine, Delia Nettinger." Letting the sheet fall, he stepped past Anna and settled into the tub.

———

"Glad you could join us, Anna" was Burgess's greeting when she had finished talking to Delia. His teeth were yellow like Jo's but smaller. A brown crack ran through the two front ones. Tobacco stains from unfiltered cigarettes had bled into his white beard, dying it yellow and traveling upward via sideburns until his whole pompadoured hairline looked varnished. Anna always had the

urge to stick his head under a faucet and scrub it with her knuckles. He wore two-toned shirts with yoked western pants and his
favorite jewelry was lots of turquoise. As Burgess often said, he'd
"made the mistake of introducing my friend Thomas O. Bryan to
Anna. He said he needed a woman who could keep her mouth
shut, and I told him there wasn't a more self-absorbed woman in
the state than Anna, and it's a big state."

Bryan bounded into the living room with a foil-covered bowl
and a tray of crackers. He swung by Anna to kiss her. "Ah,
friends." After setting down the tray on the coffee table, he
rubbed his hands and asked, "What can I get for my friends?
Josephine? Burgess?"

"A Coke," said Jo. She rested her head against the sofa.

"Go ahead and have a beer." Burgess turned his attention to
the foil-wrapped bowl on the table. "What's this? Never mind.
I know better. I brought my own hors d'oeuvres. You don't mind
if I use some of your crackers." He pulled a can of processed
cheese spread out of a paper sack. A pile of soft orange cheese spit
out of the nozzle onto a round cracker.

"That stuff's going to turn your beard orange," Anna said.

Burgess lifted his half-eaten cracker. "Make mine club soda
with a—"

"With a slab of lemon," Anna finished for him.

Jo reached past her husband to dip a cracker into the bowl.
"What a good hostess to remember what everybody drinks.
Mmm-mmm, what's this dip called?"

Anna sat down and tried to figure out what Jo and Bryan saw
in Burgess. "Hummus," she said. "Bryan's recipe."

Burgess's yellow-tinged eyes sharpened. "Lot of men like to
cook for you, do they, Anna? Ronnie Mauss cook for you when
he came by to pay his respects, did he?" He moved his legs quickly
in anticipation of Jo's kick. "Must be knee-deep in catfish these
days."

Sweat from Burgess's club soda dripped down Bryan's arm.
"Ronnie Mauss was here?" he asked. "When? What did he
want?"

"Anna's got them waiting in the wings," Burgess said.

"What did he want?" Bryan demanded.

Anna pried two beers from his protection. "I don't know," she said vaguely, gesturing with the cans. "Forgiveness, I guess." She should have known better than to appreciate Burgess's not calling Bryan earlier with the news.

Burgess's voice boomed behind her. "Did he get it?"

"He didn't deserve it. And neither do you."

Bryan entered Anna's field of vision. "Did he hurt you?"

She felt as if she were out in the front yard again with Ronnie Mauss. She'd lost control. Not accounting for Burgess's big mouth had slipped her up. "You didn't see any bruises, did you? You went over me pretty good."

"Anna," Bryan appealed to her.

"Bryan. It doesn't have anything to do with you. I don't pry into your life, so don't pry into mine."

Jo bared her big yellow teeth and nickered. "I could eat a horse. Chugalug that club soda, Burgess, and let's go."

The wail of a Russell child next door reminded Anna of the water gun. Bryan followed her into the bedroom. "Did he hurt you?" The concern centered in Bryan's brown eyes was almost undone by the outrage that tightened his small mouth. The dent in his chin puckered. "If he touched you, if he hurt you in any way—"

"Bryan." Anna clicked the trigger of the empty water gun at him. "Calm down. Nothing happened." She twirled away from his advances. Events were overlapping and she didn't want any more collisions. "Jo and your best buddy are waiting."

The whatnot shelf in the hallway shook as Bryan strode past it. When she walked outside, Bryan was wedging the fallout of toys into the Russells' ratty hedge. "I told Burgess and Jo we'd meet them," he said. Anna lodged the water gun into the hedge while Bryan whistled to tell the children that there was something hidden for them.

"I'll drive," Anna said, but Bryan walked her to the passenger door and opened it.

"You don't talk when you drive. I'll drive. I like to talk and drive at the same time. It soothes me, and I need some soothing."

"You'll be talking to yourself then. Because I'm not saying anything." She wouldn't fall for it. Bryan was bringing it on himself by trying to overstep the boundaries. "If you want soothing, drive around the loop. You can see how green the hills are."

Bryan drove past the old baseball stadium with its stone walls and painted iron baseballs, past the radio station sitting isolated in a field of grass, and followed the gradual incline of the hills past the country club, past the nursing home and back into the high trees and shadowed lawns of the big houses. He cut through the college, and they climbed even higher until they crested the hill and coasted down to the highway.

The Chisholm Club, where they were meeting Jo and Burgess, was a private club attached to a motel. For a monthly fee on top of a liquor per drink charge, members could entertain friends before or after dinner at the motel restaurant. Burgess, the recovering alcoholic, belonged.

"Don't be sad tonight," Anna said. "You'll just set off Burgess, and Jo and I'll end up paying."

There in the parking lot Bryan scrunched his shoulders and his face in an imitation of Richard Nixon. Suddenly his hips swayed and he threw his head back and spread his arms. Waves of joy seemed to emanate from his body. "How's this—this all right? This do?"

Anna laughed and resented the fact that he had made her laugh. How could she trust Bryan when he could marshal his emotions in a second? The problem was that he believed his own acting. Bryan bundled her into a hug and swept them into the Chisholm Club.

Burgess sat back in his black leather club chair until it squeaked. His elbows seemed stapled to the arms. "Anna, what'll you have to drink?" His cracked smile became so expansive it threatened to split his gums.

Although Burgess hadn't had a drink in fifteen years and hadn't missed one Tuesday evening at Alcoholics Anonymous in the basement of the hospital, he enjoyed treating people at the Chisholm Club. Anna could never tell if Burgess was pleased by his own sacrifice or if the sight of other people drinking made him feel even more superior. She ordered scotch. It had been his favorite.

Burgess smoothed and folded his stomach until he had formed a depression for a handful of oyster crackers. "That Nettinger girl still calling you, is she? Sounds like she's looking for a new mother."

Jo stood in front of the jukebox, feeding quarters into the slot. Anna wished she would finish selecting the songs and come back and give her husband a kick. "I'm not old enough to be anybody's mother."

"There's that denial again," Burgess said. "I wasn't talking about any age difference."

Bryan grinned as if he knew his best friend and his wife were only pretending to hate each other and they would all laugh about it later. Crowds of people buoyed him. He saw happy endings everywhere.

Burgess herded the cracker crumbs together and dumped them in his palm. He pitched them into his mouth and said, "Ed Nettinger ordered his daughter a brand-new Ford Escort. Ten thousand bucks. Factory air. AM/FM. Tinted glass. The girl's spoiled if you ask me."

"What was the verdict on Grace Nettinger's death?" Bryan asked.

Burgess's palm hit the wooden table. "Suicide."

"But why?"

Returning in time to hear Bryan's question, Jo shot a glance at Anna, who said, "See. I'm not the only one."

"We know why she did it," Burgess said confidently. He rubbed a squashed lime around the rim of his glass.

Anna focused on the lime pulp clinging to his beard. "Oh, really? Who's we?"

Burgess scoured his teeth with the lime rind. "The ones that know."

"How can you stand him?" Anna asked the table at large.

Jo's chin doubled as she bent her head forward to check the circuitry of her hair. "I don't know, I think he's kind of cute."

"The ones that know," Burgess continued, "are the ones that

understand why Ed Nettinger, still smelling like the Gulf Coast shrimper he is, was, and always will be, married Grace Ames in the first place. Let me give you a little lesson in history, Anna."

"Oh Lord, now you've done it," Jo said.

Burgess removed the cigarette from Jo's lips and put his hand over her mouth. "Pay attention now," he instructed. "Especially you, Anna. You could stand to learn a few things."

Jo's tongue flicked through Burgess's stout fingers. Anna ignored Jo's attempt to distract and concentrated on tearing her damp napkin into triangles. Generally she had to concede the purity and truth of Burgess's knowledge of area history. "Let's hear it, Burgess."

"Back in 1935, once Congress approved Big Bend National Park, the state had to make sure that the land the National Park Service wanted was all deeded over to the feds. So the state finally got the Big Bend Land Department going in '41, and they went out and appraised and cleared titles and bought the property. By '42 they had all the ranchers north of the Chisos Mountains signed except for Carl Ames. He just flat wouldn't sign. Not that Carl couldn't use the money. He never recovered after the 1893 depression sent wool prices down, and he never would run cattle." Burgess paused to thumb the side of his nose. Then he raised his hands. "All of a sudden he signs all his land over. Next thing you know, he's packed up Helen, his wife, daughter Grace, three hundred head of sheep and moved south of town where the Ames-Nettinger place is now, a ranch foreclosed on the month before by the Dalton bank while it was still a state-chartered bank. Two weeks after Carl Ames and his family and sheep are settled in, the Dalton bank gets a national charter."

"So?" Anna asked impatiently.

"I am *starved*," Jo said. "And you-all know how mean I get when I'm hungry."

"So?" Burgess appealed to the set of longhorns anchored over the bar. "So there was collusion. The feds want the land, and Carl Ames won't give. Carl Ames wants a ranch closer to town, not just any ranch, but this one certain ranch. The Dalton bank wants to be a federally chartered institution so they can guarantee their deposits in case of another depression. Everybody wants something. Everybody except the Cuthbersons, who just want to live where they've always lived. That was their big mistake. They didn't *want* anything. The Dalton bank forecloses, Carl Ames gets his ranch, the feds get their land, and the Dalton bank gets their national charter. There was a deal struck as sure as the deal that Carl Ames and Ed Nettinger struck between themselves over that new piece of land."

"So?" Anna repeated.

"So?" Burgess's voice rose higher. His hands patted his shirt pockets for a cigarette. Jo lit one and gave it to him. "Carl Ames had no sons."

Anna shrugged. "So?"

Burgess stared, unable to comprehend her thickness. "Ed Nettinger wanted land—bad. He stepped off that train, found out what ranchers with marriageable daughters didn't have sons, and hightailed it out to the Ames place. Never worked on a ranch before. Only knew how to net shrimp. He keeps hitting that saline water out there, he may turn into a shrimper yet again."

"That's gossip, not history," Anna countered. "Like Jo said, Grace Nettinger died by her own hand. Nobody held her down and poured bourbon and Percodan down her throat." She should have known that Burgess would sully even his beloved history to get to her.

"Carl Ames sold his daughter to Ed Nettinger. Ed Nettinger's no better than a white slaver. He didn't stay on mending fences and shearing sheep out there for the love or respect of *any* Ames —Carl or Grace. The man lusted for land." He raised a threatening finger. "Don't 'so' me, Anna."

"Maybe that's the kind of man Grace wanted," Anna said steadily. "A man who knew what he wanted and wasn't afraid to go after it."

Burgess smiled triumphantly. "Then why did she build that house in town and live apart from the man six days out of seven? Quick as Carl Ames's in the ground and the will's read, leaving the ranch jointly to Grace and Ed Nettinger, there's Grace at the Dalton bank, trying to mortgage the ranch. Nettinger gets wind of it, goes to the bank—you've never seen such a scene in your life. They had to shut the bank down for an hour."

"School," Anna said promptly. "Delia started school. It's a thirty-mile trip into town. Somebody had to stay at the ranch to take care of things."

"Like I said, the girl's spoiled." Burgess shook his head sorrowfully.

"And you're not?" Anna asked.

The sound of Jo's fingernails against the heavily varnished table drew their attention. Long and scarlet, they made noise like crickets at night. "Thomas O. Bryan," she said thoughtfully. "What does the O stand for?"

Bryan stopped eavesdropping on the next table and kissed Jo's hand. "Ah, Josephine, I got the O from my father, and like him, it stands for nothing."

Jo threw a cracker at him. "You're supposed to help me out with these two," she reprimanded.

"I thought I was." Bryan's smile widened as he caught a second cracker. "The story of my father is as sad as Carl Ames's."

"You ever run into Ed Nettinger at the bank, Anna? Both of you checking on those marriage agreements you keep locked up in your safety-deposit boxes? Is that the attraction?" Burgess patted himself on the stomach in congratulation.

Anna decided to get into the seat of the bulldozer Burgess had just vacated while the seat was still warm. "You must have been a really hateful drunk, Burgess. To have broken your wife's arm."

The only sound at dinner was the hiss of steak fat sizzling in the metal platters. Jo shingled her meat into shreds with a fork and fed smoke into the glassed-in dining room. Even Bryan was quiet, eating steadily to keep his mouth full. Burgess stared into the lime-washed football stadium, where college boys were jumping hurdles set up on heavily chalked ten-yard lines.

Anna let steak grease soak her potatoes. She hadn't gone too far in using the forbidden weapon against Burgess. Everybody had a sore spot. Without exposure to light and air, it would never heal. Jo's protectiveness and Bryan's loyalty served only to inflame Burgess's self-inflicted wound. If he wasn't tough enough to take it, then he needed to watch out who he attacked. He'd loaded the weapon and put it in her hands.

Anna knew he'd bleed on Jo and Bryan, and she would be paid back through their disapproval. She might as well keep the ball rolling. "Jo saw an ad at the grocery store for Summer Haslip's garage apartment."

"Time to powder our noses," Jo said. She jerked Anna's chair away from the table. "It's got a shine on it, believe me."

The top of Jo's hair brushed the doorway of the women's rest room. She held the door open for Anna.

Centered on the flocked red velvet wallpaper were pictures of high school girls with their grand champion steers and reserve champion fat lambs. The steers reminded Anna of stolid bankers wearing vests and spats. She wondered if Ed Nettinger kept pictures of every fish caught from his pond.

"I love you, Anna, but I love Burgess better. I forgave him a long time ago for what he did to me that *one* time. I expect more from you—yes, I do—"

"That's not fair."

"I don't care if it's fair or not. I gave that tiny piece of my life to you so you'd be able to see that there were other stories besides yours. Don't make me regret that confidence."

"I don't care if he was drunk as a skunk. I won't forgive him. I won't do that. And you shouldn't ever forget that he did that to you either."

"Stop blaming Burgess for what Ronnie Mauss did to you," Jo advised and left the room.

Anna shook the beer bottle she'd brought in with her and ran a wet thumb through her hair to sculpt a wave. She turned on the hand dryer and fluffed her hair in the hot air. Burgess hadn't stopped hitting. He'd just stopped using a force that left physical traces.

By the time Anna got back to the table, the bill had been paid and Jo and Burgess were gone. "No lectures," she told Bryan. "Let's go to the dance and get good and drunk. Some of us can hold it."

The college gymnasium came full-columned out of a mountainside like an Egyptian temple. Floodlights made the granite columns glitter. The tiled entrance hall distorted the origins of voices and music. Bryan held Anna too tightly and the dance floor was claustrophobic. She struggled out of his grip.

"I've never seen you like this before," Bryan said. "It's not only our Burgess getting under your skin. What is it? Is it Mauss?"

"No. I don't need any comfort. I just want to get drunk and dance and not talk and not think." Bryan's arm lay across her shoulders. The weight made Anna's knees lock. She tried to brace his arm with both hands.

He pulled her closer. "Anna, love, what is it?"

Anna's knuckles drilled into his chest. "I'm not the one that needs comforting, I said. Let's just dance."

"You may not need comfort," Bryan sighed, "but I do."

"I can't give it to you," Anna said flatly. "You need somebody who'll take off in the middle of the night with you. Somebody who'll be able to leave everything behind when the trouble hits. Somebody willing to start up someplace else. I've run away once. I'm not about to do it again."

"It may never come to that. If it did, you wouldn't necessarily have to leave. If anything did happen, it would almost be the same as it is now, except you'd be the one visiting every two weeks."

"And I'd have the Border Patrol on my back all the way to the river." Anna left Bryan standing in the middle of the dance floor. With a beer in one hand and her sandals in the other, she roamed the fringes, always keeping one step ahead of him.

———

Anna dawdled at the kitchen table Sunday morning while Bryan painted the cabinets. There was a new wariness in his attitude. He'd never caught up with her on Saturday night. She'd kept diving into the dance floor by herself and emerging on the opposite side.

While Bryan cleaned closets and drawers, Anna watched a baseball game on TV. His clothes and boxes and books were consolidated into pyramids. The three-by-five card advertising the

Haslips' garage apartment that Jo had taken from the grocery store bulletin board was stuck in the phone's rotary dial.

————

On Monday morning Anna leaned against the stone parapet of the bridge and sucked on a cube of frozen orange juice. She'd already been to the newspaper office to place an ad in the classified section that she would no longer be responsible for Bryan's debts.

The toes of her running shoes were wet. She had purposefully stirred up the grass under the pecan trees in back of the library. It was Claude's delivery day. Anna could see his truck blocking the alley to the side of the shop. She tugged at her pink lace-edged socks and prepared to mend fences.

Claude's eyes widened under his cap when she walked in. He whistled appreciatively. "Nice socks, Anna."

"For you, Claude," Anna told him. "For nobody but you."

Crouching like a catcher, he examined the turned-down cuffs. "Nice, Anna," he repeated reverently. "Promise me you'll keep wearing dresses for as long as you live."

"Claude, don't get carried away. Have you ever seen me in anything besides a dress?"

"Only in my dreams."

"When will I learn?" Anna jumped over his arms. A box of doughnuts sat on the appointment book. She flipped through the assortment and called, "Whose doughnuts?"

Jo appeared in the doorway to the shampoo room. "A gift from Burgess. He's got your number on sweet things."

"He bought these?" Anna asked doubtfully. "Does he know he bought them?" She uncurled a cinnamon roll and ate the still-warm center. A woman sitting under the new heat lamps patted her stomach and refused the offered box. Liz sleepily dunked a devil's food doughnut into a cup of light coffee.

"I bought them in Burgess's name and spirit." Taking off one of her stained pink rubber gloves, Jo pinched a jelly doughnut until strawberry oozed out. She sucked the jam out of her fingernail. "I told them blueberry."

"That figures," Anna said.

"I'm going to take that piece of criticism as pertaining to the bakery and not another swipe at the man I love."

"Go right ahead."

Jo snapped off her other rubber glove. "Someday, Anna, you'll go too far and you're going to wake up all alone."

Anna dug out the soft cinnamon underside of her roll. "Me and everybody else."

"You don't believe that."

"Of course I do. People break up. They separate, divorce, move. Everybody dies. It's all temporary. You lose touch. Think of all the people you've met in your life. All the people you swore you'd never lose touch with. Where are they now?"

"You've got a smart mouth, Anna."

"Probably," Anna agreed. She went to her station to separate lavender, aqua and pink curlers for a nine-thirty permanent. A word or a touch would earn Jo's forgiveness, but that would lead to Burgess's being forgiven. And he didn't deserve it.

Jo, Liz, Leo and Anna drove out to Los Olmos at the end of June. On the last Sunday of every month Luisa Olversson opened the Los Olmos ranch house to the public. Leo sat in the front seat of Anna's Valiant, trying to control the map of Texas he'd unfolded. Liz was driving. Sitting behind the wheel of a car gave her a relaxed confidence that she didn't have standing behind a customer or beside Leo.

"The turn's coming up," Leo reminded Liz. "You better turn on your signal. We have to cross the highway. Turn on your signal. There it is—you better start slowing down."

Liz maintained speed and bypassed the double line of elms that gave Los Olmos its name. Jo stuck cock-eyed sunglasses into a growth of hair three inches above her widow's peak. She tweaked Leo's curls and said, "We're going a different way. Look, Leo, look—four eyes." Leo grabbed the wheel in panic when Liz turned around instead and started laughing.

A pair of rock pillars coming up on their right supported the wrought-iron tiaralike signpost of the Ames-Nettinger ranch. The arched Ames name crowned the longer Nettinger name, which ran in a straight iron band from pillar to pillar. Two miles past the sign Liz turned left and drove over a cattle guard. Camelback Mountain sat in front of them. Anna had never been able to see the resemblance between the mountain and its animal namesake. The crest of Camelback was slightly rounded but not enough to suggest a hump. She thought whoever had named it must have been very thirsty and thinking about how far a camel could go without water.

Liz drove around the perimeter of Camelback Mountain and took a road that cut across the length of the slope. They stopped where the road ended in a natural promontory called Camel's Knees. "Aren't we on Nettinger land?" Leo asked anxiously.

Jo pulled him out of the car. "It's all right, we've got Anna with us. Lord! Look at this view!"

The lookout point gave them a view of more than a hundred miles. To the north the E-shaped adobe compound of Los Olmos was visible at the end of the double line of elms.

Leo climbed on top of the car. "It's Van Gogh on a grand scale! It's Cézanne! Monet! It's genius! Creating a precise piece of art from the earth and then letting fate and nature take over!"

Farther north, beyond the ranch house, a giant canvas measuring four square acres bloomed. Last summer hundreds of volunteers had poked holes in water-softened bluebonnet seeds to ensure germination, and the artist who conceived the idea had spread the seeds from a low-flying airplane. Tons of other wild flowers, trucked in from greenhouses privately funded by Luisa Olversson, had already been planted by volunteers from Houston and Dallas and New York. Thanks to good spring rains, the flowers that had started blooming in March were still blooming. Visitors to Los Olmos could go up in a helicopter and hover over the plot, moving closer to the artist's work or stepping back from it as if they were in a museum or a gallery.

"It's a bunch of crap," Liz muttered. "All those people and all that money for what?"

"Luisa's putting us on the map," Anna pointed out. "We made *Time* and ABC News."

"They made fun of us," Liz said. "They said our restaurants are lousy, and that there's nothing to do out here except drive out to Luisa's and watch the flowers grow."

"We can always drive out and watch Ed Nettinger dig his new bass pond." Anna rested her chin on the car door and looked down and to the west. Ed Nettinger's stock pond full of catfish shone like a dime. A yellow bulldozer sat inside the beginnings of another pond. The remains of the burned-out main house were hidden by hills. In contrast with Los Olmos, the Ames-Nettinger land seemed much more exposed and barren. Across the highway was the acreage that Grace had sold off to a consortium of Permian Basin orthodontists who visited on weekends during hunting season. The smart thing to do, Anna thought, would have been to hang on to the land and lease it out. Hang on to it no matter how much you hated it. Get something out of it.

Liz twirled the same strand of hair over and over again. "You're going to loosen the roots if you keep that up," Anna told her.

"My sister-in-law's hair went completely straight after she had her baby," Liz said.

"Your hair's already straight. Maybe a baby'll make it curly. Do you promise that you don't want Mary Frances's shop?"

"How many times do I have to swear it, Anna? I don't want that old shop. Do you know how much money we owe those Hazelwood and Hinson people?"

Not wanting to get involved in a recap of Leo's college career, Anna leaned out the window. Jo was tilting her mirror back and forth in an effort to catch the sun. "What are you doing?" Anna called. A flash of light from the high ground behind Los Olmos caught her eye.

"Making sure I don't have a long, ugly black hair poking out of my chin."

"I just saw a flash of light behind Los Olmos."

"Probably some other Indian checking his war paint." Jo scratched Leo's bag of chips. "I'm starved—share, Leo."

He crushed the bag under his arm. "Not till you apologize for that war paint remark. I can't believe you're that racially insensitive."

"Oh, pooh. You take everything too seriously."

"I feel like driving off and leaving him on the hood like that," Liz said. "Why do I want a baby when I've got him?"

Anna was beginning to wish she'd stayed home and soaked combs. She opened both back doors and stretched out along the seat.

"Peel me open a can of Vienna sausages, Anna," Jo said.

"If we stop staring at Los Olmos and go down there, we can have some barbecue," Anna said. "Burgess is probably already down there, stuffing every sparerib in sight down his throat."

"We can't go yet, so you might as well break open those crackers, too."

Anna shut her eyes and let the sun coat her face and neck. She didn't want to know how Burgess figured in Bryan's border dealings. If it was solely a profit-making venture, Burgess had probably instigated the whole thing. Greed wouldn't motivate Bryan; morality would. But if Bryan's cause required money, Anna knew he'd do anything. He was a romantic who believed in expediency.

Warmed by the sun, Anna wanted to give everyone the benefit of doubt—even Burgess. He loved the people she loved and that was some kind of a bond.

Jo grabbed Anna's ankles and pulled her out of the sun. "Time to go, get up."

Small pieces of potato chips from Leo's beard littered the front seat. "I want to go up in the helicopter," he said. "You can't see anything from here." He nuzzled Liz's neck and left crushed chips on her shoulder.

"Why do you think Mary Frances and Alfred never had any babies?" Liz asked. "What if it had something to do with giving permanents for all those years?"

"Mary Frances hasn't touched curling solution since 1945," Jo said. "Besides, you're looking at the wrong woman. Look at my two sons."

"One and a half," Leo mumbled. Anna hit him on the shoulder

and hoped Jo hadn't heard. Leo had problems with the military, but he was able to accept Jo's son Marvin being in the Marines. It was her other son Leo had problems with. For all his education, Leo couldn't understand why Bevo would prefer the sexual and emotional company of another man.

"I'm starved. Let's go," Jo said.

Liz drove down the mountain and took a dirt road to Los Olmos. They parked behind an old bunkhouse which had been subdivided into four artists' spaces and painted salmon. One artist's work had overflowed. A mural of balls of fire unrolling into tongues of flame ran from the last door to the corner of the bunkhouse. Two high-rise big-wheeled Suburbans were nosed to reclaimed hitching posts. LOS OLMOS was painted in green on their doors.

The fatty smell of barbecue thickened the air. Beans simmering in a big kettle married with the meat's richness, reducing the richness to an earthiness that made the smell bearable. Anna couldn't keep from grabbing a warm flour tortilla and dipping it into the kettle. "There are health laws," Leo said.

The Los Olmos five-dollar admission price included lunch and a tour of the ranch house and artists' studios. For another two dollars a visitor could rent Luisa Olversson's cassette version of the Los Olmos story. The helicopter ride above the wild flowers was an extra ten dollars.

They sat at a long picnic table under the elms. A teenager filled their iced tea glasses and kept stacks of steaming brown-spotted tortillas at the tables. Leo cleaned Liz's plate with a tortilla. "No shoptalk from anybody. You're out in the real world now. Feast your eyes and ears." He jumped off the bench to follow the helicopter's low path over the cattle pens.

Liz frowned at a family of six sitting at the next table. "Those children look tired. Children shouldn't look so tired."

Anna looked at the family of six. She hadn't ever been around kids long enough to know what was normal for them. Most of her clients were mothers. They all worried about their children. They worried about sugar and television. They worried about using the word "no" too much or not enough. They worried about all the streets in the world to be crossed and all the drunken drivers and freight trains lying in wait. Anna didn't want the worry. She'd survived childhood. Everybody had his or her share of scars. Some were like birthmarks passed from generation to generation and some came from a single personal event. Children were resilient. Their bones were rubber. They were closer to the ground and had a shorter distance to fall. Their minds were ready to accept what the world offered. Adults were the ones who worked and reworked the past as if it were a piece of dough that had to be kneaded and allowed to rise and then punched down again.

"They're probably just tired of being driven around," Anna said.

Liz drank half her tea in a prolonged swallow and continued to watch the family over the glass rim. "Look at that father. You can tell he pushes them too hard. Leo would be like that. He makes me so tired sometimes. I just wish he'd leave me. I keep thinking about the Christmas card divorce counts and the Beauty Operator's Syndrome. Leo laughs at it, but I know part of him believes it. He'd never leave me—I know that. It doesn't matter how much more schooling than me he's got. I think he's putting off graduating because he's afraid."

"It's those statistics scaring him," Jo said. "He puts more faith in those than his own feelings."

Liz began to stack their empty plates and stuff used napkins into the glasses. "He wants to give the Christmas cards to a computer programmer he knows. He says he wants to prove he doesn't fit the profile of a deserter. I just don't want to change. I don't want to, I don't see why I should. My hair's been the same length since I was a sophomore, and when I tell you sophomore, you know I mean high school. I'm still the same size. I can wear my old clothes, at least until I get pregnant. Isn't it enough anymore to know what still fits?"

"You do things with your hair," Anna pointed out. Liz used ribbons and barrettes and flowers. She french-braided and french-twisted her straight brown hair. She'd never come into the shop two days running with the same style. "That's what's important."

"I don't care about hair. I want a baby, Anna," Liz said impatiently. "Only I don't want Leo to have anything to do with it. He'll take it and have its IQ tested, and he'll never let it alone. He can do his part of the business and then leave me alone. Look at you. Georgia did okay on her own. It's easier now for a single mother than it was."

"You need a better example than my mother," Anna said.

"I'm tired of everybody telling me what to do!" Liz said fiercely "I want to have a baby, and I want it to learn how to crawl and walk and talk without somebody measuring it up all the time."

"It's hormones talking," Jo said. "Do what you have to do, Leo'll come around. He'll be mush in your hands once he feels that baby move inside your stomach."

Anna stared at Jo. "I can't believe you said that. They need to talk about this and get it all spelled out before they even *try* to have a baby– "

"This isn't a matter of contracts, Anna. You can't always spell things out and expect them to happen the way you wrote it out."

"You have to have a basic agreement that you're both headed in the same direction," Anna argued.

Liz yawned. She looked hot and sleepy, like a child herself. "Let's go look at the pictures of the cowboys. I like their eyes. You can tell what they're thinking. They'd be happy to go off somewhere and leave me with a baby."

A group of four in the central hall were already plugged into headsets. They could hear Luisa Olversson's unsynchronized voice following itself around and around and never catching up. The hall gallery documented the Olverssons' migration from Alabama to East Texas in the 1860's and their final move west in 1887.

"Anna and Jo!" Luisa Olversson, her arm bandaged in upholstery samples, engaged every visitor's eye and smiled as she made her way across the large open hall. "Liz."

Luisa considered every surface, including her own head, to be a potential work of art. Every four months Anna had to rectify the damage done by other hands, with the knowledge that she was sending Luisa back out into the world with a blank canvas. Luisa's hair now was so tightly curled and cropped into a square above her forehead that it looked as if she were wearing a lambskin pillbox hat.

"Why didn't you tell someone you were here?" Luisa asked. She looked around for the person who had hidden the information from her. "I've got this fabulous idea!" She gestured toward the back of her head. "We'll cut this very close to the scalp, and the color will be very much like the color of the earth in the pasture, and then we'll dye it to match the wild flowers! Don't you love it? Jo! What about Bevo to do the color? I'll fly him in from El Paso. He'll love it!"

"Don't encourage him," Jo said.

"Oh, don't be silly," Luisa told her. "A little flamboyance is a gift. I've done a video. Have you seen it yet? It's fabulous! Jo, why don't you and Liz go ahead and save Anna a seat? I want to brainstorm with her."

Liz stared at the cowboys. "You can tell *exactly* what they're thinking: 'Get me out of here.' "

Luisa cut Anna away from Jo and Liz. "By the by, Anna"—her eyes roved the hall for listening ears—"I know Tommy told me *never* to call him at your place about this, but the people he found for me, the husband and wife? Their food is getting raves at my dinner table, but I cannot communicate with them. *No hablán inglés, no hablán español, no hablán français—no hablán.* Well, a little. bit every now and then. Would you mind talking to them?"

"Bryan doesn't give trims and I don't talk to his people." Anna fought the curiosity that was rising from her legs to the small of her back and urging her to the kitchen. She was relieved to know he was smuggling wetbacks across the border and not guns or drugs. "I'll tell him you need to talk to him."

Luisa peeled the layers of material off her arm and draped them over her shoulder. Her mouth barely moved when she said, "Can't you call him—I'm at my wits' end. I like to be able to converse with my help. I pride myself on it. I don't like having to keep them hidden away in the kitchen—my guests want to meet them."

Anna smelled the synthetic citrus tang of Burgess's hair

pomade before she saw him. Since the exchange of light flashes
at Camel's Knees she'd been expecting him to turn up.

"I'll handle this," Burgess said.

"Go right ahead. Where did you say the video was?"

"I'm afraid I don't have time to show you," Luisa said. "I have
other business to attend to. Follow the signs."

Anna accepted the snub that should have been aimed at Bryan.
Their divorce was well timed. She couldn't stay married to him
much longer and remain ignorant.

Liz was standing in front of a photograph at the other end of
the hall. She put her face close to the wall and then crouched and
looked up at the picture. It showed a group of men ranged along
the rocky slope of what was now "A" Mountain south of town.
About twenty buildings were scattered behind them in the wide
and treeless valley. The courthouse was blurred and ghostly in the
upper left-hand corner; the tower of the Southern Pacific depot
rose before a two-story building; the rounded hills across the valley
where the college now sat were bare. Anna couldn't see the creek.
In 1889 it had to have had water in it. Why would anybody build
a town on the banks of a dry creek? Who would stay in such an
unfortunate place? Like Liz, she stood to the side of the picture
and put her face close to try to see more.

" 'Alpine as it looked in 1889,' " Anna read. "It looks like a
strong wind would blow the whole town away. What are they
thinking?"

"I can't see their faces. I can't tell," Liz said.

"I'd be thinking that there's not much out there. What if
they'd built everything half a mile to the west? That might have
changed everything. We might not be here now. The whole
course of history might have been changed."

"Well, they didn't," Liz said with finality. "You're as bad as
Leo."

Anna left Liz staring at photographs and went to the cattle
pens. Scaffolding twelve feet high had been constructed in front
of the pens to afford a better view of the wild flower project. All
performances had been called off until the fall. That was fine with
Anna. Calf tying and barrel racing stirred up too much dust, and

she refused to sit through any more of the nonrodeo performances. Bryan had dragged her to one last fall where a woman wrapped in aluminum foil ate crystal wineglasses.

Anna climbed the scaffolding stairs and slipped into an empty space at the railing. The elevation gave her an opportunity to study hair. A badly done raspberry Mohawk raked the air. She wished she had some cards along to drop into the crowd below.

The movement of a brick red head going around to the kitchen entrance caught Anna's attention. Nobody had hair the color of Bryan's. If he wanted to hide, the first thing he needed was a hat or a coloring appointment with Bevo. Anna concentrated on Bryan. She waited for him to sense not only that he was being watched but that he was being watched by her. If Bryan couldn't tell when a friend had him targeted, what would happen when an enemy sighted him? If their union were meant to be a lasting one, wouldn't he feel her eyes on him? Wouldn't he turn around and search her out?

Anna was so intent on Bryan that she didn't see or smell Burgess until he was beside her. The sun glanced off his shellacked head. "Where's Jo?" he asked.

"I don't see her from here. She must still be inside." Anna tapped Burgess's hammered silver armband. A square mirror studded with four turquoise stones was set in the middle. "Is that new?"

Burgess cuffed his shirt over the bracelet. "A present."

"From Bryan? You both stick out like sore thumbs. It's your hair. You should both learn to wear hats."

"Trust you not to go any further than what color somebody's hair is."

"Tell me about the *avisadores*," Anna prompted. "The people along the border with the mirrors. The message senders. That have their own special codes. Cortez's undoing."

"Garbled as usual, Anna. They probably flashed messages to Montezuma from the Pacific coast to the interior about Cortez. It was Montezuma that was undone. I don't know any Anglo who could prove there's any such a thing as an *avisador*."

Anna nodded toward the hills behind Los Olmos where the

light flashes had come from earlier. "That wouldn't stop an Anglo from thinking it was a good idea. Something was going on out there this morning. Half the county could have seen it. If you're his friend, then watch out for him."

"Hoping I'm going to slip, are you?"

"No," Anna said. "That would mean I'd thought you'd picked yourself up in the first place."

Jo called in sick on the morning of the '26, '36, '46, '56, '66 class reunions. Her chair was turned into a relay station for women on their way to or from the dryers. Mary Frances had overbooked, and appointments were running behind by forty-five minutes. To keep the women from staging a mutiny, Anna had started giving free thirty-minute conditioner packs. One head was encased in plastic and steaming under two heat lamps. Another woman had melted into the contours of the shampoo couch as soon as she'd heard the word "free."

The redhead Liz had tucked behind the manicure table was opening all the nail polish bottles and painting different-colored stripes on each nail. "Don't get those bottles out of order," Liz warned. She began undoing a section of hair she'd just rolled and pinned.

"I might as well give myself a manicure while I'm sitting here," the redhead said. She opened a drawer and searched through it. "I'd rather have that than the conditioner. Take your time, don't worry about me."

The woman in Liz's chair plucked at the damp hair uncrimping down her neck. "Is it extra to get it dried now?" she asked, pulling grocery receipts and old Kleenex and dollar bills out of her purse. "I can finish rolling it. What does your dryer take? Bills or coins? The one at the washateria only takes coins."

Anna whisked her customer's neck and spun her out of the chair. She slid the emery board out of the redhead's hands and put it back into Jo's drawer. "Authorized personnel only."

"But you're busy! I want to help!" the woman said enthusiastically.

"Follow me," Anna said. At her instruction the redhead knelt on the shampoo couch and faced the sink. She grabbed the sink rim to keep the couch from teetering. "This is fun! Now what?"

"Bend over." Anna turned on the taps and regulated the water temperature before putting the hose into the woman's groping hands. She rolled a towel and stuffed it into the gap between sink and couch so the couch wouldn't flip over. "Shampoo twice and then rinse with cold until the water runs clear."

Mary Frances's only customer in ten years had been herself, but Anna buzzed upstairs on the intercom. She kept her thumb pressed hard against the button. She could tell when Mary Frances took off her shoes and tiptoed across the apartment. A broom handle churning the ceiling finally got her to answer the intercom. "Put on your rubber gloves and get down here before Liz and I walk out," Anna advised.

"Well, really, Anna," Mary Frances said, "if you can't stand the heat, get out of the kitchen—"

"Five seconds, MF. Then we're walking out the door. Five seconds after that I'm calling Willi over in Marfa and telling her there's a shop over here ripe for the picking—"

"I don't care what you do. There are more important things happening. I am not alone up here. I am entertaining. I am taking care of my business on another level—"

"Five seconds. Or I'm taking the cashbox with me. If you want to run this shop, then run it."

Anna hung up and thumbed Willi's card with some regret. The engraved letters made her fingertips itch. She might consider working for Willi if technology made it possible for women to unscrew their heads from their bodies and still function. They could drop off their heads and operators would shake the brains into special containers and fit the empty heads on padded bases. Instead of fidgeting restlessly while the heads got worked on, the bodies could go about their business and have a dress fitted or have another headless woman order a place setting of china. The thought of dropping Mary Frances's brain into a container and storing it at the back of a shelf was deeply satisfying.

As if she'd been waiting for that cue, Mary Frances material-

ized in the shampoo room. "Let's keep our fingers working, girls."
She sidled over to Anna and whispered, "I'll go as far as comb-
outs, and that's it. These hands were not born to shampoo."

"Good, you're here," Liz said. "It's time for my break." She
carried a paper bag into the bathroom and locked the door.

"Elizabeth!" Anna shouted. "Get out of there!"

Mary Frances tapped Anna's wrist with a silver comb. "Rule
number one—my clientele's comfort is *never* compromised by my
operators' private battles."

"Even Willi's been known to shampoo in a pinch," Anna said.
"No dividing line in her shop between owner and owned."

Willi also had a procedures manual and a leather-bound portfolio of twenty styles that she changed seasonally. She had one
shop in Marfa, twenty-six miles to the west, but franchise was on
her mind. The individual stations at Willi's were prefabricated
and could be plugged into an empty room.

Every Christmas Willi sent Anna a case of imported beer and
the offer of a percentage of the franchise venture. The first Monday of every year Anna refused. She was opposed to mass production.

"In one shop it may appear to be mass production," Willi
always explained patiently. "In dealing with many shops, it
becomes quality control. I will give you free rein over upgrading
forty-five percent of the portfolio. Thirteen styles, Anna, all yours.
We will not go to the slick European magazines to see what is
happening. We will create the styles on local women and have
them photographed, also locally. They will be the trendsetters of
their communities."

"Willi's giving her stylists dental insurance," Anna told Mary
Frances. The stylists at Mary Frances's were free-lancers. Anna
preferred taking care of herself rather than taking the carrot and
the stick only to find that the carrot was so old and soft it felt like
a human finger.

"She called you again, didn't she?" Mary Frances accused. "I
knew it, I knew it. Oh, hell." She remembered that the hair
entangled in the roller was attached to a scalp and gentled her
fingers. "She gets me conditioned into expecting her attack in

December, and then she kamikazes. Well, I won't have it. I should let you go, and we'd see how long you lasted. We'd see who you appreciated after all." The roller was hopelessly embedded. Mary Frances sneaked a pair of scissors into her hand and razored hair away from the roller.

Years of standing in front of mirrors had taught Anna to keep her face neutral. The long horizontal mirrors weren't for the operators' benefit. They weren't there for the luxury of self-indulgence. The mirrors were there to calm the clients, to let them see that nothing was going on behind their backs. If a woman didn't catch Anna rolling her eyes, then she'd catch Jo rolling hers.

The redhead had finished washing her hair. Exhilarated, she paused in the doorway. "Now what?" she asked. "What shall I do now?"

Mary Frances put down her comb and stared at the woman. "Who is that?"

"Coffee," Anna said. She pushed her curler tray into Mary Frances's hip. "Make us all some coffee. Everything's in that closet under the stairs in the hall. If you can't get into the bathroom, fill up the pot where you washed your hair." The woman checked the security of her terry-cloth turban with both hands before striding to the closet.

"You hired her, you pay her," Mary Frances said. She anchored a comb in the hair of the woman Liz had abandoned. The woman, her head half set, was still looking in her purse for change. "You want to take over my shop—you manage things. Tell Liz I want to see her upstairs before you close. Then you can come up."

The bathroom door bucked open. Liz waved a test tube filled with blue liquid. "I'm ovulating! I have to call Leo!"

Anna pulled the telephone line out of its jack. "Later. You're good for a couple more hours."

Liz retrieved her comb and sucked on it. "He's in anatomy till four anyway. I'm so excited! You should feel my heart! That's what it's going to be like, like another heart inside me. Be happy for me, Anna. Cross your fingers for me. Let me see you do it."

Anna held up her crossed fingers. The woman forgotten by

both Liz and Mary Frances looked up and said, "Oh, honey, it's supposed to be the first pee of the morning you test."

Her big brown eyes tearing, Liz fumbled more rollers out of the woman's damp hair. "Well, I *know* that, I'm not stupid."

"She hasn't been under the dryer yet," Anna reminded Liz.

"Well, I *know* that, Anna, you're so smart, why don't you finish her?" She ran into the bathroom and locked the door. The toilet flushed steadily.

Liz's customer shook the remaining rollers out of her hair. "I just hated for her to get her hopes up . . ." she said sadly. "I know how it is."

"It was a hard call." Anna shielded her own customer's eyes and sent a light coat of hair spray into the air to make the woman think she'd been given extra protection. Moving to Liz's chair, she fluffed the sad woman's hair with her fingertips. "You really don't need a roll-up. I'm going to put you under the heat lamps and let the curl come through on its own."

"No, really, it's all right . . . I shouldn't ever have come in." The woman felt for the ground with her foot, but Liz had pumped up the chair as high as it would go.

Anna didn't want to let the woman go thinking she deserved to be passed from hand to hand and ignored and finally left waiting for something she had a right to enjoy. Urging a wave forward, she said, "You really have beautiful hair. It's a treat to work on hair like this."

Liz slammed out of the bathroom and shouldered Anna aside, but Anna stood her ground. She wasn't letting this woman get away. There was no resemblance to Grace Nettinger, but look how wrong they'd been on that one. "Lizzie, go upstairs and talk some vodka tonics out of Mary Frances before the supplies-have-gone-up lecture starts and the whip comes down. Go on."

"Promise me you won't tell Leo I failed that test."

Anna flipped up two dryer hoods before crossing her heart. "Send that redhead who's making the coffee back in here." The two heat-flushed customers released from the dryers looked dazed. Anna fanned them with a neck towel.

The redhead brought a tray of coffee cups into the styling room. Bending her knees, she offered cream and sugar to everyone. "Put the coffee on the manicure table," Anna instructed. "Unroll these two. Do this one first, then call me." She eased Liz's sad customer to the ground and installed her beneath the heat lamps. "Don't move. These lamps are very sensitive and very expensive." Placing responsibility for the lamps in the woman's hands should keep her from running out the front door. Once she saw herself in the mirror, the woman would never again put the care of any heat lamp above herself.

———

At the end of the day Leo stuck his head through the paneless window that separated the reception and styling areas. "Where's my Lizzie? What have you done with her?"

"How about a trim on the house?" Anna offered. "All I see is a great big hairy hole opening and closing."

"Aha! It's the Delilah Syndrome. Confronted by a man of strength and character, not to say intelligence, the women of Mary Frances's Beauty Salon seek to decimate his power." He flicked his short fingers at Anna. "Away with you, I say. Where's Liz?"

Waving the towel like a matador's cape, she said, "Come on, Leo, I need the practice."

"Is she in the bathroom again?" He sighed and walked to the bathroom door. Shifting his untidy body to block Anna's view, Leo tapped lightly on the door. "Liz? Baby? Time to go home."

There was something so tender in Leo's manner that Anna hated to tell him he was knocking on the wrong door. She decided to rinse the sinks one more time.

Leo followed her. "You've convinced her to leave me, haven't you? You're trying to talk her into leaving me before I leave her. You've got her thinking I'll walk out on her."

"What is wrong with everybody today? She's upstairs with M.F. I'll be happy to buzz." Anna pressed the intercom twice.

Clearing the wreckage on her counter, she tried not to keep track of Leo's dejected wanderings. He prowled around in the shampoo room, opening and closing cabinets. A blast of water from a black rubber hose ricocheted into one of the sinks. Anna hoped it wasn't the one she'd cleaned twice.

The thick gurgle of air being squeezed out of a bottle of conditioner sounded obscene. She could see Leo staring suspiciously at the plastic mustard bottle in his hand. He waved the pointed tip close to his nose. Mary Frances had found out that restaurant suppliers were cheaper on certain items than the beauty suppliers. There was a logic to the disharmony of red ketchup bottles filled with shampoo and those yellow bottles of conditioner side by side with the diehard pink femininity that Mary Frances peddled. Given a choice between total womanhood and the preservation of a dollar, Mary Frances went for the money, but Anna didn't think Leo was in a mood to appreciate the reasoning.

He appeared in the doorway again and watched Anna. Hands pried into his jeans pockets, he bounced his shoulder against the doorframe. "It's not very easy for a man to come in here, you know. You all stop talking. I always think you hide something when you hear me coming. I *like* women. I should love it here, I should be swimming in my element here. You-all make me feel lonely."

Anna almost started laughing. She didn't know where men got some of their ideas about women. "You're romanticizing it. I'd feel uncomfortable if I walked into Gladstone's."

"You? Ha!" Leo settled into Jo's chair. "You'd intimidate three-quarters of the men if you walked into Gladstone's. There's something about you that just puts a man on guard.

"Nope, I've made a study of this woman thing. You'll notice, for instance, that barbershops have their traditional colored poles, but how are beauty shops distinguished? You can walk down the street and look in a storefront window and see a barber at work. Not so with a beauty shop. You shroud the entrance in ivy or cutout cinder blocks, or you have to go through room after room to find the center of operations. You're perpetuating this high priestess myth."

"*You're* perpetuating the myth," Anna said. "You're the one who told me what the barber pole meant. Remember? It was a sign that surgery was done. The scissors and razors might have carried over, but we don't need signs outside our doors because we didn't get started by doing D and Cs in the back room. The idea of a beauty shop is a man's fantasy. There's no mystery. We offer more services than a barbershop does. We need more room. Period. And I offered to cut your hair, but you won't give your body as much attention as you give your brain."

Tired of letting Leo practice his senior seminars on her, Anna began sweeping the floor. She made a pass underneath his chair and glanced at the inseparable mass of beard and hair. Her fingers ached to bring order to the chaos. Peering closer, she asked, "Leo, is that a pierced ear I see in there? Did Liz do that?"

"Don't try to throw me off the track, Anna," he warned. "I know your games."

Anna didn't know exactly why she found it so hard to take him seriously. She admired his thirst for knowledge. The vision he held of himself was a grander one than he would be able to obtain. "But there is a hole in your ear, isn't there?" she persisted.

The rapid clicks of Mary Frances's heels hit the uninsulated section of ceiling. Anna and Leo clocked the impatient movement of her footsteps and waited for the slower and heavier steps of Liz to come through the rain-soaked acoustic tiles.

Anna rested her arm across the back of Jo's chair and pumped up Leo. "Are you ever going to graduate? Don't get your back up." She patted his shoulder in a sisterly fashion. "I just don't want anything to happen to you two. You check in with each other, right? You know what she wants? What you want? It's important."

Leo used the arms of the chair to hoist himself up a few inches. "No offense, Anna, but you're not exactly the best authority on a happy home life."

She pretended to consider his criticism. "Well, no. But I've read some books, I've seen some movies and things on TV. I have an idea of how things are supposed to work."

"We've got a plan. I'll finish up, and then she can go back to school—"

"What if she doesn't want to go back to school? What if she just wants to stay home and turn out babies and peach pies?"

Distress lines appeared on either side of Leo's short, wide-nostriled nose. "Not my Lizzie. How can anyone not want to learn? It's an inalienable right. That's what's wrong with you. You should go back to school."

"I went to beauty college. People either learn or they don't. School's not the only roof all the learners gather under. You're a snob, Leo."

"There you go again," he complained. "You're deliberately misunderstanding me. Aren't there things you really, really want to know? What do you want?" His arms hooped above his head as if he could channel some great shining light into her.

There was a certain grace in his attempt to harness the world that Anna appreciated. "You know what I want, Leo. I want to make this place mine. I will, too."

Leo's puffy pincushion hands fell over the armrests and dangled hopelessly. "That's *it*? That's all you want?"

Thinking about all the time and money already spent in getting control of the shop, Anna pointed fiercely to the floor. "Not *this*" —her hand flew up to slap her forehead—"but what's up here. I said I wanted to make it *mine*. And I don't just mean scraping Mary Frances's name off the door and painting mine on."

"I'm not dead yet, Anna," Mary Frances cut in. She stalked to the cash drawer and tucked the metal strongbox under her arm. "Liz, dear, you might want to watch your husband. Anna has that greedy look in her eyes again. You think about what I said."

There were times when Anna felt the chain of fate around her neck and knew there was somebody ready to jerk it. Confiding in Leo and getting caught doing it had put the chain into Mary Frances's hands. Fifteen thousand dollars in CDs were worthless if Mary Frances refused to sell the shop to her.

"I'm only a little hungry, Mary Frances," Anna said, made suddenly reckless by the realization that hard work was its own reward. "Throw me a bone."

Mary Frances tightened her hold on the cashbox. "Show the

two lovebirds out and lock up. Then we'll have a nice talk." She turned at the stairway entrance. "Don't forget to buzz before you come up."

Anna locked the door after Leo and Liz and switched off the lights. The pinkness of the shop was naturally strong in early-morning light. In the afternoons the color was bolstered by a row of pink light bulbs that were concealed behind a strip of painted wood. Without the lights the rooms took on an ashy quality. Tomorrow's sunlight wouldn't refresh the pink walls; they would be another day older. More patches of pink would have curdled into shades of orange. Waiting in the shampoo room for Mary Frances to buzz her up, Anna shut her eyes and stripped the walls clean.

By the time Anna was invited upstairs late-afternoon sun had filtered through the drawn bamboo shades on the west wall. Wearing her black velveteen hostess pajamas, Mary Frances re-clined on a powder blue chaise lounge in the center of the room. A black lacquer coffee table beside the chaise lounge held a de-canter of sherry, two matching glasses and a tray of cucumber-and-butter sandwiches cut into hearts and diamonds. If Mary Frances had broken out the sherry, then something was up.

Mary Frances rearranged her slim legs and considered the ef-fect before she said anything. "I've counted the cash, but of course, we have to deduct all those free treatments you gave away, not to mention paying that woman you were bossing around. How much did you give her?"

Anna pulled a twenty out of her pocket. "You got the question wrong. She gave me forty. I split it down the middle with you." She didn't give Mary Frances a chance to negotiate for a sixty-forty split. "She'll be back next time she's in town. She'll tell all her friends in San Antonio about it. They may even fly in just to have the experience of working in a beauty shop. You might even get written up in *Texas Monthly*."

"It's yourself you're bragging on, not my shop. I know."

A truck barreled into the alley at the side of the shop, and a gang of barking dogs greeted it. Anna took her glass over to the windows and looked down into the next yard. She felt as if she

wcrc in a tree house, hidden from the world. The upstairs apartment was another reason she coveted the shop. One sweep of the
room gave her a 360-degree view of the town. She could see two
Irish setters nipping at water as it twirled out of a sprinkler. The
yard was littered with Frisbees and a fluorescent green one was
stranded on the roof. "Who lives with the Frisbees and the dogs?"

Mary Frances had stiffened in the act of pouring more sherry.
"It's not fair," she railed. "They stick together. They see someone
in need and they get disgusted. They see someone who doesn't
want their help and they *jump* at the chance to do something—
anything they can." She advanced on Anna. "You"—she pointed
—"you're always going to have people falling all over themselves
to help you because you go *out* of your way to put people off."

Anna couldn't follow Mary Francces's train of thought. "How
much have you had to drink?"

"Oh, I see what's going on, don't think I don't," Mary Frances
declared. Reaching out to steady herself, she encountered a fern
and jumped back with a scream. "Who put that there?"

Anna went into the kitchen to make coffee. Mary Frances slid
on stockinged feet after her. "Good-bye, good-bye." She sighed,
hanging heavily on Anna's arm and waving into the trash can.
"No more musk. No more beer and Roquefort."

Six empty beer bottles rose from the full trash can, their lips
touching to form a tepee. Underncath the amber bottles lay an
almost empty bottle of after-shave. It wasn't the conventional
brand Mary Frances's husband, Alfred, doused himself with.

Anna had to rely on the kitchen sink's sturdiness to hold up
both of them. "I thought you'd stopped secing that other man
after Alfred's bypass."

"I did, I did." Mary Frances pressed the after-shave to her
cheek. "Why does everybody always want what I have, always,
always? Even Alfred. Jo wanted him at the Christmas dance of
1971, fifteen years ago. She almost got him, too. I'd like to see
what she would have done with him," Mary Frances said indig-
nantly.

Jo and Alfred didn't belong together. There was a height difference of four inches in Jo's favor; but then Mary Frances and

Alfred were a proportional couple, and that seemed to be their only point of compatibility.

Mary Frances put on her shoes again and let the right one dangle off her heel and tap the tile floor. "I love this sound," she emphatically struck the floor, "don't you? I do. You want my shop. Jo wants Alfred. Alfred wants me. If Jo can't have Alfred, then she wants you to have my shop. I know she does. I wish she wanted it. I wish she wanted it and she wanted Alfred."

"What about Burgess?" Anna asked. Jo didn't want the shop or Alfred. "They're so tight you couldn't slide a nail file between them." She found the coffee and measured spoonfuls into mugs. Mary Frances's small body had an amazing capacity for alcohol.

"*Burgess?*" Mary Frances cast off the idea. She displayed her hands and admired. "I was good out there today, wasn't I?"

"It's not like you're a brain surgeon or anything, Mary Frances. You only combed out one head today and you almost botched that."

"I'm sure you loved it. You had the whole place to yourself; you could just pretend it was all yours." Mary Frances threw the after-shave bottle into the trash and waved at it. "Good-bye, good-bye. You're no fun, Anna. No coffee. I can't drink coffee and conduct business."

Clouds streamed in unraveled braids across the sky and glowed from the fiery touch of the sun. Anna wished she could reproduce the effect of color and texture on earthbound hair. From the windows she watched a bare-chested man in cutoffs as he played Frisbee with the Irish setters. He looked up once and Anna drew back from the window. "Who lives down there with the dogs?"

"Oh, who cares?" Mary Frances had huddled herself into a ball. "Some young college thing. From the smell that comes out of there, all he knows is dogs and marijuana. Sit, Anna. We have business to discuss."

"Just tell me how much you're going to dock me and do it." Anna was disappointed that the man below wasn't Mary Frances's lover. Somebody with a headful of hair and unbuttoned Hawaiian shirts might be good for her.

"Sit down and shut your eyes," Mary Frances commanded.

"Don't peek." Anna heard her tiptoe over to her wall safe. The dial scraped through the combination. "All right, open."

The purple and pink batik of a woman pouring a pitcher of water was back in place. The nail it hung on was too short and the safe's dial made the pitcher's spout protrude. Mary Frances had put on her glasses and was unfolding papers in her lap. "I was going to offer it to you after Jo, but after your highhanded behavior this afternoon, I've given Liz second opportunity."

Anna believed there was a certain amount of justice in the world. She believed that having a goal and working hard to achieve it were what kept people going, but what she knew was that what she believed didn't matter. Having a clear vision of what her own shop would look like didn't matter. Guarantees from both Jo and Liz that neither wanted the shop didn't matter. Money in the bank didn't matter. Everything hinged on Mary Frances's decision.

"Liz wants a baby," Anna said and waited for Mary Frances's deal.

"What do you think this shop means to me? This is *my* baby. I have borne and raised it and you want to take it away from me. You treat me like I'm some unfit mother! You do! You want to take every ounce of me out of this place. You want to destroy everything I've built here."

If the shop was the child that Mary Frances had never had, then she'd grieved long enough. The shop should be a vital thing, not a monument to the past. "What about Willi? Leo'd sell out to her in a second if it came down to financing a Ph.D. You know I'd never sell."

"Why can't you and Jo go in together and buy it?" Mary Frances wailed. "She's the only one I know who could keep you from tearing it all down. I don't know what would happen if you touched that ivy of hers. . . . Bevo could come back and work here—"

Anna shook her head. "Jo doesn't want the shop. She's only working till Burgess retires. And you know Bevo won't ever move back here. Tell me your terms. Financial."

Mary Frances sighed and handed Anna a sheet of paper.

"Here's the inventory from the last quarter. You helped on that, so you know it's accurate. It's a fair market price. One hundred thousand for the building, fixtures and inventory. That also includes the hospital and nursing home contracts. Twenty thousand down. Cash. Interested?"

The terms were what Anna had expected. "I'd like Bob James to look at the books and the contract."

Mary Frances waved her hand. "That's fine. I want everything closed by the end of August. That gives you almost two full months. Don't ask me for a raise between now and then."

"Why now?" Anna asked. The deal, long anticipated, seemed to have snowballed out of nowhere.

"Alfred's taking early retirement from the university. He wants to buy a houseboat and put it on Lake Amistad. We're going to sip gin and tonics and putt-putt around the lake."

The thought of Mary Frances and Alfred cruising around the lake made Anna laugh. "Are you kidding?"

"I've never been more serious. My life is *over!*"

"Take my money and run. Take your lover and go."

"Easy for you to say, Anna. The only thing you've ever been committed to is my shop." Mary Frances stroked the skin under her eyes. "Turn on the lights—slowly."

Anna smiled and her whole body participated. The shop was hers. She was five thousand dollars short, but she had more than two months to get the money. Only an act of nature could stop her now. Only a tornado reducing the building to a stack of Popsicle sticks could stop her now. And this wasn't tornado country.

In the second week of July Anna's lawyer sent her the divorce papers. When Bryan called to say he was sending someone to move his things, she was relieved. Their divorce was on schedule. It appeared that Bryan, at last, had given up his fantasies and his deceits.

Two days after Bryan's call a tall, silent man appeared on Anna's doorstep. He handed her a letter signed by Bryan. The signature was witnessed and notarized. Fingering the seal embossed on the bond paper, Anna wasn't sure who Bryan was trying to get the better of—her or the Border Patrol or the INS.

Distrusting the mover's lethal silence, she followed him to Bryan's new home. She watched him load the boxes marked "Jenny Lind, AR" and "Evening Shade, AR" on the dumbwaiter that Summer Haslip's son had had installed when his mother had gotten too sick to fix her own meals. The garage apartment was still filled with Summer's furniture—rocking chairs whose seats were puffed like rising loaves of bread, a four-poster canopied bed and hand-painted lamps with double globes.

Anna put the last box, "Anadarko, OK," on the dumbwaiter herself. As the box sailed to the second floor, an impulse to stop its flight overtook her. She ran up the steps and snatched the box before it reached the man's hands. Holding the box tightly, she felt an uneasiness that might have been regret at seeing Bryan's things finally going or suspicion about the mover, who was now standing right behind her. Anna waited for the man to say something to her, but he didn't. She wondered if he would stay so quiet if she ran away with the box.

Suddenly the secrecy that Bryan had imposed upon their relationship and that she had been only too glad to uphold was unbearable. Anna tore the lid off the Anadarko box. She rummaged through Chamber of Commerce brochures and and newspaper clippings as if the key to understanding and believing Bryan could be found in them, but the only clue she found was a matchbook with a telephone number penciled on the inside cover. Her discomfort expanded. She told herself she was getting hysterical. She was out of control. The clear-cut ache of a broken heart would have been a more welcome feeling. Her initial sense of relief was unexpectedly becoming intertwined with a sense of loss.

The man sent the empty dumbwaiter down to Anna. Vibrating, the metal tray waited for the last load. With the help of deep breaths Anna forced the craziness out of her body. She returned the matchbook to the "Anadarko, OK" box and felt the man's light eyes burning into her back.

Confident that Bryan had schooled him in the art of not answering, Anna fished. "Where did you meet Bryan? Anadarko, OK? Bossier City? Sydney? Texhoma? Durban? Pátzcuaro? El Paso? Boquillas Canyon?"

The man ignored her and took the last box into Bryan's new home. He made a point of shutting and testing the glass-paneled door behind him. Anna bet he'd heard steel doors slam behind him in the Huntsville prison. She waved to Summer Haslip's son as he watered red and purple petunias. He jiggled the hose in response until the water snake-danced. Knowing that somebody had seen her in the company of a man who looked as if he made his living by preying on highway-stranded women made Anna feel better.

She jumped when the man came out and locked and tested the door. Swirls of dust were trapped in his eyes, and it was hard to make out the irises' true color. Unwillingly she bumped down the steps before him. "You must be a driver, too How long have you known Bryan?"

"I move things," he said. "Something's over there, I move it over here. I don't ask any questions, so I don't answer any." He patted the El Camino where the dull tan paint was skinned off the hood. The left headlight was walleyed. "I'm headed your way."

The man's eyelids dropped until Anna couldn't tell which part of her body he was dismembering. "No thanks. I'm not stranded." She was angry at Bryan for sending a man who frightened her and angry at herself for being frightened.

Another flash of his dusty eyes and he was rattling out of the driveway. Restless because she hadn't found out anything about Bryan now when she had had the chance, because she wouldn't be able to tell the police what kind of accent the mover had, because she should be feeling free and full of accomplishment after successfully completing a two-year project, Anna decided to visit Cheryl Long and let herself be talked into buying something ridiculous.

Keeping an eye out for snakes, Anna crossed the floodplain between the hospital and the country club golf course. She hated snakes. In her mind a red racer carried the same potential as a rattlesnake. Striped lizards with soft bellies were warming themselves on the rocks. She didn't mind those, or horny toads as long as they were babies. It was the big prehistoric-looking horny toads that she chunked rocks at. Part of her still believed that the big ones could spit blood up to a distance of twenty feet.

A small paved road surged out of the floodplain and took Anna past the hospital. She cut over to a wider street where there were sidewalks. A ten-block walk took her to the business district, which everybody called downtown.

Gladstone's barbershop was next door to Labrette's. A cardboard sign in the window read, LIKE TO READ: ESQUIRE, GQ, CONSUMER REPORT? SO DO I—BRING 'EM IN! Gladstone's magazine collection was as bad as Mary Frances's. Anna peered in the window and wondered if the magazine with a huge pink-mouthed fish on the cover was Ed Nettinger's contribution.

Homer Gladstone had salvaged four green leather chairs from a bankrupt dental college. Leo was right; anybody could stand across the street and tell who was sitting in the chairs and getting a haircut, but the openness of the shop, as if men had no vanity, didn't fool Anna. She liked to put her nose against the plate glass and stare at the men until she got somebody's attention.

When Homer signaled her to come in, Anna tapped her watch. "Are you going to HairExpo in Chicago?" he yelled.

She shook her head and rubbed thumb against fingertips. "I'm saving my money this year."

The thick blue plastic shades at Labrette's were being drawn against the afternoon sun. Three mannequins in the window wavered and looked like big dolls at the bottom of a swimming pool.

"Anna!" Cheryl exclaimed. "I don't believe it. Come in this *instant!*"

"I need something frilly and ridiculous," Anna said.

"Well, you've come to the right place. Sit down right now." Cheryl Long placed Anna between a standing ashtray and a rubber plant. Cocktail dresses and long formals rustled in the cool air. "Let's see now. Something in an Ava Gardner, I think."

"Don't start trying to sell me. I just want one thing."

"Just because you don't do anything with yourself, don't laugh at me. A little lipstick wouldn't kill you, weed out those eyebrows —you know what I mean." Cheryl Long bent over and popped a contact lens into her palm. One eye was hazel and the other was an emerald green in contrast. "Look here, you think I've got green eyes? *You've* got green eyes."

"Show me something ridiculous. Quick. I didn't come in for a complete make-over."

Cheryl Long paused before a drape-covered doorway that led to dressing rooms and an office. "A little blush on those cheekbones would do *wonders,* believe me."

Anna wandered around the shop. China bowls heaped with rose potpourri sat on the glove and scarf counter. The clothes hung on padded blue hangers. Casual wear started near the front door. The degree of style increased in formality to better dresses, suits and after-five wear and culminated at the back of the store with lounging pajamas.

The heavy blue window shades made car fenders buckle and the necks of passersby lengthen as if they were caught in a fun house mirror. There was no traffic noise. Anna decided Labrette's must be soundproofed. The combination of cool, gently scented air and blue-filtered light made her lethargic. It was unthinkable that anyone would speak above a whisper. Everything would be kept confidential.

Anna couldn't fit Cheryl Long into her surroundings. At least Mary Frances had stripped away all the padding; all the tricks and tools of that trade were visible. Cold shampoo and hot dryers kept the women alert. Labrette's was the place for Leo to be uncomfortable in. A sudden picture of Ed Nettinger grabbing an armful of soft clothes and breathing deeply made her thighs tighten, and she frowned at their mutiny.

"Did you get an okay from Alan Lehrmann on doing Pete Nelson's Plumbing Supply for your class project?" Anna called.

"He said yes, *finally.*" Cheryl's voice sounded muffled and preoccupied.

"Was this before or after you had dinner with him?"

Cheryl stuck her head through the drapes. "Are you ready? I am going to make you look *so* good!"

Anna counted eight hangers dangling from Cheryl's fingers. "It's a good thing your fingers aren't any longer. Remember—only one thing. This is to get over a divorce."

"You don't look very heartbroken to me. And it doesn't cost a *thing* to try clothes on." Cheryl slipped each hanger off her finger and twirled it before slinging it across a chair. "The most terrible, horrible thing happened to poor Pete Nelson."

The pile on the chair grew, and Anna was disappointed to feel no charge of desire. "Why make up a plumbing supply company when you've got your very own dress shop?"

"That's *exactly* why. I already have this. Think of poor Pete Nelson and his plumbing supplies. His partner's cleaned out the office safe, and their bank account, and he's left town with poor Pete's wife."

A spill of cream-colored satin caught Anna's attention. She reached out and felt herself smiling in wicked delight at the splash of satin. "You're in trouble in that class as it is." The satin skirt billowed as she rescued it from the pile. "What's this?"

Cheryl Long arched a well-tended eyebrow at Anna. "I knew you had it in you. 'Voilà! The perfect nightgown for a soon-to-be-divorcée. Try it on this *minute!*"

Anna stalled. She wanted to hold the nightgown across her arms and get used to the feel of the material before trying it on. "You do remember that you made up Pete Nelson, don't you?"

"Professor Lehrmann is the one who said to expect the unexpected in business. Just think of poor Pete Nelson. He needs somebody to get him on his feet again."

"You and Bryan would be perfect for each other," Anna said and went through the blue velveteen drapes to a dressing room. All the rooms were covered in gray carpet. When she tried to rub out an old cigarette burn in the thin pile, her actions were reflected in three mirrors.

The dressing room curtains shook. "Are you all right in there? I'm thinking of making Alan Lehrmann mine. What do you think? A Jewish man. My mother would *die*. Hurry—I'm dying to see."

"What about Bryan?" Anna asked. "He and poor Pete Nelson are in the same boat. Both of them abandoned by their wives."

In the shadowed pleats of the deeply cut bosom, the color of the nightgown approached copper. She knew without trying on the gown that she'd take it. A celebration present for outwaiting

Mary Frances and not giving in to Bryan. Anna molded the nightgown to her body and whirled around.

Jo and Burgess had stood up for Anna and Bryan when they were married in El Paso. Despite her previous assurances to Anna, Jo had issued a prenuptial warning to Bryan. "I just want you know," she had said, "I'm keeping my eye on you. I'll know if you don't treat her right."

The fact that Anna refused to take any money and that Bryan seemed to have fallen in love had disturbed Burgess. "I don't know what your game is here," he had told Anna, "but if you think you're about to turn him in for a big reward, you've got another think coming."

Jo and Burgess's son Bevo, who lived in El Paso, had joined them for the wedding dinner. Bevo had brought a date, a young man. It was the first visual confirmation of Bevo's preference that Burgess had had.

"You promised!" Jo had hissed at her son.

"I'm supposed to be the lonely one?" Bevo had said. "Look at Anna and Bryan—what a sham—at least I'm honest about what I do."

Anna and Bryan's presence hadn't been enough to keep anybody in check. Jo's lips hadn't been free of a cigarette or a salt-encrusted glass rim the whole evening. Bevo had taken potshots at Anna, but he jumped on his father when Burgess went after her. Halfway through dinner Bevo's date disappeared with someone else.

Now Anna and Bryan were back in El Paso for their final weekend. Jo and Burgess were two floors below, and Bevo was meeting them for dinner. But this time Bryan had his green card, and they could go across the river to Juárez, where the steaks and margaritas were cheaper.

Bryan unpacked a framed photograph of himself and an older man standing in front of a house shaded by palms. They were both bare-chested and grinning. Anna still didn't know who the other man was. "Is that your father?" she asked for the second time. "It can't do any harm now for me to know."

"Thanks to you I'm a free man now. I can come and go as I please," Bryan answered.

Anna ignored the double-edged reference to freedom. "A Canadian passport, an Irish passport, an Australian one. You've always been a free man." She knew that his route from South Africa to Texas had been a roundabout one. He'd deserted the army and made his way to Australia and then Singapore. Jo had been able to tell her that much.

"Freer than most," Bryan agreed, "but that's not good enough."

Anna looked out the window. Sunk low in its channel, the Rio Grande looked too tired to accept the burden of separation Mexico and the United States had imposed on it. The river had changed course more than once to escape the responsibility. "I don't think you really have anything to hide. I think you just like being mysterious."

"You were a good partner," Bryan said. "Don't stop now." The next picture he set out was a picture taken at their honeymoon dinner. The flash had caught both Anna and Bryan red-eyed. Meanwhile, Jo's face was turned away from the camera and Burgess's eyes were shut. Only Bevo had faced the camera squarely. The flash had given his teeth an enduring phosphorescence.

"That's a great picture of Bevo," Anna said. "We should crop everybody else out."

"This is the picture that should have been taken across the border, but the bastards wouldn't let me in. They hadn't bestowed their precious green card on me yet."

"It's nothing personal," Anna said. "I don't think either the United States or Mexico would much care if you went over and came back or not."

"It's unnatural," Bryan said. "They think they can manipulate geography; they think they can hand out scraps of paper and call them passes; they think they can uproot people—take them *physically* out of their homes, or they take the other tack, try to seduce them, play with their minds, convince them that that place over there is the promised land. America—you can't imagine how much the sky over this country shines. People for thousands and thousands of miles see the glow, and they think they will be happy and healthy and *rich* here."

He laced his fingers together. "It's all tied together. Ripples in the pond. What happens here, in this room, happens because of what happened halfway around the world. We can't avoid it. The unwillingness to admit that does not put an end to the responsibility. The inability to commit yourself, on any level, is a failure of the spirit. They rely on that failure to keep people in check, that's why they've set up townships and iron curtains and tortilla curtains. They've destroyed the trust between people."

Anna could smell the difference between personal and political coming out of Bryan although he would say there was no difference between the two. "I vote," she said. "In March and November the politicians are at my mercy. What am I supposed to do? Follow your lead? Do whatever it is you're doing? No. If there's so much wrong in South Africa, then why did you come here? Where's your loyalty?"

"Loyalty! You're confusing loyalty with guilt. Staying in one place does not indicate loyalty. If you choose to stay out of spite, that's a misplaced sense of duty. The true test of loyalty is the ability to maintain distance." He hoisted Anna's small bag. "May I?"

"You should run for governor," Anna said. "Doing something shady is a real vote getter these days." She plumped up the king-size pillows and watched Bryan's big hands gently transfer her clothing to a separate drawer. He unpacked more completely for an overnight stay than she and her mother had for half of their moves. The negligee was folded in tissue paper. "You can peek," she encouraged.

The cream-colored satin lay across his arms as if Anna were already in it. "I believe I'll leave this out. Ah, now that's lovely, draped over the chair like that."

"You're like a little boy at Christmas," she teased.

"It's not every day a boy gets divorced, love."

"The trouble is I don't know what divorce means to you.

Maybe we should have the lawyer draw up a postdivorce agreement." The idea of seeing in black and white what Bryan expected from their relationship appealed to Anna. Words printed on a stiff piece of paper wouldn't put limits on him, but she'd like to preserve the bones of his intentions.

"I know when to give up, and I know how to give up without deserting. I don't need a legal document to tell me what my responsibilities to a friend are. It's the documents that got us into this mess. There's not one that can't be doctored."

Small boys selling newspapers and Chiclets paved the road from the bridge to downtown Juárez. The cab created holes in the traffic and quickly plugged them, but, racing a bus to a left-turn lane, the driver stalled the engine. Two young men carrying torches climbed onto the cab's hood. One drank gasoline from a clear bottle, spit it out and held a torch close to his mouth. Fire roared from his mouth. The other one appeared to eat the flame of his torch. Bryan paid the cursing driver. The dry summer heat charged Anna's skin. All it would take to breathe fire was a lung full of air. She kept turning around to see what the two young men would do next, but Bryan wouldn't let up the pace.

Neon signs screwed to the close-fitting buildings were almost colorless in the evening sun. The crowd swallowed Bryan, and Anna had to trust the hand she held was his. The river did make a difference. Juárez and El Paso were sister cities, joined by bridges, bringing out the best and the worst in each other. Mexico was another country, a foreign landscape, a place that to some Americans promised cheap celebration. Everything was bright and loud and in motion. There was nothing in the bank; it was all spent in a Saturday night. Soldiers from Fort Bliss and White Sands with closely shaven heads and sunglasses bargained with vendors for onyx chess sets and donkey piñatas to send back home.

Anna felt a reverberation beyond sight and sound. Something was happening that was beyond her understanding. The marketplace was a mask and the face behind it was unknown. For a second she wanted to shake free of Bryan's hand and throw herself into the crowd to see where she would surface.

But Bryan held tight and pulled them into the quiet courtyard of a restaurant. Jo was seated in a rattan chair with an overgrown back. Her hands hung off the armrests; her nails had grown so long that the tips had begun to curl. A turquoise parrot in a cage hooked his beak over the bamboo bars and tried to get at her hair.

Bending to raise her hand to his lips, Bryan exclaimed, "Ah, Josephine, you look like the dowager empress sitting there."

"I believe I'll snap you up myself, Thomas O. Bryan. Keep up that chatter at your own risk."

Anna was finding perverse pleasure in tempting the parrot with her fingers. "You're too late. Cheryl Long's got her eyes on him," she said. Careless talk was tumbling out of their mouths, but crossing the border seemed to flesh out fantasies and to make their desires real. Everything, every look and word casually thrown away had a different value assessed on it here. The waste would be consumed by somebody.

"You run along and keep Burgess company," Jo commanded. "Anna and I are going to have a little girl talk." For the past month she had seemed drained and remote, but some strong inner source powered her tonight.

Anna was glad to see the alteration in Jo. "Don't worry. I'll be good. When are Bevo and his date coming?"

"Charles, his name is Charles. I never should have let Burgess saddle him with that nickname. Nobody should have to answer to the name of a football team's mascot."

Good, Anna thought. The remark about her son's date hadn't caused Jo to flinch. Either Bevo wasn't bringing anybody or he was bringing a girl. Or Jo had finally gotten sensible and refused to referee the relationship between her husband and son. Tonight might not be so bad after all.

Suddenly Jo's nails clicked around Anna's wrist. "Don't you forget—we're going shopping all day tomorrow. I'll meet you in the lobby at eight A.M. sharp. Here's a list of what I'm coming home with. I've got the sizes and colors—it's all written down—

all you have to do is buy everything for me. There's a check there to cover it. I'll meet you in the plaza at five-thirty. And don't you say one word about this to *anybody.*"

Anna no longer trusted her ability to understand. There seemed to be too much at stake, and she had no idea why. "What are you up to? If this has anything to do with Bryan's business—"

Jo's face cleared. "Oh, pooh, Anna! You see a snake under every rock. Nothing's wrong. Here's Charles now—oh Lord. He's brought a Negro with him. Burgess may fall off that wagon yet."

Thousands of oiled black curls swam toward Bevo's fair-skinned forehead. His linen pants and cotton shirt were fastidiously pressed. Bevo had compounded Burgess's doubts by going to beauty college in San Antonio, where he'd tapped into a flair for coloring hair. Instead of dropping the nickname given to him by Burgess—"First full sentence out of the boy's mouth, I swear, 'Hook 'em, Horns' "—he had Frenchified it, turning Bee-vo into Bay-vo. The time line of his friendships was marked by the pronunciation of his nickname.

Bevo touched cool cheeks with Anna and introduced his friend, Paul, whose drooping eyelids lifted at the sight of Jo's hair. He was as immaculately dressed as Bevo. His skin had the color and matte texture of cocoa. Anna envied their crispness. Arm in arm, Jo and Bevo passed through the dining room and out French doors to the courtyard. Paul's hips barely moved, but they had a life of their own. Anna thought it had something to do with knee action.

Jo stopped and sighed in admiration at a waterfall pouring out of a rock wall. With a surefooted instinct Paul stopped a split second behind mother and son on the uneven flagstone walk. Disoriented as she was, Anna felt the hush and stir their entrance had caused. She knew what color Burgess's face would be before she saw it. Bryan jumped up and began to deal out chairs to people.

Anna lingered behind as if she weren't a part of the scene. She was one of the outsiders at a family dinner, but those family members were outsiders at her divorce dinner. Paul was outside of everything, and Anna wouldn't have been surprised if an hour before he had been a lizard sunning himself on a rock, transformed for the night by Bevo to bedevil Burgess. He was present as a friend to Bevo, in the same way she was a friend to Bryan. Neither friendship was acceptable to Burgess.

Bryan was there for Burgess. She was there for Jo. Jo and Burgess had each other. It all worked out. Tomorrow she would be shopping all day by herself, creating a lie for Jo to give to Burgess, and Jo never lied to Burgess. None of it made sense, but tonight, on this side of the border, that seemed all right.

Bryan placed a gardenia beside Anna's plate. "I remembered" —he beamed at her—"I remembered about the gardenia bush always going with you."

"It's my mother's flower," Anna said. She left the gardenia in its plastic bag.

"What's your flower?" His hand roamed her shoulder in a gesture of intimacy as he whispered, "Help me here. We are a community now, not a group of individuals."

"Ooh-la-la, Anna and Bryan," Bevo said.

Feeling slow and stupid because she didn't have a flower, Anna spent some time with her glass of champagne to show Bryan that she was making an effort to be a good and productive member of the group. She thought of orchids with their long curling tongues, tightly furled roses, carnations like wadded-up tissue, the honkers of gladiolas and daffodils. Irises and the sweet smell of hyacinths reminded her of Grace Nettinger in her bronze coffin. She breathed heavily in thought and the scent of gardenia was trapped in her nostrils. A vine by the waterfall caught her eye. "Hibiscus," Anna said triumphantly.

"You were starting to worry me," Paul said. He smoked a thin brown cigarette the color of his eyes. "Every woman has to have her own flower."

"What if a woman wants to change her flower?" Anna asked. Paul considered the question for so long she thought he'd fallen asleep.

"I don't think she can," he finally decided.

Two waiters ushered Bryan away from the hibiscus vine as he tried unsuccessfully to pick a flower for Anna. Another waiter motioned madly for the flower vendor. Using the waiters' white-jacketed shoulders as backdrop, Bryan deliberated between yellow and red flowers, begging opinions from all sides in fluent Spanish. By the time he chose two flowers, the waiters and the vendor were his great friends. Pitchers of margaritas and plates of *asadero* cheese wrapped in green chiles and bowls of guacamole appeared on the table.

Bryan left the gardenia with a woman at a table close to the waterfall who had helped him choose Anna's hibiscus. He returned to the table and tried to slide an orchid behind Jo's ear, but the stem wouldn't puncture her hair. "Your Spanish has gotten a lot better," Anna said.

Shut out of Jo and Bevo's conversation, Burgess turned on Anna. "Too bad they didn't have any oleanders. You'd look good covered in oleanders."

"But they're poisonous," Paul objected.

Bevo stopped in mid-sentence to stare down his father. "You can't stand being left out, can you?"

"She can handle it," Burgess said.

Bryan fixed his eye on Paul. "And what about South Africa?"

Paul drawled, "It's taken me twelve years to get this far from the cotton fields in East Texas, and the man wants to send me back to Africa." He leaned to Bevo in mock appeal. "Who is this man? Help me! Help me!"

Burgess slapped the table. "Hell, I sympathize with a good struggle. Guess who built the first house in Alpine? Go on, take a shot. Even Bryan wouldn't get this one in a million years."

Bevo ignored his father and assured Paul, "Don't worry. Thomas is persona non grata in South Africa. You two could take turns kissing a white woman in her own bedroom, and he's the one they'd go after. They would. They'd go after this white guy here before they even thought about you. Don't worry. Just keep thinking: Los Angeles."

"A Negro, that's who," Burgess announced. "A one-armed Negro ex-sergeant at Fort Davis, early, early 1880's. J. M. Watts. That's right. He operated the stage stand between Fort Davis and Pena Colorado. There now."

Jo repeated Bevo's last words. "Los Angeles? What about Los Angeles? You're not going back out there?"

"We might," Bevo said.

"Don't think of it as losing a son. Think of it as gaining a place to stay in Los Angeles," Paul offered. He rubbed his wrist and smelled it. "Think of it as the stage stand between here and Hawaii."

Anna decided there was opium in Paul's brown cigarette, and the smoke was getting to her. She painted her mouth with a chile, and her eyes watered.

Burgess thumbed the air. "He can call himself black, and you can call yourself gay—it's nothing but playacting. You go to California with this nut, don't bother to come back."

Bevo let his hands crawl across his cheeks. "Oh no! Forgive me. Don't leave all your mufflers and your carburetors to Marvin the marine! My heritage—lost!"

"That's far enough," Jo said.

"What will I do?" Bevo wondered. His fingers drummed the table. "*How* will I be able to stand it? I know—I'll become an alcoholic and then recover—like my daddy!"

"Oh, waiter," Paul called, throwing back his neat head and looking at no one in particular. "Oh, Mr. Waiter! *Más* margaritas, while there's still time. *Andale! Andale!*"

"Shut up!" Burgess slammed his palm against the table and glared at Paul. "Not at my table. Not at my goddamn table!"

"Drunk," Bevo retaliated.

Burgess rose halfway out of his chair.

Jo pulled him back to the table. "Hush," she said.

"No," Bevo said. "Say it. Let him say it. I want to hear it. Say it!"

Burgess's head seemed to swell with blood. "Faggot."

Jo's hands kept them both at the table. The strength of that grip was considerable, but even she couldn't take the excessive charges of energy from her husband and son. Bryan grabbed Burgess's other hand. Paul reached for Bevo. To complete the circle, Anna joined hands with Paul and Bryan. Jo held fast against all attempts to break free. Anna saw the jolt of Jo's will travel into and subdue both Burgess and Bevo. The tremors passed through Bryan and Paul and fused inside Anna.

———

Anna's left thigh was cramping. The hem of the long satin night-gown was bunched under her knee. For almost an hour she and Bryan had been exchanging lazy kisses soured by the taste of tequila. The clock's fluorescent glow kept catching her eye. Their movements were restless and out of rhythm, caused not by passion but by a desire to claim comfortable positions before the time was up and they drifted off to sleep. The drugged sensation Anna had experienced in Juárez was long gone. Her flesh sandbagged around her. The thought of taking on Bryan's solid weight was unbeara-ble, but she kept hoping his hands and lips would help to make her weightless.

Finally Bryan dropped his head to Anna's shoulder. "This isn't going to work, love," he groaned. "I had thought we might go on all night, but not like this."

Anna slowly ruffled his neck hair and kissed the top of his head in relief. "Here. We'll have a cigarette and I'll get us some water. We'll work our way backwards." She walked confidently through the room. Her eyes had been wide open since the light was turned off.

Bryan sat on the edge of the bed. "Why did you marry me?"

Not again, Anna thought, and ground her head into the mirror. "You needed somebody to marry," she recited. "I liked you. I didn't want anybody taking advantage of you. It seemed like the perfect relationship. Everybody knew the rules and the time limit. You were gone enough of the time so I was glad to see you when you came back, and I knew you would be leaving soon. It was perfect."

His cigarette glowed long, short and long as if he were sending Morse code. "Are you going to impose legal limits on all your lovers? What happens if getting Mary Frances's shop isn't enough? What if you wake up one morning and decide you want a family and no one's there and it's too late?" He flicked sparks

into the ashtray Anna held. "Here's another deal for you: I'll stake
you for the down payment to Mary Frances. We'll be partners;
I'll be a silent partner—I can keep quiet if it's worth my while,
you know. We'll sign a new agreement, move my boxes back,
things can go along—"

"Why do you want to do that to yourself?" Anna interrupted.
"You've been letting Jo put ideas into your head. You don't
have to settle for me just because I'm handy. You *say* you want
a home and a family. I don't. I want the shop. I won't be sidetracked from that, and I won't be seduced by your money. I
know you.

"What if you wake up one day and you decide you want a baby
and the wrong woman's there and she won't unlock her legs for
you?" she continued. "You love the idea of what I could give you
—what any woman could give you. You've pretended that you
loved me so the people you had to fool were fooled. You don't love
me."

"I do," Bryan affirmed. "In a certain way I do."

They sat shoulder to shoulder and thigh to thigh. "Because you
know I'll say no to you, Bryan. You know I won't let you get away
with more than you want to get away with. That's not good
enough," Anna said. "Not for me and not for you."

"It's better than nothing."

"No it's not. It's worse. Think, really think about how it would
be. I won't run away with you when trouble hits. I don't want to
operate a beauty shop out of a Winnebago."

Bryan rolled to the other side of the bed. "Don't you ever think
you're pricing yourself out of the market? Don't you ever think
a little compromising may be in order?"

"Never," she said firmly.

"That's convenient for you, love, isn't it?" He pulled the sheet
around his shoulders and anchored it under his chin.

Anna lit a cigarette and concentrated on keeping the ash attached as long as she could. The face of the clock dominated the
room. It wasn't the transitory nature of relationships that scared
her. It was the thought of being beside somebody and knowing
it was all wrong, having to resist the use of a word or a touch

because that was easier than getting up and going, being reduced
to watching the clock and waiting for morning to come.

———

Hauling two shopping bags filled with purchases she'd made for
Jo, Anna left the store. She narrowly escaped being gunned down
by a perfume-wielding saleswoman. The glare and exhaust of the
hot afternoon made her wish she'd grabbed the atomizer to
sweeten the air. A car rental agency across the street looked
inviting. It was only four blocks to San Jacinto Plaza. She had
plenty of time to walk, but the idea of meeting Jo in a sealed
air-conditioned car where no one could hear their conversation
seemed appropriate—assuming Jo told her anything.

Anna shifted the bags in annoyance. She disliked providing the
alibi. There wasn't another man, although Burgess had given
enough cause. If it had anything to do with Bevo, Jo would have
come out and told her. Three blocks were gone, and the only other
possibility she could think of was that Jo was doing something for
Bryan. The idea of his pressing Jo into service angered Anna. As
far as she was concerned, his movement of people might be moral,
but the fact that he'd use anybody to advance his cause made him
an immoral man.

At the plaza's edge she stopped to shift bags and tried to
remember any significant looks exchanged at dinner. The fight
between Bevo and Burgess hadn't been planned, and there hadn't
been time for anything else to happen.

A bench opened up on Anna's second lap around the plaza.
Ignoring a shouting man selling the *Daily Worker* and thanking
whoever held the strings that Bryan wasn't there to debate the
record of the Communist party with him, she shielded her eyes
against the cloudless sky. The wires of an aerial tramway were
tacked to Ranger Peak and glistened in the sun. The Franklin
Mountains ridged the horizon like a half-buried arrowhead. A
shadow fell across her face.

"There you go again," Jo scolded, "staring into the sun again."
She settled on the other side of the bags. A large manila envelope

rested across her thighs. She fiddled with the metal clasp until one of the wings broke. "Did you get everything?"

"Two bags full." Anna wanted Jo to go through the purchases. Warnings against hearing confessions started going off in her sleep-starved mind. "Let's go. I've got this urge to take another crack at married life." She stood up abruptly.

Jo remained on the park bench. She tapped all the cigarettes out of their red leather case. Using a fingernail, she carefully slit the white paper of each cigarette. "You might as well sit down. I've got three other packs in my purse."

A man with raw edges to his clothes and hair was transfixed by the loose tobacco swirling like bits of hair around Jo's feet. His blunt, begging fingers questioned the air.

"Isn't this a little drastic?" Anna eyed the man. As his mouth worked, the light shuttled in silver flashes across his unshaven cheeks. "If you're finally quitting, you could unload those packs in a hurry."

Jo spread a slit cigarette and shook out the tobacco. "That's not the point. One of your favorite expressions. The point is"—she narrowed her eyes and stared through the man—"the thing is— if it's bad for me, it's bad for everybody. Nobody gets singled out. Nobody gets special attention."

Anna watched Jo gather the loose filters from her lap and squeeze hard before throwing them into the trash can. The smell of tobacco was bound to be floating around the plaza; they'd be surrounded soon. The man's hand went to his matted head. He brought it before his eyes again and again and was surprised each time to find it empty. Anna willed him to go away. She was tired of everybody's needs.

The sheets in the envelope rustled like tin. When Jo thrust the X rays between Anna's eyes and the sun, Anna saw the curved milky shapes of ribs and the ghostly presence of the lungs. "No. I don't want to know."

"Too late." Jo tapped the X ray, and a cloudy blot came into focus under her nail. "TB scars from an undiagnosed case when I was younger—Harrison over in Marfa thought that one up. TB, my foot. I've lived in West Texas all my fifty-two years. This is where they send people to get over TB. Now, this little baby speck didn't show up in the pictures he made two weeks ago." Her fingers fed across the surface and stopped. "Now this one down here did. But it's bigger than it was. That's the one.

"A little Valium plugged into your arm, a little tube stuck down your throat, in one lung, then the other, they can tell you all kinds of things." Jo turned the flame of her lighter up and sent it across one edge of the X ray. The sheet melted before the flame and fire hung suspended in the air.

"Swear to me you won't tell anybody. Cross your heart," Jo said.

Anna's mind shut down. The blots Jo had pointed out looked like clouds. They would disappear. "There's nothing to tell." She walked over to the circular fountain in the middle of the plaza. Pennies with blue-green halos were embedded in the dry concrete bottom. The tattered man had brushed away the gum wrappers and was using a Popsicle stick to try to pry the coins up. Once alligators had been kept in the fountain to give the sun-blessed city a more tropical air, but eating the pennies and Popsicle sticks and chewing gum had killed them.

Looking back at the park bench, Anna realized that it was true. Jo had already lost ground.

It's girl talk," Anna said, easing Bryan back into the hotel room and shutting the door.

Halfway down the hall she felt his big hand on her back. "Pay attention to Josephine when she tells you what a fine man I am and what a lucky girl you are."

"Don't you ever stop? What if I said yes? Where would you be then?"

"Ah, paradise." Bryan reached through the elevator's electric eye for Anna. She pressed her palms against the metal doors and pushed to hurry their closing. He snatched his hand back before the doors shut.

Jo was waiting in the bar on the top floor. Anna flipped the stop switch between the twelfth and fourteenth floors to give herself more time. She hadn't been alone since her shopping trip for Jo. Instead of hanging between two floors, the elevator continued to the fourteenth, where a group of people got on. The quivering doors remained open and an alarm rang.

"Hell, I'm calling room service," a man said and

reached over Anna's shoulder for the emergency phone. She leaned against the control panel to undo the stop switch. When the doors met, the closeness suddenly made her claustrophobic. She battled her way out on fifteen and walked up the remaining three flights.

A closet plant's hooded white flowers hid her while she looked around the bar and tried to shake off a feeling of doom. Jo's hair had dissolved in the darkness of a corner table. Her remoteness gave Anna a vision of herself running on a treadmill, never able to reach the table. At the bar she turned her back on Jo and ordered a Carta Blanca with lime as if the appearance of indifference could fool the illness and mask a fast move later.

Jo joined Anna at the bar. "Give this woman a glass for her beer and me an amaretto sunrise."

"No glass," Anna told the bartender. "Let's go back to the table. It's more private."

"I don't have a thing to hide," Jo answered. "We've found a haircutting seminar that goes on all day tomorrow. I want you to send Thomas back and get him to take Burgess back with him."

"What exactly did the doctor say?" Anna asked. "And how do you know he's any good?"

"It was Dr. Laurence, Anna." Jo fingered a pretzel stick and placed it between her lips.

"Why does everybody practically cross themselves whenever his name's mentioned?" Anna refused to believe Jo trusted Dr. Laurence. Anybody in West Texas who believed they needed a miracle went to see Dr. Laurence. It was Jo who'd christened him Last Hope Laurence.

He was wrong. In Jo's case he was wrong. He wanted to cure cancer. The fastest cure would be for an illness that was diagnosed but not present. He was seeing what he wanted to see. He must have sensed Jo's skepticism and thought he had to prove something to her. How did they know the X rays were really Jo's? "You'd think he was Jesus Christ or something. You ought to see another doctor."

"How many doctors do I need to see before I accept it? Two? Six hundred?" Jo held her drink up to the light. "Now this is a pretty drink." The weight of a top layer of amaretto was sending red grenadine drifting into the orange juice base.

All right, it's cancer, Anna conceded to herself. The initial shock had driven Jo to consult him. Pessimism had made her consult him before it was necessary. She didn't need a miracle. She needed a cure. "What exactly did he tell you? What kind of treatment? What time are we going in there tomorrow? Josephine. Give me something."

"Oh, I don't know. Radiation. Chemotherapy. I don't know what all." Jo closed her eyes and took a long sip. "I'm not doing it. I'm not having all my hair fall out, that's all there is to it."

"Are you crazy? It'll grow back."

"How do you know, Anna? How do you know that? Can you give me a guarantee?"

Anna saw that she'd fallen behind. It wasn't a question of challenging a doctor's diagnosis or choosing between various forms of treatment; the question was whether or not Jo was going to do anything to save herself. "What did he tell you?"

"I don't have a head for figures, Anna. Besides, they're liable to tell you anything."

"What about Burgess?"

"I'm not going to have him helping me in and out of cars. He'll want to bundle me up and throw himself between me and any old germ—I want a husband, not a nurse."

"It's the least he can do," Anna said, but Jo didn't rise to the bait. "Look. If you trust Dr. Laurence, then do what he says. Let him take care of your lungs. Let Burgess bring you breakfast in bed. I'll take care of your hair."

Tables of cigarette smokers surrounded them. Jo's eyes followed the currents of smoke. "You aren't that good, Anna."

"Bevo will help. There are things we can do. There are tricks. Scarves, switches—what do you think happens when you're dead? It stops. That's some guarantee."

"I won't care then. Don't look at me like that."

"I can't believe you have so much Grace Nettinger in you."

Jo's eyes narrowed and her chest filled with air as if she were holding a cigarette between her lips and both fighting and accepting the smoke. "Saturdays are treatment days. Come with me if you don't believe me—I don't care. Lend me a quarter for the jukebox, I want to hear about somebody else's problems."

———

Dr. Laurence's clinic was downtown. The vanilla block building looked as if it should house government agencies that had low budgets, but the directory listed doctors, dentists and lawyers. As Anna and Jo walked down the sixth-floor corridor, their footsteps seemed to make the closed doors of frosted glass vibrate. The emptiness magnified every sound. None of the other offices was open on Saturday. The other doctors weren't setting themselves up as saviors. Dr. Laurence must know what effect traveling down the long, silent corridors would have on his patients. Did the man think he was God or the Wizard of Oz? How many more corners would she and Jo have to turn before they found Dr. Laurence's office and heard his judgment?

Two corners later, when Anna saw the line of people waiting patiently outside his door, she knew it was a setup. A man in a green army jumpsuit alternately swallowed pills and orange juice. A Mexican family at the head of the line was spread protectively around a thin little girl; tiny gold crosses hung from her pierced ears. The other patients were reading magazines and newspapers and drinking coffee out of plaid thermoses and star-burst paper cups with fold-out handles as if there were nothing wrong with just standing there and waiting.

It was only seven-thirty. Jo had said treatment days were first come, first served. Anna counted ten people ahead of them. She didn't like that idea or the cowed acceptance of the people in line. She didn't like the hard-set waves in the hair of the woman standing in front of them. The smell of the woman's perfume made Anna's eyes water. Jo didn't belong in the line. She grabbed Jo's arm and started to say, "Let's get out of here," but the woman ahead of them, favoring her left side, turned slightly.

"He's supposed to open his door at nine," Anna said. "Does he?"

She was glad to see the woman straighten herself in response to the implied criticism. "He does what he's supposed to—and more." She leaned forward out of Anna's range to address Jo. "First time?"

Anna couldn't believe that the woman had targeted Jo. Dr. Laurence was a fraud, and so were his patients. They'd do as well with someone who pretended to pass his bare hands through skin and pull out the offending tumor.

"We know the order," the woman said. "We operate on the honor system. Count on about thirty, forty-five minutes a person. Most everybody brings their own food and beverage. We clean up after ourselves. There's a Chinese restaurant downstairs, but they don't do takeout. We usually donate any magazines we bring. I'm Kitty." Her duty done, the woman faced front again.

Anna was surprised that Kitty hadn't gone on to admit to having cancer. As if acceptance were the first step toward recovery. As if Jo had been awarded membership into a club that excluded any of her friends.

Jo didn't seem to be paying attention to anything except the beat of her own heart. All the AA and Al-Anon meetings must have taken their toll. The constant reinforcement of confessing to alcoholism at every meeting had definitely narrowed Burgess's sight. At breakfast with Burgess and Bryan earlier that morning, Jo had grumbled about Anna's making her go to the seminar, and then she'd hidden behind a cup of coffee, looking up once to remind them all that she had never been a morning person. Burgess had laughed, and Anna had wanted to snatch out his beard for not noticing that something was wrong.

The door to Dr. Laurence's office opened from the inside. A tall hunch-shouldered man with gray Napoleonic curls gripping his forehead peeked out and then opened the door wide.

Kitty turned halfway around again. "Dr. Laurence," she told them.

There was too much reverence in the woman's voice to suit Anna. Dr. Laurence held the door open until everybody was seated. His eyes brightened and settled on each person. He looked as if he wanted to say something, but the hands clasped behind his long, curved back prevented him from speaking out. The last in line, Anna paused to give him a chance to prove himself. He entrusted the door to her and walked into an inner room.

The little girl's family separated enough to let her slip through and follow Dr. Laurence. Her red patent leather shoes avoided the black tile squares and always landed within the white ones. The man wearing the green army jumpsuit got up to shut the inner door softly when the family nodded.

Anna couldn't believe they'd let the little girl go with Dr. Laurence by herself. "Is there a nurse in there with them?" she asked and turned toward Kitty. A portion of the woman's chin was caved in. Anna felt everyone staring. "Is there anybody else back there?"

"It's her first time," Kitty explained to the room. The right side of her mouth angled down as if it were about to slide into the hole. "His wife used to help him."

There was no need to ask what had happened to Dr. Laurence's wife. The protective attention of the room returned to focus on the door to the inner room. The patients and their families responded like one organism. Good, Anna thought. Let them attack me then. Let me be the enemy.

A green light over the inner door flashed on. Five minutes later the little girl, walking on her heels, reappeared. A bandage circled her small wrist. The pride of the room was centered on her. Kitty produced an iced cupcake. The top of a TV tray passed from hand to hand among the family until it reached the little girl. Her mother or sister or aunt tickled her toward Kitty. Everyone had something for her. The tray was piled with a roll of nickels, ring-pull suckers, a crocheted pencil holder filled with map colors and an Ysleta Bobcats pennant. She stopped in front of Jo and stared up at her hair. Jo bent forward to let her touch it. The little girl squealed and whispered excitedly in Spanish to her family. Jo dug a black hairpin out of the curls and put it on the tray.

The ritual warmed Anna. Maybe she'd been wrong in gauging their behavior. Maybe there was a kind of healing going on. She dug in her purse for a sample tube of perfume to contribute, but the little girl passed her by. "Oh, wait."

The little girl paused and looked uncertainly from her family to Anna. *"No está enferma,"* one of the family said. *"Vengase."* What difference does it make that I'm not sick? Anna wanted to ask. I can still give her something. Why should good health isolate me? She would have liked to touch the little girl's hair just once to boost Jo's chances.

The room was quiet after the family left. Jo tucked the headset of the cassette player that was Burgess's twenty-sixth anniversary gift under her chin. The headset wouldn't reach over her hair. Anna was stuck listening to the rustle of waxed paper and air escaping from plastic containers as lunches were unpacked. There wasn't a scrap of aluminum foil in the waiting room.

As a child she'd used waxed paper to make the playground slides more slippery. One Easter she'd sandwiched Crayola shavings between sheets of waxed paper and ironed them to make stained glass windows. It had taken her a whole boxful of sixteen colors to figure out the setting and the amount of pressure to use, but by that time burned wax had ruined the iron and Georgia wouldn't let her do it anymore. She'd spent a whole weekend arguing nonstop for a chance to prove that she'd learned how to do it right. She should have known better than to argue with a woman who'd waited half her life for somebody who was never coming back.

"I'll be back in five minutes, maybe ten," Jo said. She gripped her purse tightly. "Don't you time me, Anna, and send your hounds after me—I'll be back."

Anna didn't trust Jo, but at least she was breaking away from the group. To keep herself from following, Anna had to hook her foot around the skinny steel leg of the couch. She wanted to walk past Dr. Laurence's office with Jo as if it were any other office. They could peek in and laugh with relief because they didn't need Dr. Laurence's services; they could feel guilty for laughing, and then they could walk away scot-free. They could ignore the flashing green light. They wouldn't give over responsibility for their lives to a word-stricken man, to a man who couldn't even greet his patients by name, who had room in his head for all the names of chemicals but no space for the word "Jo." Dr. Laurence didn't deserve respect because he kept an open waiting room on Saturdays or because he kept working despite his wife's death or because he gave the illusion of control by letting his patients police themselves. Anna wanted to take away their misguided faith and teach them how to dig in their heels.

Jo came back in fourteen minutes. Standing by the outer door, Anna heard fingernails clicking along the wall and made it back to the couch before Jo saw her.

"I called Burgess and told him to go on, I wanted some time with Charles. Bryan's driving him back this afternoon. You like to drive by yourself anyway. You can leave first thing in the morning," Jo said when she sat down.

"I'll wait and drive you back."

"I want some time alone with my son. If he can't drive me back, I'll take the train." Everything settled to her satisfaction, Jo carefully positioned the headphones and turned up the volume.

There was nothing Anna could do about Jo's withdrawal except sit on her hands and watch the people's faces as they came out of the inner office.

The man in the jumpsuit was released by Dr. Laurence. His pockets bulged with more pills. A middle-aged man went inside. So much of his scalp showed through his hair that the strands seemed to be hovering, rootless, above his head.

As the afternoon wore down, Anna's brief glances around the room had settled into a pattern. She felt as if she were a bank camera high in a corner capturing all their expressions, recording the sudden twisting of lips in pain and anxiety. Next time she would bring something to keep her hands busy. Maybe Dr. Laurence would award the hair concession to her.

After crocheting a steady six inches per hour, an older man stopped in the middle of a row. He glared sightlessly, and his hands hovered over the afghan in bewilderment as if he realized it was useless to take comfort in a red steel hook and shades of yellow and gold wool. His fingers refused the yarn again and again until finally he wrapped the strand of yellow wool so tightly his fingertip turned purple, and the hook tugged at the afghan again.

Pretending not to watch a woman wearing a badly blocked wig, Jo clicked her long fingernails together. Kitty was keeping her eye on Jo. Anna wanted to tell her to mind her own business.

Jo opened her mouth and picked a strand of tobacco off her tongue. Anna held out her palm. "I can't believe it. Give it to me." Jo smeared her fingers across the lines of Anna's palm.

By four o'clock only the man crocheting and Kitty were left in the room with Anna and Jo. The man worked doggedly on the afghan; he had switched to caramel-colored yarn. Every time he came to the center of a row Anna willed him to the end and on to the start of a new one.

When Kitty had been called and they were alone in the waiting room, Jo restriped her eyebrows and lips. The same feeling of loneliness that had threatened Anna the night before while Bryan was sleeping hit again. Seeing the sun rise wouldn't help this situation any. She had thought she would be able to relax once the waiting room was empty, but her shoulders ached.

The green light flashed. Jo brushed the front of her blouse. The rapid motion of her hands against the black and green and red jungle print made Anna dizzy.

Concentrating on straightening her pants seams, Jo said, "I'll meet you at that Leo's on Montana at six. Have a margarita in a fishbowl ready for me, lots of salt, not too much ice."

"I'm not going anywhere," Anna said. "Except into that doctor's office with you."

"No, you're not," Jo stated calmly. "You were watching. You know as well as I do he doesn't let anybody but patients back there. You're going to get us a booth in the back at Leo's. I want you tanked up on hot sauce and tequila by the time I get there."

Anna didn't want Jo to go through that door alone. She had to make sure that Dr. Laurence understood what Jo feared about the treatments. He had to stop and listen. "You expect me to leave you now? You expect me to believe you'll go in there and ask the right questions? Either he makes an exception or I'll wait my turn."

"I just needed a push-start, Anna. Thank you very much, but the bottom line is that your questions are not my questions. You ask a lot more than I do, you always do. This is happening to me. I'll take care of it in my own way. I know what I'm doing. Now scat!"

"Look—" Anna said.

The inner door swung open. Dr. Laurence stood in the doorway. "Josephine?"

Looking at Dr. Laurence's curved back made Anna realize how tired she was. After Jo went into the inner room, he held the door protectively close to his body. "Would you make sure the outer door locks after you?" he asked Anna.

She had to stand on tiptoe to look over the doctor's shoulder and see Jo. There was no way to get past either of them. Holding out her hand to Dr. Laurence, she said, "I'm Anna. A friend of Jo's. Don't let her—"

"Leo's at six," Jo reminded her.

"Don't let her talk you out of doing anything."

Jo pressed the inside bend of Dr. Laurence's arm and sprang his hand out of Anna's grip. "Lord! She's just dying to get her hands on your hair, but you're all mine." The door closed.

Anna pressed her ear against the frosted glass until she couldn't hear Jo's voice anymore. A wad of waxed paper shifting in the trash can startled her. The waiting room had been peopled all day, and now she was the only one left.

She wanted to slam the outer door behind her until the glass shattered. She wanted the glass to leap up and reassemble so she could slam the door over and over and over again until something inside was satisfied. Part of her wish had maliciously been granted. Here she was walking away scot-free, but where was Jo?

————

The only things Jo had discussed at dinner was how Leo's made its chile rellenos and what time Anna was leaving in the morning. "Don't look at me like that, Anna," Jo had said. "I know how you like to drive without anybody in the car with you. Charles can drive me back."

Driving alone suited Anna. Jo was right. The demands of conversation and the added responsibility of delivering somebody else safely home eroded her concentration. But any distraction on the three-hour trip back to Alpine would have been welcome. She had tried unsuccessfully all Saturday night to take a reading of what Dr. Laurence had had to say. The absence of cigarettes had seemed to be a hopeful sign.

Anna rolled down the windows and ignored the air conditioner. The cassette player Bryan had installed hung silently under the dashboard. She liked to feel the place she was passing through. It didn't matter if the wind tangled her hair. Radio stations fighting static in the long stretches didn't bother her. Late-night evangelists preaching into the morning from Mexico and overexcited sportscasters had their messages garbled and intercut and shuffled into new combinations. There was a natural pattern to the combinations that Anna didn't want to tamper with. Hearing certain words shouted through the interference made her strain to hear the whole urgent message.

Much of her life had revolved around the workings of cars. Her mother was fond of pointing out that half of Anna's blood was fueled by the blood of a mechanic, but Anna discounted Michael Leandros's influence. She laid it at her mother's feet. Georgia had always worked in auto supply stores. Her mother's secondhand knowledge of the bits and pieces that made a car whole was as great as Burgess's. Every new town they moved to had a different favorite. Some towns had a strong GM dealership; the next town over might favor Chrysler. There was never an even distribution within any single town.

Anna's first job, when she was sixteen, had been doing the bookkeeping at a body shop. Cars were dragged in, crumpled beyond make identification. The shock of collision was frozen in their shattered windshields. One of the mechanics had a cigar box full of loose teeth he'd found inside the wrecks. His most precious find was a front tooth marbleized by fluoride. Wanting to have a matched pair of cuff links made, he mourned the missing twin tooth. Anna had always hoped there was somebody else walking around with the other tooth still firmly rooted.

Working at the body shop had formed her habit of walking in

town whenever she could. Despite the fact that most wrecks happened on the highway, a couple of cars in town had been reduced to tin cans by freight trains. Anna didn't see any use in pressing her luck. She was a good driver; by the time she was twelve she was spelling Georgia at the wheel. She learned to honk the horn before rounding boulder-plastered curves and cresting rises.

In all the highway time she and her mother had logged, they had never been involved in an accident. It seemed miraculous that they had escaped injury. After hearing Delia's account of her mother's night driving, Anna had wondered at the odds being so much in Grace's favor. What had kept her on the road when anybody else would have been slung around a curve and sent plunging through the delicate guardrails? Grace had been spared time and time again only to turn around and abuse the privilege. Jo would never show such ingratitude; she'd fight for a second chance and recognize it when it came.

Anna found herself passing a lone mountain that rose outside the field of the Guadalupe Mountains. Its slopes were scarred by dull reddish-purple streaks that looked like the claw marks of a giant animal. The mountain was one of her landmarks. As soon as the slope came into view, she charted its shifting progress along the horizon until the scars were no longer visible in her rearview mirror.

She was angry at herself for letting Grace Nettinger take her attention from the road. The speedometer read 80. She slowed the Valiant to 55, and the roadside park with its tepee-covered picnic tables came into focus. One slip, Anna reminded herself. That's all it took. Grace didn't need any company.

Two cars heading in Anna's direction appeared briefly at the top of a hill and then disappeared into a distant valley. Water mirages shimmered in her lane. She honed the cat-and-mouse feeling that the sudden appearance of another car on an empty highway triggered in her. It could be anybody. It might be Ronnie Mauss. It might be Michael Leandros, her mother's long-lost love. It might be an operator she'd known eleven years ago in Kingsville. If she realized twenty miles down the road who it had been, it would be too late. Whoever it was would be gone.

It might be another Grace Nettinger bent on destruction.

———

To get the garage door closed, Anna had to step on the bottom latch and rock it down with the full weight of her body. She lay on the slanted door with one hand curled overhead, staring at the pearled moon. It seemed natural to be lying at an angle six inches above the earth. Other passages should be available. Jo should have a whole corridor full of doors to choose from or at least one window to crawl through. Death wasn't a passage. It wasn't an escape. It was the end. Impatient wih her own lassitude when there was so much to be done, Anna stretched her arm toward the top of the garage and used her body to bring the door down.

She thought briefly about going to the Haslips' garage apartment to enlist Bryan's help. One of the closets might hold shelves of remedies left over from Summer's knock-down, drag-out fight that Jo could inherit. But she'd promised secrecy to Jo, and any nighttime visit to Bryan would be purely selfish.

Too restless to sleep, Anna walked to the shop. She hadn't considered the shop to be Mary Frances's for years, but superstition kept her from calling it her own yet. The two heat lamps she'd persuaded Mary Frances to buy still sat in the reception area, their coils packed into chrome hoods. Anna checked each cord from flat saucer base to plug. She flexed their gooseneck stems. Since their arrival, the lamps had been used only three times—twice by Anna and once by Jo to dry a pair of black hose she'd rinsed out in the back. Saying it was inconvenient and unnecessary and all Anna's doing, Mary Frances refused to set them up in the styling room. She tried to prohibit their use in the reception area by insisting that her clients would feel that they were on display.

The ringing of the telephone spooked Anna. It was after eleven o'clock, bound to be a wrong number, but the urge to answer got the best of her. She placed her hand on the receiver to try to get a sense of who was calling. Just pick it up, she told herself. No sixth sense had visited her last night at dinner with Jo; there was no reason to expect it now.

Georgia's voice came out of the receiver. "Anna? Anna? I hear breathing. Who's there?"

"It's not Ronnie Mauss again, is it?" Anna asked. Her mother's voice sounded too normal for anything to be wrong with Frank.

"You haven't been home all weekend. Burgess said you were due back this evening, but you weren't at home, you weren't at Jo's," Georgia's vague voice accurately picked places out of the air, "you weren't at Mary Frances's house. You weren't at that Mexican food restaurant you took us to that Frank liked so much . . . I can never remember the name, but the operator—"

"Those directory assistance calls cost money," Anna interrupted. "You should have waited."

"Frank got me an Alpine phone book. It makes me feel better seeing your name and address somewhere. You'll understand when you're a mother—"

"I was in El Paso. Celebrating my divorce."

"He seemed like such a nice man . . . that one time we met him. Is it—"

"They all seem nice to you," Anna said. "How's Frank?"

"Fine . . . he's really the one that wanted to speak to you."

"Where is he?"

"He's out back. He'll be here in a minute."

There was silence on the line. Anna wondered if her mother was holding the phone, waiting for Frank to come in. "This is costing money," she reminded Georgia.

"Honey, I just want you to be happy. Are you happy?"

Anna wished her jaw would relax. She wished that she were free to confide in somebody about Jo. She wished she wanted to confide in her mother about Jo. "Yes, yes, yes. I'm happy. Where did you say Frank was?"

Frank's voice boomed into her ear. He spoke into the receiver as if it were the velocity of his voice that mattered instead of the miles of cable. "Anna? Anna! Hold on—wait—what? Georgia, I can't talk to you both at the same time. Hold on."

The sound of Georgia's muffled voice came over the receiver. Anna wondered if Frank had his hand over the receiver or over her mother's mouth. "Anna? Anna! Hello? Hello! She wants me to find out if you're happy." He paused and then asked awkwardly, "Are you? Happy?"

"You don't have to do everything she asks you to, Frank."

"I know where my own line is, Anna. You don't have to do the opposite of everything she wants either. Between the two of us I guess it works itself out. But that's neither here nor there. That's not what I want to talk to you about. Well, in a way it is, it's about your happiness. I think I can help. I want to help."

Anna let the receiver drop to her shoulder for a second. Frank was having one of his spells where he wanted to be a good father to her. Adoption papers were probably in the mail again. The rims of the dryer hoods reflected like crescent moons in the wall-length mirror. She roused herself enough to say, "Frank. I'm happy. Are you happy?"

"I hate these things," Frank said in near despair. "I tried to write you a letter. But I'm a face-to-face man, that's all there is to it. Here's the cut of it: What I really want to do is talk this out with you in person, face-to-face, but you know how she hates those ten-hour drives—"

"You know how many of those ten-hour drives she's committed in her life?"

"Anna, let's just get on to the cut of it. Here's the deal. I've thought a lot about this, so here goes." He cleared his voice and began his speech. "You're more than Georgia's daughter to me. I don't exactly feel like you're my own daughter—because you were already grown up when I met Georgia—but I love you. I never wanted to take the place of—you know, your father—your father, or whatever, but I feel like there's a good, strong bond between us that's there naturally and not because our both loving Georgia's forced it on us. This is getting away from me here—"

Anna nodded in agreement. "Please, Frank. You don't have to say anything. I know. Let's not go into that whole adoption thing again—"

"That's not it. Here's the cut: I want to stake you to your shop. I want to give you the down payment. I can do wire transfer or I can do cashier's check."

"No!" Anna was as shocked as Frank by the violence of her answer. He should have known better. She felt as if he'd just slapped her in the face. She resented his offer. "I don't need your help. Just take care of my mother and stop her from spouting all those lies about that two-bit mechanic she went to bed with. That's what you can do for me—"

Georgia's voice broke in. "It's all been true. You're the only one denying anything! He was a wonderful man!"

"Goddamn it, Georgia," Frank shouted, "get off the extension! I'm talking in confidence to Anna. Hold on!"

Slinging the cord around her neck, Anna bent over to let the blood circulate to her scalp. "Look. You know how I feel about you. Let's not complicate the issue. I respect you. You respect me. Let's leave it at that."

"Anna? Anna! Why? Why? My money's good—I got lucky in that one field. It's only right to pass some of it on. I don't fritter it away. If there's something that needs doing and I think it's a good, sound project—well, that's the important thing. I see the shop as a good, solid investment."

She steeled herself against his hurt. "No. I don't want any partners. I've already got the down payment. It's in the bank earning interest. The loan's on track. I appreciate the offer, but it's all been taken care of." She was still four thousand dollars short on the down payment but confident of negotiating with Mary Frances. Her drive and intent were worth that much. The shop was within reach. Anna knew in her bones that the shop was hers. Remodeling money would be tight, but if it came down to it, all she needed was a sledgehammer and a crowbar.

Frank's voice was quiet. "There's nothing wrong with accepting what someone offers you, Anna. The gift of acceptance has never been your strong suit."

The buzz of disconnection coming out of the receiver made Anna's shoulders hunch involuntarily. She couldn't believe Frank had hung up on her. He had brought it on himself. He should have known better.

Telling Frank about Jo would have helped; he would have felt like a father, and tonight Anna felt as if she needed one, but Jo had sworn her to silence. After rejecting his offer, she couldn't confide in him without being accused of looking for sympathy— not for Jo but for herself—and following the easy path to forgiveness.

Anna balanced on the balls of her feet and knelt. On a strip of pink wood inside her cabinet were sample slashes of paint. She'd been smuggling in small cans of aqua paint on the weekends and early mornings for nine years without finding the right shade. Rubbing the slashes, feeling the raised surface of paint under her fingertips, was tangible evidence. These were the marks of her ownership, set down slowly, from the inside, to guarantee her eventual possession of the shop. The pieces were falling into place. Nothing would stop her.

Jo would always have a chair here. She could come in whenever she felt like it. Bevo would be a guest stylist whenever he was in town. If Liz got pregnant and had her baby, they'd work out a schedule. Mary Frances would drop by whenever she was in town; she'd see that change could be positive. Nobody would lose anything because of the shop's transition.

Anna sat in Jo's chair and rubbed the black plastic arms, offering the heat of her own body's resistance to Jo.

———

The next morning orange teddy bears sat in each operator's chair. Liz stood in the doorway to the shampoo room, wiping her hands on a towel and smiling sleepily. "Don't take it so hard, Mary Frances," she said. "I promise we weren't thinking of you when we were getting this baby thing off the ground."

Mary Frances let the sole of her open-backed sandal slap the bottom of her heel repeatedly. "Getting this baby thing off the ground?" Her shoulders reared and collapsed. She fluttered her hands as if she were drying her nails. "It's much too early in the morning to be discussing the subject of hiring a new girl, and babies and things. I suppose now you'll be pleading morning sickness and Leo will be mooning all over the place. I'll have to lease out the bathroom to you. Anna," she said, turning suddenly, "I can count on you to take precautions. Can't I?"

Anna sat in her chair, holding a teddy bear by its arms and flipping it over and over. "You made me get my tubes tied before you'd hire me. Remember?"

"I most certainly did not!" Mary Frances gripped the arm of the dryer chair so tightly that the black plastic bar came off in her hand. "That's right—joke. Give people more to talk about."

"The husbands are next," Anna predicted. "Vasectomies. Tell Leo he got out from under the knife just in time."

Liz's dry eyes widened. "Oh, no, poor Leo, he'll be so relieved."

"Forget Leo. Poor you!" Anna said.

"That's right—laugh." Mary Frances toyed with the back of her neck. "As if you two didn't have anything better to do. Two ladies of leisure—it must be nice. The gay divorcée and the knocked-up one."

"Don't worry, M.F. You don't have to worry about a thing. By the time Liz starts feeling bad, I'll own the shop and you'll be putt-putting around the lake with Alfred."

Mary Frances averted her face and spoke into her padded shoulder. "Go right ahead and enjoy yourselves at my expense, while you can. Jo's not coming in until later, so—"

"Jo called? When? From El Paso or home?" Anna asked.

"Really, Anna, I thought you knew so much," Mary Frances said. Her face had gone pink and almost matched the walls. "It looks like there's a lot you don't know. And this is still my shop."

Jo's early return could be a good sign. It could mean that she had decided to fight and that the decision had energized her. She might be returning to town only long enough to pack a bag for a longer stay in El Paso. The next time Jo came home to stay her body would be clean throughout. A little frayed at the ankles where her veins darted and spit blue, a little more give under her arms, a little normal wear and tear, but nothing alien corroding her organs and bones.

The cowbell over the front door rattled and was followed by a burst of clapping. "Okay, girls," Jo yelled. "Clean it up! Man on the floor!"

"Leo!" Liz guessed. Her face softened.

Jo cocked one fist on her hip. "I said man, Liz. Man." She swept Bevo into the styling room. "He is, too," she said, sounding almost surprised as she held him at arm's length. "He sure is."

Bevo jiggled Jo's upper arms until she slapped his hands away. Hugging Anna, he said, "Anna Leandros Mauss Bryan, that angora sweater of yours won't hold too many more initials. You better slow down, girl." He twitched his hands and lunged at Mary Frances. "I always save the best for last." She leaned into his embrace and raised one foot.

While Jo watched every move her son made, Anna tried to see into Jo's body. "Don't stare, Anna. It's rude," Jo said.

Released by Mary Frances, Bevo picked up the teddy bears one by one and raised an eyebrow. Liz blushed and hurried to rescue the bears. She hadn't met Bevo before, but she'd heard Jo talk about him. Mary Frances always tearfully supplied the parts Jo neglected.

"That's Liz," Anna said. "Chair number three for almost two years now. A record. She's deserting us for motherhood."

"You'll never desert me, will you, Anna?" Mary Frances asked anxiously. "I meant, of course, in the few, short months I have left."

"Not unless you welsh on our deal."

"Even if Anna got pregnant and went into labor," Jo said quickly, "she'd go right into the shampoo room and pop it out and come back out in time to put on the neutralizer. Like shelling a pea."

Bevo examined Liz. "Husband in college? Graduated? Big job in Dallas? Houston? Doctorate program at UT? A&M? No? Yes? Which? All of the above? None of the above? A and C? Talk to me." Liz's brown eyes began to water.

"Take it easy," Anna said to both mother and son.

"*Preg*-nant!" Bevo exclaimed. He led Liz to her chair. "Sit. Sit." He sat beside her in Jo's chair. "Who's the father? Anyone I know?" He clasped his knees and twirled around. "Anyone I care to know?"

"Down, Bevo," Anna commanded. Jo had turned her back on all of them, but her set face was visible in the mirror. "Down, boy. There's enough competition in this town as it is."

"But, Anna," he protested, "it's my understanding you've gone through just about every man in town. Don't be so greedy. I know! How about Budge? Mom! How about Anna and Budge? Wouldn't they make a cute couple?"

"She could do a lot worse," Jo said briefly. An abrupt motion of her hands sent a wave of plastic rollers tumbling down the counter.

Jo hadn't told Bevo. He must think he was here because his mother needed a ride home and it was time for her annual attempt to talk him into coming back.

"Let's leave the men at home and go visit Bevo again," Anna said. "He can take us to the dog races. Let's go to El Paso a *lot* this summer."

"Count me out. I'm tired of that place. I've got no intention of going back there for a long, long time." Jo reached into the back corner of her drawer and pulled out a pack of cigarettes.

"Not even to visit me? Your only normal son?"

Jo sparked a kitchen match with her thumbnail. "You'll have to come here if you want to see me."

Anna snatched the cigarette out of Jo's mouth. "Don't you dare light that!"

"Free will, Anna." Jo snared Anna's wrist and forced her hand to raise the cigarette.

"Girls, girls," Bevo said.

"Oh, I knew it! I knew it!" Mary Frances wailed.

"Don't say another word," Jo said.

Anna fought uselessly against the pull. The match had flamed down. She could smell Jo's burned fingernail. "Help me," she called to Bevo.

He stopped laughing when he realized they weren't joking. "Mom, no big deal if Anna wants to play junior health aide. We'll sneak out behind the barn and light up. Hey. Hey!"

Anna's hand was almost numb by the time Jo released it. She massaged her skin to renew the circulation. "You're making a mistake. You don't have to fight me. I'm not the enemy."

On the first weekend in August Anna rode out to Lake Amistad with Bevo to see Mary Frances and Alfred's houseboat. Burgess and Jo drove ahead of them. Anna's houseboat-warming gift for Mary Frances was a cashier's check for fifteen thousand dollars, a good-faith deposit on the down payment until the bank loan came through.

Bevo's car, a 1957 Plymouth, was the dull greenish gray color of a June bug out of sunlight. The steering wheel had a knob screwed onto one of its spokes. Floating beneath the knob's plastic bulb was the picture of a blonde falling out of her blouse. Woven plastic mats of tan and green and wild, patternless streaks of orange protected the front seat, and a scalloped and fringed shade edged the windshield. Jo had made Bevo take the plastic Virgin Marys off the dashboard. Anna felt as if she were riding a second-class bus in Mexico; she expected them to pull over in an unscheduled stop to pick up the first person who appeared at the side of the road.

Since his return, Bevo had started trading half days on Tuesdays and Thursdays with his mother and was now working her full hours on those days. So far he hadn't offered a reason for his extended stay, and Anna hadn't asked for one yet. She didn't want to give Jo's illness any more power than she had to, but the time when they'd all have to band together to make Jo fight was getting closer. It didn't matter which treatment Jo chose—chemotherapy or cobalt at M. D. Anderson in Houston, peach pits in a Mexican clinic, or breaking a raw egg into a dish and putting it under her bed to draw out the evil eye, *mal de ojo*—as long as she chose to fight.

Bevo beat the heel of his hand against the steering knob. "Look at that. Look at that! Budge is going all over the fucking road trying to keep us in his rearview mirror."

The outside wheels of the car ahead kicked up a storm of dust as Burgess overcorrected his path. Anna was surprised he hadn't chained the two cars together. "Maybe he's afraid we'll elope," she said.

Bevo tapped the horn in long and short bursts. "At least you've got all the right equipment. If we ran off together, it would mean I'd come back. I'd come back and admitted I was wrong. I'd admitted I could love women. But you know that still wouldn't be enough for old Budge. If I turned up with a woman and that woman was you, pretty soon he'd get antsy and wonder why, with all the women in the world, I chose you. He'd think we dreamed it up just to spite him."

Anna dropped her head until it rested on the seat back. "He'd be right. I can see his face now. It would be worth it. Just for that."

"You don't think he's reformed at all, do you?" Bevo asked.

She'd had both Jo and Bevo turn on her before in defense of Burgess. It wasn't worth spoiling the trip. "Jo does. You do—more often than not. That's what counts."

The dry, chalky land flashed past, marred only by outbreaks of scrub brush. The hills and mountains had broken apart into isolated clumps. Three parallel strands of barbed wire ran along fence posts made of steel pipe. That a lake, fed by the Pecos and Devil rivers, had been man-made in these barren hills seemed inconceivable to Anna. She couldn't get over the feeling that the water in the lake wouldn't last any longer than the water in the creek had. She could picture Alfred and Mary Frances's houseboat stuck in a huge mud puddle. Three to four hours from Alpine, depending on which speed limit a driver obeyed—the legal speed or the higher one dictated by the long stretch—the lake had a hard-core weekend following. Forget oil, Anna thought. Forget gold. Out here, it's water.

"I know why Mother came to El Paso," Bevo said.

Anna willed time to slow. The eroding soil and the hard blue sky wouldn't care. A change of seasons meant nothing to a treeless plateau. The breakdown of Jo's body had to stop until everybody else's caught up. The illness could wind its way through her body, cutting the channels deeper, but let the process be gradual. Let the process of decay be proportional to the decay of the land. Twenty, thirty, even forty years more for Jo wouldn't upset the natural flow of things. Time had to slow until they figured out what to do.

"Did she tell you why she won't go back?" Anna asked.

"She just won't, that's all. Anna—promise me you won't flip out—about anything that happens." He pulled over to join his parents at a lookout point above the Pecos River. "Listen, we'll tear up Mary Frances's. Okay? We'll have a good time. That's the name of the game. To have a good time. We'll do that for Mom. No matter what else happens."

Before Anna could answer, Bevo was out of the car. He leaned against the retaining wall beside Burgess and Jo and stared into the canyon. The span of the Pecos River Bridge glinted in the sun. She watched them closely. From the back they appeared to be a a harmonious whole. Burgess and Bevo favored each other in their sturdy, compact builds and in their peculiar earth-grabbing stances. Jo's hair reached for the sky, and her body looked ready for flight. Anna wanted to call out to Burgess and Bevo to grab Jo's arms so she wouldn't shoot into the sky. Her body was capable of deceiving them all. Not trusting husband or son to know when to hold on, Anna walked to the wall and stood behind Jo. The old river road twisted downhill until it broke abruptly at the water's edge. Its smooth-coated surface and inner layers, rough and striated, looked like a half-eaten candy bar.

Jo's sharp chin was blunted by her fist. "I remember when that road washed out last," she said. "A couple from New Jersey got washed away. Their little baby girl got caught in between those two big boulders; they found her, hollering away. I wonder what happened to that little girl." She freed her chin and nestled closer to Burgess. "You remember that?"

Burgess nodded. "It was a miracle."

"No, it wasn't," Jo said flatly. "That's just the way it happened to turn out. It could just as soon have gone the other way."

Bevo started doing push-ups against the wall. "If Alfred's still wearing as much after-shave as he used to, I'm staying out on deck. I'll gag if I'm in close quarters with him."

"You don't have to worry, now do you?" Burgess's eyes rested reluctantly on the play of his son's shoulders. "I don't know too many men who'd want to get caught in close quarters with you."

"Don't be too sure," Bevo said and grinned.

For a moment Burgess seemed to study his son as another man might do, trying to judge what the attraction might be. The effort redirected Burgess's blood flow and turned his cheeks and forehead a reddish orange.

"Let's get this thing over with," Jo said. "Let's go ooh and aah over Alfred's ship."

"I don't think this is going to work," Bevo said.

"Sure it is." Burgess clapped a hand on his son's neck. "It's what your mother wants."

Jo reached out to brush the hair out of Anna's eyes. "Let's go. Mary F.'s already got those eggs deviled. There's no turning back now."

"Yes, there is," Anna said, but Jo had already started for the car.

Anna, Bevo and Burgess watched Jo walk toward the car. Bevo hoisted himself to a sitting position on the flagstone wall. Pressing the backs of her legs against the wall, Anna knew that Burgess and

Bevo shared her reluctance. None of them agreed with Jo's decision. Now was the time to challenge her.

"You're not making this any easier," Jo said. She stood by the side of the car with her arms folded, looking at them, until Burgess pried himself away from the wall.

Anna tried to catch Burgess's arm to pull him back, but Bevo stopped her. "Don't," he said. "Let him go."

"No! We can't let her do this—"

"It's what Mom wants. Case closed."

"Why don't we just throw her off the ledge then?" Anna asked. "It's the same thing."

"I *said*—case closed." Bevo jumped off the wall and walked to his car.

"No, it's not," Anna said. She refused to accept Jo's version of the future. They didn't have to feel that there was no other way, that they were being dragged into a hole by some more powerful and unknown force.

The roadside gravel crunched as Bevo inched the Plymouth toward Anna. Burgess honked his horn impatiently, but the Plymouth kept rolling slowly. Anna wouldn't budge. She could feel the heat of the front fender against her thighs. Another inch on Bevo's part, and she would be pinned against the wall.

"Face the other way," Bevo called. "You're going to make a great hood ornament." Anna shook her head. "Don't make me go through this alone," he said.

There wasn't any sense in staying behind. The only way to change Jo's mind was to work with Bevo and Burgess. Anna climbed over the hood and got into the car.

———

Mary Frances yoo-hooed them out of the two cars and down the marine trails to the white houseboat. Her elevated platform sandals acted as springboards for the rest of her body, and her arms pedaled madly. Anna couldn't tell if she was trying to keep her balance, direct them to the houseboat, or warn them away.

Alfred was on the top deck. The set of his back suggested he was about to be saddled with unwanted cargo. Anna longed to get her hands on his hair. The thick waves were offset by a nervous and staticky fineness. There was an ashy element to the whiteness, a smudginess, that came out of nowhere. She couldn't figure out how the individual strands blended together to produce the effect. Even Bevo couldn't figure it out, but then Alfred never tolerated his presence for long.

"Well, blow me down!" Burgess exclaimed. "Lookee there at the admiral."

Lagging behind Jo and Burgess, Anna and Bevo prodded each other into laughter. Before he could catch himself, Burgess turned around and winked at them. He jolted the marina planks with a booted jig.

"That's enough!" Jo said sharply. "I don't want you riding Alfred today." Anna laughed outright. Bevo kept his lips shut, but aerated laughter issued from his mouth. "You two stop lollygagging and straighten up. I want peace today."

"Josephine," Anna protested. "Stop acting like you're my mother."

"Stop acting like you need one then," Jo said.

Even Burgess fell back a little. He recovered quickly to slide an arm around her waist and promenade them past bare-masted sailboats. "We'll be good, Mommy," he promised.

There was a deeper quality to his playful contriteness, almost a plea, that Anna looked away from. Bevo stared steadily at his parents. He reached out for his mother's shoulder, but his hand hung in the air. Anna pressed Bevo's dazed hand close to her side.

"Over here! Yoo-hoo! Over here!" Mary Frances signaled from the houseboat's back deck. "We're going to have so much fun! Over here!" The water behind the houseboat began to churn. "Hurry!" she called frantically. "Over here! Hurry!" She tried to calm the foaming water by patting the air. "Alfred!"

Bevo vaulted onto the deck. He and Mary Frances bumped cheeks in greeting as Alfred revved the motor again.

"Tell him to stop this goddamn thing until your mother gets on board!" Burgess thundered.

"Hush," Jo commanded. Using her husband's shoulder as a base, she stepped onto the ladder. It was harder for Burgess, in

his workboots, to get a toehold on the narrow metal rungs. "I told
you to wear tennis shoes," she said.

"You've been telling me too damn many things lately." Burgess
bit at Jo's offered hand, and she withdrew it.

Anna had never seen Jo turn away from Burgess before, not
even when he'd been drinking. For the first time she felt sympathy
for him.

Bevo went to the front deck and spread himself across the green
plastic cushions. Mary Frances watched anxiously as he stripped
off his shirt. "He's not disrobing . . . is he?"

Jo tried out three deck chairs before she decided on one. Aiming
her head toward the front, she called automatically, "Keep
those pants on and put on some lotion."

Mary Frances flew to the side and peered down at Anna, who
still stood on the dock. "Anna! You're coming! Aren't you?" She
turned to Burgess and Jo, both already tucked in and determined
as if they were embarking on a long voyage. "She's coming. Isn't
she? You *are* coming. Aren't you?"

Anna smiled and waved, but suddenly she felt beached, without
the means or inclination to rejoin civilization again. There was too
much tension for one houseboat to handle. The uncertain and
urgent motion of the water worried by the motor didn't calm her
any. She didn't move. That was one way to stop things. But a lack
of motion wouldn't solve the problem. "What's for lunch, M.F.?"

Alfred blasted the horn. Mary Frances was close to tears.
"Anna! You have to come! Don't leave me out here with him!"

Hoping there was plenty of beer, Anna climbed on board. She
wandered into the main cabin while Bevo cast off from the cedar
pilings. A table sprang out of the wood-paneled wall when she
punched a button. Alfred was visible from his knees down. His
feet were stationary, but his knees were rocked by imaginary
waves.

Mary Frances squeezed in beside Anna. "Here you are!" she
said brightly. "Here's Anna, Alfred!" She crooked her neck and
pulled off her scarf. Hundreds of new tiny curls had spawned on
her scalp. Her fluttering hands skewered several curls.

"What have you done to your hair?" Anna asked.

"Really, Anna, is that all you ever think about?" Mary Frances rolled and rerolled the collar of her striped T-shirt. "It wouldn't hurt you any to pass around a compliment every now and then. Why don't you stay in here awhile and keep Alfred company? Alfred," she called, "Anna's out here to keep you company."

Alfred's knees jiggled. Anna accepted the beer Mary Frances shoved into her hand. Rooting in the side pockets that ran along the cabin wall, she found and bypassed the book of letters to the editor that Alfred had paid to have typeset and bound in black leather. *One Man's Conscience* he called it. Mary Frances had passed out autographed copies with their paychecks last Christmas. Anna had hoped for profit sharing.

"Lunch, Alfred!" Mary Frances called. "Dock or anchor or moor, or whatever it is, and come down."

"Boat won't steer itself," Alfred said. His knees bent and swung suddenly to the left.

Anna braced herself for a big swell. She should have known better. Alfred's knees snapped to attention again after weathering the storm.

Mary Frances had packed different lunches for everyone, including two kinds of potato salad, one with mustard for Anna and one without for Jo. She stood on the narrow side deck to pass deviled ham sandwiches through a porthole to Alfred.

"The man's an asshole," Bevo said. He pushed sunglasses up his nose to dismiss the scene.

"She's like a little hummingbird," Burgess said. "She's running herself silly." Elbows splayed, he scooted deeper into the canvas chair and continued to chew a bacon and pimento cheese sandwich. "I've got no use for him." He inched forward. "Now, if Bryan was here"—he paused to burden Anna with a significant look—"he'd give him an airing out. *If* he was here. *If* it was possible for him to be here."

"You don't know the other side of it," Jo said. "You don't know what Mary Frances gets out of it. It takes two."

Empty-handed, Mary Frances trotted to the back deck. She seemed at a loss when no one needed anything.

"What happens if we cross into Mexican waters?" Bevo asked.

"Will there be a scene?" He flexed his arms high overhead. "I could use an international incident right about now. What do you say, M.F.? Let's talk the admiral into dangerous waters."

"I don't think so, dear. Alfred sets his own course." Mary Frances patted his shoulder. She blushed and murmured at her contact with Bevo's skin, "Oh, my . . . "

Bevo displayed himself to greater advantage. He arched his eyebrows at Burgess. "What do you think, M.F.? Think I'm an asset to the shop? Think I could make a woman feel good about herself? That's the name of the game. Right?"

Anna pressed her thighs into the cushions and connected with the pulse of the houseboat's engine. She sometimes wondered how far Bevo would go. His body rather than his face registered emotion. The stringing of muscles and tendons tightened or loosened in a rhythm that attracted the eye. Right now there was something caught between his shoulder blades that wouldn't work itself out. She moved behind him and pressed her palm into his back.

When Bevo was sixteen and still Charles, Anna had entertained the idea of leading him into her bedroom. He had gone to Boys' Town in Ojinaga instead, a windowless and roofless series of cinder-block rooms where Mexican girls led American boys across another kind of border. He'd come back drunk and sick. She'd held his head over the toilet and let him sleep on the couch. Burgess had been ready to kill her until he found out she hadn't initiated his son.

Thinking of her own first encounter with Ronnie Mauss in the back of a pickup parked beside an abandoned loading pen at the railroad tracks, Anna couldn't decide who'd gotten the worse deal. Ronnie also had been schooled at a Boys' Town in Piedras Negras farther south. He had had a businesslike approach, which he'd probably picked up from the breeding pens in Future Farmers of America. She hadn't had time to learn how to stretch the economy of Ronnie's motions to her own satisfaction.

Bryan was like a friendly puppy, all tongue and sprawl, which, when she was loose and floppy herself, had been fine. The idea of molding a lover appealed to her. The velveteen chaise lounge in Mary Frances's upstairs room held a new promise. But it would take more than a body and something to support and cushion that body. Could she teach a teenage boy, first of all, to hide his truck, take off his boots, tiptoe up the back stairs and spit out the wad of chewing tobacco before he kissed her?

The outside staircase leading to the second floor was worth the extra ten thousand that Mary Frances had suddenly tacked onto the original asking price earlier in the week. She said Alfred had set his sights on ten more feet of boat. Anna didn't want to have to backtrack and ask Frank for the money. Her banker had squeezed his nose when she'd gone in to change the figure on her loan application and said he'd think about it. The cashier's check in her purse should convince Alfred.

A silver fishing boat bucked the houseboat's wake. "Look who it is!" Mary Frances cried. "Ed Nettinger! Everybody—it's Ed Nettinger!" Leaning far over the side, she grabbed for him as if she were drowning.

Except for blue canvas boat shoes, Ed Nettinger was dressed for dry land. Bobbing up and down, he looked ridiculous wearing a long-sleeved shirt, khaki pants and a straw hat, as if he'd been caught riding the range when the floodgates lifted.

His sudden appearance startled Anna. Since Bryan had moved out, she'd been avoiding Ed. He required too much. Although he appeared to accept fate, to in fact gain control somehow by an acceptance of it, Anna distrusted his lack of need. There was something too comfortable about the man, and she didn't trust that either. She didn't need any more surprises. Nobody else's future was going to reel her in.

Ed tipped his hat. The gesture infuriated Anna. She wanted his politeness to drop and his seams to show so she wouldn't be tempted.

He maneuvered the small boat to within a speaking distance. "I didn't think I'd see you out here. Do you like to fish?" he asked.

Excess sunlight bounced off the water. Anna stared into the brilliance. "Probably not."

"Anna—Mary Frances, get her some sunglasses," Jo directed. Alfred kept the houseboat even with Ed Nettinger. For the first time all day the houseboat idled as Alfred called Ed Nettinger on the City Council's handling of the low-income housing project. When Alfred gunned the houseboat's engine every few seconds to make his point, Ed had to hold the sides of his rocking boat.

"Hold on, cowboy," Anna said.

Mary Frances hailed a cabin cruiser approaching on the other side of the houseboat. "It's the Owenses. Oh, you'll love them! Yoo-hoo! Esther, Jim! Over here! It's Alfred and Mary Frances!"

Bevo shouldered his radio and a towel. "I am *not* believing this." He stretched out on the cushions beside Anna. "So that's your widower. He's a little stringy, isn't he?"

The sides of the cabin cruiser and the houseboat bumped. Abandoning Ed, Anna responded to Mary Frances's summons to meet Esther and Jim. Bevo ignored the company. Glued to their chairs since leaving the dock, Jo and Burgess nodded and smiled and waved. Anna extended her hand for a shake and found herself being hauled over the railing to the cabin cruiser's deck.

Mary Frances had already climbed over. Esther and Jim wore saucer-brimmed straw hats and had zinc-coated noses. With the sun behind their backs, it was impossible to make out their features. Jim Owens shouldered a golf club. Anna looked around for stray balls rolling along the deck.

"He's got the best putt on the lake," Mary Frances confided. "Show Anna your putt." She looked as if she wanted to send Esther Owens over to the houseboat and stay on the cabin cruiser with Jim. Esther could go around and around the lake with Alfred until the stopper at the bottom of the lake was pulled and they were sucked down.

Anna eluded Jim's helping hand and climbed back to the houseboat. "Wait there," she told Mary Frances. "I've got something for you." She jerked her purse from under Bevo's head. "Break out the champagne."

Bevo whipped the towel off his eyes and sat up. "You're going to have Alfred marry you and the widower! Mom! Anna's adding another initial. She's up to L.M.B.N. now."

"Don't be silly. I can't remember what I've got now." Anna
snapped the cashier's check before his eyes. "Take a look at that."
"Oh, shit. Oh, shit!" Bevo fell back on the cushions. "Oh,
shit."

"Calm down. It's only money," she said to Bevo and hurried
to present the check to Mary Frances before Alfred entered another squall. "Take it and run, M.F. It's only got your name on
it."

Mary Frances clutched the check to her throat and looked
frantically around the lake. "What's this—it isn't for—? I *told*
you—" She backed away. "Alfred made me—and Jo practically
threatened me. Didn't you?"

Anna felt seasick. Her vision was suddenly bleached of color.
"What are you telling me?"

"Let her have her money back," Jo told Mary Frances. "Pass
it to me if she won't let you put it in her hand. Go on and pass
it to me." Jo smoothed the check and placed it on the cushions
in front of Anna. "We've given Mary Frances twenty-five thousand. Bevo and I own the shop."

"Alfred needed the money for the houseboat," Mary Frances
explained desperately. She hung on to the houseboat's railing and
tried to keep the cabin cruiser from drifting away. "Anna! I told
you I'd offer it to Jo—I warned you—I was as surprised as you are
that she wanted it."

"I can't believe it," Anna said bitterly. "You set me up. You
told me to go ahead. You gave me your blessing. You told me you
didn't want it."

"Things have changed," Jo said. "I don't have to explain that
to you. I want the shop for my son."

"The shop's not going to make you well." There was no place
on the houseboat for Anna to go. She climbed onto the cushions
and dived into the lake. Surfacing, she kicked for the nearest
shore. The opaque green water was composed of cold, snaking
currents and lukewarm pockets. Her clothes dragged, especially
her tennis shoes, but she knew she'd need them on the rocky
shore. She wasn't going back for anything.

Flashes of silver were appearing on her right side. Her strokes grew more frantic as she attempted to gain speed, but the silver maintained its pace as she tired herself. She fought the craving to stop, to turn around and paddle back to the familiar. There was nothing familiar on the houseboat to return to. Jo had been betrayed by her body, and in turn she had betrayed Anna. The push and pull threatened to swamp her. *Go,* she shouted to herself. Stop thinking and just keep moving. A wave engulfed her as she breathed to her right. She dogpaddled in place and coughed.

Ed Nettinger sat in his silver fishing boat and waited for Anna to focus. "I'm heading in. How about a ride?"

Drops of water from her shaking head splattered him. "Leave me alone."

He floated an orange life vest to her. "There's a cove over there by those trees. You can touch bottom about thirty feet out. Can you see where I'm pointing?"

Nodding, Anna treaded water and waited for him to go. The part of shore he pointed to seemed to recede as she looked at it. In refusing to look back at the houseboat, she had nothing to gauge distance by.

Water skiers in tandem knifed through the water. To survive the wash, Anna had to reach for Ed's boat. She became uncomfortably aware that there were no pedestrian lanes in the lake. Boats of all shapes, sizes and speeds crisscrossed.

"Not much of a pattern to all the traffic," Ed observed.

Anna hooked her elbows on the boat's rim. Just the idea of trying to flip herself into the boat required too much energy. Ed moved to the front for balance and extended an oar handle. She stared at the steadiness of his hands for a long time. She faked a movement toward the oar, but he held it stable. When Anna finally grabbed it, he brought it in hand over hand until she was halfway over the side. Water scraped off her stiff legs as she finished the job by herself. Ed changed places with her and headed for the cove.

Keeping her back to Ed and the houseboat, Anna stripped down to her bathing suit. A plastic pickle bucket at her feet held live fish. "Don't you have enough fish at home?" she asked.

"I'm comparing the lake water with my pond." He nosed the boat toward his station wagon, which was wedged in between a stand of cedars and the base of a cliff. A piece of tarpaulin covered the rear windows. "I've got an extra towel in the car," he said.

When the water was shallow enough, Anna slipped overboard and waded to shore. Ed shifted position to compensate for the lost ballast of her body. "You must not like boats too much," he said, keeping pace with her.

"I guess not." Anna stepped onto dry land and left him to moor the boat.

"I'll have to remember that." Ed lifted a string of fish from the water. They overlapped on the line in the shape of a Christmas tree. "Taste test," he said.

"Are you serious?" The man didn't know what he was doing.

"As serious as you are. The tools of our trade might be different, but the same thing drives us, a certain vision, a love."

"Don't be too sure. A dream doesn't have one thing to do with the real world." She grasped a catfish and worked its mouth against the line hook. "What happens if your fish taste like cardboard?"

"I'll have to convince people that cardboard tastes better than they ever thought it would." Sunlight prismed into Ed's eyes and crystallized the gray irises as he stared out at the houseboat. "What happened out there?"

"I got restless. We weren't getting anywhere. Can I get a lift back to town? I'll put in for gas."

"We'll work something out," Ed said. "Did you get a chance to eat?"

It would take him hours to put a meal together. Anna needed to be in motion. "Is there a bus stop on the highway?"

On Anna's fourth lap around the station wagon, Ed disengaged himself from the back bumper. "Here," he said, holding out a set of keys, "take the car down that left fork and meet me at the Texaco marina. Let me load the fish in their tanks. The water starts spilling over at fifteen miles an hour on this road."

Anna let the keys fall into her open palm. "How do you know I'll meet you there?"

Ed lashed the tarp to the rear bumper. "You don't strike me as the kind of woman who'd want to be stuck with a bunch of catfish to take care of."

"You don't know me very well."

"In fifteen minutes we'll both know whether I'm a fool or not. That left fork there." He spread a towel across the driver's seat for her.

Once the fishing boat had jumped away from the shore, Anna started the engine. She considered letting the fish go and driving away, but the memory of Ed's concern for them took that choice away. The sun glanced off several silver fishing boats in the vicinity of the Texaco marina. None of them was Ed Nettinger's. She broadened her field to include the body of the lake. He was headed for the houseboat.

Anna gunned the station wagon down the wrong fork. Two miles later she ran out of road and had to back up and go down the fork that went to the marina. Ed Nettinger hadn't been a fool to give her his car and a choice of two roads; he'd rigged the choices. Two forks and one dead end. The only real option led straight to him.

———

Anna and Ed drove into Sanderson at six. Late-afternoon sunlight tanned the hills. The thickened light bestowed the town with a rich and shadowy beauty. Houses were randomly thrown upon the slopes, and commercial buildings were caught halfway between the highway and the banks of another dry creek. Parked cars lined the main street, but no one was in sight.

Highway towns were deceptive. Travelers flashed through and assumed no residential life existed. Cafés, gas station/rock stores and motels were there to court those who had the time to stop. The life-span of a tourist's attention in a town like this was thirty minutes tops. Anna's experienced eyes searched out the clusters of trees set at spaced intervals behind a line of one-story buildings whose crowned façades hid flat roofs. Families lived behind the shelter of trees, not in rooms tacked onto the back of a drugstore.

"Can we drive around and look?" Anna asked.

"We've got plenty of time," Ed said. "I don't see why not." She always broke long trips by turning off the main highway and browsing through a town. On Sundays there was always an unair-conditioned church with a door open to release uneven voices into the afternoon air. Front porches were her specialty. They might shelter hand-holding couples and solitary rockers. Her greatest find so far had been a whole family reunion with sprawls of people zipping corn on the cob through their teeth.

Late Sunday afternoons unsettled Anna. She'd spent hundreds of them in her best dress, petticoated until the skirts pointed stiffly, and black patent leather shoes. Home from church and from pretending to believe, Georgia would rock the afternoon away, hidden in a corner by a living-room window. Thousands of cars must have passed every one of their front porches without slowing down. Still, Anna twirled and tapped the Sunday afternoons away as if her footwork would be enough to catch somebody's attention. One evening, in the middle of a pirouette, she suddenly understood that nobody ever would stop. Her house wasn't anybody's final destination. The knowledge had come to her unbidden and easily after so many years of longing. Shimmying out of her dress and kicking off her shoes, Anna began to leave behind the sound of her mother's rocker to prowl through backyards and vacant lots. Georgia could wait all she wanted for the promised permanence of a future that Michael Leandros was supposed to bring back with him, but she wasn't about to.

Anna had learned to embrace the temporariness of the present. She progressed through all the subsequent moves hand over hand as if she were involved in a square dance where she wasn't supposed to meet the same partner again. She learned to pack before her mother's symptoms became full-blown. Georgia, always so careful not to shortchange Anna out of half her history, would say, "You get it from him, your wanderlust."

"It's you." Anna would retaliate. "I get it from you."

Although her mother's reasons for moving might have been

faulty, the episode on the houseboat made Anna realize that
Georgia's instincts had been right. There was no one place, no
right place. Anna saw she'd made a serious mistake in assuming
that Alpine was her final destination. That was the same as believing a car would stop and someone would discover her dancing on
the porch.

"Remember the flood?" Ed asked. He pulled into the grocery
store's empty parking lot and pointed to the sharpened remains
of a billboard. "You can still see traces of the damage. The remains of Grace's grandmother were washed away. Grace had it
put in her will that she be buried fifteen feet down."

Anna had been eating macaroni and cheese when the words
"Sanderson, Texas" had come out of Walter Cronkite's mouth.
She remembered the cheese sinking into the ditch under her
tongue. It was as if he'd pulled up outside her front door, but it
was too late. She had been suspicious of Walter Cronkite for
trying to trick her into thinking the rest of the world cared about
a place where she'd once lived. They hadn't cared when there'd
been no trouble. Ed Nettinger was beginning to make her feel the
same way. A man who inspired confidence because of the way he
competently handled tragedy.

"Why did she do it?" Anna asked. "Why did Grace kill herself?"

The shift in conversation didn't seem to faze Ed. "She couldn't
get comfortable."

"A lot of people can't get comfortable. That's not a good
enough reason."

"Maybe not, not for you or me," he said, "but for Grace it
was."

"You don't feel guilty?" she pressed. "For not stopping her?"

"I stopped her a lot of times. And I finally came to realize that
there was nothing I could do, except protect Delia from the
unhappiness as much as I could. I've done my mourning. I had
fifteen years to do it in. I'm not a perfect man. I didn't marry
Grace out of love. She knew that, she didn't love me either. That's
probably part of why she married me. I loved that land, and she
thought she wanted to be taken away from it."

He restarted the station wagon and pulled out of the parking lot. "I'll tell you a story on Grace's grandmother over a hamburger. It might help you see—unless it's safer for you to believe that I drove her to it. Then we'll drive around town."

Anna had been hoping that he would stop the station wagon and tell her to get out. He hadn't asked what had taken her so long to pick him up at the marina. Her belief in motion was fading. Everybody was a step ahead of her. For ten years she'd been running in place. All she had to show for it was the nice ditch she'd dug.

She needed to find another town and another shop. Fast. The wrong future had seduced her. She should have been able to foresee Jo's illness. Anna hardened her heart. There were millions of people left behind in small towns by those who'd gone on to other places. There were probably hundreds of people she'd never see again. They might as well be dead, but she'd never grieved for them. Leaving them behind had guaranteed their immortality.

"Tell me about Grace's grandmother."

Ed opened his door. "I want to check on the fish. Then we'll eat and I'll tell you." He surprised her by appearing at the window again. "Are you sure you want to hear it? You're not just being polite?"

Anna ruffled her hair. The more she heard about Grace, the more unlimited and unbelievable Ed's steadiness seemed. His capacity for diffusing abuse appeared to have no bounds. Grace must have flung herself against the granite hardness of his unfailing support, wanting to weaken him, until she'd exhausted herself. But this person at her window, with jug ears and sarcasm embroidering his words, had taken care of himself first. The question was, Had it been at Grace's expense? For the first time that day Anna looked him straight in the face. "I want to hear the story."

Four elderly women in a 1965 Mercury Comet sat next to them at the drive-in. Heads up and necks stretched to see better into the station wagon, they looked like hungry baby birds waiting in the nest. "Do you know those women?" Anna asked. She didn't recognize them.

"Jealous?" Ed grinned. "Here's the food. I'll tell you the story after we eat."

Anna watched him sip a soft drink. His eyes watered, and he said, "That first sip always burns going down."

His vulnerability strengthened her. She curved into the warmth of the seat and began to eat. The Comet backed up with the tray still attached to the driver's window. The back seat women shrieked. Flustered, the driver shifted gears and ran the front tires over a concrete ledge designed to keep cars from crashing into the kitchen.

Ed tapped his horn for the carhop. "You might want to take the ladies' tray first and then come back for this one," he said when she appeared.

"Do you always think women need your help?" Anna asked.

"I don't think you want my help. I don't think you'd take it even if you needed it."

"I'm glad to see you're a sensible man." She could do without his criticism, too.

———

While Ed drove the eighty miles from Sanderson to Alpine, Anna fiddled with the radio. The strongest signal was a mystery theater out of Oklahoma City. The quiet, uninflected voice of the narrator colored the night.

Soothed by the disembodied voice, Anna remembered switching towns with her mother. They moved long distances, never putting fewer than four hundred miles between one town and the next. Georgia always traveled with the sun at her back. Depending on the direction, they either started or ended in darkness. Until she started to help with the driving, Anna would fit herself into the back seat between boxes and press her ear against the seat and release it so the sound of tires meeting road made her whole head tingle. Certain voices on the radio comforted her. She would rub the gardenia's slick leaves and pretend that her mother had company in the front seat.

Anna turned the radio off in the middle of a scream. "Tell me about Grace's grandmother. The one they didn't bury deep enough."

"That's the other one, the one that floated away, her mother's mother, a real ball of yarn if ever there was one. Nell, Carl's mother, is buried on the ranch. She was originally buried on land west of the Rosillos Mountains where the park is now, but the government wouldn't give them exclusive rights on her grave, so they dug her up and moved her when they got the ranch outside of town. That's a story in itself, but I'll save that for later."

"I've heard it already," Anna said.

"There was a period there of two years when Nell didn't get into town. Town was a five-, six-day trip by wagon, so they'd usually stop at ranches along the way to break it up."

Anna felt as if she had gotten a third-grade mathematics problem instead of a story. Distance = rate × speed. "Burgess told me about the depression in wool prices. So?"

He looked at her and seemed pleased. "I'm getting to it. Nell was an import from the East—I don't mean East Texas, but from *the* East—totally unprepared for life out here. She arrived in Alpine by train, expecting the worst part of her trip to be over with, and there it was just getting started. Grace used to call that trip six days to nowhere.

"Nell stayed in her bedroom and cried for a month straight, and then—"

"She never shed another tear," Anna interrupted.

"This is my story, not yours. She walked downstairs and started getting to know the ranch," Ed continued, "inch by inch, making it hers. Owning it. It was another two years before she got back into town because that's as long as it was. There were other priorities. Some people see what can be fought and how and when to do it. Some can't. Nell taught all the hands how to read and write; she taught herself Spanish. She respected the land, she saw what it offered, and she was glad to take it and to give back in return."

"Did she approve of you marrying Grace?"

"She died before I came out here, but I feel her presence very strongly when I go down to the park. She's present in a way that Grace never was. She was a transplant, but she was tied to the land in a way Grace never was. What Grace held to in that story was that it took Nell two years to get back into town. She fixed on that part of the story like it was a family curse that was going to be brought down on her head one day. Nell knew what to fight. Grace—Grace fought everything."

"Why did she marry you if she knew all you wanted was her land?"

"That's not *all* I wanted, Anna, or want, for that matter. But to answer your question—I don't think she ever really wanted to leave, and she never could admit it. No place was ever right for her. We traveled. She lived in San Antonio for a few months, and she hated it. But the thought that she would be trapped on the ranch, by acts of nature, by me, by anything besides herself, that's what she wanted. To have no other choice but that last choice, that's what she wanted all along, to have no more choices."

"And the ranch is worth all that?"

"I'd have done anything to get that land. I'd do it all over again if I had to," Ed said matter-of-factly. "My father was a shrimper, and the Gulf wore him away. I wasn't going to go that route. You can't own a piece of the ocean. There's a sweetness and a dryness in the air here that comes from the land. This is my home, my place. This is where I was meant to be. This is where I can use and appreciate the things my father taught me. That was the main difference between Grace and me. I don't fear the past. I don't believe it's something that's going to be visited on me."

Fool, Anna thought.

"I'd like to check on the fish. Do you want to get home right away?"

Mary Frances would be calling all night. Bevo would be throwing rocks at her window. She'd rather deal with Ed Nettinger and his fish. "No, I'll come with you."

"Your husband—"

"Ex," Anna said promptly.

"Your ex-husband used to take quite an interest in our council meetings. I haven't seen him lately."

"He's around."

The brightness and density of the stars made Anna's throat tight. Light shed by the moon was so strong that her hand cast shadows on the road. Ed parked close to the reinforced earthen lip of the two-acre catfish pond. The unfinished bass pond was a black spot behind the legs of the windmill. Catfish kicked, and the skin of moonlight on the water flaked into tiny pieces. Ed reshaped the pond surface with the palm of his hand.

Anna pointed to a plastic hoop about ten feet in diameter that floated in the middle of the pond. "What's that for?"

"That's a feeder. I use a floating feed. Ordinarily, I like to throw it by hand, that way I can see how they're coming along. You also don't tend to overfeed so much that way. If I'm not here, the ring keeps the feed from washing back up on shore. I've got a couple more to pull in."

Anna waited. She'd be gone tomorrow, but she had all night to seduce him. Ed transferred the lake catfish to a small, square, steel tank close to the pond. While they watched the fish acclimatize themselves, she stroked his back, and when she was sure the ceremony was finished, she opened his attention to the rest of the world by drawing his head close and painting his lips with her tongue.

Ed's belt buckle dug into her stomach and his hand moved to protect her skin. Anna had forgotten to take his own need into account. She had to reach for the tailgate when he kissed her to keep her balance.

He caught her shoulders before she toppled. "Is this what you want?"

Anna concentrated on unsnapping his shirt. The action kept them apart and sped things up. She wanted to see if his chest and back were raw and exposed like his hands. "I want you to stop talking," she said.

They slid headfirst into the back of the station wagon. Ed never did stop talking. Anna had to resist the physical and mental engagement of making sense out of what he said and believing his words mattered.

A nna rang Willi's after-hours bell. The Trend-Setters shop wasn't open for another hour, but she had been in Marfa since six o'clock, driving up and down the wide streets. After Ed had dropped her off, she'd taped notes of cancellation to the doors of all her Monday appointments and then driven twenty-six miles west to Marfa.

She hated the shop's door. WILLI'S TREND-SETTERS down-stepped in three lines. The first letter of each word was painted to resemble a hank of curled and frosted black hair. The rest of the word was scripted in black across the glass. Anna moved to a clear spot of glass so Willi could see who was at the door.

By the time Willi opened the door, a look of shrewdness had replaced surprise. Her long hair, pulled back in a high ponytail, was stained Chestnut Sunset. The planes of her face were wide and pronounced and could take the severe hairstyle. It was her fifty-plus hairline that bore the strain.

"I'm available," Anna said.

A gold cigarette lighter rode in Willi's left hand. A thin, brown cigarette, unlit, was between her cocoa-colored lips. "Your timing is excellent. Come in."

Willi's shop consisted of two rooms railroaded together. The waiting room was unadorned by plants or a soda machine. Steel-legged director's chairs with taut chocolate-brown canvas seats and backs were lined up on either side of a Plexiglas coffee table. Current issues of plastic-covered magazines, *Town and Country*, *Vogue* and *Glamour*, overlapped with even edges on the clear top. Two steps led up to the styling room. Sliding glass doors separated the rooms. Before its conversion the waiting room had been a carport.

Anna counted four chairs, four dryers and three heat lamps. Each chair had its own station with a Formica counter colored in streaks of butter and cream. The hinged counters lifted to reveal yellow sinks. Column windows of leaded glass sided the mirror at each station. Hidden behind the mirror was a deep supply cabinet. Three poster-size head shots were framed in plastic and mounted on the wall above the dryers.

The shop gave Anna the same hungry feeling that new houses in subdivisions gave her. The smell of new paint lingered, and there was a silent vibration in the air as if the painter had just gone out the back door. She reminded herself that she didn't want to buy the place. It would be a temporary situation that provided a chair, a mirror and a sink so she could do her work.

After the tour they sat in the waiting room. Willi tamped her still-unlit cigarette against the gold lighter. "I don't wish to have a war on my hands. Mary Frances has accused me of being a scalphunter more times than I care to remember."

"Don't worry," Anna said. "She's got no grounds."

"Then this is my proposal. I know these chairs are not comfortable. They are not for a reason. There is also a reason for the steps and the glass doors. I want my clients to see what awaits them. Yes. When they arrive in the styling room, I want them to have that sense, that privilege of having arrived. And they are never—never—to be disappointed upon their arrival or departure."

"If you mean the customer's always right, you can forget it,"

Anna said. "I don't play politics. I don't wipe chins and I don't coddle neurotics. You rent out space to me and I'll keep my chair filled and hand over thirty-five percent."

Willi paused in bringing together her lighter and the same cigarette. "I have something else in mind," she said. "Twenty percent of total net profits for two months. Yes. As manager of Trend-Setters."

Anna looked at Willi critically. She wondered if the cigarette and lighter were designed as a distraction. "Yes? And where will you be?" She couldn't picture Willi staying in the background like Mary Frances.

"On a Florida honeymoon with my golfer sweetheart," Willi answered, without a trace of pride or excitement.

"I don't want that kind of responsibility. I'm not a baby-sitter. What about your other operators? Don't you trust them?"

"Make no mistake, my girls are good. I don't reward average performance. Elidia and Susie each have their strengths, and weaknesses. Yes. I don't want to create a division between them. Bringing you in will unite them. If they turn against anyone, it will be you."

In a move that reminded Anna too much of Jo, Willi squinted against imaginary smoke. "You were negotiating for Mary Frances's shop."

"She got a better offer."

"You don't have some Svengali running his finger along your backbone, do you?"

Anna raised her hands from the armrest and produced her palms for Willi. "No strings."

"I assumed, of course, that your marriage was a business arrangement. Those things can be more trouble than they're worth. I've often thought of writing a manual about obtaining citizenship in this country."

Willi's assumption irritated Anna. Despite its legal foundation, she hadn't considered her marriage to be a bloodless pact. Nobody saw it in the proper light. Including Bryan.

"You understand I have to ask these things. I have worked very hard and I am very careful. Yes. My accountant handles all the finances, including the daily till. Thirty percent of total plus a bonus of twenty-five dollars for every new client you bring in and set up with a weekly appointment."

Anna didn't care about dickering over financial details. She had a damp cashier's check somewhere to fall back on. "Fine."

"I am not convinced, Anna." Willi tapped the gold lighter end over end against the steel arm of her chair. "Why am I not convinced? Surely, failing to bargain successfully with Mary Frances hasn't broken you. No."

"I've told you what I wanted. I'd advise you to put one of your operators in charge and let me rent out a station. I'll split my profits with you down the middle."

"I am in need of a manager, not a free agent. No. This is what we'll do. You'll take my manual home and read it overnight. If you are willing to follow my procedures, then we have a deal. If not . . . come back in two months."

The manual was bound in light yellow vinyl that was padded. Anna had no intention of reading through an inch's worth of paper on how to maintain a shop. Tonight she was getting some sleep. Her muscles were beginning to ache from adjusting to Ed Nettinger's body.

"We have a deal," she assured Willi. "I'll swear on your manual but I won't sign anything. No written contract."

"No? For my protection purely then. My accountant will fill in the blanks." Willi picked up a cordless telephone. She punched in numbers with her powdery fingertips. "Vernon, please fill in these figures: thirty percent total, twenty-five dollars for every new, confirmed, weekly. Chair number three. A unilateral agreement. Yes. And the prenuptial agreement will also be ready? Good. That one will be signed by both parties. Yes."

Anna flipped through the manual. She should have loaded the Valiant and saved herself a return trip. As it was, checking into the Paisano Hotel was three or four hours away.

Willi plunged the phone's antenna down. "A few more details, Anna. Are you planning to commute?"

"I'll stay at the hotel."

"No. I have a house in mind for you. We'll look at it and then drive to the newspaper office."

They rode in Willi's yellow and white Cadillac down the wide avenues. Anna sent her electric window up and down. No matter how fast or how hard she pressed the switch the window's response was too slow. She'd take a hand-cranked window whose speed was under her control over that any day.

The house Willi had in mind sat behind a large two-story winged house and looked tired and runted in comparison. The east wing of the large house hid the smaller house from the street. Its only access to the street was an unpaved alley.

"I'll take it," Anna said. "I'll be back with my things in a couple of hours."

"If you are always so easily persuaded, perhaps I should have Vernon sign the supply orders."

The weight of the procedures manual was making Anna's thighs numb. "It's your shop."

They continued on to the newspaper office where Willi took out an ad in the *Big Bend Sentinel* announcing Anna's arrival. She signed two blank checks when she returned to the car and handed them to Anna. "Your first official act as manager," she instructed. "Put an announcement in the Alpine newspaper and one on the radio."

Despite her hurry to relocate, Anna parked on a high limestone bluff that overlooked Marfa. Her newest town. Burgess subscribed to the theory that every town had been born for a different reason. He called Marfa a white-glove town. It had been a station located close to the point where the overland trail crossed the railroad. A community of merchants had sprung up easily. There hadn't been the hard push to bring the railroad through town, as in Alpine, where thousands of dollars were raised and acres of land given to persuade the Orient Railroad Company.

Burgess was wrong. Despite the wide-avenued gentility of Marfa, Anna was looking down into another dry creek bed. Towns sprang up because people got tired and thirsty. The free-flowing water had seduced them and made them lazy.

Mesquite, with its insatiable roots that went down forty feet, was blamed for the loss of water. Some swore dry creeks flowed again once the mesquite was cleared away. Others said the success of communities and the increased need to tap into underground streams were responsible for the disappearance.

All those theories were wrong. It was a natural deception. Sensing need and desire, the water had withdrawn into the mountains, where the source was protected until it was time for another flash flood and the overgratification of everyone's prayers for rain. In a climate of deception like this, was it any wonder that people gave up?

———

Anna closed her bank account and tore up her loan application. She placed the Trend-Setters' ad in the *Avalanche* and canceled her newspaper subscription; she rented a U-Haul trailer; she left a general delivery change of address at the post office and picked up deposits at the utility and telephone companies; she called and canceled her Tuesday through Saturday appointments.

It didn't take long to pack. Bryan's move had spurred a weeding out of her own possessions. When the trailer was completely loaded and her boxes filled only a third of it, Anna realized she'd been living for the past ten years in anticipation of this day. She plugged in the telephone only long enough to call the landlord in San Angelo and leave instructions on his answering machine to mail her security deposit to Willi's shop. The telephone book that was wedged under the screen door went into the trashcan at the side of the garage.

When Anna rounded the garage, she found Liz staring into the open trailer. Her tears spattered the boxes; She hadn't had a dry day since February.

"I'm not working for him," Liz declared. "I don't care if he is Jo's son. He's making fun of all of us. I'm sick and tired of people picking on me and thinking I'm too stupid to see it." She lifted the flap of a cardboard box. Her voice got soggier. "What are you doing? What's going *on* with everybody?"

"Change," Anna said. She didn't want to hear about Jo or Bevo or the shop. Jo had made her choice. This was hers. She knew the reasons behind both actions. This move might have been delayed but it was no different from any other she'd made. "Everybody needs change. Even you."

Liz unloaded the last newspaper-stuffed box that Anna had loaded. "Nobody's ever satisfied anymore. They always have to go faster and learn more, and they never stop, they never stop to look at anything."

Anna shot the box back into the trailer. She wished she hadn't been so optimistic at the grocery store in grabbing too many boxes and thinking she had so much to carry away with her. "Go ahead and have your baby," she said. "You think that won't change things? If I were you, I'd find out all I could about coloring from Bevo—"

"Don't you dare tell me I can learn a lot from him. I don't want to go any further!"

"Fine. Go on crying. See how long Leo puts up with it. Maybe Bevo'll start looking pretty good to him." Anna congratulated herself on making this a clean move. No danger of exchanged addresses or made-to-be-broken promises to keep in touch. No regrets.

Liz kicked a trailer tire. "You'd sleep with him, you would, and you'd call it a learning experience." The Kleenex she tried to pull out of her waistband shredded. "Where are you going? Why are you leaving us? What *happened?*"

She pulled up her blouse. The flat moles on her stomach arranged in the shape of the Little Dipper were shiny. "I really am pregnant. You can't leave, you'll miss everything."

Knowing she couldn't afford the link to Liz and a mailbox full of baby pictures, Anna got in the Valiant and drove off without answering. She intended to leave Alpine with its population stable. The promise of a birth wouldn't offset a death.

In her rearview mirror she saw Liz rubbing her stomach. "You're on your own," Anna said. "You're all on your own."

In spite of the line of cinder blocks that ran from wheel cap to wheel cap to keep the boxes huddled together, the trailer still wagged. Traffic was light on the four-lane highway, but Anna had

visions of the trailer willfully drifting into another lane. She regretted briefly not having accumulated more possessions that could
act as stabilizing weights. The roadside park at the foot of Paisano
Pass was deserted. She pulled over to check the hookup. This is
it, she told herself. Last chance. You can't be stopping every five
feet. Get out. Check it. Get back in and *go.*

The hitch took Anna's full weight. Sitting on the Valiant's rear
bumper, she placed her feet against the trailer and pushed. A dark
green Delta 88 the same color and make as Mary Frances's
streaked westward. She heard skid marks being made. The grassy
ditch behind her was tempting. Chancing a rattlesnake bite was
better than having to face Mary Frances's guilt.

The Delta 88 angled back end first across three lanes of highway. Anna smelled scalded rubber. Mary Frances reluctantly left
the heavy armor of her car. "I've been calling and calling and
calling. Look, see, there's a blister rising up on my finger."

Anna remained unmoved. "You're wasting your time. Hire
yourself another girl. If Jo and Bevo haven't already. I don't know
who has jurisdiction now."

Mary Frances clutched her collar. "That's a blow, Anna, a real,
low-down blow. I never thought I'd be reduced to having to call
a client, and not one of my more favorite ones, either, I might add,
to find out what's happened to one of my employees. I knew you'd
let *them* know—bread and butter over friendship."

"You're walking a fine line, Mary Frances," Anna warned. "I'd
watch that if I were you. We had a verbal agreement."

"Alfred doesn't understand verbal agreements. He only under-
stands cash in his hand. He can't put verbal into a strongbox."

"Alfred's *your* problem. Don't try to palm him off on me."
Anna climbed off the trailer. "Send the cashier's check and my
last paycheck to Willi's."

"*Willi's!*" Mary Frances screamed. "Willi's! Well! I like that.
Here"—she extended her arm, filigreed with lavender veins—
"here, rip my veins out, too, while you're at it. Go ahead, you
might as well. Willi's! Nobody even knows where she came from,
and that accent—does that accent even have a country behind it?

She could be a Nazi wife. And that Cadillac! People don't want to do business with somebody who drives a *Cadillac!*"

"Then the ads in the paper and on the radio won't bother you. Maybe they'll think twenty-six miles is too far to drive. Anyway, you won't have to worry too much longer. It'll be just you and Alfred paddling around the lake. Enjoy all your time together." Anna began to inch the Valiant past the Delta 88.

"Anna!" Mary Frances held on to the door and trotted beside the car. "There's something wrong with Jo—tell me what it is."

Anna braked. Her knee had locked instinctively. She hardened her heart. "Why would she buy a beauty shop if something was wrong? The only thing wrong is you two screwed me."

"Don't be like this. She wants it for Bevo. She wants him to stay and straighten himself out. You don't understand—it's a continuation. It'll be like her grandchild."

"He won't stay," Anna said. "Jo won't want to hang on to it. Where will your shop be then? With nobody to take care of it. All the years you put into it—right down the tubes. You don't even care. And you were worried about me." In an independent move the trailer flicked the Delta 88's bumper.

Mary Frances followed as far as the abandoned air base. She turned off the highway quickly when Anna braked suddenly and then put the Valiant in reverse.

Although nobody knew where she was, Anna unloaded the trailer quickly. After hiding the Valiant deep in the alley, she decided she could afford the reward of a nap.

Lying on a double bed pushed into a corner, Anna realized the small house was built like a hideout. Wood-framed screens swung on side hinges. Horizontal slats of glass in the windows could be cranked open or closed, but she'd have to be two inches thick to crawl through them. There was no back door; the front door was the only usable exit.

Deep breaths weren't helping to bring sleep any closer. In a sudden fit of panic Anna threw her pillow at the door. She felt as if she'd drunk a hundred cups of coffee. It was the lack of sleep that was making her so jumpy. Twenty-six miles and she was acting as if it were the moon and she had no other choice. There was no point to staying in bed and mourning.

Anna pulled all the drawers out of the dresser and set them on the bed. She opened all the cabinets and drawers in the kitchen and bathroom and the closet in the big open room. And then she opened all the cartons. For such a small house, it had an overabundance of storage space. Within ten minutes something of hers sat in every drawer and cabinet. Summer and winter clothes were mixed, cups and glasses sat side by side on the shelves, but it didn't matter. She broke the cartons down, tied them with string and slid the flattened pieces underneath the bed.

When Anna lay down again to take a nap, the mattress coils dug into her back. She had to put a padding of quilts beneath her. Scenes from the day before kept playing in her head. Voices from the big house sounded like Jo and Ed Nettinger. Anna sat up.

Nobody knew where she was. But just in case, she got up, opened all the cabinets and drawers, dragged the boxes out, wrapped her fist in string and repacked everything. And timed it.

———

After turning in the trailer and buying some beer, Anna stopped at a pay phone outside the telephone company building to call her mother. Armed with exactly three minutes' worth of change, she listened to the number ringing and tried to pry open a beer bottle by sticking the head into the coin return slot. When the bottle got stuck, she tried to lever it down.

Georgia answered as Anna cursed the bottle and the phone company. "Anna? Where are you? What's happened?"

"Goddamn it—I've got a beer bottle stuck in the coin slot. A perfectly good bottle of beer gone to waste. You should get my change-of-address card by Saturday. No phone yet. Love to Frank."

"I don't know what good it'll do," Georgia said doubtfully. "I'll try, but I've never seen him so upset with you. What's that noise? Where are you?"

Anna had succeeded in cracking the head of the bottle. Beer foamed out of the fissure and ran down her arm. "I have to go. There's beer running all over me. Tell Frank a million bucks wouldn't have gotten me that shop. Even if the Phantom Mechanic had been Howard Hughes, I still wouldn't have gotten that shop. Maybe the Phantom Master Mechanic really was Howard Hughes. How tall was he? Did his feet stick out of the bed?"

"Anna, are you intoxicating yourself in public? Where are you? Are you at a bus station?"

"Why? Is Ronnie Mauss in the neighborhood again?" Anna almost wished she had two more minutes' worth of change. Two more minutes and she might have her mother on the defensive. She licked beer off her wrist. A train whistle rattled the telephone company's windows.

Georgia raised her voice. "You're wasting good money. You'd think a woman on her own could find out the train schedule and call in between trains. At least you're not at a bus station. I can't stand bus stations—"

"Time's up." Anna clicked the receiver hook and hung up. Picking a fight long distance wouldn't work. High school basketball courts were good places to pick fights. Words were no substitute for the physical release of a shove. Knowing how to jab an elbow into the soft space between ribs and whirling away were part of the game. Words were only good for inciting the physical. The fights men had in movies where they wound up respecting each other weren't anything like the fights Anna had seen or been involved in. Bruises appeared instantly on the screen and somehow managed to adorn the huge face.

She wondered if women in general were more unforgiving because their fights usually weren't physical, or if men were born wearing the possibility of uniforms and guns, knowing that they were expected to inflict damage before they were provoked. But then she couldn't imagine Ronnie Mauss and Bryan fighting and shaking hands, buying drinks for each other and toasting their new understanding and respect for each other. That was the movies. Anna moved her body to hide the bottle jutting out of the coin return as a car passed.

And fights between men and women. She didn't even want to get started on that one. The small part of her that wanted to take responsibility for Ronnie Mauss's blows insisted on testing other men's limits. She'd pushed Bryan more than once to see how far he would go. Red-faced, he'd fling his clothes off until a piece littered every room and reappear in shorts and running shoes. After negotiating his own one-sided truce, he would return light-headed and clean-lunged.

Bryan took displacement hard. He would think she had deserted Jo. He would never forgive her for that.

———

Willi left for Florida the next day. After leafing through the manual, Anna saw Willi envisioned a future with Trend-Setters franchises from coast to coast complete with a fleet of yellow and white Cadillacs with personalized WILLI T-S license plates.

"There are always rules and regulations," Willi's introduction to the manual read. "I'm constantly impressed by the creativity with which guidelines are followed. There is a great amount of flexibility between two points."

The two points of opening and closing and everything in between were spelled out clearly in the manual. Anna almost chucked it, but she made herself follow the pages of starred and single-spaced instructions. The individual sinks and the cordless yellow telephones with their own extensions gave the appearance of privacy and independence until she stepped back and saw the conformity of the whole. A desire for the rivalry for sink space and telephone time at Mary Frances's hit Anna. She looked at the spotless yellow kimono that had ANNA embroidered across it. Forget about sending down those deep roots, she told herself. Go for the ones that spread shallow and fast.

Step 16, page two of the section on opening detailed the making of coffee. Ten tablespoons were to be scooped, leveled by a knife blade, and emptied into the filter. Anna used eight heaping tablespoons and bypassed 16c, which was the adding of a rounded teaspoon of cinnamon. What if the mirrors were two-way and

Willi's accountant was hidden behind one of them, tallying her mistakes? She spun around to face all corners of the room. The face reflected back to her was sharp and suspicious. Lines were making themselves at home on her forehead. Anna tried to roll the tension out of her neck. All she had to do was obey the rules. It was Willi's shop. But she had a feeling that Step 243 would land her inside a closet with a locked door.

As Anna was remeasuring the coffee, the back door slammed. Elidia, one of Willi's operators, silent and unblinking, stood beside the washing machine. Her thick bangs, swatches of auburn, gold and beige, followed the curve of her rounded eyebrows and met in a V at the bridge of her nose. Her black, heavily fibered eyelashes seemed woven into her bangs. Halos of cover stick highlighted her obsidian eyes. The markings always reminded Anna of an owl. They had met at a convention in Houston, where Elidia had taken notes and Polaroid shots of all the demonstrations. Lifting her chin in greeting, Anna continued to measure.

"Scab," Elidia said.

Anna shaved the knife blade across the last spoonful of coffee and ignored Elidia.

Ten seconds later Susie barreled in the door. The collar of the man's shirt she wore rode an inch above her shoulders as if somebody had tried to pick her up by the neck. Her short platinum hair spiked in different directions. Earrings flowered along the borders of her ears.

"Let's just get this straight right off," Susie said. "Elidia wanted to be manager—*wants* to be manager—got it? She'll never tell you to your face. You'll find out when her mother slits your sheets at the Laundromat. You get on Elidia's bad side, you get on Elidia's family's bad side, and you don't get the good dryers at the Laundromat. You get fatty pork chops from the butcher at the grocery store and forget about getting your yard mowed. They wouldn't leave a tree standing. You might as well forget the sweet tamales at Christmas and her grandmother's tea, which is too bad, because I haven't had bad cramps since I started drinking it."

"I line-dry my clothes. I'll manage the other things."

"Let's get this totally straight," Susie lectured Elidia, "Willi's decided she's the manager—it doesn't matter if she's out-of-town talent—Anna's the manager while Willi's gone."

Elidia turned to face the back door. "A lot can happen in two months."

Susie palmed her ears closed. "There is no way—no way—I'm getting in the middle of this mess. My chair may be between you two but I ain't passing notes back and forth. There is no way."

Anna approached Elidia's chair. "You can be as obnoxious here as you want as long as it doesn't affect your work. If that's too tough for you, then I can recommend a shop in Alpine that's short somebody." She was beginning to feel like the warden in a women's prison movie and enjoying it.

Elidia remained impassive. "I don't run away when I don't get my way."

Anna carefully rewrapped her kimono before answering. She stared steadily into Elidia's eyes and swore not to say anything until the woman blinked. Her own eyes began to burn. Elidia's thick eyelids shuttered quickly. "The only thing I expect from you is good work. If you want to take over as manager, go ahead and try it."

"Let me tell you"—Susie sighed—"it's going to be a *long* two months."

"Step twenty-two has your name on it," Anna said and tossed the manual to Elidia.

———

Elidia used her customers as guinea pigs. Anna couldn't tell yet if Elidia was searching for a technique, trying to hide the fact that she didn't have one, or if variety was her technique. She used cloth twists to roll her first customer's hair. The woman remained as impassive as Elidia, out of fear, sleepiness or complete confidence.

Susie was all repetitive action. She drew a roller's worth of hair with surgical precision, but the section of hair would droop over her thin, ringed fingers and dry while she talked on the telephone and groped madly through her jumbled curler tray, stopping long enough to choreograph her words in the air. Every time Anna felt like snatching the comb out of her hand, Susie would rewet the section and instantly have a line of curlers embedded, smoothly rolled and securely anchored. Anna had never seen hands flash so fast once they were in motion. Then another tail of hair would wave while Susie got sidetracked again.

Anna preferred a steady rhythm. She never tried a new procedure cold on a customer. She practiced on wigs and switches until she knew how any type of hair would respond—permed, tinted, thick or fine. "You'd think she was a doctor," Jo had cracked, "worried about malpractice." But on slow days they had sometimes raced to see who could finish a customer first. The women had been spun out of the chairs so fast they complained of dizziness. Anna could see that dizziness wouldn't be condoned at Willi's.

The telephone at her station rang. Each operator had a different number in addition to the central line at Willi's desk. Anna kept thinking that the yellow instrument hanging on the wall was a cordless neck razor or a cordless broom. "Hello." Her fingers, reaching automatically to walk the ridges of a cord, were disappointed.

Delia's voice came out of the receiver. "I hear my father fished you out of the lake. You better watch out. He's got this thing about trying to save people. Only he's not very good at it."

Anna hated having the events in her life teletyped and then garbled in the process. "Who gave you this number?"

"Not my father. God, was he surprised to find out you'd left town."

"Bevo," Anna guessed. "You called Mary Frances's."

"He's a gold mine. He must know tons of stuff—"

"I don't want you to call me anymore."

"You know what? I got an A on that biology test—"

There was a call waiting click on Anna's line. "This isn't Mary Frances's. Don't call me anymore. Somebody's trying to get through."

"It's probably my dad. Just remember," Delia said quickly, "I found you first. You were my friend first."

Anna pressed the dial tone button twice to disconnect all calls.

She left the receiver on the counter, buttons up, and finished combing out her customer.

At six o'clock, after Elidia and Susie had left, Anna reactivated the phone for Willi's call. She sat under a dryer to get a new perspective. Susie's cluttered station looked lived in. A postcard from Epcot Center was stuck in one corner of her mirror, and a plastic lei, a memento from a client's Hawaiian vacation, dangled from a drawer knob.

There was no personal decoration at Elidia's station. It was so clean and neat that it looked brand-new. Willi must have a rule in the manual somewhere listing the amount and types of personal possessions that were allowed at the stations. Anna couldn't find a trace of herself on the counter Willi had assigned to her. She wanted to keep it that way. Nobody would send postcards, and no client would feel obliged to bring her back a souvenir. She wasn't about to get on anybody's list.

Willi called at six-thirty, on schedule. "How did it go?"

Anna thumped the manual with her thumb. "It's pretty straightforward. It seems Elidia considers herself manager material."

"Elidia relies on the specter of her family to get what she wants. I don't have the time for people who cannot take care of themselves. How can they be trusted to handle something outside of themselves, something bigger and more important? No. Elidia is not manager material. You may have to go to Alpine for a week or so to buy your meat. Vernon said the daily figures were good. I'm pleased. I will call next week."

Willi's small parking lot had once been a tennis court. The rusted net poles were dented by years of car fenders. Anna had driven to work, something she never did. In Alpine a hard rain usually wasn't enough to convince her to take the Valiant out of the garage. Cars were for the long hauls, but this shop, this move made her uneasy. She was out of practice; she couldn't tell if she had gone too far or not far enough.

That night not even pink-rimmed brisket in a warm flour tortilla was satisfying. Anna wandered out to her slab of porch and finished a cold beer. A grove of pecan trees with straight trunks fronted the small house. Limbs branched from their trunks at six feet. They weren't good climbing trees. When a foursquare pattern of light from the main house slanted across her legs, she went inside to watch the black-and-white television Bryan had left behind. By the end of the first show the wig stands were unpacked and clamped to the wide-lipped kitchen counter.

Anna could hear Ed Nettinger's car radio from clear across the street. A straw hat was tilted low over his gray eyes. One elbow stuck out of the driver's open window and the other arm was stretched across the back of the front seat. The reception of the Alpine station on his radio was poor as if he thought she wouldn't be able to resist the urge to come out and tune it.

Willi's was the only commercial building on the block. There was the possibility that an irate neighbor might order him off the street. The surrounding residential community had a history of complaints about fumes and parking problems and the firing of Willi's neon sign. A brief paragraph of neighborhood rezoning attempts and restraining orders appeared in the Trend-Setters' manual. If Ed didn't turn down his radio, he might be included in the next edition.

Anna fingered the dent in her scalp that a pair of pliers in his station wagon had made. She remembered her hand shooting through the air, reaching for something to hold on to. Ed's lips had been dry and their last kiss off-center. "When will I see you again?" had waited behind his teeth. Grace Nettinger had probably been hovering over them, staring through the windshield while they tussled with the tarp, her ghost trying furiously to rip the air apart and burst back into her old dimension.

"Are you trying to get me fired?" she called across the street to him.

He tipped his hat back and started a grin. His whole weathered face participated. That smile was trouble. Anna crossed the street without looking. She wished she had bet money on whether or not he'd check both directions for her. His door opened in case he had to bound into oncoming traffic.

"Lucky nobody was coming," he said.

Anna leaned against the station wagon and rocked the open door. "How long do you intend to stay out here?"

Ed inhaled appreciatively. "It's a good day to be sitting outside with the radio on, waiting for somebody."

"Why didn't you come in?" She swung her body close to him but avoided his hand. "Don't you want to know how Willi's smells?"

He smoothed her thigh. "I thought I might be able to pick up the scent from you."

"Think so?" Anna bent down and inflicted a kiss upon him. His passion surprised her again. Daylight and occupied houses on their blankets of lawn didn't faze him. Her actions had backfired again. One more try. She bunched her dress and began to hitch it up her legs. "Maybe I should just lift my dress over my head and let you bury your face?"

Ed sat back. He cradled the steering wheel and squinted through the blue atmosphere high on the windshield. "Whichever way you want it, Anna," he said. "You pull your dress up over your head and I'll bury my face. Is that the way you want it?"

Anna let her dress fall. "I'm just trying to figure out what you want."

"I don't need a punching bag, and I don't need a green card. Somebody to have dinner with tonight is as far as I've gotten. How about some of Hallie's chicken?"

"Not Hallie's. And it's only four-thirty," Anna pointed out. "Hallie's doesn't even open till six."

Ed found the soft spot behind her knees. "We could go someplace else."

Anna's body became less generous. "I don't like crumbs in my bed."

"It was a serious dinner invitation, Anna. If all I wanted was to get you into bed, I would have said so. There's no reason for me to sugarcoat it."

"But I bet you used to dissolve aspirin in orange juice for Delia. Here." Anna handed the frosting kit she had been holding to Ed.

"Collateral. I'll meet you at the hotel for drinks at seven-thirty. Then we'll see about Hallie's."

———

The right side of Anna's bed was pushed against the back wall. Propped up by pillows, she could look out the window into the backyard of the big house. A volleyball net in the middle of the yard threw a grid across her view of staked tomato plants and kinked watermelon vines. A game would start in thirty minutes, at seven, even though the sun was still high enough to put the eastern team members at a disadvantage. They usually couldn't return serves until the sun sank lower in the sky and was diluted by apple and pear trees.

The volleyball thumped against Anna's back wall with the leathery sound of a rotting gourd. A lone player was serving practice balls over the net, and two on the eastern side were practicing spiking. When the constant bombardment of her wall stopped, it meant practice was over and it was time to meet Ed Nettinger at the hotel. She hoped he'd gotten them a room and had given up the idea of Hallie's in favor of room service. They needed neutral territory.

Willi's manual was propped against the windowsill. Anna wanted to memorize it quickly. Her arms ached from carrying it around for reference all week. The weight of it was the only thing keeping her at Trend-Setters. She held the telephone receiver against her stomach and tried to dial Jo's number without looking.

Coming out of a spike, a woman on the eastern side got her ring caught in the volleyball net. Deflected by the raised slats of glass in Anna's window, the ball was ignored as the other two players tried to untangle the ring without damaging the net. Anna couldn't remember which three in Jo's number she had gotten to. She replaced the receiver and decided to call if the ring was free by the time she had to leave.

Ten minutes later Anna had her scissors case unsnapped and was about to go out and cut the ring loose herself. The players were too much like Jo, wasting precious time to save one string of netting, one strand of hair, one fingernail, at the expense of stopping the whole game. She shook the scissors off her fingers and dug her backbone into the pillows. "There," she said aloud. "Free will. Free will." Whatever made the earth spin and the stars shine and the sun rise and set, whatever it was—she hoped it had seen her back off and was busy recalculating her points.

Ed snapped his fingers in front of Anna's face. "Am I supposed to put on my pants and go now?"

Anna plumped her pillow. Resting against the headboard, she could see the snipped panes of volleyball net etched across the night sky. She was disappointed that the diamond ring wasn't dangling from an uncut net. "What about your reputation?" she asked. "Don't city councilmen have reputations? What if the newspapers got wind of this?"

"This is another city. I think I'd weather it." He unfolded a long leg and entwined one of hers. "What about your reputation?"

"This"—she flopped her hand—"this whole thing can only add to it."

"Well, as long as you get something out of this—this whole thing," Ed said. "I still don't know if I should put on my pants and go yet. When am I going to get the poke in the ribs?"

Anna shifted restlessly. "Pretty soon now, if you don't keep quiet." She rocked her free leg and watched as shadows liquefied and spilled down the sheet. "A woman got her diamond ring caught in that volleyball net this afternoon."

The pressure of Ed's body remained constant. "Let's talk about what's going on in here. You left town awful fast. Something happened on that boat. I might be a little rusty but not enough to send you screaming into the night, never to be seen again. What was in that envelope Jo gave me to give you?"

"You shouldn't take it personally." Anna didn't want to talk about the cashier's check in the envelope or what had happened on the houseboat.

"That's it?" He drew the top sheet away from their bodies.

"There's nobody else in this bed, there's only you and me. One of these days—listen—one of these days you're going to have to decide whether this is personal."

The desire to confide in Ed was too strong. He could be her ally and keep watch over Jo. He could teach her how to grieve properly for someone. Feeling herself being pulled back by his presence, Anna separated her leg from his. Holding the soles of her feet, she was able to conjure up Grace Nettinger sitting in the armchair. If she could summon Grace so easily, Ed must see her everywhere.

Anna resisted the urge to inflict Grace upon him so soon. She rolled out of bed and found his pants. "Here. You'd better go."

———

The appointment book confirmed that Anna was free on the second Tuesday in September. "Sorry. That day's booked solid. I'd stick with Mary Frances if I were you—" She cradled the telephone and almost cut off the woman when her chin hit the redial button. "Sorry. . . . Right. . . . Be-Jo's, Styles Unlimited. I wasn't sure which name they'd decided on. . . . Uh-huh. A friendly split. Time to move on. I'd recommend Jo. . . ." Anna let the sentence hang, but the woman at the other end of the line didn't volunteer any information.

A crochet hook clamped between her teeth, Susie looked over Anna's shoulder. "I thought Willi was giving you a piece of the action."

Elidia's hair dryer shifted to a quieter speed.

"I'm not interested in money," Anna said. She had deposited the cashier's check in the Marfa bank that morning. "Mary Frances had a great pension plan. I took early retirement."

Susie turned back to her chair and seemed surprised to see a woman sitting there. A frosting cap was tied under her chin and strands of hair sprouted through the holes. "Sounds like a *real* friendly split to me."

Tremors shook Elidia's bangs. "You don't care about money, you don't care about being the manager—what do you care about?"

Anna tried to consider the question carefully, but her attention wandered to the sky visible through the front door. Thunderheads had been building up all morning. The change in atmosphere gave the walls a greenish cast. Three months ago she would have thrown off the question with a shrug and a flip "Not much" just to get a reaction from Elidia.

Well, she had learned her lesson. Now, when she knew better than to chance defiance, she had nothing to protect and so nothing to sacrifice. Her inner slate was wiped clean. There were no images and there was no pain when she looked at Elidia and said in a neutral voice, "Not much."

very afternoon during the first week of September clouds banked to the north. Staring out Willi's front window, Anna began to feel like a drought-stricken rancher. The daily standoff was getting on her nerves. She wanted to yell at the clouds to stop sending out their scouting parties. They should either drop their heavy loads of rain or move on.

On Monday of the second week a few isolated clouds finally broke away from the mass. By mid-afternoon they had drifted over Marfa. Water gushed out of the clouds; washes of sunshine alternated with the downpours. Anna had to drive to work on Tuesday with her window rolled down, sticking her head out if she wanted to see anything farther than five feet ahead. The Valiant's wipers were useless against the solid line of rain drilling against the windshield. She wished, briefly, that she were back at Mary Frances's, watching the water rise in the creek. And then she reminded herself that there was a perfectly good creek in Marfa that would fill up today and dry out tomorrow. There was no need to go back to Mary Frances's.

While Anna sat underneath two heat lamps to dry out and read the manual, Elidia handled cancellations as they were phoned in. Its back cracked, the appointment book lay open to her smoothing and confirming touch. An entry distressed her and she sniffed at the page. "You booked Amy Dominguez and Roxanne Schieder on the same day."

Anna didn't look up from her reading. She was hoping the heat lamps would set the manual on fire. Single pages of it were scattered all over the shop, marking the spots where her attention had died.

"You're not supposed to book them on the same day. They hate each other."

"Too bad," Anna said.

Susie slapped a king of hearts on the manicure table and anchored the card with a bottle of cuticle softener. "Elidia's right —they've got lawsuits out on each other, and let me tell you— I am too young to die."

Elidia shook the appointment book and loose pages of the manual fell out. "What are you going to do about it?"

Anna slammed the vinyl binder shut. "Nothing."

"This isn't your place," Elidia said. "You have to do what the manual says. When Willi gets back—"

"How can I get this thing memorized if you keep interrupting me all the time?"

Susie tried to twist her hair into her ears. "Here we go again."

"Then I'll reschedule them myself," Elidia threatened.

"You're just making more work for yourself," Anna said.

As Elidia made the first call, Susie rolled closer to Anna. "Are you doing what I think you're doing? Making her mad could backfire. It won't work anyway—Willi doesn't want to make her manager. You may be handing the reins over to her, but—"

"Look. This is a beauty shop. Not a court of law. Not a boxing ring in Las Vegas. Not group therapy. I'm not here to handle anybody's dirty laundry. If somebody needs a cut and set to push-start herself—fine. It's my hands, not my mouth, that're

going to get her going. I won't make allowances for them. It's
encouraging weakness—I won't do it. I don't want to hear about
anybody's problems."

Fanning through the deck, Susie found a jack of diamonds to
play. "Is everything always so black and white with you?" The
close crack of thunder made her spill the cards. A second later the
lights went out.

Elidia hurried around the room and pulled all the electrical
cords out of the walls. She unplugged the coffeemaker, the dryers,
Susie's radio, the heat lamps and her own curling iron. "Don't use
the phones either. They carry electricity."

Watching Elidia's movements made Anna tired. She wished
the armrests between the dryer chairs folded up the way the ones
on airplanes did so she could stretch out. "Do you know what the
chances of your getting hit by lightning are?"

"Forty-eight, forty-nine, fifty—damn," Susie said. She stood up
and shook out her shirt. "Lift your feet, Anna. I'm missing a
queen. So what are you going to do when Willi comes back? Lift
up your other foot. Do you really have enough money so you won't
have to work?"

"Texas isn't even number one in the nation when it comes to
getting hit by lightning," Anna said. She lifted her feet for Susie
but ignored the financial questions. "Florida is. All those golf
courses."

Elidia brushed her long black hair. The bristles ignited tiny
silver and blue sparks from her crown to her shoulders. "Willi
would never let her man play golf in the rain."

Anna laughed. "Is that written down in the manual, too? What
if she's got him insured? If he doesn't get hit in Florida, she can
bring him back here, and he can play on the only mile-high course
in the world. The lightning won't have to go so far to get him."

In search of lost cards Susie's platinum head bobbed underneath each dryer. A residue of light seemed to be trapped in her
hair. "I knew somebody once that got struck by lightning—where
is that goddamn card? Anna—you aren't hiding it from me, are
you?"

"Are you sure you had fifty-two in the first place?" Anna asked.

Elidia would pick up the thread of Susie's story. The two operators were a good match. Susie had more talent, but Elidia had more skill. Without Susie's constant search for entertainment Elidia's blinkered precision would be deadly.

"What are you going to do when Willi comes back, Anna?" Susie asked. "You don't really have enough money so you don't have to work . . . I just thought I'd try asking again. . . ."

The fluorescent hands of Willi's battery-operated clock read "3:15." Anna swore it had been 3:15 an hour ago. If time had slowed down, then she had nothing to worry about. But if it hadn't, she would have to decide soon where to go next. Ed Nettinger was her only loose end, and she had delayed too long in cutting that last tie.

"What did the lightning do to your friend?" Elidia asked. "He was probably close to a place he shouldn't have been, someplace where there was a death or where somebody was buried."

"Oh, he can't hear out of one ear, and all the change in his pocket melted together. He's fine. Really, Anna. What are you going to do once Willi comes back?"

"Nothing," Anna said.

The day after the storm was clear and bright. Anna decided she'd been getting too lazy. It was time to pay Ed Nettinger a house call. She took the phone back into bed with her and called the shop to make Elidia manager for the day.

When Anna drove up, Ed was standing in the middle of the newly filled bass pond. Baggy plaid shorts hung precariously from his waist. There was something so ridiculous about his standing knee-deep in water and talking to fish that Anna felt ready to defend him. She had to remind herself that if he needed defending, it would be from her. The last thing she needed was to be around somebody who made her think she could work without a net.

Anna took off her sandals and waded into the pond.

"It's the first time you've come out on your own." Ed smiled.

"Don't take out a newspaper ad or anything. I've come to treat your hair." Fish nuzzled her ankle. She sidestepped a wide underwater mouth. "Have you fed these things lately?"

"They're just excited." Ed helped Anna onto the bank. "Do I get a shampoo, too?"

"The works. Wait." She dabbled her toes and then washed off the mud that flecked his pink heels.

Ed backed up and stepped behind Anna. "How about I shampoo you?" He engaged her arms as if they were about to tango toward the white-washed adobe bunkhouse where he lived.

Capturing the lead, Anna negotiated him toward the charred remains of the ranch house. The rock spine of a chimney rose above the trees but its alignment was way off. Most of the second story had fallen into the first, and bowlegged porch supports held the sagging lap of roof. Delia had said that nothing had been touched since the fire; kitchen drawers still held complete table settings of silverware. This was a hopeful sign. The fire had been five years ago.

"Was it really an accident? Or did she set it on fire?"

"It was an accident all right. Grace didn't like pain."

"Why don't you rebuild?"

"I thought once, if Delia wanted me to, I would, but I don't imagine she'll ever come back out here to live. She feels more comfortable at the house in town. I've got the bunkhouse. It's not a priority."

The answer didn't satisfy Anna. Leaving the house in ruin had to be either a sign of slothfulness or a monument to Grace. Ed didn't look as if he had anything to hide. Maybe he really didn't think he did. Maybe that was his fatal flaw. She renewed her search of the landscape and was rewarded by a wrought-iron fence overgrown with rosebushes. "What's that over there?"

"The old family cemetery. "Let me go get my clippers and we'll take a look."

Anna went on without him. She parted the long, thorny branches and looked for the unmarked space that should have been Grace's. Nell Ames, Grace's grandmother, had been reburied with a simple granite marker. The three upright headstones behind Nell's were too worn to read. Two impacted marble plaques were pressed into opposite corners of the plot. GIRL CUTH-BERSON's life-span of three days had been one day longer than BOY CUTHBERSON's.

Dressed in overalls and still shirtless, Ed came up the grassy incline. He tested rocks with his boot and rolled loose ones out of the way. A bottle of beer was stuck in each pocket.

"Which Cuthbersons are these?" Anna asked.

"They're the grandbabies of the Baylors, the people who used to live here. The two on the left are Mr. Baylor's parents, and the other one standing is Mrs. Baylor's aunt."

"They just left them here? Where did they go?"

Ed threaded a rose branch through the iron railings. "They were repossessed. I don't know that they had that much of a choice." He broke off a rose and tucked it into one of Anna's buttonholes. "And no matter how much people meant to me, I don't think I'd want to keep digging them up and carting them around with me. They're looked after. That's my spot over there in the first row."

"They've never come back to visit them?" There was something wrong about all this. The marking of a grave meant nothing if there was nobody left to recall the name. Leaving the living kept an infinite number of possibilities open. Deserting the dead sealed their mortality.

"Are you thinking about that whole side of family that you don't know, your father's side of the family?" Ed asked.

"No. That's different," Anna said impatiently. "I never knew him. It's not the same as knowing somebody. Knowing them and seeing them die. And then leaving them."

"Then I'm a little surprised you're taking this so hard. You don't strike me as a woman who'd spend much time around the dead."

Anna was stung by his implied criticism. "So why didn't you bury Grace out here?"

Scratches reddened the tender skin of Ed's inner arm. He reached in again to twine another branch. "She'd never have let me have any peace if I'd done that to her, stuck her out here forever and ever, so she'd never get into town again."

The harshness in Ed's face that Anna had seen at the funeral home as he looked down at Grace hadn't been anger or the need for retaliation as she'd first thought. The harshness was only a physical product of sun and wind. But Grace was bound to have had the same erosive effect on him inside. Her death couldn't have left him with nothing to settle.

"Don't you hate her for what she did? Somewhere? Deep down?"

"She didn't do anything to me. She did it all to herself."

"She did something to Delia."

"Just who do you care more about—Delia or me or Grace?" He pocketed the clippers and started down the hill.

Anna had no choice but to follow him to the water trough. "Didn't you want to fight for her at all? Didn't you love her? Ever?"

Ed flipped his handkerchief into a rope and wet it. He halved the length and swabbed his arms. "I did everything I could. I learned a lot living with Grace that maybe I never would have learned from another woman, but I'm not going to drink myself into a ditch for her, and I won't do it for you. I won't do it for anybody. I grieved for her a long time before she died."

"When did you give up on her?"

Ed slung the handkerchief around his neck. "Are you asking me if I'm capable of love, if you can trust me to stick by you? Is that what you want to know?"

Anna couldn't believe that he thought she was so transparent and that he thought he didn't have anything to prove. "It's just hard to understand." She shrugged. "You wonder, you know . . . what happened."

"Don't judge either Grace, or me, by what you think we did to each other."

"Fine." This wasn't getting her anywhere. It was time to change tactics. She pointed to the short-haired moss that was attached to the trough's sides. "That water doesn't look too clean."

"It's nice to see you're so concerned, I've got some hydrogen peroxide at the bunkhouse."

"Good. I can use it to put streaks in your hair."

"Hold on," Ed said. "What are you going to do to me?"

The beginning of suspicion was a good sign. "Shampoo. Trim. Conditioner. The works. You can trust me with your hair," Anna said truthfully.

While Ed doctored himself, she sat on the front porch steps. Several weeks' worth of the Alpine newspaper were folded beside a rocking chair. Anna ran through them quickly, hunting for Jo's name in the "Hospital Ins and Outs" column first, but it wasn't listed there. Next she skimmed the one-paragraph local items spotted in between wedding stories, nursing home news and beef recipes to see if Jo and Burgess had gone to El Paso or Houston for the weekend. A SIESTA sign had been drawn in under Mrs. Long's "Longitudes and Latitudes" by-line. The college had given Alfred a retirement lunch. She found Willi's ad but none announcing Bevo's arrival and the change of ownership.

Ed sat beside Anna. He tapped the newspaper. "If you want to keep up, I'll bring them over after I'm done with them."

"No." Anna refolded the paper and unfastened her scissors case. "I wasn't looking for news. I just needed something to catch the hair."

Anna received a packet of mail forwarded from Mary Frances's. Jo had inked out the addresses and written in Willi's address. The heavy back slant seemed as strong as ever.

"Does your grandmother know anything about reading people's handwriting?" Anna asked Elidia. "For signs about the future. Love. Money. Health. Anything like that?"

"She's a *curandera*, not a Gypsy," Elidia said. "You're so superstitious."

Susie had dealt out Anna's forwarded correspondence by last name and ended up with six piles. "Are these all you? Bryan, O'Bryan, Rawlings, Mauss, Leandros, Gebhardt."

"Second husband, second husband misspelling, mother's maiden name, first husband, father's name, stepfather's name."

"Well, which one are you?" Susie pressed.

"None of them."

Susie didn't look convinced. "You have to be *one* of them— you have to have a *name.*"

"Rawlings then. My mother's maiden name is the closest I would come. It costs too much to keep going back to court and getting it changed." Anna turned to Elidia. "I am not superstitious."

The front door warning bell rang. A young woman wearing a maroon scarf and sunglasses stood on the welcome mat. The grinding of her heels kept tripping the bell. She passed a leather-gloved hand in front of the door to disable an electric eye.

"It stops once you're off the mat," Anna called.

Susie looked over Anna's shoulder and whispered, "Not one of mine. It's almost ninety outside—what's she doing in that getup?"

Elidia dismissed the woman with a heavy-lashed blink. "You're the manager," she told Anna. "You decide which one of us gets her, or I can call my grandmother and see what her crystal ball says to do."

The woman sat down in one of the uncomfortable cloth chairs in the waiting room. She looked like someone who existed in a shell of comfort. She looked as if she were used to being waited on. No way, Anna thought. She'll have to come to the doorway and ask for an appointment.

"Are those *diamonds?*" Susie whispered when the woman hiked her sleeve to check the time.

Old bruises, fading to brown and yellow, colored the woman's wrist. "That's not all she's got," Anna said. The injuries made her heart speed up.

Susie shrugged. "If you've got diamonds to cover them up, who cares?"

"It's no joke," Anna snapped. There was no way she would take the woman into the shop. Willi's wasn't a halfway house for battered women.

Susie blushed and hunched her shoulders and twisted her bangs until they cowlicked. "I didn't—"

Anna wiped her hands on a towel. "Never mind. I'll see what she wants."

The woman beat her to the doorway. "You're Ronnie's ex-wife." Her long, thin lips, planed smoothly across her delicately boned face, split in satisfaction. "I knew it. I knew it had to be someone like you. I could tell." She looked Anna up and down. "He was right. He was absolutely right about you."

Anna wanted to tell the woman the joke was over; it was time to wash the makeup off her wrist and take off the sunglasses, but her attitude of assurance and lack of emotion were too familiar. Ronnie Mauss had learned a lot from this woman. "I'll meet you outside in two minutes."

"I have three twenty-six." The woman modeled her wrist without shame again. "Two minutes then."

Good, Anna thought. Let's get this over with. She finished squirting neutralizer on her customer's hair, fitted the plastic cap over the curlers and set the timer. "Elidia, check her in ten minutes if I'm not back."

Susie brandished her telephone. "What should I do? What do you want me to do? Do you want us to go out there with you?"

"Look out the window in a couple of minutes. If there's a guy out there with us who's got curly brown hair and a sweet face, call the police."

The woman was standing next to the silver Volvo Ronnie had been driving in June. Anna recognized the Louisiana license plates and the dent in the rear fender. Feeling as if there were a target pinned to her chest, she swept the area for any sign of him.

"What do you want?" Anna asked when she had crossed open ground safely and reached the Volvo.

"Ronnie Mauss," the woman replied.

"It looks like you've already got him."

"What did you do to him?"

"Not nearly as much as he did to me." Anna nodded toward the woman's bruised wrist. "Or you. Is that the first time?"

The woman clenched her fists. "I want to help him."

"You've got your work cut out for you."

"You're just like he said you'd be. I'm not giving up on him. I'm not running away when things get a little tough."

"You better have something else planned then."

The woman nodded. "I see now. I see now what it was all about. I never believed it was his doing. You're the one. You are the one."

Nothing in Anna responded. Any marks left by Ronnie Mauss weren't her fault. The little part of accepted responsibility that she had kept in reserve for Ronnie Mauss's defense could go over to this other woman's side. Anna felt generous. "Look. If it's easier to blame me—fine."

"It's not easier. It's the truth," the woman answered.

"What's your name?" Anna asked. "Where do you live?" Somebody should be alerted. She stopped herself. It was their dance. Maybe it was a good thing for the rest of the world that they had found each other.

"I used to try to get him to talk about his father, to see if his father hit him, if his father hit his mother. All he would say is 'Anna. Ask Anna.' "

"You can't save him. The only thing you can do is protect yourself."

"And then I talked to your mother. It explains a lot, but it's no excuse. You abandoned him. You're the one who was reliving everything. You wanted him to leave you, and he wouldn't, so you climbed out a window. You abandoned him, you deserted him, when he needed you the most. You never loved him."

The news about a visit to her mother jolted Anna. She hoped the visit to Georgia was a lie supplied by Ronnie. If he couldn't be there to deliver a blow in person, the next best thing would be to have his girlfriend be the courier. "And what about your mother? Has she made a career out of getting hit?"

"You can't hurt us," the woman said. "You can't hurt us anymore."

Anna had nothing left to say. Words of sympathy or advice or self-defense would be wasted. The woman seemed as satisfied as Ronnie Mauss had been to blame somebody else. When Ronnie hit her again, she would have a picture of a third party to project her anger and humiliation upon. Anna's business with Ronnie Mauss was finished. Standing right in front of her was a future she'd managed to escape. The account was closed.

The woman took off her sunglasses and displayed a black eye that looked several days old. What she wanted to see must have registered on Anna's face because she smiled and walked to the Volvo.

———

Anna spent the rest of the morning taking inventory of Willi's supplies, which were stored in a prefabricated shed in back of the shop. Crape myrtle bushes separated the shed from the main building and disguised the fact that she was having to count the packages of butterfly hair clips for the third time.

"Coming through!" Susie shouted. "Urgent call for Anna!" Snapping her fingers to inner music, she box-stepped through a break in the crape myrtle bushes. "Here—long distance. It's a man, but not Mr. Catfish."

Waiting for Anna to take the phone, Susie ran her fingers on a search-and-destroy mission through her bleached hair. "What do you think about a purple streak here—and here, like that crape myrtle when it blooms?" Her hand dropped. "I guess not."

Anna considered tossing the receiver into the bushes, but that didn't seem as if it would be as instantaneously gratifying as jerking a phone cord out of the wall would be. It looked like only half a thing. She hated the fact that the phone's mobility made her so accessible, and despite that accessibility, her mother hadn't told her what was coming.

"Anna!" Bevo's voice exaggerated his relief. "I didn't think you were *ever* going to answer. This *is* long distance after all."

Anna's heart seized up at the sound of Bevo's voice, but she thought the exaggeration in his voice was a good sign.

"Anna, don't hang up. We have vital information for you. *Vital.*"

The telephone was so weightless that she couldn't imagine anything vital being transmitted through it. Paying attention to Bevo's "we," Anna thought she caught crosscurrents of breath from Mary Frances's upstairs extension. "What vital information could you possibly have for me?"

Bevo's voice strolled. "Don't be so impatient—"

Jo interrupted. "Some woman came in today wanting to know which one of us was Ronnie Mauss's ex-wife."

"Naturally we thought of you," Bevo said.

"She's been and gone," Anna said. "What did you do? Draw her a map? Between you and Georgia—" The instrument in her hand was connected to nothing, but there was Jo's voice coming out of it, strong and clear. She wanted that voice to go on talking and never stop.

"I take it you were addressing my son," Jo said. "I didn't send her over. You understand? No matter what's passed between us, I would never have sent her over."

Bevo broke in excitedly. "You should have heard Jo. She tried to convince her you'd moved to California. She was a *scream*. I almost wet my pants. Of course, Mary Frances blew the whole thing. She swished in in the big middle and saw the diamond watch and just spilled her guts."

"Did that Mauss character put her up to it?" Jo asked.

Anna tried to let Jo's concern slide by, but her throat suddenly wouldn't cooperate. The sound of her own breathing had become more suspect than Jo's. "I think he's met his match with this one."

"Well? What did she want?" Bevo demanded.

"Hush, Charles, leave Anna alone." There was silence on all three lines until Jo continued. "Willi's pretty busy?"

"Pretty busy."

"Anna! Wait until you see! I did this fantastic—really fabulous —raccoon cut and color. It's a circle shag with a ringed tail and everything. You'd have died. It's my zenith."

"If you're letting your son get away with things like that, everything must be all right."

"It's great—" Bevo continued.

"I was talking to your mother," Anna said. "You're no judge of when things are normal."

"I'm still here," Jo said. "Talk to her, Charles. I've got a woman with cotton balls stuck between her toes I've got to tend to."

The sudden absence of Jo's voice created a buzz in Anna's ear. She couldn't tell if it was the connection or a heavier frequency being tuned out. "Is she still smoking?"

"She's cut down a lot," Bevo said. "You'd be surprised. She's doing great—hold on. Next week? Absolutely . . . bring in all the pictures of Elizabeth Taylor you *want.* Sorry, it was Faye Ballinger."

"Don't encourage Faye Ballinger," Anna advised. "You look more like Elizabeth Taylor than she ever will."

"I believe that's one of the nicest things you've ever said to me."

"Try to get her to fight. Promise her a grandbaby if you have to." Anna pushed the seven, zero and redial buttons before she managed to cut Bevo off.

According to the manual, Step 13's estimated time of completion was 6:28 P.M. By 7:28 Anna still had Step 5 in front of her. She'd swept the same pile of hair from one corner to the next and then rounded it into tighter and tighter circles. There was enough hair to outfit two women if they weren't particular about color. In a shuffleboard move Anna sent the hair flying. She knew how Grace Nettinger had felt about being fixed in the wrong spot and that wrong spot being her life. But unlike Grace, she'd diminish the forces of the past. It wasn't Ronnie Mauss who'd brought her to this point; it wasn't Jo's decision not to fight; it was her mother who'd led her down this path.

Reckoning that the long, comfortable habit of guilt had sent Georgia into a back door vigil, Anna called at seven-thirty to interrupt it. "What are you doing?" she asked when her mother answered.

"Anna! There was a woman—"

"She's long gone."

"I didn't want to worry you . . . last time, you said you—"

"Why did you even talk to her?"

"Oh, baby . . . I don't know, I thought I could stop her from going on to you—"

"What did you tell her?"

"She had things completely mixed up. . . . She had the whole story wrong. And she was so—she seemed so . . . lost, and I thought, What if it was Anna in her place?"

"*Lost?*" Anna had to press the receiver against her mouth to stop herself. "I will never, never, be in her place."

"You don't know what it's like not to know!" Georgia cried. "Stop making me pay for what you did!"

"That's not it—that's not what—"

"You betrayed me," Anna said. "You've lied all your life. You're the one who ran away from Michael Leandros. You're the one who broke contact with your family—"

"Don't—it's true! You don't know what happened. He was a wonderful man! Anything could have happened to him, to keep him away from us! You don't know what we had—"

"Nothing. You had nothing because that's the way you wanted it," Anna said. "I won't pay for that anymore." She shoved the phone into a jar of Barbicide. It bobbed gently in the blue liquid disinfectant among the combs. Tiny bubbles escaped from the seams of the phone as if Georgia were still trying to convince someone to believe her.

———

It was almost ten when Anna finished closing. Light fanned into the sky above the high school football stadium. A window-shaking cheer from hundreds of human voices fused into one made her shiver. She thumped the Valiant's gas gauge to get a true reading and drove north. The burn-off jetting from a gas well half an hour away became her beacon. White lights strung along the derrick became visible, and she could see floodlights hitting the trailers that housed offices and living quarters.

Lying against the cold windshield and watching the well burn sapped the heat from Anna's body. She spread her hands in front of the distant flame for warmth. What was she doing in the middle of nowhere? A fifty-eight-mile drive didn't constitute a practice run for her next move. She had fifteen thousand dollars in the bank. She didn't need to drive anywhere; she could hop on a plane and fly around the world. But then she'd have to get to the airport in Midland or El Paso, and either of those places was a three-hour drive. Why not pitch a tent right here? There was a pair of pretty good scissors in the glove compartment. The men stuck out at the well were probably dying for haircuts.

The October chill finally forced her back into the car. Cold air sprayed out of the heater onto her legs. She punched in the lighter and, when it popped out, set it in the ashtray. There was nothing on the radio except high school football, and she was close enough to Marfa to roll down her window and hear a game.

The odometer rolled closer to ninety thousand miles. Anna gunned the accelerator and two tenths of a mile were eaten. With her foot off the gas, the car traveled on its own velocity another tenth of a mile before rolling to a stop. The last number on the odometer, a three, wavered. She concentrated on the numbers as if they were about to click into a winning jackpot. She'd win if the Valiant hit ninety thousand exactly as she pulled up in front of the small house. Everything would be all right then. She zigzagged through town, alternating right and left turns, shaving tenths of a mile off in alleys, then throwing all the savings away in a freewheeling figure eight on the Baptist church parking lot.

The bottom loop consumed more miles than she'd calculated it would. Numbers disappeared as if somebody were holding a giant magnet in the Valiant's direction. Anna shot across vacant lots and a corner of the elementary schoolyard in her race to get home. The last alley dead-ended in the heart of a block.

She'd blown it. Backing out would cost her too much mileage. She left the Valiant where it was with ninety thousand about to click into place and walked two blocks to her own alley. Bevo sat on the front porch, rolling joints.

"It's about time," he said. "Where have you been?"

Anna kicked the Baggies under his legs. "Are you crazy?"

"Let's go inside then. Holy shit, Anna, since when are you so hysterical? Is it that time of the month or what?" He grabbed the key out of her hand and opened the door.

Anna pulled the key from the lock and switched on a lamp. Bevo snatched a red bandanna off the dresser and centered it over the lampshade. "No lights. N-O. No." Holding a joint behind his back, he breathed deeply from the covered well of the lamp. "Nice smell. Whose is it? The widower's? How many men have you had? Do you remember?"

"Nowhere as many as you've had." Anna turned on the overhead light. The way Bevo had of tucking a joint in the corner of his mouth and tilting his head to escape the smoke reminded her of Jo.

He narrowed his eyes. The shadows of his eyelashes knifed across his cheeks. "At the rate they're dying off . . . is that how you like it? With the lights on?" He cuffed his shirt sleeves down and began to unbutton his shirt. "Let's do it, Anna. Let's just get it over with. I can't take the process anymore."

Anna wanted to touch his back where the shoulder plates almost came together. She didn't see why she shouldn't. She didn't see why they shouldn't take things out on each other if they found some comfort in it. "No," she said. "No. It would never be over with."

"Don't worry, Anna. I've taken the test five times. I'm negative for the virus." Bevo begin to flick his blue jeans open, button by button. "I thought you said I should give Jo grandkids."

Anna put her hands on her waist, underneath her blouse. She thought about placing Bevo's hands there. If he had tested negative five times, the only risk between them would be emotional. What if he had said he tested positive for AIDS? The risk would graduate to include the physical risk of death. Would a positive test have made Bevo more seductive to Grace Nettinger?

"Five times? Are you taking after your mother?" she asked. "Are you going to keep pushing your luck and taking the test until it turns out positive? It's taken a long time with her. She's been smoking for more than thirty years. It won't take that long with you."

"Tell me about it. What's the matter?" Bevo asked. "Don't tell me you're being faithful to old Nettinger?"

Anna slid the cold beer bottle into the widening V of his jeans. "Maybe it's more like being faithful to you." His stomach contracted, and he dodged away from her.

It would be so easy to bring him back, two steps. She didn't see why she shouldn't The bed stretched behind a fanfold screen Ed had given her. Chinese men in fishing boats stared up at Chinese women simpering across a curved bridge. "Is Burgess out there with a camera? Are you trying to get a picture to take back to Jo?"

Bevo sat in the wing-backed wicker chair. "Is that how you like it? With other men watching you do it? Ever done it with another woman?"

They were just going through the motions. Anna knew Bevo didn't have any more energy than she did. He wasn't sixteen years old and a fugitive from his home. How could she take him in when she was a runaway herself?

Her body felt tired and depleted already. "You're just like Burgess," she said. "You can go to California. You can go to Timbuktu. Nothing's going to knock it out of you. It doesn't matter who you sleep with."

Bevo dragged the bandanna off the lamp and tied it around his neck. "I know four men who've died in the past year because of who they've slept with. It matters. You're afraid to sleep with me for all the wrong reasons." He sent smoke rings to the stained ceiling. "Can I take a bath?"

Anna went into the bathroom and turned on the bathtub faucet. "What temperature?"

"Hot." Bevo sat beside her on the edge of the tub until it was full. "What are we going to do without her?"

"I don't know," she said and let her head rest against his.

They sat together on the rim of the tub for a long time, staring at the water as if they could capture the heat as it rose.

When Anna finally tested the water, she felt cheated. "It's cool."

"I'll sweeten it," Bevo said. "It'll be fine." He piled three of

Anna's towels on the toilet seat. "Do you want me to run one when I'm done?"

Anna nodded and left him alone. She stacked the extra throw pillows against the wall by the dresser. The tub emptied and was filled again. Sitting by the window and waiting for her turn, she felt like a little girl again when on certain nights another person in the house had seemed like a charm against the darkness.

E · L · E · V · E · N

According to Willi's manual, the shop had another eighteen months to go before its biannual spackling and painting. Twenty years from now this Trend-Setters and a hundred others scattered around the country would look as fresh as the day they had opened.

Willi was due back in a week. So far Anna had fought the urge to take a fingernail file to the walls, although she thought gouges in the Sheetrock would be convincing evidence that Elidia had had to take over as manager.

Anna missed having something to scratch off the walls. Jagged pieces of amber-colored tape left by styling posters whose edges had defied adhesion decorated Mary Frances's walls. Some of the tape strips were so old that the adhesive had crystallized. She missed the sparkle of the old tape on her fingertips. She missed confronting Mary Frances with evidence of the shop's deterioration. At least the decay of Mary Frances's shop had been honest. Nobody had to hang a sign over her door that read: DON'T EXPECT MIRACLES.

"Don't forget to change the liner," Elidia said as Anna upended a straw hamper and dumped damp towels into the washer. "I expect my operators to know all the closing steps."

Susie slapped her counter with a towel and sent hair flying. She shimmied to shake off the bits that stuck to her shirt. "You've about managed us into the ground, Elidia. Let me tell you—I wouldn't say a word to me about a broom right now."

"How do I know you won't try to muscle your way back in here?" Elidia asked Anna.

Anna steamed her face over the wash cycle until it was time to add bleach. "I've got a deep kitchen sink that's good for shampoos. All I need is a chair outside and a sunny winter and I've got my own operation." Thinking about all the small towns stranded beside dry creek beds that potentially lay ahead was exhausting. The anticipation of new beginnings held no excitement. She just wanted to sit on a front porch, drink beer and aim a hand-held dryer in the general direction of somebody's head.

"What's in it for you? Making yourself look so bad?" Elidia asked. "This sounds like some kind of Anglo thing. Why should I trust you? How do I know you'll really tell Willi that I managed the shop while she was gone?"

"Because I put it in writing and I had it notarized and I gave it to Vernon, the accountant, to hold until Willi gets back."

"She'll think I blackmailed you into doing it," Elidia objected.

"What difference does it make how it happened? What's important is how you handled the shop. Look. If you don't want it bad enough—fine." Anna set the dryer and pushed in the knob. "Check off Step Twelve."

"Hurry up!" Susie said. "Thirty-seven minutes of hotel happy hour are gone. How can we celebrate Elidia's promotion in an hour and twenty-three minutes? That's not enough time to celebrate *anything!*"

"I deserve to be manager," Elidia said. "A real manager would have called Willi the first time you started acting up."

"*Make* her give it to you," Anna insisted. "Fight for it or walk away. Don't stand around moaning about it."

"I don't moan. I have a very sad-looking face. I can't help that. I have my own way. Nobody has to tell me what to do or go over it again—"

"Yeah, yeah, yeah, yeah, yeah," Susie muttered, "only there's about four billion things a person's got to get done in about an hour." She slumped into her chair. "You-can't-do-one-thing-at-a-time or you'll just get buried. They'll never dig you out. Let's go! These celebration minutes are ticking away!"

"What makes you think Anna's really going away?" Elidia asked. "She could be setting me up."

"You've already been set up. Willi's got you exactly where she wants you," Anna said.

The thin metal bracelets Susie wore collided with each other. "You two are driving me *crazy!* I need a Harvey Wallbanger— oop, here's Mr. Catfish."

Ed had learned to step over the mat after hours to surprise Anna. She attributed the strong rushes of pleasure his appearances caused to the success of the conditioning treatments. His hair was softer and brighter. She wanted to touch the strands to reassure herself, but he stopped at Elidia's station.

"Tell your grandmother I came across some popotillo in my north pasture. It's reddish brown, so she ought to get some good tea out of it. I'll pick her up whenever she wants to come out."

"Finally," Anna said when he shut the laundry room door behind him. "What do you have for me?" she asked, reaching for his head.

Ed caught her hand. "Burgess called me. Jo's put herself in the hospital. He thinks you'd better see her."

They drove past the old men dressed in khaki who leaned against the corners of the pool hall and saved the wall of main street businesses from collapsing. Anna wished Ed would drive faster until subtle changes in the landscape verified that the next pass would bring Alpine into view. She couldn't go back.

"Stop the car. Stop the car!" As the station wagon slowed, she opened her door and put one leg out.

Stepping onto solid ground made Anna stumble. She reached for the back door to steady herself and was pulled forward. Ed kicked in the emergency brake and bolted out the open passenger door. "Don't you *ever, ever* do that to me again!" he shouted, shaking her by the shoulders.

The force pushed Anna against the station wagon. Now that Ed had reached his limit, she didn't know what she'd done to cause the explosion. She could feel each of his fingers exerting a different amount of pressure. "Let go of me."

"Why the hell couldn't you wait for me to stop? That's the kind of stunt Grace would pull."

"Let go of me." Her actions had had nothing to do with Grace. He didn't recognize a lifesaving action when it was there in front of him.

"Just when I think I've got you figured out, you throw something else at me. Here," Ed said, handing over the keys. "You drive us wherever you want to go. I don't care where it is."

A west wind blew the clink of glass empties from the bottling company on the outskirts of town. Anna rubbed a muscle in her stomach to keep it from twitching. It wasn't Ed's fault. She'd placed too much belief in his indestructibility and his prolonged experience with death, as if that and half an hour's distance would be enough protection. Grace hadn't died a quick unexpected death, and neither would Jo. Acknowledging his wife's condition might have made Ed think he was prepared for her death and for his life after her death, but despite all the preparation, Grace was still ambushing him.

Anna couldn't find the middle ground within herself to accept Jo's decision not to fight. Leaving Alpine was supposed to have been the end of their friendship; it was the only way she could see of letting Jo go. The idea of going back now, of resurrecting Jo in order to see her body fail was too much.

Anna handed the keys back to Ed. "I don't know where I want to go. Just give me a minute, okay? Drive five miles and then come back and I'll be ready. I promise."

Ed surveyed the mountains as if he could foresee having to track her. "Five miles fast, or five miles slow?" he finally asked.

"Slow. Jo's killing herself as sure as Grace did. I don't know what to do to save her."

"Get it out of your system," Ed said briefly. "There's not a thing you can do about it." As he continued staring at the mountains that Grace had hated, his lips tightened until their rough outline disappeared.

Anna had begun to learn what constituted puzzlement and happiness and concern in Ed's face. There were hundreds of clues to his emotions in the spare movements of the skin around his eyes and mouth. The fluidity of his face was always a surprise, but this was the first time she had ever seen him in his pain.

"I think I'll take ten miles each way," Ed said. "Medium speed." He tried to smile, but his mouth lacked the flexibility.

Anna watched the station wagon get smaller and smaller as Ed drove toward Alpine. She couldn't rely on him not to come back. The decision was hers. Going east to Alpine meant she wouldn't give up on Jo; going west, to Marfa and beyond, meant she had accepted the situation and that Jo had already died.

There was no choice. She had to go back. When Ed's station wagon reappeared on the horizon, headed in her direction, Anna ran to meet it.

On the way to the hospital Anna ran two stop signs and rolled through another. The important thing was to get to Jo, fast. Ed flinched each time and pumped imaginary brakes on the passenger side of the floor. "Don't worry," she said in an effort to comfort him, "I've been driving since I was twelve. We'll get there in one piece."

The one-way highway traffic on Alpine's main street was heavier than normal. She turned off onto the dirt road that roller-coastered in and out of the creek. "Hang on," she said before the station wagon shot into the creek. The stomach-plunging descent made her giddy. Anna wished Ed wasn't in the car so she could release the inappropriate laughter that was building up inside her. Jo would be all right. They would all band together, everyone that loved Jo, to make sure she didn't give in. "Don't worry. I know this road."

Ed shut his eyes and didn't say anything. For his sake Anna tried to slow down, but she was riding the brakes as it was. At the last intersection before the hospital cars were approaching from the right and the left. She ignored the stop sign and pressed down on the horn. "Don't worry. They see me."

"There's a space over there," Ed managed to say when they pulled into the parking lot.

She stopped close to the wheelchair ramp and shifted into park. "Thanks for coming to get me."

"I'll wait in the lobby," he said.

"No. I'll be awhile. Go home."

"I'll wait."

"You shouldn't be here. I didn't mean what I said about Grace and Jo. This doesn't have anything to do with you."

"You might need a ride back."

"I'll either catch a ride with Bevo or I'll get Burgess to loan me a car off the secondhand lot. Go home," Anna said and slammed the door. She didn't have the time to outlast his obstinance.

A short-haired, stern-looking nurse was sitting at the front station. The dinner trolley came out of the kitchen, and Anna shadowed the movements of the LVN who accompanied it. Jo's tray was on the top shelf. When the LVN delivered her first tray, Anna slipped Jo's out and walked to room 302.

Through a crack in the door she saw Burgess bent over Jo's feet. The crook of his elbow was cradling one foot as he carefully outlined and painted Jo's toenails. Veins in her swollen ankle, branching and stained purple, were pressed beneath the iridescent skin like a slide section. When Burgess blew on Jo's toes, her back arched. Anna couldn't tell if the response was caused by pain or the memory of pleasure. She was embarrassed and angry at having caught them in such an intimate act. She didn't want to see Burgess's tenderness and end up having to feel sorry for him. It would be hard enough to break through the territorial ring he was sure to have drawn around Jo.

Anna willed a smile to appear on her face and then knocked. "Have you seen what that LVN has done to her hair?" she asked as she breezed in. "There should be a law against rubber bands."

Jo's head was wrapped in a green satin turban, and her face looked fragile without the intricate architecture of hair. She looked as if she had aged twenty years. The pupils of her eyes were dilated and cloudy. As she motioned Anna to the bed, the sleeves of a bright green Chinese bed jacket were tunnels for her thin arms. Smoke fanned out of her lips in greeting.

"You're smoking," Anna accused. Burgess would let Jo get away with anything and call it love. Couldn't he see what was happening to her?

"Relax," Jo said thickly. "Relax, relax, relax, relax. Relax." Her hands tried to orchestrate the sharpness out of Anna's voice.

They were obviously overmedicating Jo. She needed relief from pain so she could build up her resources. The medicine was slowing her down; she was having to fight it, too. "I feel like I'm in some whorehouse opium den," Anna said.

Burgess tilted his head to get a better look at Jo's foot. "Flashing back to one of your previous lives, are you, Anna?"

Jo rested the the great weight of her turbaned head against the pillows. "There," she said, "that's good . . . that's better. . . ."

Anna could almost see the air ripple heavily around Jo's fingers when she summoned Burgess. "Get the cards. Charles and his friend should be here soon."

"I'm getting the cards," Burgess said, "and Anna's getting the coffee. *Anna's getting the coffee,* you understand me?"

"You're getting the cards and *I'm getting the coffee.*" She went over to the bed and jiggled Jo's fingers. "I'll see if I can't drum up something a little stronger."

"It's a shock, ain't it?"

Jo's hand wouldn't take a denial. "Some," Anna admitted. She bent to kiss Jo. "Anything to get a man to paint your toenails." Jo's lips gathered in a moue. Her eyelids closed and stretched. "I'll be right back," Anna promised.

Burgess's palm beat against the open door. "Come *on,* Anna." He hustled her down the hall. "I don't want her upset."

"Then don't upset her," Anna said.

"No backbiting in front of her, I mean it."

"What you mean is you're the only one who gets to dish it out."

Burgess extended his hand. "I'm serious. Truce." The gap in his misbuttoned shirt yawned. He looked terrible; it looked as if fat had congealed in the pockets beneath his eyes.

"Okay. Truce." Anna took his hand reluctantly.

He blocked her entry into Jo's room. "Don't forget the coffee. I like lots of sugar."

When she returned, Burgess was rubbing baby cream into Jo's ankle. The skin was turning waxy. "What about that golfer husband of Willi's?" he asked.

Despite their truce, Anna didn't trust Burgess's social chatter. There had never been anything idle about his speculations. "They freighted his golf cart in last week. Who could resist a mile-high golf course?"

"Good." Burgess nodded and remained totally dedicated to his wife's foot.

Jo's fingers impatiently mimicked lips. "Call Charles . . . tell him to bring his friend over."

Burgess rolled his eyes and pursed his mouth. He let his wrist go limp. "If you get my drift," he said to Anna.

"Always." Jo spoiled the men in her life. They were untrustworthy. Bevo, waking fresh and untroubled, had laughed at Anna for sleeping in the chair. "No control, huh?" he'd said and poured the last of the half-and-half into his coffee. Now Burgess, in a burst of false alliance, was trying to catch her in a trap against Bevo, so he could then turn his son against her.

"Don't think about it so much," Anna suggested.

"Maybe you could snuggle in between them and show them what they're missing," Burgess said. Tiny threads of brown had drained from his irises into the yellowed whites of his eyes. "Show them what a real woman's like."

"Tut, tut," Jo warned slowly. "Tut, tut, tut, tut. Let's just all relax, relax . . . relax. . . ."

Burgess took the smoldering cigarette from Jo's hands and revived it. At that moment Anna thought the malignancy in him was stronger than the cancer in Jo's body. It wasn't fair that Burgess should be the one to thrive on his own body's poisons. She looked hard at Jo's body and could almost see the delicate molecules popping under the pressure of her eyes.

The strongest and most reliable force in the room was the conflict between herself and Burgess. Hate seemed to be easier to maintain than love. It was an emotion that inspired fidelity. People weren't tricked into giving the object of their hatred freedom to decide what was best; you couldn't get away with an open embrace where hate was concerned. Burgess was loving his wife to death.

Jo brushed something away from her face. "Buzz for me," she said.

Burgess jabbed the call button. "Go rustle her up, Anna," he instructed. "Make yourself useful."

Anna was pushed out of the doorway by the LVN with the mistreated hair. Burgess took two large orange pills out of the pleated and starched paper cup she handed to him.

The damage to the LVN's hair was extensive. Some of the hair shafts had six or seven split ends feathering all the way to their roots. She probably tried to bite off her split ends, too. Anna's fingers burned to section off the brittle platinum hair and to cut away the unhealthy growth. Only three quarters of an inch of the hair could be saved, but healthy hair grew back quickly.

"Honey and egg and mayonnaise," Anna advised. "Whip them together, get yourself a plastic shower cap and a magazine and sit under a dryer for thirty minutes."

The LVN scrabbled for her thin ponytail with nail-bitten fingers to protect it from Anna's lustful gaze.

Burgess jostled the pills. "These things are too big. She can't swallow these horse pills. Can't you give her a shot? How in hell is she supposed to swallow these things?"

Jo gestured and Burgess was drawn as irresistibly as if he were attached to the end of a wire she held in her two fingers. "Let me see what I can and can't do."

"If you're not family, you shouldn't even be in here," the LVN said. "I don't know who let you in here."

Jo's fingers grasped for the ledge of Burgess's outstretched hand. "I can do it if you stroke my throat. Like you did Connie's."

"She needs her privacy right now," the LVN said and held the door open.

"I'm setting her straight on that hair. I'll be back in a minute," Anna said. That stroking act of persuasion might have helped their poodle, Connie, to swallow antibiotics, but she didn't trust Burgess's fingers on Jo's throat. How far would he go to help her die?

The smell of ether in the hallway made Anna sick. She wanted to slide down the wall and rest her bare legs against the cool tile. To avoid hearing any sounds coming from Jo's room, she cupped her ears and made the ocean roar inside her head. She flapped her hands, and the sound of waves rushed through her ear channels.

Maybe Burgess deserved some credit. If he could bear to stroke Jo's throat into convulsions of acceptance, Anna knew she should be able to watch without shame or contempt or suspicion. His hands on Jo's throat could be a life-affirming gesture. He wanted Jo to live; his refusal to press treatment on her must signify a greater, more selfless love than Anna had imagined him capable of. Her sympathy flickered out. She had almost fallen into the trap. Burgess was misguided; it was wrong to respect Jo's wishes. If ever there was a time for selfishness, this was it.

They should try everything—guilt, the threats of mutual acts of self-destruction, force—everything. Burgess had done it before when he'd been drinking and Jo threatened to leave him. Maybe selfishness was too closely tied to drinking in Burgess's mind. Maybe he thought one was no longer possible without the other.

Anna prided herself on a strong respect for individual privacy, but Jo was abusing that right. If she refused to fight, then everybody else had to do it for her. It was wrong to give up. It was irresponsible. The smell of ether and the lines of responsibility so clearly drawn made Anna sock her fists into her hipbones and double over.

Bevo and his friend walked down the hall, carrying a card table between them. The skin underneath Bevo's eyes was indented and shadowy. Her head still down, Anna stared at the square-toed boots of his friend and the metal chains slung around the heels. Not the kind of man Bevo needed.

"This is William," Bevo said, "but you can call him Weasel. I know I do."

"If it's good enough for you, Charles, then it's good enough for me," Anna said.

Weasel dropped to his knees and stared up into her face. His blue jeans were so new that they creaked. "What do they call you?" he asked. A wedge of clipped lead-colored hair grew into his forehead, notching two vertical lines above his eyebrows.

Anna pulled away from the sharpness of his face and voice. "Just Anna."

"Anna what?" Bevo prompted. "I saw old Nettinger out there. Don't tell me you haven't tacked his name on. Hasn't it been six months since the first Mrs. Nettinger died?"

"You're getting more like Burgess every day," Anna said.

"Anna what?" Weasel asked, looking up at her.

"Anna None of Your Business." She watched Weasel's thumb cruise Bevo's knee.

"Hey—Anna—you don't want to open up to me—that's fine. That's fine. Some people are open; some people are closed. I understand in full."

"How come you're in the hall?" Bevo asked. "What are they doing in there?"

"Could be making out," Weasel guessed. "Could be a little heavy petting going on." Fanned out behind Bevo's knee, his fingers rose and fell in sequence.

Bevo jerked his knee away from Weasel's hand. "Sure, right." He stared at the closed door. "Stand up, Anna. What is wrong with you?"

"I'm circulating the blood in my scalp so my roots will be healthy and happy. Did you see that LVN's hair?"

"A dime a dozen in Vegas," Weasel said. "Platinums should never wear white. They fade right out. Especially fake platinums."

"What other kind is there?" Bevo asked as he paced in front of the door. "You brought the cards, right?"

Anna bent lower and twisted her head to see Bevo's shoes. "Are those *taps?* Are those *taps* on your shoes?"

"They protect the heels. Leave me alone." He absentmindedly stroked the thin tail of hair that snaked down Weasel's neck. "How do you think she looks? I think she looks great! She won't let me touch her hair, but I bought her the turban. Did you see it? I think it looks great on her! She should really play up the exotic."

"I think it looked better on me," Weasel said.

The air swam and sparkled when Anna finally raised her head. This would never work. It would be worse than the dinner in Juárez. Bryan was missing and Weasel looked more lethal than the naroleptic Paul had. Jo's body wouldn't be able to absorb the jolt this time. "We're not really playing cards."

"Mom wants to play cards," Bevo said. "We're playing cards."

Weasel flexed his fingers until they cracked. "Let's do it."

Reluctantly Anna followed them into Jo's room. This mix of people would never work; there was a collision in the offing that would only further deplete Jo. She should leave and come back in the morning. But there would still be a collision because Burgess and his son and his son's boyfriend would be together. And if Anna disliked Weasel on sight, she could imagine Burgess's reaction.

Bevo and Weasel were already setting up the card table. Stacks of poker chips sat on the rollaway tray in front of Jo. An orange pill knocked against a stack of blue chips. Burgess pocketed the pill and carefully transferred the chips to the card table.

"Got five bucks you can stand to lose, Anna?" Jo croaked.

"Five bucks, hell! She better've brought her goddamn checkbook!" Pulling out the chair with its back to Jo, Burgess said, "You sit here, Anna."

His false heartiness wasn't convincing. Anna had been counting on the solid reliability of Burgess's hostility to get her through the game, but the helplessness of his expression as he stared over her shoulder at Jo was too much. She pushed herself away from the table. "It's too crowded in here. Weasel and I can go play two-handed something in the sun-room."

"Two-handed something!" Weasel said and squealed like a pig. "My favorite!"

Burgess shoved Anna's chair close to the table again. "What's the matter? Our money isn't good enough for you?"

"You are crazy if you think I'm leaving you alone with this man," Bevo said. "Listen to her. Nettinger's out in the lobby and she's gunning for my man."

Weasel patted Anna's hand and winked at her. "Sorry, hon, some other time. I don't mind women."

"Deal, deal, let's see what you're made of," Burgess said.

Weasel sent the cards skidding across the table. "Five-card draw. The lady on my left goes first." As everyone studied their cards, he popped his back.

The sound raised goose bumps on Anna's arms. It looked as if they were stuck with Weasel; Jo must be desperate for entertainment. Unless she had forced a promise out of Burgess to sanction Bevo's life-style and this was the test. That would partly account for the I-can't-do-it look in Burgess's eyes.

"Let's go, Anna, pick up your cards, or you'll all be here till midnight," Burgess said. He reached over for one of her blue chips and threw it into the kitty. "Now place your bet and draw your cards."

Anna knew enough to hold on to the two kings, but of the nine and six of clubs and the two of hearts, which should go?

"Bet, Anna, let's hear your bet." Burgess waited a few seconds and then took five red chips off her pile.

The cards buckled in her hands. As she was about to retrieve the chips, Weasel grabbed her wrists. "Stop bending the cards. They'd kick you out of the casino. In Reno, they'd think you were trying to mark the deck. They'd think you were cheating."

Bevo started laughing. "Anna doesn't need to cheat. Why should she cheat?" The table jumped.

"My fault, crossing my legs," Burgess explained. In reorganizing everyone's fallen chips, he swept some of Bevo's into the kitty.

"Are you going to let him get away with that? He just kicked the table and stole half your chips," Anna said.

"I'm just saying that Anna's *lucky*. Anna's *always* been lucky. That's all I was saying. Right, Mom?"

Burgess slapped Anna's hand away from the kitty and Bevo's repossessed chips. "Just bet and throw away your goddamn cards!"

"He dumped half your chips in the pot. Are you going to let him get away with that?" Anna asked Bevo.

"Like the man says"—Bevo leaned across the table and tried to pull two cards out of Anna's hand—"just bet and throw away your goddamn cards. Well, then, bet and throw something away. Remember, this is a high-stakes game."

The table jumped again, Bevo yelped and everyone looked at Burgess. "All I'm saying is we don't want any sissy bets," Bevo clarified. He moved a tower of his own red chips into the pot, and Anna followed his lead.

Weasel sighed. "It's not your turn. Ms. Slowpoke here still has to discard."

Anna couldn't believe that the game was helping Jo any. The room was too small for all of them plus a card table. Smoke from Jo's and Burgess's cigarettes had stagnated in the corners. By turning sideways in her chair and pretending to protect her cards, Anna was able to check on Jo. She was watching the game with more alertness than she had displayed since Anna had walked in.

"What should I do?" Anna asked, fanning the cards so Jo could see.

"You know what to do. Throw those three at the end away."

"Well, that tears it!" Burgess slapped his cards facedown on the table. "She's got a pair, I'm out."

"Burgess, you wait your turn," Jo warned. "You don't know what Anna's got. She could be bluffing. Pick up those new cards of yours, Anna."

Weasel had dealt her another king and two threes. This is good, Anna thought. She flashed the cards at Jo for confirmation. "I forget what it's called."

"Show your cards," Weasel said impatiently. "Show your cards. King's high wins it. Anna wins the pot." He forced the chips to her side of the table. "Are you just going to let them sit there or what? I can't deal until you clean up your side of the table."

Bevo began to build Anna's chips into multicolored towers. "Come on, Anna. Give the rest of us a chance."

Burgess jerked his chin at Weasel. "You. Deal, deal, come on, deal. Pay attention, Anna." His hand collided with hers in midair and two stacks of chips toppled.

Jo's fingernails tapped out a message on the tray top. "A nice, little nice game . . . that's all. That's all, that's all."

"Okay," Burgess agreed grimly. "Deal, deal. Let's see if Anna lands on her feet this time."

Jo had saved up; her voice sounded strong and clear. "Anna, what are the rules of conversation?"

Mary Frances had taped the ten rules of conversation to their counters, but it hadn't done any good. They'd memorized the rules and recited them back to Mary Frances. "Number one," Anna began, "patron's interest in herself, her personal grooming and cosmetic needs. Number two: patron's own activities. Number three, four, five, six: fashion, literature, art, music. Seven: education. Eight: travel. Nine: vacations—" Unable to remember number ten, she turned to Jo for help. "I forgot number ten."

"Civic affairs—you forgot civic affairs."

"Sleeping with a city councilman, you'd think she'd get that one right off," Bevo said.

"And what do we never, ever discuss?" Jo prompted.

"Our own personal problems," Anna said. "Religion. Other patrons' bad behavior. Our love affairs. Our own financial status. Poor workmanship of the other workers. Our own health problems. Information given us in confidence." She threw chips into the growing pile in the middle of the table. "Never, never, never."

The cards shot out of Weasel's hand. The velocity of his arm made Anna glad that the edges weren't sharper. She was dealt three jacks on her second hand. "What beats what again?" she asked. Burgess and Jo and Bryan played poker on the Saturday evenings Bryan was in town, but she'd played with them only twice. She couldn't stand being at the mercy of the odds.

Burgess grabbed an envelope off Jo's bedside table. "Goddamn,

Anna"—he dotted *i*'s and crossed *t*'s so violently that the table jumped, "there. There's your goddamn list. How many cards? Cards, how many cards?"

"Back off. I'm thinking." Looking at Burgess's scribbled list, she knew she could throw away the two or the seven and try for a fourth jack or she could toss either one and try for a full house. At one Saturday evening session Burgess had accused her of playing recklessly when she had asked for four new cards every hand. In her mind, since she had no control over the outcome, it hadn't mattered how many cards she asked for. If she needed a three, it didn't matter how much she wanted it or needed it; she couldn't increase her chances of getting the card by any action on her part. If the card wasn't there, it wasn't there. It had nothing to do with her. She understood about the law of averages, but she took the loss of power personally and refused to put herself in a position where she fought something that couldn't be fought.

Jo moved restlessly. There was a powerlessness in the scrape of her fingernails against the sheets that made Anna unable to decide which card to toss. The sounds of Bevo's taps and Weasel's boot chains and Burgess's pocketful of change and Jo's clogged breathing, metallic in its own way, filled the room. Anna couldn't decide. The choice seemed crucial, as if it would make a difference in all their lives. She traced the diamonds and hearts with her finger, hoping to get a sign from the cards themselves. She told herself it was a game and it didn't matter what she did.

"I *said* don't mutilate the cards. Bevo, stop her." Weasel tugged at the hair arrowing into his forehead. "Why did I agree to this?"

"Shut up." Bevo shook Anna's wrist. "How many cards?"

"One," she answered without bothering to throw a card away.

"Either pull it or I will," Burgess said. "This hand makes me or breaks me."

Six columns of chips curved in front of Anna. She didn't remember winning so many chips. "I don't want any cards after all," she announced. "I fold."

Jo's toenails scraped against the sheet. Her fingernails worked the table. "Anna doesn't fold. Nobody folds. My rules."

Weasel dealt two cards to Bevo. "Jesus Christ!"

"You didn't even give him a chance to say how many cards he wanted," Anna objected.

"We're very close." Weasel rested his forearms against the table. His point of hair dug deeper into his forehead. "I *know* how to give him what he wants."

Blood rushed into Burgess's face and turned his skin orange. He concentrated on letting his chips fall one by one into the center of the table. "All of it," he said. "I want this game finished."

They all wanted the game to end; Anna decided not to prolong it. She pushed all her chips into the center. "If he can do it, so can I."

Bevo hissed at them from behind the half circle of his cards. "Suckers." He lounged backward in his chair. "Mom—look at this hand, look what they're doing." Jo's eyes were closed, so he manufactured a response. "I know—they're crazy. Give me your pen, Budge. I need to do an IOU. Don't worry"—he stemmed Burgess's protest before it was made—"I'm good for it."

Weasel popped his knuckles. "Show your cards. Let's get this bloodbath on the road."

Burgess swept his cards off the table. "I was bluffing, I didn't have a goddamn thing."

Bryan had told her that Burgess never bluffed. He had a hand to play or he folded. "I didn't have a goddamn thing, either," Anna said. "I was bluffing, too."

Bevo jerked the cards out of her hand and almost drew blood. "Let's just see those cards," he said. "Liar. Look at that. Three jacks. Beats me. I had two tens and two aces. Congratulations, Anna. Mom! Look at that! Anna won." He handed three five-dollar bills and his folded IOU to Anna.

"That was a nice little game," Anna said. She wrapped the money around the IOU and returned it to him. "Let's just call it even. No winners. No losers."

Bevo wouldn't take the money. "No. This is yours, fair and square. You won it. I won't take it. You can let it rot. I'm not taking it back and neither's Budge."

The IOU sat on the table between Bevo and Anna until Burgess grabbed the piece of paper and unfolded it. "There," he said and threw down the IOU in front of Anna.

Bevo had bet the beauty shop. It was a setup. "I don't want it. I didn't do anything for this. I don't want it." She pushed away from the table.

"Fixing to run away again?" Jo rasped.

Anna moved to her bedside. "Look," she said, throttling the metal guardrail. "I know what you're doing. I don't want the shop. I don't want the responsibility. I need somebody like Mary Frances telling me what to do and taking care of the little shit details."

Jo reached up to brush the hair out of Anna's eyes, but Anna caught the plastic identification bracelet and returned Jo's hand to the bed. "I really don't want it," she whispered. "I really don't. She tilted her head back to stop her tears from dripping on the bed. "I'll see you tomorrow."

The hall was deserted. Despite the sound of television sets and human voices that were warped by the closed doors, and the rubber squeak of the dinner cart in the other hall, Anna felt as if Jo were the only person in the hospital. The anemic nurse was probably biting the ends of her hair and talking on the phone to her boyfriend. Dr. Laurence was probably curved over his desk in El Paso, eating greasy takeout chicken and writing a case history on his wife for some medical journal. He might even stop in mid-sentence to wonder why he bothered. Was he grateful that the burden of her faith was no longer on him? Or was guilt forcing him to work harder for a cure? What would he do once he found it? Take that long-promised vacation? Swab himself with a high-number sunscreen and sit in the sun and drink planter's punches?

Anna realized that she had been staring into a glassed-in portion of garden between the two hospital wings. The glass walls formed a cube where the controlled humidity inside supported orchids and bromeliads. There was probably more moisture inside the cube right now than had been in the outside atmosphere for a whole year.

She saw unfastened fishing boots scuttle through the bark chips and a plastic rain hat drip as the gardener stooped and pinched the hairy sphagnum moss that held the plants to their weathered pieces of board. The quick movements began to look suspicious.

Anna backed along the glass wall to get a better look at the gardener. The reflection of Burgess's face in the glass made her jump. The gardener, an Oriental man, froze.

"You'd better jump," Burgess advised. "You're not getting out of this. If she wants you to have that shop, you'll take it and you'll be grateful to her for thinking of you."

"Fuck you, Burgess." Anna pulled her arm out of his grip. "Am I supposed to be grateful to her for not fighting?"

"You're signing the goddamn deed and title transfer in front of her tomorrow morning, and you're doing it with a smile on your face. You're keeping that shop for as long as she lives—"

"No! No way. I'm not doing anything to make it any easier. I want her to get pissed as hell. You've probably got the fucking coffin already picked out and paid for. Right? She's doing all this legwork for you, and you're keeping your chin up for her and none of it's helping any."

Anna thought Burgess was either going to hit her or plunge his fist through the glass. But he pressed his hands into his face until spasms traveled across his shoulders. When he showed his face, his cheeks were wet and wrinkled. "She called Pullock herself last week. He came by with a catalog and swatches and cross sections of the caskets. There's nothing I can do. She's going, she's made up her mind. I have to give in to her. I can't keep her here. The last time I tried to hold on to her, I broke her arm. You understand me? There's nothing I can do."

A sudden surge of hope smoothed his face. "Take the shop, Anna," he said. "Bevo won't take it, but if you do, she'll at least know he's got someplace to come back to. Take the shop and come by every day and ask her for help. If she doesn't think you're ready to take it over, then—she'll—she won't—she won't go . . . she won't let herself be taken so soon—"

Anna willed herself to stop crying. Burgess and Bevo were so obviously unprepared to deal with each other in Jo's absence, but that hadn't convinced Jo to accept treatment; difficulties at the shop wouldn't change Jo's mind. Bevo and Burgess must have

talked Jo into transferring the shop so they wouldn't have to deal
with it later on. They needed a temporary caretaker until the shop
could be refurbished and sold. She could do that much. Nobody,
not even Mary Frances, knew the particulars of inventory and
square footage as well as she did.

Carefully she sponged Burgess's damp beard with her palm.
"Okay," she heard herself say. "Okay. Where do I sign?"

He allowed her touch for a second. "That's Chaivant," he said,
waving into the terrarium. "Thomas brought him in."

"From where?"

"Don't ask questions. I just told you so you wouldn't ask any.
If anything happens to him, it's on your head." Burgess signed a
greeting into the terrarium and disappeared down the hall.

Chaivant unhooked a moss-bound bromeliad. Cradling the
board, he parted long, serrated leaves to reveal the bromeliad's
bronze heart. He beamed at her like a proud parent. Anna
smeared the glass with her wet palm. "Give it up," she said. "It's
no use. No matter what Bryan told you. Nobody gets away with
anything over here either."

Cantinflas was starring in Wednesday's Spanish matinee at the
Palace. Anna carefully examined the posters that hung behind the
ticket booth. The snatches of Spanish dialogue coming from inside the theater increased her restlessness. She knew enough Spanish to catch a word now and then, but the pleasure of
understanding was defeated by the next series of words that sped
past her. The desire to understand wasn't helping her comprehen-
sion any.

The ticket seller, a high school girl, came out of the faceted
glass booth as Anna's reading took her closer to the entrance. "I'd
go ahead and buy a ticket if I was you and I was just waiting on
them," she advised. Her hair was streaked and crimped like crisp
bacon.

"You're sure they're in there?" Anna tapped her watch to make
sure the hands hadn't stuck. The feature was supposed to be over
in fifteen minutes.

"Every Wednesday. Just make sure you don't look yourself right through that entrance," the girl warned.

Elidia and her grandmother were the last ones to come out of the theater. The light circles around Elidia's eyes glowed when the sun hit her face. The grandmother's black-scarved head barely reached Elidia's shoulder.

Anna grabbed Elidia's arm to stop her. "Elidia, I need a favor." She didn't have time to wait for Elidia's eyes to come out of the depths and focus. "I need your grandmother to cure somebody."

The two spoke a Spanish too fast for Anna to translate. She didn't have time to learn another language. Minutes were precious and she was losing the weapon of speech. Politeness was a formality. If she had to, she'd physically carry Elidia's grandmother to the hospital and make Jo swallow whatever the old woman concocted.

"Does your grandmother have a cure for the lungs?" Anna asked. "Please. It's important." She appealed directly to the grandmother. "Ed Nettinger said you might."

Sadly the old woman closed her eyes. The lids were so thin the pupil and iris of each eye cast a shadow on the skin. *"Que lástima!"*

Anna didn't know whether the old woman was grieving for the Nettingers or for the potential loss of Jo. "It's not sad," she insisted. "Not if you help her."

"There's no magic in what she does, Anna." Elidia said. "She knows how to use certain plants for certain things. Don't expect a miracle."

"I'm not asking for a miracle. I just want a cure. Why is everyone—"

"You Anglo women are so impatient. It's so easy to feel sorry for you, all those thin blue veins of yours. You think screaming and yelling and ordering people around shows you have great passion. You don't know what you're dealing with."

"I helped you—"

"You don't understand. Your help will not help me. It doesn't matter what your intentions are. You don't have that kind of power over me."

Anna spoke again directly to Elidia's grandmother. "Please, please. *Por favor.* Help Jo."

Elidia's silver nails and pale fingers showed like X-rayed bones against her grandmother's black sleeve. "You're not here because of Jo. You're here to help yourself."

She and her grandmother began talking at the same time, but Elidia finished first. Ed Nettinger's name separated itself from the tangle of the grandmother's Spanish several times. "She says maybe. Come by tomorrow."

The odor of potatoes and onions fried in lard lingered after the two were gone. Anna hadn't been aware of the smell while Elidia's grandmother was standing beside her, but she felt the comfort of it now. Her stomach contracted as she imagined a kitchen full of people, eating lunch and laughing, happy to be alive, enjoying today and looking forward to tomorrow.

———

The tea was wrapped in a brown paper bag that had been crumpled into softness. Anna tucked the package under her arm, grabbed the plastic bottle of black Redi-Dye for Jo and locked the door of the small house.

Willi's long Cadillac nosed up the alley. There was no way to get the Valiant past the bigger car. The mason jar of tea was still warm; Anna wanted Jo to drink some before it cooled, although Elidia's grandmother had said its temperature didn't matter.

The Cadillac's front passenger window was powered down. "I was sorry to hear about Jo," Willi called. "How is she doing?"

"Fine," Anna said. "I'm on my way there now."

"A minute, Anna." Willi extracted a fresh cigarette from her purse. "I'm disappointed in you."

"I don't have time for this. I told you I wasn't cut out to be a baby-sitter. Elidia makes a good—"

Willi and her mirrored twin joined in laughter. "Anna, please! No. In another three years, perhaps, it will be within her to manage Trend-Setters, then—I'll see. No. Mort will have to winter here instead of in Florida."

Holding the jar of tea to her chest, Anna looked around and saw that the October time change had allowed shadows from the blue spruces in front of the big house to spear the opposite street curbing. High school kids in a small pickup scoured the vacant lot for old tires and lumber to throw on a bonfire. Hit-and-run chills alternated with sunlight and teased her skin. She had the tea. Its temperature didn't matter. There was time to make a pitch for Elidia.

"Where will you find all these women to memorize your manual?" Anna asked.

Sitting high and sighting down the Cadillac's long hood, Willi said, "I'll find them, and Trend-Setters will be a good thing for them, a stable business in which to invest their time. I will give them the illusion of independence." Coupling the cigarette and lighter in one hand, Willi tapped the leather-bound steering wheel. "Not everyone is called. Not everyone has a vocation. It's a way to make a living. It's a job that many women do for a prescribed number of hours, they shake out their capes, they rinse out their sinks, and they go home and forget about it. Susie. Yes. They make no vows. Some women like to be around other women, they like to entertain. There's nothing wrong in that. Elidia wants respect and power. There's nothing wrong in that, except that she's too obvious about it. She cannot use her family to extort what she hasn't yet earned. You—don't fluff your hair so—you are single-minded, to a fault. You want the freedom to attend to hair. You forget a woman is attached to a head of hair, a woman completely at your mercy, you think. It's the other way around. You don't manipulate them. No. You ignore them. They won't stay with you. It won't matter how good you are.

"Anna, what's the function of a beauty shop? To offer hope, to make a woman *believe* in herself. You want to operate a shop on reality. It cannot be done. We operate on fantasies. Your talent, your skill will not be enough. The women will walk out of your shop believing themselves unworthy of the hairstyles you have given them. They will know that you don't trust them with what you've done for them. What good is a doctor who treats only the most obvious symptom, who refuses to consider the whole person? Don't you want Jo to be given the most comprehensive treatment available, to—"

"It's not the same thing and you know it. It's not life and death."

"It is the same. Only the matter of degree differs. Where do you go, Anna, when you need to take care of yourself?"

"I don't *need* to go anywhere. I'm after built-in protection."

"A friendly warning, Anna, this is what I offer to you. If you want a successful shop, you're going to have to bend. I like thinking of you as competition. Yes. I wish you luck." Without looking over her shoulder, Willi backed straight out of the alley.

Anna tailgated the Cadillac in reverse and kept the bigger car at bay, getting the jump on forward motion while Willi was still switching into low drive.

———

Connie, Jo and Burgess's black poodle, greeted Anna with stiff-legged hops. As Burgess had instructed, Anna poured heated milk over the dry dog food. Sad, low sounds came out of Connie's throat while she ate.

The day's mail was stacked on the dining table. A note from Bevo topped the pile. "Gone to El Paso for the weekend. Back soon. XoXoXo, Bevo." She hoped he'd gone to put Weasel on a plane back to Las Vegas because Weasel had repaid his favor. The thought of Bevo's owing Weasel for dealing a marked deck made her uneasy.

A load of Jo's nightgowns were huddled in the bottom of the dryer. Anna laid a sheet of fabric softener on the pile and set the machine for ten minutes to warm the gowns. She folded Burgess's undershirts and socks and placed them in a duffel bag on top of a paperback mystery she hoped would draw his attention from Jo for a few minutes. He didn't know anything about the tea Elidia's grandmother had made. And to distract Jo, Anna had begged wallpaper books and chains of ceramic and linoleum tile samples from the lumber company.

Burgess was trying to retouch Jo's roots with a cotton ball. He swabbed with one hand and wiped drips with the other. An inch-wide band of soot-colored roots separated Jo's high pale forehead from the rest of her black hair. A turquoise silk turban, its top caving in, sat on the bedside table.

It was the first time Anna had seen Jo without the turban. She had the same head of hair, but it looked as if her scalp had shrunk and exposed the roots. The crescents of white that already lined Jo's cuticles, too, gave Anna the feeling of shrinkage and not growth.

Holding a fresh cotton ball to the rim, Burgess shook the bottle of dye. He glared at Anna. "Think you could do a better job, do you?"

Anna smiled but kept her lips together so nothing inflammatory would come out. The sight of his ministering to Jo always unnerved her. Every day, right after lunch, he shooed her out while Jo slept. Anna would have liked to watch Jo rest, but she felt the same jealousy that Burgess was displaying. In the afternoons she would run errands for Burgess, memorizing faces and stories to tell to Jo in the evening after dinner and before the next to last round of medication.

"I've been around cars all my life," Anna pointed out. "I've got the credentials, but do I come in and tell you how to do your business? Bevo should be doing that."

"He's not here, is he?" Burgess's elbow kicked out in warning.

Jo's eyes opened suddenly. "Charles?" She turned her heavy head out of Burgess's hands. "Charles? It's too hard on him. . . ."

"It's only me," Anna said quickly. She walked into the narrowing range of Jo's focus and displayed a box of candy. "Look. A going-away present from Willi. A five-pound sampler. I need somebody to mush the centers to see what kind they are. What are you doing tonight?"

"Ann-na," Jo said. She rallied to demand the candy. "Hand it here. I'll squash till kingdom come."

"Good." Anna smiled and stepped around Burgess. "Why don't you go out for dinner?"

"I ate off Jo's plate."

She tried to take the cotton ball out of his hand. "You're dripping all over the place. Let me do that."

"*No!*" Burgess backed into the cot beside Jo's bed where he slept. "Leave us alone!"

"Budge, Budge," Jo whispered. The words whistled out of her throat. She lifted her finger from a chocolate and it remained stuck to her nail. "Here."

"No," he said.

Anna knew he hadn't left the hospital in almost a week. "I'll wait outside till you're done. I can read the paper to Jo while you go out for some air."

"We don't need air. We need privacy."

"Burgess. I'm telling you you need a change of clothes. How do you expect Jo to breathe?" Anna saw that normal bickering or an appeal to take care of his own health wouldn't get him to hand over the baton. She didn't know if he was capable of responding to a plea from her. "Please, Burgess. I'd like to be alone with her for a little while. I won't upset her. I promise."

Burgess looked at Anna for a long time. "Let me finish up here," he grumbled with more grace than she expected.

"I'm not blind—don't think I am," Jo said in a version of her old voice. "I see what's going on between you two, you can't wait till I'm in the ground. It won't be two minutes before you're rolling around on that bearskin rug in the bedroom. Lord! You might as well take me now as later."

Burgess blushed. "Go on out there and let me finish this." He bent close to Jo and motioned toward Anna. "She's afraid I'll do a better job than her. I've got her running scared."

"He's got me shaking," Anna said before she walked out the door.

The hall was deserted. The hall was always deserted. Anna couldn't tell if that was a good sign or bad—if it meant people were healthy and didn't need the hospital or if all the patients were too sick to move or they died and were carted away in the night. She listened to a series of shoe squeaks and identified them as the night nurse's. That nurse, whose short, severe haircut was all wrong for her head and body, always sent out quick, efficient squeaks. There was a pink rawness exposed all along her hairline that made Anna suspect the nurse used her husband's electric shaver to shear away the neck hair.

She lost track of the squeaks. In the last week her senses had become too sharp. Noises were suspect. Details burned her eyes. They focused on objects nearby and then those in the distance, telescoping out of control, as she attempted to capture the essence before the motion had played itself out.

From a distance of fifty feet her vision separated Chai from long streamers of orchid leaves in the glass cube. His cheek rested on the top of a transplanted stump and his arms encircled the base. Anna couldn't tell what he was doing—using the stump as a pillow, hugging it, or trying to will the roots deeper into the two feet of topsoil. But when she went up to the terrarium and knocked on the glass, he rose eagerly. Did they ever let him out of the cube? So much for the promise of freedom. It looked as if Bryan's good intentions had backfired again.

Careful that only Chaivant could see her open wallet as she held it to the glass, Anna asked, "Do you know this man? Bryan. Thomas O. Bryan?"

The smile left Chai's face. "You go!" he shouted before disappearing behind a nest of staghorn fern.

Moving at another angle to the glass, Anna saw too late that Burgess was right behind her.

"What the hell are you doing?"

"You're always sneaking up on everybody." Streaks of black dye ran across his forehead. "There's dye on your forehead. I hope you got some on Jo's roots."

Burgess banged the glass. "It's okay! Hey, in there, it's okay!" He gentled the vibrating pane. "It's okay. She didn't mean anything by it." He circled his forefinger close to his head. "Loco. You understand? Crazy!"

"I just wanted to know how he gets in and out of there," Anna said defensively.

"If he gets caught and sent back, I'm holding you personally responsible." The fleshy pockets underneath Burgess's yellow eyes distended as he glared at Anna. "You and your friend, K. O. Browne, Jr."

"Wipe off your forehead before some of that dye seeps into your brainpan." Burgess was right. She had slipped.

"I told Thomas this was too close, you'd be here all the time, you wouldn't be able to keep your nose out of things. But Thomas won't listen and Chai won't leave. He loves his goddamn garden too much. He thinks it's his goddamn home—"

"Don't try to set me up. If anybody finds out anything, it'll be because you don't know when to shut up. I don't know anything. I can't tell what I don't know." K. O. Browne, Jr., had already tried his best and failed. If the right-mindedness of his position hadn't been enough to convince her to talk, then Anna didn't think the patrolman spent any time thinking up ways to make her talk. She wasn't worried that he might unlock her nightmares and find snakes and fire. Those things were tangible and could be fought. Either learn to like the snake or bash in its head; either walk into the flames or put them out. The only way K. O. Browne, Jr., could get anything out of her would be if he were the one behind Jo's rapid aging. If she could make a deal in exchange for Jo's life, she would. The worst torture of all was seeing pain inflicted and fear practiced upon someone she loved.

Burgess brought his face close to Anna's. "You'd tell, too, wouldn't you? You'd tell and probably get a microwave oven out of the whole deal to dry all your little wiggies, all your little children. You'd land on your feet all right."

"You're cracking up, Burgess."

"Even Thomas sees that he's better off without you now."

"Good," Anna said. "Then we all agree and we're all happy."

"I don't want you upsetting her any. She doesn't have any little plant to hide behind and tend to."

"You're not the only one who loves her. It's not me she needs protecting from. You're the one smothering her. You're the one using up all her air."

"She makes allowances for you," he said. "You know what you

are to her? You're nothing but a stray she took in and fed and tried to paper-train."

Anna didn't think they'd ever run out of hateful things to say to each other. One day they wouldn't be able to stop. The momentum provided by their love for Bryan and Jo would be gone, but their mistrust and jealousy would continue to grow as the emotions fed on themselves. She and Burgess shouldn't be left alone together.

"She'll be here when you get back," Anna promised. "I'm not taking her anywhere."

"That's what you don't understand, Anna. That's what you haven't clicked to yet. You can't promise me she'll be here when I get back."

"Yes, I can," she said steadily. "No matter what happens, she'll hang on until you get back. She wouldn't do that to you."

Burgess's eyes filled with tears. "You think so?" he asked anxiously. "I'm afraid she's going to slip away while I'm gone, that she thinks it'll be easier on me that way. That's why I can't leave. You can have five minutes with her. I'll be right outside the front entrance."

"Ten minutes. Please, Burgess. Make it ten. If anything changes before then, I'll send somebody to get you."

Without agreeing, he walked down the hall toward the entrance. Anna rested her forehead against the glass wall and saw Chaivant standing with a hoe upended in his hand, ready for a possible attack. "It's all right," she said and patted the glass. "It's all right."

Jo's left hand found her mouth, and her right guided a cigarette to her lips. "Light me up, Anna," she commanded.

"I've got something else for you. Here's a piece of candy first."

"Light me up here, Anna."

"No." Anna broke the piece of candy in two. The orange center reminded her of Burgess's skin. She glued the two pieces together again.

"I need a light here," Jo insisted.

Anna unwrapped the tea and poured some into a plastic cup. "I don't have any matches. Here. Try this."

"I want a light." Jo kneaded the thin bedspread. Her heels rode up and down the mattress but failed to catch hold. "So goddamn gullible sometimes, Anna. I don't want any of that crap."

"Why don't I just go to the kitchen and ask for a butcher knife so you can slit your throat?"

"Because I'd rather do it myself. I'm not bawling over any should-haves, I know what I'm doing. I don't want to hear any lectures. You worry about keeping your own house in order, and we'll get along."

"What's that supposed to mean?"

"Listen to me—you might as well get something out of watching me waste away. You hear me? You do something, you stand by it. No regrets, that's all—no regrets. There's not a thing I'd change. Now get me a light."

"No. I'm not going to regret not bringing you matches on your deathbed. Believe me. Let Burgess do it. He's the traitor. He'd sell his soul if you asked him to. He probably already has."

"I don't want to hear that kind of talk," Jo said sharply. "I don't want to hear about souls. Let me go. The more you try to save me, the more I want to go."

"Say hello to Grace Nettinger for me then. You two are going to have a high time together. A lot of laughs. Here. One sip of tea. That's all. Here."

Jo knocked the cup out of Anna's hands. "All I want from you is a match—that's all. If you can't do that for me, then get out. It shouldn't be hard. You've done it before."

"I'm not moving. I'm pouring more tea. We'll each have a little sip. I'll read you the paper and then I'm showing you the tile samples. Buzz that hair-biting nurse. See if she'll get you a match. Get her to call your doctor and have him put it on your chart." Anna's hands were shaking. She made a show of tasting the greasewood tea. It was terrible, bitter and tongue-coating.

"Are you sure about those sinks?" Jo asked suddenly. "You give every chair their own sink, there's no extra chair to set anybody in while they're waiting for a comb-out. What if all your operators turn out to be as funny as you are about sharing their chairs?"

"I never saw you moving for anybody." Anna willed the cigarette to fall forgotten from Jo's lips. "I'm thinking of leaving one sink in back and extending the shampoo room to the first dryer and then pushing the front wall that much farther into the reception area."

"Where's the soda machine going to go?"

"Don't worry. Claude's safe. He'll get that Hawaii trip off us. He'll tell me how many cases he needs to unload to win. Same as always. I'll store them upstairs if I have to. Don't worry. I know my responsibility to the community as a businesswoman. Here. I've got some tile samples for you to look at."

Jo's face tightened in pain. The cigarette dipped and jabbed at Anna like an accusing finger. "Light me up. Just a puff—if you love me."

"Not until you try the tea."

"Look at me—one puff's not going to hurt me any more than a sip of that tea's going to help. I've accepted that. It's about time you did."

Anna could see the struggle was wearing Jo down. She had been prepared to go on all night to work Jo into a healing fury, and all she was doing was speeding up the process. "I won't," she whispered, but her hand struck the match and shielded the flame until the cigarette was lit.

On Halloween Burgess stroked Jo's throat for half an hour, but she couldn't swallow. Anna wrapped the orange pills in a handkerchief and pounded them into a fine dust with the bottom of a glass. Burgess then rubbed Jo's rigid neck cords with baby cream to erase the red frustration of his fingers. Jo couldn't take the crushed pills mixed with water. Bits of the orange coating dribbled off the teaspoon and down her chin.

"I'll go get somebody," Anna said after they had rung the call button. She ran down the hall, divided in her feelings about what Jo needed more—a steadfast refusal to let go of the pain or a final acceptance of death as the end of pain. This pain was a trick; death shouldn't be the only easement available to Jo. The constancy of pain could overcome the best resistance; pain should be an affirmation of life, a struggle of the body to heal itself. In Jo's case the absence of pain now would mean death. The wrong kind of shot might sink Jo, but Anna didn't think there was a medicine potent enough to offer the dual benefits of relief and recuperative strength.

The night nurse came down the hall at a run. Anna started moving backward, then sideways in basketball defensive action to keep up with her. "She can't swallow. At all. Nothing. We've got to do something." The nurse pushed up her sweater sleeves and slammed the door open.

During the night Jo's blood pressure dropped, and by the next morning she was in a coma. Wide-eyed yet sightless, she managed six loud, hard breaths every minute. Anna continued to clock each breath while she was in the coffee room, where the only sound was the bubble of a percolator that was off Jo's rhythm.

Burgess held one of Jo's hands, massaging her fingers and talking as if she could hear him. Bevo held the other, secretly pinching the fleshy part of his mother's palm. Standing against the wall, Anna beat the time with her fist. She patterned her breathing to Jo's, pushing deeper for air to add seconds of life. Longer silences began to come in between the breaths. They were all quiet until the deep, loose noise caught in Jo's chest again.

Anna spelled Bevo. Jo's eyes were the worst sign. Their very openness proved she was still alive, but their lack of responsiveness said she was gone. Please don't let her be caught in some kind of limbo, Anna pleaded. She squeezed Jo's hand as if a desire to live could pass through the blood and skin of one person to another. As if that would be enough to bring her back.

Burgess wouldn't leave the room. He rested his cheek against the guardrail in acceptance. In the light of Burgess's grace, Anna felt ashamed by her own denial. The desire to see Jo live at all costs now seemed selfish, a test of will rather than love.

After Bevo took over again, Anna paced the halls and happened on the nursery, where two full-haired babies slept. She tried to tell who would fight and who would accept defeat and which would survive the longest. Without the benefit of sight or speech, they were locked in a world of privacy as surely as Jo was. Anna tapped on the window. Somebody should warn them.

It was midafternoon when Jo took her last breath. Anna moved closer to the bed and waited with Burgess and Bevo. For several seconds nobody breathed. "Mom?" Bevo whispered. "Are you all right?"

Burgess let down the guardrail and sat beside Jo. Gently he closed his wife's eyes and then, using both hands, pressed her cheeks and kissed her forehead.

"I feel so relieved," Bevo said in wonder. "I can't believe I feel so relieved. I didn't expect that."

"I'll go get somebody," Anna said. Medically there was nothing to be done. Bevo was right. The cessation of Jo's breathing had brought a certain peace to the room. She was reluctant to leave and have the peacefulness become a memory, but Burgess and Bevo's time with Jo took precedence.

"You don't have to go, Anna," Burgess said. "We'd like you to stay."

Bevo moved over to give Anna room at the guardrail. She kissed Jo's forehead and was surprised by the warmth.

———

Late that afternoon Burgess called Parris Island to tell Marvin that his mother had died. Anna and Bevo searched through all the kitchen cabinets for any secret stashes of liquor. Anna pulled open the drawers and tried to forget the sound of Richard Pullock zipping Jo into a black plastic bag.

Holding on to the cabinets' metal handles, Bevo did standing push-ups. "What the hell," he said. "So what if Budge starts drinking again? He wasn't such an obnoxious drunk."

"No," Anna said. "Don't even start to think that way." Squatting under the sink, she unscrewed a plastic bottle filled with clear liquid and sniffed. The smell of ammonia made her grab for the drainpipe.

"He only quit for her, because she said she'd leave." Bevo pressed the cabinets closed with open palms. "I used to wish he would. I got a bottle of scotch once and almost planted it, but Mighty Marv stopped me. He was a marine even back then—a thirteen-year-old marine." He batted the chrome joystick faucet. "It wouldn't have mattered. She wouldn't have left him. Never. Him or us, and it would have been him."

Anna didn't think that was true. She felt comforted by the sound of Burgess's voice coming from an extension in the bedroom. Any emotion in his voice was ironed out by the living room wall, but the steady rhythm and tone were soothing. They were all in motion, and that was a good sign. Burgess was calling relatives; once he got off the phone, Bevo would call the motels to make reservations. Anna had already delivered Jo's obituary to the newspaper and the radio station.

Things still had to be done. She and Bevo were due at the funeral home early the next morning to take care of Jo's hair and makeup. Time progressed. The fall sun, which had manufactured heat for them all day long, was setting in such vibrant coppers and golds against the blue sky that Anna's heart ached.

"Are you calling anybody to come down for you?" she asked, in the hope that Bevo had been hiding the best and most important person in his life from them. She hoped for somebody nice, somebody who would show up at the funeral wearing an ordinary gray suit.

"I leafed through my little book and just couldn't *decide.*" Bevo flipped the gas burners on and off, playing the blue rings of flame against each other, making one flare up and another cower. "Half of them are probably dead by now anyway. Aren't you glad we never really did anything?"

We did things, Anna thought. We did some things. But she knew what he meant. And she knew if they had slept together that night, she wouldn't have been able to use his leg as a support to help herself up. They were freely bound to each other and, unlike lovers, careful in the uses of their bodies. "You're not my type. You're too short."

"What about that shrimp Ronnie Mauss?"

"That's why you're too short. I learn from my mistakes. It only takes once." Anna looked over the counter into the living room. What she could see of the house looked immaculate. On her twice-a-day visits to the house she hadn't been able to do more than blow dust off the end tables.

The living room didn't look like Jo or Burgess; it looked like something out of a magazine—tan carpeting, orange couch, yel-

low armchairs and drapes patterned in orange and brown. High
school graduation pictures of Bevo and Marvin, airbrushed until
their enlarged teenaged pores had vanished, hung above the
piano. A faint blush colored their cheeks. Instead of conveying
high spirits and good health, the pink tint looked as if someone
had put rouge on the photographs and then had decided to wipe
it off.

Burgess walked out of the bedroom. "I talked to Glynn. Ruth
left this morning. He said she'd had a dream. They're flying
Marvin into Midland early tomorrow morning."

"I'll pick him up," Bevo volunteered promptly. "Anna won't
mind going to the funeral home by herself."

Anna did mind. It was one thing to confront Grace Nettinger,
a woman she had barely known, packed in a coffin and another
to see her best friend. The warmth of Jo's face was still too real.
Anna had counted on shoring up herself by shoring up Bevo.
There was still a feeling of imbalance, as if a train she'd been
riding on had reached its destination, but the forward motion of
her body hadn't been checked.

"I think your brother'd like that," Burgess agreed and then half
a second later turned deferentially to Anna. "Say the word, and
I'll have Marvin rent a car and drive in." He seemed calm and
centered. The lines scored across his forehead had softened, but
Jo's illness had taken its toll.

There would always be a challenge in everything Burgess said
to her, but Anna realized she didn't always have to take it up.

"If Bevo wants to pick up Marvin—then he should. I'll take
care of everything tomorrow morning. I can take the dress and
everything now."

"Dress!" Bevo hooted. "Pantsuit, you mean. I think the last
time I saw her in a dress was when I was ten." He jerked his thumb
at Anna. "And this one never wears anything but."

Burgess looked toward the hall. "She never let me see how she
put up her hair. She always said it was part of the mystery."

Anna hoped Burgess wasn't waiting for an invitation to the
funeral home so he could see how it was done.

Bevo tossed Burgess a peppermint from a dish on the coffee

table. "Even Anna may not be able to pull this one off. I think Mom was the only one who could defy gravity."

"If I don't get it right, she'll plague me forever," Anna said. It was a ridiculous hope, but without some provocation Jo might never give them a sign that she was all right.

"It's Halloween," Burgess said suddenly. "I just now remembered that it's Halloween. We'll need some more candy. These peppermints won't last once those trailer park kids start heading over here."

"I'll go," Bevo said and walked out the door.

Burgess stood by the front window until Bevo's car disappeared. "He'll be all right."

"Sure," Anna agreed. "He'll be fine." She couldn't get over how neat the living room was. The room seemed bigger, too, as if it had cleaned itself and expanded in preparation for the day of the funeral.

Connie clicked across the kitchen floor. Burgess scooped her up. "She knows," he said. "Connie knows, don't you, girl?" He carried the poodle across his chest and sat on the piano bench. Her pink forehead ribbon bobbing, she rode quietly on his arm.

For ten years Jo had made a show of buying sheet music, but she never had learned to play. "Nobody could hear over the racket of these nails," she'd said. "I can scratch Burgess's back or I can play the piano—one or the other—but I can't do both. Besides, I like watching part of myself growing, just growing and growing. I can't wait to retire and just sit there and watch my hair and my nails go to town. I can't stand the thought of Mary Frances sweeping part of me up and stuffing me into one of those pillows of hers."

Mary Frances would listen in horrified fascination. "I suppose you'll let the hair on your legs sprout, too." Anna would remind Mary Frances not to forget about Jo's armpits. They would keep it up until Mary Frances, running her hands up and down her own bare calves to check and recheck the rate of stubble growth, started to melt the leg wax.

"Did you ever hide in the closet and try to watch how she put up her hair?" Anna asked.

Burgess concentrated on centering Connie's pink ribbon. "She didn't want me to, so I didn't want to."

"You men always make such a big deal out of what some chemicals and heat can do. It's very scientific. Plus having the proper tools and knowing what you're doing. That's all. Like anything else. Like tuning a car."

"Men and women don't need to know everything about each other," Burgess said. "A man and a woman between them can decide what to tell and what not to."

A month before Anna would have challenged Burgess's knowledge of women in general and Jo in particular. There were things about Jo that she had been sure he hadn't appreciated enough. No matter what their degree of silent communication was, things were bound to fall through the cracks. But now Anna no longer knew if it was worth it to turn around and try to tie up the loose ends. How could you get ahead of the game if you went back and had to cover the same ground over and over again? Was it possible to leave things undone and unsaid and escape? If not, then it wouldn't matter how long a bus ride she took or how far a swim. Anna didn't think she had ever known what she needed to about another person. Either the desire to know or the knowledge itself was always too late in coming.

Burgess turned on the lamp beside the piano. "I'll get Jo's bag. Pullock's picked up her clothes already. She packed everything herself just like she was going into the hospital to have a baby. There's a note for you in the makeup bag. I didn't read it."

"You should have," Anna said. She suddenly felt like a thief, ruthless in her greed, wanting to steal the answers from everybody for all the questions she'd never asked.

———

The gold curling letters that spelled out Mary Frances's name had been scraped off the front door glass. BE-JO'S was painted in navy blue horseshoe letters on the door. Below the name, stroked in the same color but with finer lines, ran what must have been Bevo's promise—STYLES UNLTD.

Holding the suitcase filled with Jo's hairpieces and a paper bag full of candy corn, Anna tapped her foot on the Astroturf welcome mat before the front door. This is mine, she thought, and felt no desire to enter the shop. She decided to go upstairs first. Having access to the private areas of the shop was the real mark of ownership; taking possession of the upstairs first might spark her desire for the shop.

The outside steps seemed to sway beneath Anna's feet. She had visions of the staircase separating from the building and gliding off, but the steps held. Cautiously she set the suitcase and bag down. The landing was a perfect place for a trapdoor. Suppose she put the skeleton key into the lock? The shop wasn't meant to be hers. Like Wiley Coyote, she might hang in the air for a second as the truth of the situation slowly dawned; once it had, with nothing to support her, she'd plummet to the concrete car porch below.

Leaving the key in her pocket, Anna sat on the landing and looked down into the next yard. Whoever lived there had posted a sign guiding trick-or-treaters into the alley. Snaggletoothed pumpkins sat on each fender of a beat-up truck topped with a wooden camper. The Irish setters were dressed in plaid sweater vests and bow ties. Welcoming light beamed out of every window in the house. Good, she thought. There was no reason to go in and turn on the lights. She would catch the children as they went next door. Pleased with the plan, she opened the candy corn and bit the white tip off one piece.

On Halloween Anna used to spend hours on her hair and impatiently step into the costume Georgia had reshaped at the last minute from her own wardrobe. "What do you want to be?" Georgia would ask, too late pulling belts and ribbons and earrings out of nowhere. With her top lip outlined in lipstick, Anna would back out the front door to join the other children, pouting so Georgia could draw in the bottom lip and finish applying the color.

The sign wasn't luring any trick-or-treaters into the alley. Anna was disappointed but not surprised. No parents in their right minds would send their kids to the house next door. The risk of receiving drug-laced candy was too great. If the shop had been open that day, some of the customers would have brought their children in for Mary Frances's jack-o'-lantern cookies. And even if people had known that Anna was there, out of respect for Jo, the shop would have been the last place they'd send their children.

Finally, when the lights next door went out and she found herself holding a bag of candy corn that had all the white tips and yellow bottoms chewed off, Anna knew it was time to go inside.

Mary Frances's jasmine perfume still retained possession of the walls. Anna opened all the windows with screens. A canvas cot, sheeted and blanketed, was pushed against the far wall. It was a poor replacement for Mary Frances's chaise lounge, but not having the chaise there reconfirmed the feeling of temporary occupancy.

The telephone started to ring. Anna tracked the sound to the kitchen, where the phone nested on a long cord.

Mary Frances's voice streamed out of the receiver. "Anna! I can't believe it. I mean I *knew*, but I never really expected her to die, and so soon. I thought she'd hang on and on just out of sheer stubbornness. I can't talk long. Alfred's got the motor running. I don't think he's set foot on dry land since he bought that big toy of his. It's all he can think about. It's nothing but a big windup toy, that's all it is." She lowered her voice as the houseboat's horn became more insistent. "I'm about out of quarters—I'll meet you at Richard Pullock's tomorrow morning. Burgess sounded better than he's sounded in a good while. How are you? I'm *coming!* Bye-bye, sweetie."

Anna continued to listen to the buzz of disconnection in case Alfred had driven off and Mary Frances needed somebody to come pick her up. The drive to Del Rio would take about four hours; they would be back in time to repair whatever damage Richard Pullock had done to Jo. But Mary Frances didn't come on the line again, and Anna knew she had to hang up and see what was in Jo's bag.

A light tan envelope rested on top of the two chignons that had been cut from Jo's hair after each of her sons was born. Both chignons had retained a soft luster. Anna had never seen Jo wear either of them. "I've got more than I know what to do with," Jo would always boast.

The note probably gave detailed instructions about what to do with the chignons, whether to tuck them, still boxed, into the casket's satin lining, or to work them into her existing hair.

Anna smoothed the envelope. There had to be instructions in Jo's note. She wouldn't have to rely on pure skill to decide what to do. Jo had taken care of everything else. Weighing the envelope in her hand, Anna was reluctant to open it. This was the last contact, the last secret to be revealed. After being close to Jo for so long, she should know without being told what Jo's wishes were. Part of her wanted the envelope to stay sealed forever, so the message would be preserved forever. Unread, it contained the only possibility of new communication with Jo.

Greedy strands from the chignon rose with the envelope. Anna wet her fingers and smoothed the hair into itself. The envelope had picked up Jo's scent—a sweet and sharp blend from the shampoo she'd always mixed herself.

Well, Grace Nettinger didn't leave a note, so I thought I'd better or else you'd never forgive me. Hope you can read my chicken scratching. I wanted to do you a tape, but then I remembered the tape recorder was Thomas's.

I know how you are about these things—wanting to know everything, always going on about things that don't have any answers. And then not asking somebody about whatever it is they're dying to tell you. (That drives Mary Frances the craziest. It used to drive me crazy as I was always looking for a way to get to that woman and you managed without half trying.) Anyway—

I liked my life. I had a good time. That's something that's too much on everybody's mind these days (sometimes a good time just comes out of nowhere—you've got to learn to recognize when it comes instead of trying to make it happen and missing it when it sneaks up on you). I know you think I'm wrong about not taking the chemotherapy and the cobalt, but if I'd done that, it would have been doing the same thing that Grace did. You think about that until you understand it. I don't want to die, but the cancer is a part of me. I OWN it in a way I couldn't ever own any chemicals and X rays. Going through all that rigmarole would kill

me. I can't change now. I'm the same as I ever was. And I can't do it.
I can't give myself over to them. Jo without hair is nobody I know or
care to know. I can see your face now—those greeny brown eyes starting
to squint and your pretty, pretty hair starting to fall into your face. I don't
want to hear it, Anna. Now—

Down to business. Hire yourself some good girls and then leave them
alone but not too much alone. You're going to need one who likes to talk
and one who likes to listen (two who know how to do both are even
better). Don't expect them to be you. Charles might be tempted to stay.
Don't let him—he won't ever be happy here. He doesn't belong to the
town, but he needs a place to stay when he visits. Give it time. Get to
know the shop. It's going to take more than one day. Don't walk away
from it, Anna. I want you to have it. It belongs to you. In a funny way,
it always has.

Only a couple more things. One—I don't know about this Ed Nettinger business, but you better make up your mind one way or the other
what you want with him. That daughter's still one to reckon with, too.
Be nice to your mother—Georgia's not so bad. Let her carry on if she
has to. She's a jealous woman.

Fix the chignons on me whichever way you can. Stuff them under my
feet if you have to. I don't want anybody else wearing my hair, and I don't
want Burgess sleeping with it under his pillow or keeping it in some
drawer someplace.

Wear those sunglasses I gave you. I'll be watching—don't think I
won't be. I love you. Jo.

Anna rubbed the paper against her chest in relief. Pleased by
Jo's resurrection, she locked her knees under her chin to guard the
note.

———

Close to midnight, after the sound of car doors slamming and
children laughing and shrieking had died, Anna went downstairs.
She uncapped a bottle of neutralizer, careful to hold the upended
spout away from Jo's letter, and took a sniff of the solution to
sharpen her senses. She couldn't give in to sadness now. There was
too much to be done.

Despite Jo's note, the quick, secret thrill of ownership refused
to strike Anna. Bevo's attempts at redecoration didn't help much.

One of his friends in Los Angeles who was trying to crack the costume design union in Hollywood had made an anorexic black poodle outfit for Bevo's can of mousse. Silver glitter sparkled in the black net. The poodle didn't favor Connie at all.

Instead of scrapping Mary Frances's *Photoplays*, Bevo had expanded the racks with his own collection of *Silver Screen* and the *Star*. His additions made Anna angry. The changes weren't cosmetic; they were designed to showcase the very things that were wrong with Mary Frances's. The shop needed revitalization, not Mary Frances's ineffectual preservation and not Bevo's sly enhancements.

The softening effect on the face of pink lights or a magazine hairstyle copied on the wrong head wasn't behind a woman's transformation. Every woman walked out of a shop carrying what she'd brought in with her. Sad walls and cans of mousse hidden in burlesque costumes compounded the problem. Nobody came into a beauty shop to be reminded of deterioration or to be laughed at. The most she could do was to make sure her customers left the shop better armed against the excesses of either hope or despair.

When the phone rang again, Anna knew information about Jo's death must be getting around. The best place to call for news and advice was the shop. She tried to straighten out all the relevant details in her mind before answering. Burgess hated anything with cream of mushroom soup in it; the service would be held Thursday in the Presbyterian church at ten o'clock; the shop would be closed indefinitely; memorials should be sent to the library.

"Who's this?" Claude asked. "Is that Anna? Everybody just says, 'Hello?' over there now and I never know if I'm calling the right place. I heard over the radio. I was halfway back to the plant when I heard. I pulled over and I just sat there for a half hour. But then I remembered her legs from when Mary Frances had those pink nylon uniforms. Her knees were on the knobby side and the insides of her calves were kind of pared away—but she was the kind of a woman that made you think she had great legs. I just wanted somebody to remember her legs with. I'm glad it's you, Anna. There's not another one like her. I won't be able to load strawberry soda without thinking of her. You two—you kind of go together in my mind, the shop and all. And your legs." He sighed. "From knee to ankle's a little shorter than I ordinarily like but the curve of the calf more than makes up—"

"Claude. Don't you ever, ever think about anything else? Maybe I should start a waxing service here at the shop just for you."

"Oh no, Anna, don't do that. That's a violence a leg shouldn't have to take. By the way, there's no need to tell Burgess what I said about Jo's legs. Some men don't appreciate the appreciation."

"I'll leave that part out when I tell him you called."

"I've been over there already. Bryan was over there. He'd just drove in. Ed Nettinger was over there with some catfish, all skinned and cornmealed. I took a case of strawberry soda over. That reminds me—the funeral's on Thursday, so I'll have to deliver to you on Friday."

"Only half," Anna said. "Don't worry. Hawaya's nice in the spring."

The glass in the front door rattled. She had forgotten to turn on the outside light over the door. With the lights on inside, she couldn't see who it was. "Hold on, Claude. I've got a trick-or-treater."

She switched on the front porch light and caught Ed Nettinger leaning against the doorframe. When she let him in, he was careful not to reach out to offer sympathy. A certain reserve had surfaced in Ed since the day he'd brought her back. The reemergence of Grace had a hand in his caution, but Anna wasn't sure where he saw his wife—in Jo, in herself, or in the fact of another premature and unnatural death. During Jo's illness Ed had dropped by the hospital every day. Anna suspected that his sense of duty had only temporarily overcome his sense of self-protection.

"I've got Claude on the phone. He said you took some fish over to Burgess."

Ed produced a bottle of strawberry soda. "I was going to surprise you." He wandered around the shop until she finished talking on the phone. "Why don't you stay with me tonight? We can stay in town or we can go out to the ranch."

Where would they be if she let Ed comfort her? Seduction of the body was one thing, but what he offered was far more dangerous. She didn't belong with him any more than she belonged at the shop. He had to understand that she was doing fine. "There's still a lot to do. Maybe I'll come out in a couple of weeks and play in the pond."

"It can sneak up on you, Anna. Don't ignore it."

"It's a different situation. Jo wasn't Grace. I'm not Grace. I don't need saving." Anna counted a space of three tiles between them, then five and then six. Stuck in one spot, she was succeeding in backing Ed Nettinger out the door.

"I'll be in town tonight if you need me, otherwise I'll call you tomorrow."

"Tomorrow's fine," Anna said.

Ed twirled his hat around one finger. "Bryan was with Burgess."

"I know. Burgess called him. He's the buffer between Bevo and Burgess now. That'll keep him pretty busy. If that's what you're wondering."

"For a second or two there, I wondered. I'll see you later."

The shop seemed emptier after Ed left. Anna went upstairs and immediately wished she were downstairs again. Only when she had gone downstairs did the upstairs seem to be the better place. Deciding that fatigue was causing the dissatisfaction, she lay down on one of the shampoo couches. Every shift of her body threatened to throw the couch off-balance. Mary Frances's chaise lounge would have been perfect to sleep on.

Ten minutes later Anna had gotten into the Valiant and was on her way to Marfa to pick up a canvas wig stand for Jo's chignons. Everything was still in Marfa, half unpacked from the move there and half packed for the next move forward.

Anna drove sixty miles farther west, away from Marfa and Alpine, to Lobo for a cup of coffee. Jo's note sat propped on the café counter. Reading the words for the tenth time was as frustrating as reading them for the second. She had lost the feeling of

hearing Jo's voice. The rising sun was in her eyes all the way back
to Alpine.

———

Mary Frances kicked off her black spike heels. She ran a stockinged heel appreciatively along a green satin stripe in Richard
Pullock's couch. "So I told Alfred he could just wind himself up
and putt-putt around that lake till the cows come home for all I
care."

The exterior of the coffin was black steel. Jo rested on pale green
velveteen. A strand of pearls kept slipping toward Jo's shoulders
so Anna made a knot and tucked the excess necklace under a satin
pillow that supported her neck. Jo wore a black cashmere sweater
set and black wool pants.

Mary Frances had washed Jo's hair and smoothed it into a top
knot. Anna wanted to use one of the chignons as a foundation and
work Jo's hair into it. Bevo had redone Burgess's dye job two days
before his mother died. He had matched the color to the chignons. Anna prodded a curl into position and asked, "What did
Alfred say?"

"He didn't hear me. He was on the boat at the time, and I was
in a motel room. I was not alone at the time either."

"Good going, M.F. That's getting tough with him."

The November light slanting into the room from the garden
window released the chrysanthemums' earthy smell. Footsteps
and slamming car doors and vague voices joined the background
of Mary Frances's voice. It was the first time since the beginning
of the summer that Anna felt that things were normal. She was
at work, concentrating on the head in front of her, while Mary
Frances reclined and moaned about Alfred and hinted about
afternoons spent in motel rooms. They could have been back at
the shop again except the rhythm was off. Anna kept expecting
Jo to take Mary Frances's bait.

"Well, I can't very well throw him out after almost forty years
of marriage," Mary Frances said. She thought for a while. "Can
I?" She got up to rearrange a spray of white and red carnations

that Burgess's mechanics had sent. "Let me know when you're ready to twine and pin."

"What about your motel man?" Anna asked. "Go off with him."

Mary Frances curled her fingers over the coffin's open edge and looked down at Jo. "It's not as easy for me to change partners in midstream as it is for you. She looks exactly right. I've never seen a job like this. Sharon Pullock's never been any Elizabeth Arden. It's like Josephine was planning her whole life how she'd look today."

Anna held the chignon in her hand. She had no idea where to start. "Mary Frances, if you don't shut up and start twining and pinning, I'm going to call up Alfred and tell him everything you've been up to."

"I wish you would." All the years of working with a comb clenched between her teeth had given Mary Frances clear diction. "This is where they laid out Grace Nettinger. Well, of course—because she's a woman. There's another room where they lay out the men. Sharon bought a red leather couch for *that* room—an uncomfortable thing, too. I've had those couch buttons dig into my back a time or two. It's really very sexist. No windows in there either. Remind me to ask Alfred if he wants to be buried at sea."

"Why don't you just conk him over the head and toss him into the lake?"

"Oh, Anna, really. I could never do that," Mary Frances said reproachfully. "I'd be the first one they suspect. When is Burgess coming over, that poor man? Now there was a love story. I always envied her—not her appearance certainly but the way life treated her."

"More like the way she treated life," Anna corrected. "She didn't sit around waiting on somebody to give her a break. She had rough times with Burgess. His drinking. The thing with Bevo. She just never let the water close over her head is all. Not even at the very end. She knew how she wanted to meet it and she did. Even if it was the wrong thing to do."

Mary Frances took Anna's arm and asked, "Do you think she

really truly *knew* how we felt about her—really truly?" Tears fed
into her eyes. "I shouldn't have made fun of those nails and that
hair."

"She knew." And when Jo didn't sit up and shout triumphantly
at Mary Frances's admission, Anna knew Jo was really dead.
There was no use in letting the comb tap accidentally against Jo's
shoulder and expecting a response.

The Pullocks had done a good job. The Jo lying in the casket
resembled the Jo of a better and healthier time. Burgess would be
pleased that her mystique had survived. Her skin looked as warm
and soft as it had immediately after she had died. For a moment
Anna wanted to take the pocket mirror out of Mary Frances's
hand and hold it up to Jo's mouth to see if her breath would mist
the glass.

The Pullocks had done too good a job. Screwing up the part and
adding too much rouge were the kind things to do. Make the
person *look* dead. Nobody wanted to say good-bye to a lifelike
corpse.

Cheryl Long arrived at the shop with four black dresses in Anna's
size.

"I'm not leaving till you try them all on," she said. "Just
because your best friend died is no reason to let yourself go any
further than you've gone." She unsheathed a black sweater dress
and twisted the hanger. "Try this one on first. This is the one—
I absolutely feel it. I hope you appreciate this. I don't make house
calls for just everybody."

Trying on clothes always made Anna's stomach feel hollow. She
stepped onto the towels Cheryl had laid on the styling room floor
and pulled the dress over her hips.

"I brought over three belts, too," Cheryl Long said. She anchored the buckles on her fingers and let red and gray and black
patent leather unfurl. "It's not like it's a wedding dress for God's
sake—wear it once and pack it away. I bet you never even had a
real wedding dress. If you get the urge again—*promise* me you'll
let me pick out the dress." She paused and twitched the soft fabric

around Anna's hips. "Perfect. Look at yourself. There's nothing that says death has to be dowdy. Jo would be so happy to see you gussied up."

The gold-threaded label scratched Anna's neck. "Don't tell me she told you to put these away for me."

"Well," Cheryl Long admitted, "she called . . . but I had this one put back for you already. She liked the one with the straight skirt and the dolman sleeves better, but I convinced her this one would be nicer to your hips. Don't tell me you don't see a hairstyle and think of a particular woman. What did you think of her sweater set? Did you feel how *soft* that cashmere was?"

"No!" Anna felt guilty enough for liking the dress without being reminded of her growing reluctance to touch Jo at the funeral home. The warmth in Jo's body had been replaced by a dry coolness. "I'll take this one."

"At least try on the others," Cheryl urged. "Don't give me that look. All I'm saying is they're here and you might as well. It's not going to *kill* you."

————

The Presbyterian church was filled with the warm, toasted smell of wool suits heated by the sun, but the scent of closely packed flowers hadn't reached the back of the church where Anna stood. She twisted the cuff of the black sweater dress and waited for Bryan.

He was trying to seat Shirley, one of Jo's Tuesday afternoon appointments. A green hat with a round crown and a curled brim was glued to her orange sherbet hair. From the back of the church, Anna couldn't tell who had styled Shirley's hair. Jo's funeral had given all the beauty shops in town and probably the ones in Marfa, Fort Davis and Marathon a busy morning.

Claude scooted the people in his row down as if they were bottles in a soda machine. He waved for Anna to fill the empty space. She shook her head and waited for Bryan to usher her to a pew. She suddenly wasn't sure where she belonged. There didn't seem to be a row reserved for somebody not technically family. Claude craned his small, slick head again to see Anna's legs. He circled his thumb and forefinger and winked.

The windows that ran along the outside aisles of the pews had been cranked open. A stream of air from a hole in the stained glass window over the altar flattened the organist's bangs. The hole, a pattern of sky and tree trunk instead of Jesus' bare left foot, had been made when a hailstone crashed through the window in late May.

In the middle of the five rows of beauty shop owners and their operators sat Willi. The snap and rustle of the fan she held were constant. Susie's black and white plastic bracelets tinkled as she tried to figure out what Elidia and her grandmother were saying. The rise and fall of the low voices were almost visible as if wind were fingering a field.

Liz and Leo were sitting beside Mary Frances and a man Anna couldn't place. Pretending to search the rack in front of him for a hymnal, Leo leaned close to Liz's expanding stomach and listened. Liz wet her finger and twisted the ends of Leo's mustache. Cheryl Long sat with her mother on the right side of the church. Mrs. Long discreetly turned her head by eighths, right and then left, recording everything in a hand-held notebook. If Cheryl had her way, Jo's sweater set would probably be the lead item in her mother's "Latitudes and Longitudes" column next week.

Ed and Delia sat behind Cheryl. Delia had tied a red and black checkered scarf around her head. The scarf ends peaked over her right ear.

Ed wore the gray suit that matched his eyes. It must be his funeral suit. Despite Anna's influence, he had poured Vitalis all over his head for the occasion. His left arm extended along the back of the glossy pew and a gray dress Stetson sat beside him, saving a place.

Anna waved a persistent usher away. His eyes had that kind of lying-on-the-ground and peering-through-the-weeds look that Bryan's friends usually had. "I'm waiting for him," she said, nodding to Bryan, who was still trying to maneuver Shirley into a pew. Her green hat bobbing, she kept jockeying for a pew closer to the casket. She flagged Bryan back to her three times with a lavender handkerchief and pointed out empty spaces ahead of her. Half genuflecting at the pews Shirley had specified, Bryan negotiated without success for her transfer. She held him a minute longer to talk, and he looked as though listening to Shirley's sorrows was exactly what he wanted to be doing. Anna had discouraged that look when he lived with her, but she was glad to see that she hadn't killed it.

Finally Bryan held out his arm for Anna. Feeling suddenly paralyzed, unable to locate her place in the church, she wanted Bryan to tell her where she should sit, or better yet, that there was no place for her in the church at all.

Bryan stared straight ahead. The flared edges of his red side-burns crinkled as he smiled. He looked longingly at the congregation as if he'd rather be with any one of them. "The family wants you to go in with them."

"No," Anna said firmly. "I'm not family. Burgess would have a fit."

"You underestimate Burgess," Bryan said. "Where would you like to sit? Ah, there's a space available next to the widower Ed Nettinger if I'm not mistaken."

"You're mistaken. If you can get Leo to stop lying all over Liz, I'll sit with them. I'll sit with the operators."

"Stylists, Anna. You always told me stylists."

"Some are stylists and some are operators. Who's that usher back there? The one with the funny eyes. Is he one of yours?"

"One of my what? Put your hand in my elbow. That's the way it's done. We have to link up; it doesn't mean anything. Proper form, that's all."

"Don't take everything so personally," Anna said. "That usher. Is he one of your people? Does he speak English?"

Bryan swung her around gently. "Here we are—safe and sound next to Liz and Leo and baby. I'm in need of a ride to Burgess's after."

Anna felt Liz's stomach against her when they hugged. She hadn't expected it to feel so hard and solid. Liz's eyes were pink-rimmed and there were swipes of brown beneath her lower lids. They sat down. "We're going to name the baby after Jo," Liz whispered. Leo nodded, and she continued, "Do you think she'd like that?" Anna nodded, and Liz beamed. "That's what I thought." Her fingers played along her stomach. "Tell Anna your poem. Leo's started a poem. It's beautiful."

He blushed, and the ends of his mustache disappeared into his mouth. "Sleep weighted women/Stumbling blocks to their own desires," Leo recited and stopped.

"Go on," Anna urged.

"That's it."

"That's it? What's it supposed to mean?" Anna hoped he hadn't written the poem about Liz or anybody else she knew.

"I don't know," Leo admitted. "I can't know everything. It just came to me."

Liz rested her cheek against his shoulder. "That's all right," she said. "You don't have to know everything. You know enough for a while."

Mary Frances interrupted impatiently. "This is Walter," she whispered and blushed to indicate the seriousness of her intention by bringing him to a family gathering.

At an unseen signal the organist straightened her spine. Her playing broadened and deepened and the congregation fell silent. Anna felt the vibrations of Jo's casket being rolled into the church. She was sitting on the aisle and had to lean sideways to avoid being brushed by the pallbearers. The sound of the gurney wheels locking into place was too loud.

Burgess walked down the aisle by himself. Side by side, Bevo and Marvin followed him. While Burgess waited for his sons to enter the first pew, his hand rested on the casket's cover of red and white carnations. Bevo bowed his head slightly to move Burgess into the pew after Marvin, but Burgess hesitated at the separation from Jo. Bevo worked a white carnation free from the cover and put it into his father's lapel. Burgess gave in and let his two sons bolster him.

A procession of cars headed by the Pullock's pearl-gray hearse bumped across the railroad tracks. They drove past the strip of tall-grassed land that kept Mexican Town from jumping the tracks and up the hill, where they turned left at the Catholic church. Built of large earth-colored stones, the church seemed to unfold from the rounded mountain like a cutout greeting card. The procession continued along the slope of the mountain to the cemetery and turned right after the last house, where a miniature cemetery filled the Fletcher front yard. Walter Fletcher had been the local representative for a monument manufacturer in Dallas. A pink granite obelisk adorned Walter's own ten-month-old grave.

Anna drove her newly washed and polished Valiant past Holy Angel, the low-walled Mexican cemetery, and through the iron gates of Elm Grove. Wanting to be at the end of the procession, she had dawdled at the church until most of the other cars had turned on their headlights and pulled into line. Being farther away from the casket and Jo's family gave Anna a better sense of the life in the day, of what was happening rather than what had happened. In front of her was a long line of people who had come to pay their respects, and surrounding all of them was a landscape that with gentled hills seemed to cradle the town.

Because of good weather, the burial tent was open on two sides. Anna found a space at the back of the tent and crunched the bright green Astroturf under her feet. It was the biggest welcome mat she'd ever seen. Ignoring the words spoken by the minister here, as she had at the church, Anna kept the focus on what was going on around her.

Delia and Ed stood outside the tent. Ed studied the horizon. Years of shrimping and ranching had taught him to keep an eye out for clouds. Delia who was also studying faces, smiled when she caught Anna looking at her.

Marvin wore his marine dress uniform. The strap of the white hat bit into his chin as he played "Taps." He held the notes and then cut them without warning so that they sliced the air. As

Anna struggled to hold on to the disappearing notes, she saw Bevo
arch his neck against the music.

The ushers stood in a semicircle behind the pallbearers. Sweat
was beginning to rim Bryan's collar. Anna made another sweep
of the cemetery to see if K. O. Browne, Jr., was watching, but
there was no sign of him. Along the route from the church to the
cemetery she had expected to catch his tan car idling at one of
the unpaved intersections as he waited for a chance to slip in.

Three Mexican men with shovels sat smoking cigarettes on the
concrete border of the Haslips' plot. One of the men pressed his
work boot against his shovel blade and made the handle rise and
stand at attention as Marvin played. Richard Pullock's smooth,
shiny forehead wrinkled in warning at the gravediggers. When the
burial service came to an end, he nudged the double curve of
pallbearers and ushers into action with his right elbow. He shook
hands with himself and sent the same signal to the young minister.

Jo had sent the minister to talk to Bevo when he came by the
hospital every Wednesday on his weekly rounds. "My soul's way
too old," she had said and waved him away. "There's not any use
trying to run any interference for me. Talk to Bevo. See that it's
not too late for him."

Graveside, the minister watched Bevo put on his sunglasses.
Tucking the prayer book firmly under his arm, he skirted Jo's
casket and clasped Bevo's shoulder. Too soon, Anna wanted to
warn. Too soon. She wished someone had come for Bevo, but
there wasn't anybody wearing a trench coat who was discreetly
watching. Bevo slid the sunglasses down his nose and gave the
minister a once-over.

Anna moved quickly. "Nice service. Reverend . . . ?" She didn't
know what to call him. His occupation while Jo was still alive had
seemed like an intrusion, an unwelcome preview of coming attrac-
tions. Today there was no harm in letting him dress up and say
a few words.

"Michael is fine. Just Michael." The minister smiled hugely
and swallowed his upper lip.

"Uupp—Anna," Bevo said, "where are those sunglasses?"

Heat surged into Anna's chest, the same mixture of pleasure and irritation she had always felt when Jo had said the words. Now there was disappointment as well. It was the words that held the power then, not the speaker. "I'll see you at the house later," she said shortly.

Tears blurred her vision but she concentrated on the separate progress of her black patent leather high heels until her eyes dried. Dust from the unpaved cemetery roads coated her shoes. Her ankles ached from trying to maintain balance against the small rocks and ruts.

Bryan leaned against the Valiant's hood. "Are you ready then? Shall I drive?"

Anna handed him the keys. "There won't be any surprise visitors today, will there?"

He leaned across the front seat to open her door. "Our friend Patrolman Browne wouldn't disrupt our day of mourning. That would be wrong, and he's a man who knows his rights from his wrongs."

"And when does our day of mourning end? At midnight? Is it all over then? What about tomorrow?" A one-day ritual of public grief wasn't going to convince Anna that Jo was all right.

She cleaned the windshield from inside and saw a figure standing in the road. "Stop. That's Delia Nettinger."

"I was hoping you'd stop," Delia said. She leaned against the car and twisted the rearview mirror toward her. Dust had relightened her mascaraed eyelashes. "God! You'd think they'd do something about paving these roads out here. Dad says it's up to the county commissioners." She bent down and whispered, "Is that Bryan?"

"Delia Nettinger, I believe?" Bryan reached across Anna to extend his hand.

Delia went pink. Her voice dropped to register her thrill. "He knows who I am? He knows?" Her voice went lower still. "Oh . . . because of Dad?"

"Because you were standing in the middle of the road," Anna said impatiently. "Who else would do a thing like that?"

"Oh." Delia grew pinker. The tears in her eyes were the color of quicksilver. "Mom's headstone finally came in, we have to go look at it, but we're coming by the Andersons later. That's okay, isn't it? I didn't know Jo all that well, but I liked her. I liked her a lot, and she was your friend." Her straying eyes suddenly returned to Anna. "Are you okay?"

"I'd be a lot better if people stopped jumping in front of my car."

Delia placed her hand firmly on the car door as if Bryan might drive off. "No—I mean really. Are you really okay?"

Anna wished she had sunglasses to hide behind. Being the target of Delia's concern threatened to undo her. "Fine. We have to go."

"I'll see you later," Delia said and stepped back. "Okay? Okay, Bryan?"

Bryan winked. "Absolutely. We've got a lot to talk about, you and I."

They drove through town in silence. Anna repositioned her outside mirror and caught the reflection of K. O. Browne, Jr., following in his unmarked patrol car. "Your friend's back there. I thought you said he would drop it for today."

Bryan stared briefly into his rearview mirror. "Coincidence. He's probably on his way to lunch."

"I don't believe in coincidences," Anna said. "It's getting too close. I know it."

Stretching his arm along the seat back to tickle her shoulder, Bryan asked, "What do you believe in, Anna love? The law? Legalities? Stiff pieces of paper bound with black cord? Artificial restrictions, artificial boundaries."

Anna stuck her arm out the window. "Maybe I'll just flag down K. O. Browne, Jr., and see what he thinks you believe in."

Bryan rubbed her shoulder with the heel of his hand. "I would never jeopardize the safety of anyone I loved. Never. You're safe no matter what happens."

"I can take care of myself," Anna said. "Don't worry." She willed the border patrolman to turn right or left, to decide on a hamburger or Mexican food for lunch, but when they passed the western city limits, he was still behind them. Bryan signaled well before the turnoff to Jo and Burgess's house. K.O. ignored the cue and continued west.

"Of course," she said. "El Paso. He's going to El Paso for a long weekend to see his wife and his kids."

"Absolutely," Bryan agreed. "A man needs the support of his family. And a man willing to sacrifice so much has to keep his family well out of it." The Valiant skittered to a stop under his heavy foot.

From the intensity of Bryan's expression as he stared through the windshield, Anna wouldn't have been surprised to see platoons and battalions and companies of men leaping over the chained mountains.

The sun highlighted milky streaks in the salmon mousse Mary Frances had brought. The mold she used had jelled a fish in mid-jump. The tail kicked toward the openmouthed head in an effort to bat itself higher into the air. There was a sliced and stuffed Spanish olive for an eye. Pale iceberg lettuce set around the copper platter had begun to roll toward the mousse. The living room was full of people as if it were a party. It was like a party except everybody was being particularly careful to keep napkins under glasses and to pick up any crackers dropped on the rug. A corps of women whisked empty plastic glasses and white cocktail napkins off the tables. Plate loads of food were rearranged and replaced. The dishwasher chugged in the background. Anna didn't know where all the women had come from. She tried unsuccessfully to find some kind of physical resemblance to Jo or Burgess in them.

Bryan and Delia were in deep conversation on the couch. Two gin and tonics had given Delia the courage to drag Bryan's loosened tie away from his neck and sling it around her own. Intercepting Delia's third drink, Bryan exchanged it for his empty glass.

Marvin wandered over to Anna. She spotted the whorl of a potential cowlick in his crew cut blond hair. His chin was still stained with a double set of red marks from the strap of his white dress cap. "Hey, Anna." Dressed in the white shirt and dark pants of a civilian, he seemed trapped uncertainly between shyness and aggression.

"It was nice that you played," Anna said. "I never heard you play anything before except for Herb Alpert. Remember? 'The Lonely Bull' or something like that?"

He smiled and showed large white teeth. " 'Spanish Flea'."

"How long will they let you stay?" Anna asked.

"They gave me ten days . . . so"—he looked around the crowded room and rocked his upper body—"so . . . so I guess ten days."

"Then where?"

"Wherever they send me." He looked down at Anna and his translucent blond eyebrows struggled. "I miss it here. Man—sometimes . . . I just can't believe how much I miss it here. You know?"

Anna didn't want to know. "It's a place. Most places are about the same once you dig down a little."

"That's my problem, I guess," Marvin confessed. "I don't dig down far enough. Man—sometimes . . . just give me three wishes and I'd be back. You know?"

"You bring yourself back here and you better hang on to those other two wishes. It's changed since you left. You can't go back to the way you thought things were. Most of the time that's not even how things were in the first place." Looking at the disappointment in Marvin's face, Anna reminded herself that she could let these things slide past without the bedrock of her own life being threatened. It wasn't her responsibility to shoot down Marvin. He was entitled to shoot himself down.

"Burgess would be glad to see you come back," she finally offered. "Maybe you should. How much time do you have left?"

Marvin's face shifted into bewilderment. "We just can't be together. . . . I don't know why it is exactly. I think about it a lot. You know? I try . . . I write Bevo, I tried to help Mom with the two of them. Do you know—seeing us from the outside?"

"I don't know . . . families . . . you know," Anna said lamely. "Everybody means well, but . . . I don't know." She wished

Marvin wouldn't look at her with such bare trust. She hoped that wasn't how he'd face the enemy. "Everything'll be fine."

"Bevo picked me up at the airport. Man, I couldn't get over that one! There he was stepping on and off those automatic doors. . . ." Marvin's eyes found Bevo in the crowd. His eyebrows peaked and pulled his lips into a smile. "Things'll be okay. Yeah . . . things'll be *o-kay.*" He hugged Anna awkwardly. "OK—zero killed. You'll see."

Anna looked at all the plastic-covered casseroles waiting in line on the kitchen counter to be heated in the microwave and she realized warning Marvin wouldn't do any good. He'd survived growing up under Burgess's hand and Parris Island besides that.

Bevo smirked and mouthed words across the room to them. Marvin squinted. "What's he saying? I'll go find out."

Anna was positive that he would be the first to fall in battle. Marvin didn't understand anything about playing dirty, and Bevo was a moving target they'd never hit. She sipped scotch and tasted the metallic sweat from her fingers on the rim.

Ed Nettinger appeared at her side. "Delia and I thought you might like—"

"How's Grace's headstone?"

"Standard," Ed replied. "No surprises there, just the dates and her name. I think Delia thought it would have the reason carved on it, Grace's last chance to leave a message with somebody."

"Her parting shot more like. Who's doing the headstones now that Walter's gone and died?"

"Nobody yet, I had to call Dallas direct. I think old Pullock's trying to get the concession." Ed considered the pairing of Bryan and Delia on the couch. "Your ex-husband and my daughter seem to be hitting it off pretty good."

"They're both talkers. They both like to dig."

"Maybe I ought to join them," Ed said.

"You better watch out. I think you'd wind up with lots of little holes dug in you."

"Is that why you're staying so far away?"

Anna couldn't take close looks from either Nettinger. The bond of grief could unite father and daughter, but there was no way she'd join them. She had had to send away Ed and his need to comfort three times since Jo's death. "They look like they're doing all right. They don't need any company."

"How many times do I have to come to you before you trust me?" Ed asked.

"Until you don't come by anymore," she answered.

"And then it'll be too late."

Anna nodded in total agreement. "And then it'll be too late. And then I'll know I was right not to trust you. So go away now."

"I don't believe you. You think it's already too late. You started out thinking it was too late. I don't know if it's because of Grace or what."

"Look. You're wasting your time. I'm not going to be here that long."

"It's my time to waste," he argued. "The problem with you is you think if you say something long enough, it's liable to come true. That's why you won't talk about what's going on between you and me, you won't tell me about the shop. You can try to pretend nothing's happened, but that doesn't work on me." Ed took her glass and worked his way to the card table bar.

Good, Anna thought. And the long-suffering, patient act's not going to work on me. She walked out the back door.

On the night of Jo's funeral, against the protests of all the relatives, Burgess marinated a leg of lamb and piled charcoal in the barbecue pit. He told the protesters to go to their motel rooms for a rest and then come back at eight o'clock for dinner. Bryan and Anna were entrusted with the transitional care of Burgess and his sons.

The mountain set behind the house wasn't visible, but Anna felt the land massed there. Standing inside the house and staring hard through the screen door, she fooled herself into thinking she could see the double craters of Twin Peaks molding the horizon.

Burgess used a pair of tongs to turn over the briquets with their red-hot hearts while Bryan cranked the spit. Fat from the lamb fed the fire. Side-stepping the sparks, Burgess continued to prod the coals.

Twenty feet away Bevo and Marvin chucked pea gravel at six rusted license plates nailed to individual fenceposts. The brothers' heels scuttled against outcroppings of rock as they side-armed gravel again and again at the license plates. Their white dress shirts were unbuttoned and the sleeves rolled up.

"Man, oh man," Marvin grieved when his shots missed metal and thumped wood. The deep, solid sound of Bevo's gravel hitting the plates where they were backed by wood sent Marvin into a congratulatory crouch.

His shirt twisting into itself in back, Bevo just threw and threw and threw without bothering to stop and listen to see if he hit the target.

"Trying to hit that mountain out there, are you?" Burgess laughed. "We don't own it. Careful you don't wake up tomorrow morning and find out it's all pocked and pitted."

Relieved of duty at the spit and seeing that he was needed elsewhere, Bryan scouted for small rocks to keep the piles at both brothers' feet replenished. The guarantee of an unending supply made Marvin looser; like Bevo, he stopped aiming and launched one rock after another.

His hits and near misses were driving Anna crazy. If only he hit one plate head on, she felt sure something inside herself would be taken care of. The men's bodies were inclined toward Marvin in attitudes of anticipation and support. When Anna thought she wouldn't be able to stand it any longer, Marvin connected with a large stone that rocked the post.

"Whoa! Mighty Marv!" Bevo shouted. "There's that aim that's true, that's true, that's true, that's always true! Damn! Goddamn!"

The four men stood quietly for a minute, listening to the fading echo of Marvin's successful hit and looking into the night together. There seemed to be no space between them. Despite Bevo's black hair and fair skin and Marvin's height, Anna couldn't factor Jo out of either of them.

She hadn't been able to factor Jo out of anything. There was no hole in the universe that was growing smaller and smaller, nothing she could reach through to bring Jo back. Jo was gone. There was no sign of her—no flash of color, no true smell, no voice in the night, no vibration.

Anna didn't believe in life after death. She didn't believe in long tunnels lit by bright white lights and departed relatives and friends acting as tour guides on the other side. She didn't believe in God. She didn't believe in the Holy Ghost; she had never known exactly what the Holy Ghost was. She had no intention of having to apologize her way into anybody's good graces. Still, for all that, she had expected some kind of sign, some kind of bone-deep comfort or knowledge.

Looking outside at the four men standing together and staring at the mountain as if they were experiencing something, Anna was afraid that a sign was being received and she was unable to recognize it.

A nna pried open the can of turquoise paint she'd had mixed the day after Mary Frances offered her the shop. A small paintbrush she had used to apply the mudlike henna was still in her old drawer downstairs. Without bothering to change out of the black dress or turn on the light, she painted a stripe across an upstairs wall. The wet streak picked up a shine from back porch lights along the alley. Trusting that the shade would be too powdery or too glossy once it had set, Anna blew on the wall to speed the process. The sooner the paint dried, the sooner she could leave.

What she had wanted for her shop was a sun-shot swimming-pool-bottom turquoise. A clear decision about the shade of the walls might have jinxed the deal, so over the years she had accumulated paint samples of every color. One strip of pink combinations was so old that some of the colors had faded and now matched Mary Frances's walls. Or whosever walls they were.

Anna lightly pressed her finger into the paint. Jo

said the shop was hers. Burgess said the shop was hers. Bevo said the shop was hers. The shop was *not* hers. A deed was only a piece of paper. That morning, as she dressed for Jo's funeral, the desire to own the shop had flared up, but she had squelched it. The desire was only a habit that was hard to break after so many years.

The deal had been jinxed, and her premature decision on what color to paint the walls had had nothing to do with it. That was superstitious. The shop was not meant to be hers. She wasn't cut out to be the owner of anything. The temptation to leave without looking back, another reliable habit, was growing stronger.

But nobody in her right mind would take the place as it was. Bevo might start renovations, but if the contractor was a man, they'd probably run off together; Burgess was in no shape to handle selling the shop. That left her.

The money saved for the down payment would go into remodeling it instead. She would stay long enough to supervise the renovation and the selling of the shop. With any luck, both she and Burgess would get most of their money back.

There was no reason to watch the paint sample dry. It wasn't an omen of the future. If the shade was off, all that meant was the person who mixed the paint had a different, more chlorinated vision of a swimming pool bottom than she did. And if the shade was perfect, that didn't mean the shop had been destined to be hers.

Before locking up the shop, Anna sprang a beer and a Coke out of the soda machine. She drove east on Highway 90 because heading west would take her past the unpaved road that dived deeply into the creek, and tonight she didn't feel lucky enough to attempt it. A trip east also meant that the sun would be at her back when she returned to Alpine.

When Anna was awakened by the phone the next morning, the first thing she saw was the paint streak. There was way too much green in it. She wasn't surprised. You couldn't scoop out a handful of pool water and capture the turquoise. How could anybody be expected to duplicate such a color?

Without getting up, Anna reeled in the telephone by its long cord. The receiver clattered to the floor, but she kept pulling in the line.

"I know better than to ask what's going on over there," Burgess said when she picked up the receiver. "You'd think you could disappoint me just once by behaving politely."

Anna put the receiver on her chest. Burgess was back to normal. "Don't think you have to clean up your behavior for my benefit," she said to the room. "I'm sorry. I dropped the phone," she said to Burgess.

"I've got a contractor for you. Name's Jerry White, does good work, doesn't charge an arm and a leg, he'll be over there at eleven-thirty."

"Fine. Does he know what you want done?" Good. This made things easier. They didn't have to pretend anymore that the shop was in her hands. All she had to do was follow Burgess's instructions.

An exaggerated sigh came over the phone. "It's your place. What do I care about any of that beauty shop stuff? I'm just trying to help you out."

"Burgess—look. This isn't going to work. You have to tell me what you want done."

"Jo wanted you to have that shop. You won it fair and square. I can't figure this out for you, what you should do with it."

Fairness didn't enter into the picture at all. Mary Frances was the only one who had legitimately gained possession of the shop. "All right. Fine. This is what I'm going to do then. If you don't want me to do it, or if there's the slightest chance that Bevo wants the shop, you have to tell me."

"Well, hurry up about it—I have to take Ruth to the train station. She'll fly one-way, but she thinks flying round trip's pressing her luck."

"I'll talk to your contractor. He'll do minor renovations—ceiling, walls, counters, floors. We don't need to worry about paint or tile or any of the fixtures. Whoever buys it'll want their own color scheme—"

"You're the expert," Burgess said. "Just remember, don't pass any of those bills on to me. It's your shop."

"It is *not* my shop!" Anna wished Burgess would tune in to what the living were saying. Jo had trained him too well. "Look. Just tell Bevo to call me. I'll explain everything to him."

Jerry White, the contractor Burgess sent over, turned out to be the man next door who wore Hawaiian shirts and owned the Irish setters. His business outfit consisted of overalls and colored T-shirts. Anna watched him pencil estimates on a restaurant check pad and wondered who trimmed his mustache. The side bars of the mustache had been allowed to grow long and beardlike under his long jawbone. It looked as if his jaw were being clamped shut by the extensions of hair.

He hummed before beginning some sentences as if that were the only way he could unlock his jaw. "Mmm, I don't work on every other Thursday, but I make up the time on Saturdays—if that's okay with you. Burgess told you . . . cash only?"

"No. How much is this whole thing going to cost me in terms of time and money? I'd like to have the remodeling done by the end of the month."

Jerry White searched his gray-streaked curls for the pencil he'd stashed there.

"How much?" Anna wanted to rip the pad out of his slow-moving fingers and estimate the project herself. His fingernails looked too clean and his hands too unmarked. Burgess's recommendation suddenly seemed suspect. "What other jobs have you done in town?" she asked.

"Luisa Olversson uses me a lot out at Los Olmos," he said.

"And she pays you off the books?"

The contractor hummed and looked uncertain. "I don't know if I can tell you that."

"How'm I supposed to explain all this unaccounted-for cash flow to the government?" Anna asked. "What did Burgess tell you to say about that one?"

Jerry White raked his bottom lip with his long white teeth. "I'd check with him on that." He folded the restaurant check and handed it to Anna. "Tops."

The low figure disappointed her. "You're the only one who'll be working here? You won't need to hire anybody else to get everything done by the end of the month?" There was no way Jerry White could get all the work done in four weeks. Just looking at him made her want to take a nap. "What if you get hurt on the job? Who pays? Who takes over?"

"If I don't watch what I'm doing, then it's my own fault."

"But who finishes the job if you can't?"

"I guarantee that no matter what happens, the job gets finished in four weeks."

"We'll see," Anna said doubtfully. "Just out of curiosity—what if it turned out that you had to paint and put new tile on the floor and finish the cabinets and put in the fixtures—how much more would that be?"

"Mmm, you pick out the paint and the tile and the fixtures, and I'll tell you what kind and how many to get, and you order it through the lumber company in your name. I've got all the catalogs. They get kind of hinky at the lumber company if you use their books and don't contract through them."

His bid covering the tiling and painting seemed too low. "What about cost overruns?" Anna asked.

"If it's my fault, I pick up anything five percent over the original estimate."

No wonder Jerry White lived in an alley and drove an old pickup truck with a camper attached to it. He must spend what little money he earned on the Frisbees that littered the roof of his house. Anna was beginning to feel sorry for him; he was getting himself into a bind. "What if I wanted to extend this wall between the waiting room and the styling area? And I wanted to get rid of the inside stairs and turn the hall into a big walk-in closet? What kind of time and money are you talking about then?"

That estimate was a welcome jolt. She didn't have enough money to carry out the original intentions for the shop that she'd dreamed of while Mary Frances still held the deed. For a second the contractor had made Anna believe that anything was possible; that wishing for something was enough to make it happen; that there might be delays, but anything was possible.

"Deal?" Jerry White asked. "I can start this afternoon."

"You don't have an agreement we both sign?"

Jerry White pulled a bundle out of the back pocket of his overalls. "Bryan said you'd feel better with lots of paper—"

"Bryan? You know Bryan?" It figured. Without Jo, Burgess needed somebody to tell him what to do. They were probably planning to turn the shop into an underground railroad.

"Mmm . . . I wasn't supposed to say that. Ignore that. Which bid?"

"The first one. The plain vanilla shop."

"Let me just fill in the estimates." He fought the curling paper and started to pencil in amounts.

"Use pen," Anna said.

———

Strong woody stems of ivy grew out of a jade green planter that after twenty years had almost rooted itself to the linoleum floor in the waiting area. The ivy had woven itself through the slats of the venetian blinds on the window facing the creek. In an attempt to train the plant, Jo had stapled runners around the the front doorway, but occasionally a long strand of ivy would suddenly drop. More than one woman had hesitated before walking through that door.

It would take Jerry White forever to expose the wall. He'd probably want to coax each tiny feeler into letting go and there wasn't enough time for that. In memory of Jo, Anna separated one stem from the mass and tried to track it from beginning to end. Her fully extended arm was swallowed up, her fingers could no longer tell which trail to follow, and she had a horrible feeling that the ivy was about to whip itself around her.

She grabbed a fistful of ivy and pushed herself away from the ingrown wall. Plaster rained down on her. The ripping sound grew louder as she yanked and reeled in hanks of ivy. Backed against the opposite wall, Anna began to think the whole front wall would come crumbling down. She dropped the ball of ivy and began to haul it in hand over hand. Spider babies dangled from the long runners. Rust from the staples had dribbled down the walls and looked like blood. The sudden flood of light coming through the window made her blink. That job was done; Jerry White could do the cleanup.

Thanks to Claude, the soda machine was stocked. A locked front door hadn't stopped him from delivering his standard six cases every week. Anna found the weak place in the machine's mechanism and freed a root beer. She turned around to see Delia Nettinger peeking through the door.

"God!" Delia said as she entered the shop. "What happened? Who did all this?"

"I did," Anna said.

"It's pretty drastic, if you ask me."

"Pretty drastic? That's pretty good coming from you."

"And look at your dress! Is that the one you wore to the funeral? It's all ruined—"

"What do you want? I've got a lot of work to do."

"I need a haircut. I'm leaving tomorrow, and I don't know when I'll be back. See, I brought a towel and a comb and shampoo and everything."

"Let me see your money."

"Anna! I thought we were friends."

"I want to see how serious you are about getting your hair cut. I'll do it for twenty."

"Twenty dollars! Are you kidding! I'm a poor student. Did I tell you I changed my major? It's social work now. I thought I had problems—you should get a load of some of the mothers that manage to stick around." Delia dug into her pocket and then held out her hand. "There." A balled-up twenty began to stir in her palm. "Daddy gave it to me. I bet you never charge him. I won't have any left over for your tip."

Anna remembered the five dollars Grace had thrown at her in this same room. "I don't take tips from Nettingers."

"Well, what *will* you take from us?"

"A lot. Too much." Anna walked into the shampoo room. The

cabinets still held the towels and capes that Mary Frances had used. Nothing had changed. The shop would endure. It always had. Anna's stomach felt hollow as she reached for a cape, an action she must have done more than a thousand times before without feeling strange. Now it seemed as if she were trespassing and, as punishment for her intrusion, would be denied the comfort of the familiar. No matter what she did, the shop would continue to decay, and it would be her fate to watch the deterioration.

A hundred years might have passed since Delia's arrival. Anna was surprised that the shampoo hadn't soured and congealed. The smell released by the lather made it too easy to pretend that everything was the same—that Liz was locked in the bathroom, that Mary Frances was upstairs, and that Jo was giving a manicure in the styling room. Anna soaped Delia's thick hair again and tried to convince herself that the shop hadn't gone bad on her. There wasn't that much work to be done. She wasn't stuck here forever.

Eyes closed, Delia sighed. "This feels great. Your fingers are a lot nicer than your mouth."

"Social work. Why social work?"

"I'm not the only one something bad's happened to. I want to lean against the structure and help people through." Her eyes flew open. "I stole that. Thomas Bryan said it first. Isn't it beautiful?"

"Beautiful. Is that what you two were talking about on the sofa?"

"That—and other things," Delia said. Her eyes remained closed and she smiled.

Anna let a little cold water dribble down Delia's neck. "Up. Let's go."

Rummaging in her paper sack, Delia followed. "Wait a minute."

"How do you want it?" Anna rubbed the ends of Delia's hair and was surprised. "You've been taking care of it. The ends feel a lot better."

Delia sounded aggravated. "Of course I have. What do you take me for? I pay attention. I take care of myself."

Anna accepted the comb Delia handed her but didn't start cutting.

"Well, what are you waiting for?" Delia asked.

"You."

"I'm not saying a word until my hair's cut and you've put those scissors down."

"Fine." Anna sectioned and clamped Delia's hair. "You still like the layers?"

Delia nodded. Her fingers drummed the black plastic armrest through the cutting of three sections. "See," she said abruptly, fanning her fingers, "I stopped biting my nails."

"Good for you."

"Maybe next time I come down you'll have a manicurist."

"Maybe. Just don't breeze in here and expect to get a bikini wax."

"Not me. I'm like my mother, I hate pain." Delia wrinkled her face and studied it in the mirror for a few seconds. "Daddy really, really likes you. He likes you a lot. He's worried about you. And I know he's worried about me, and I worry about both of you."

Anna recombed a section of hair and slid her fingers to the ends. "Some people make a profession out of worrying."

"Just say you like him. Just tell me it's okay for me to not be here," Delia begged. Her eyes filled with tears. "I can't help it. I think sometimes that it's all his fault, that he could have stopped her. And then sometimes I think he's trying to make up for her on me. She's right there between us, everything we do for each other, everything we say—"

She wiped the tears off her face. "There was this balance when she was alive, me and him on one side pulling against Mom, and now there's nobody there. She let go and it's like I've flown way over here and he's still standing up over there. He needs me here, he needs somebody here, and I just can't stay here. I can't. I mean, I can see that he's still going through the whole thing, but I really, really can't come back here. You can help each other. If he's happy with you—and then I think, I'm the one that found you —I don't want to be left out—"

"I'm not taking Grace's place for either of you," Anna said

flatly. "Alive or dead. There's no way I'm turning into the thing between you. What I do with him is none of your business and what I do with you is none of his business. I've told you that before." She couldn't stay any more than Delia could. The potential for damage was too great.

Delia's face, freckled and splotched with pink, looked like the wall in the waiting room. "But it is, Anna. It is my business, and his. We're all in it together. No matter what we want or where we go or what we say. I'm so afraid of having to come back here, of finding out maybe how much I'm like my mother—but I would if he needed me."

Anna let Delia's hair slide through her fingers. She wished she could locate the invisible bond between them and cut it before it was too late.

————

Jerry White was as good as his word. By the end of the first week he'd torn out the baseboards, pulled up the linoleum and scraped most of the paint off the walls. Anna took the can of turquoise paint back to the lumber store. The man who had mixed it listened again to the description of the color she wanted. Instead of saying it would be impossible to reproduce, he assured her that he would temper the green and add a little more white.

At midnight Anna jimmied open the second mix of paint. She dipped her fingers into the cool paint and then smeared them against the wall. Three hours later, unable to sleep because the image of a swimming pool bottom wouldn't leave her mind, she got up to examine the new sample by flashlight. The streak had dried to a chalky blue. The man at the lumber store was either a liar or a fool. What she should do was break into the lumber store and mix the paint herself.

Wide awake now, she circled the room and looked out each window. The thought of driving made her tired. In the two weeks since Jo's death the Valiant had logged more than a thousand miles. She would be leaving soon enough anyway. All her things were still packed. There hadn't been any reason to open the boxes except to put away Jo's chignon. She and Mary Frances had had to use only one of the hairpieces. Anna had said that she would return it to Burgess. But what would he do with Jo's hair? Lay it on the pillow next to his and go to sleep? She could make better use of the chignon.

To prove her point, Anna unpacked the hairpiece. She held the long hank of hair under the bathroom light. The individual strands, cut after Bevo's birth when Jo must have been twenty-two, hadn't faded. Jo's natural color hadn't been a true black even then. Anna found shadings of red as she gently combed her fingers through the hair to get the tangles out. Knotting it quickly, she held the chignon up to her own head for comparison. It didn't take a coloring genius to see that the two tints were entirely different.

Anna shook out the knot and then braided Jo's hair. With the braid draped across one shoulder she worked until dawn on a synthetic hairpiece that refused to defy gravity and spiral into a ten-inch crown. She had to stop frequently to touch the braid for reassurance.

———

The lumberyard was deserted at lunchtime. A forklift with a load of pine stood frozen, its prongs halfway between a truck and a pyramid of boards. Anna swung the empty paint can onto the wooden counter. "Where's the man who mixes paint?"

"Lunch," the bookkeeper said. "Say, Anna, how many more weeks? I can't take much more of this getting burned by a curling iron at Yolanda's."

"Where's he having lunch?"

"I can't tell you where James Bailey's having lunch," the book-keeper said. "I hear talk you're going unisex."

"I'll find him on my own then," Anna said.

The bookkeeper lifted the paint can. "What am I supposed to do with this?"

"I don't care. It's not my paint."

James Bailey, master paint mixer, wasn't eating lunch at home. He wasn't having a pimento cheese sandwich at the drugstore. DairyLand hadn't seen him since morning coffee. Anna hadn't heard he was having an affair with anybody, so she stuck to the restaurants. The Lions Club filled the Sands Motel restaurant, but James Bailey wasn't among them. The Yucca Flats Motel restaurant was Anna's next stop. She turned off the highway in front of a cattle truck.

A kidney-shaped swimming pool was planted in front of the dining room's full-length windows. Leaves and drowned dragonflies washed against the concrete sides. James Bailey was sitting at a table by the window and staring at the murky water. Anna hoped the color was haunting him, too. Settling into a chaise lounge by the pool, she waited for the man to finish his bread pudding.

"Still no go, huh?" James Bailey asked when he finally wandered out. "I thought sure I had it that last time."

Anna sensed a shifting in the cloud cover. Shadows were becoming more distinct on the hills. "Do you even know what I'm talking about? Can you see what I'm talking about?"

The man sat down. "I sure do." When the clouds redefined themselves and the air lightened, he stared intently into the water. "And that pool of water is sure not what you want."

Anna leaned her head back and shut her eyes. Why should she have any faith in him? She saw how hopeless it all was. The pool water was too stagnant; the season was wrong. Walls were solid. A coat of paint wouldn't dissolve them.

"I used to paint some, you know, on canvas," James Bailey said. "The thing I always wanted to do was lay down this one color on the canvas and have people feel about the color what I felt. For me, it's the color of a cold glass of beer. To be able to put that down on a piece of canvas and have people look at it and feel . . . relief, I guess. You know, some sort of pleasure at the end of a long day. But I couldn't get it down, so I quit."

"Can you do the turquoise or not?" Anna asked. Hope or no hope? She needed the answer to that question.

"I know the color you want. I just don't know if I can turn it into latex."

From the way he was staring into the pool, Anna believed he did see the color. The answer was "no hope." It shouldn't matter;

she had already made her decision. No paint was going on the walls. It would be a bare bones shop offered for sale.

"But I've got my oils out," James Bailey continued, "and I figure if I can come up with the right mix of colors that way, I can sure transfer it."

"Don't," Anna said. Her eyes teared. She couldn't bear to hear the man's optimism. The shop seduced people into dreaming. "It doesn't matter. It can't be done. It doesn't matter anymore."

James Bailey offered his handkerchief. "One more try, what do you say?"

"No. Forget it. Forget about the paint." Anna put on the sunglasses Jo had left her. Bailey finally walked off, but she stayed in the lounger, staring at the horizon and sky. When the sun set, she forced herself to drive back to the shop.

Jerry White came to the front door of his house. "We're on schedule!" he shouted as Anna climbed the back stairs. His cheerfulness made her start crying again.

———

Anna lay on her side. A candle cast the ridges of her body upon the whitewashed wall. The formations were unfamiliar to her. When she reached for the wall, the shadow of her hand, separating from the general mass of her body, got smaller and denser. The wall was cold to her touch and textureless as if her shadow had no impact because her body was unable to project warmth or substance. She wondered if she had expected Jo to stay with her like shadow on a wall.

Using red lipstick, Anna traced her outline on the wall. Her shoulders looked square and strong, but her jackknifed knees made her hips jut and round too soon. She rolled away from the wall and considered calling Jerry White to put on his Hawaiian shirt and come over to tear the stairs away from the outside wall. The dominoing steps could be his final payment, good lumber for a doghouse or a new camper for another truck.

She wanted to be stranded. She wanted the thunderheads to gather north, east, south and west over the mountains and to bombard the earth with rain until water slashed the curves of every dry creek, until there was so much water that the mesquite couldn't suck it all up and the parched ground got its fill and overflowed, until the shop's second floor was flooded and she floated away from herself. Like Grace Nettinger, Anna didn't know what to do with herself. Neither motion nor stillness satisfied.

She wanted to see and touch that part of herself that missed Jo. She wanted to master it, but the effort required too much. Everything had been spent in trying to ward off Jo's death. There was nothing cleansing in the kind of sorrow she felt, nothing that would fill in the gaps and repair the damage.

———

"I thought I'd invite you out for the weekend," Ed said. "I could use a trim." He looked at the boxes piled in a corner, the smears of turquoise paint on one wall and the blurred lipstick horizon outlined on the other wall.

Anna wondered if he carried that concerned look with him everywhere—to Grace's grave, to Delia's dorm. No wonder they all wanted to get away from him.

"Don't look so worried," she said. In order to give Ed a place to sit, she jerked the top covers off the cot. Oversize styling magazines from Europe and empty boxes of gingersnaps spilled to the floor. A canvas wig stand that Jo's hair braid was anchored to rolled under the cot. Grabbing the tail of the braid, Anna dragged the wig stand out.

"If I look worried, it's because I am. I don't know what you're doing," Ed said.

"Cleaning up the place. Rebuilding it. Out with the old—in with the new."

"There's a lot of demolition going on," Ed agreed. "Then what, you'll leave? I'll come waltzing by and you'll be gone? I'm not any too stable these days myself, so I'd appreciate a warning."

That was impossible. How could she tell Ed that if anybody could convince her to stay, it would be him? The timing was wrong for them. Between them they had too many ghosts. And there was Delia. Anna didn't feel capable of being the conduit between father and daughter.

"I've told you I'm leaving once the shop's sold. Unless you just want somebody to sleep with, there's no point in—"

"You're a coward," Ed said. "When I heard that story about your climbing out the window to get away from your first husband, I thought that was a brave thing, that you weren't so blinded by love you'd hung on to something when there was no hope—"

"Does something bad always have to happen to make you feel brave?" Anna interrupted. She didn't want to hear about hope and expectations, especially from him. "I think you thrive on other people's troubles. You act like you're everybody's guardian angel. But you're not. You feed on trouble. Just like a buzzard. I feel like some cow you're circling. Like you know ahead of time I'm going to wander out onto the highway and get hit by a truck. And you can't wait to pick my bones clean."

"I don't need another Grace on my hands. There's not a damn thing I can do if you want to sink—no matter how much I may want to and no matter how wrong that would be. You keep fighting the wrong thing. I know. You may bottom out, and you may not. But there's no way in hell I'm going with you. I'm climbing out that window before you do."

Anna had nothing to say. It was about time that Ed Nettinger learned when to leave.

He paused at the door and crimped the edges of his Stetson. "Delia'll be calling you about Thanksgiving dinner. I'll try to head her off. Whatever you do, don't do this to her."

Anna pressed a pillow over her face. Relief at Ed's final departure was slow in coming. Pressing the pillow tighter, she welcomed the darkness until a wash of pure turquoise spilled behind her eyelids. She hoped the internal flood of color would burst through her skin.

———

Anna started the third week of renovations on Sunday by tearing out the pink banquette that sat under the dryers. She dismantled the thin chrome bars supporting the black plastic armrests, and the armrests, bolted in back to the wall, flopped uselessly. When she reached into the crevice between seats and pulled, the banquette toppled forward to expose a sheet of brittle plastic hanging behind it.

A can of paint sat on the newly sanded counters. James Bailey had tried a third mix and dropped it off on his way home from church. Anna retrieved Jo's braid off the counter and twisted it around her hands as if the hair were a talisman. Everything depended on the paint's being the right color. The difference between giving up and letting go continued to elude her. If the paint was the right color, then there was hope. Jerry White would finish his job, and she would be able to hand the keys over to the new owner with no regrets. If the color was wrong, she might as well go back upstairs and nail blankets over the rest of the windows so she could stay in bed all day without having to resort to wearing sunglasses.

With the braid dangling from one hand, Anna pried open the paint can. Telling herself that the mix didn't have streaks of yellow in it, she pressed the lid against a primed wall and left a shiny oval. The paint dried to a high gloss. There was enamel in it. He had put enamel in it. Light rebounded from the dried paint. She couldn't believe it. The walls were supposed to dissolve, not throw the sun's glare into everyone's eyes; the color was wrong on a grand scale.

Anna dipped the tip of the braid into the paint and brushed it across the clean walls. The wisps of paint left by the hair didn't satisfy her. Slowly, she dunked the whole length of hair into the can, letting the paint seep into the strands. No matter how much she wanted to stop and snip the ruined hair from the good, Anna relentlessly pushed the last juncture of the braid under the opaque turquoise surface until her own wrist had disappeared into the paint.

Jo wouldn't let this pass. If she was ever going to give a sign, this was the time. Anna sat very quietly, attuning herself to receive some sort of indication that Jo was watching out. The minutes passed, and nothing happened. "Look what I've done," Anna said out loud. *"Look* at this." She swabbed the mirrors with the paint-soaked braid. "Look!"

There was no response. "I won't do it then. I'll leave right now and let Burgess and Bevo deal with this mess." Again stilling herself, Anna waited for a sign—the smell of a burning cigarette, a heat lamp turning itself on—but nothing happened.

Then this was it. There was only this—a present with no guarantee of a future. No hope.

Looking around the shop, Anna inventoried what she had done so far. Not enough. Not nearly enough. She dumped paint over the torn-out banquette. She splashed the dryer hoods. The sound of dripping paint filled the shop. She took short and unsatisfying breaths. Not liking the sight of her face under the lights, she threw the empty can into the mirrors and shattered them. She retrieved the can as it rolled backward and shot it straight overhead. She shielded herself, but the explosion of light and glass temporarily blinded her.

Anna sat in her old styling chair and continued to cover her eyes to avoid seeing what she'd accomplished. The pleasure brought about by the act of destruction was fading rapidly, but the memory frightened her. She'd felt the same elation after hitting Ronnie Mauss back. She hadn't learned anything in these ten years.

———

Congealed paint curled in front of Jerry White's paint scraper. He stopped when he got to the paint-stiffened braid which was stuck to the counter. "Wow . . ."

"Just get this place presentable enough so I can unload it on somebody else," Anna said. "I don't care how much it costs. I want it done. Fast."

"You were thinking of getting new dryers anyway, right?" Jerry walked over to the line of dryers and straightened one of the dryer necks Anna had tried to twist off. "This'll slow things up some. I can't promise the first full week in December anymore."

"It doesn't have to be perfect. Just get it done." The smell of paint coated Anna's nose. She went upstairs to start on a three-week nap. From the windows facing southeast, she saw Jerry take a load of splattered dryer hoods out to the alley. He fit the hoods into the indentations of the U-shaped couches he'd torn out of the shampoo room. Anna let the blanket she'd nailed over the window fall into place. At this rate, unless Jerry White managed to keep one step ahead of her, she would be here forever.

————

The groan of the drainpipe attached to the back of the shop woke Anna. She looked out the window and saw Bevo hanging twenty feet above the ground. He had one arm around the drainpipe and was reaching for the thick cords of wisteria that climbed the wall. The twisted arm of wisteria he chose couldn't take the weight and snapped. His feet scrambled against the yellow stucco wall for a foothold. Anna doubted the drainpipe could hold his weight much longer. He began a swing toward the staircase's support structure. His boots hooked around a beam, but his body remained fully stretched between the wall and stairs.

"Jerry!" Anna shouted. "Bring a ladder around back. Quick!" It would take him forever. Suspended a foot below the landing, Bevo was within reach. She sat on the landing and slid her legs through the balustrades. "Lift your stomach," she instructed. "I'll grab your belt."

In preparation Bevo let his stomach cave in. He then took a deep breath and arched his back. Her upper body pressed against the balustrades, Anna extended her arms. Bevo started laughing as her fingers scrambled across his stomach. "Stop laughing," she said.

"Stop tickling me then. I think you want me to fall." He let his stomach collapse again.

Hoping that the railing would hold, Anna wedged her face between the balustrades and braced herself for another try. "Lift your stomach."

Bevo relaxed his leghold on the stair's support beams. The reduction of tension allowed his body to arc more fully and Anna was able to catch his belt with her hands. As Bevo inhaled, her body was forced against the railings. Either the railings would give or they would split her into three pieces.

Bevo made his stomach buck upward, and she pulled backward
with all her strength. For a few seconds there seemed to be no
motion as they balanced each other. Then Anna felt her body
being forced forward again. She resisted, but Bevo's belt started
to slide through her hands. Losing hold of the leather completely,
she fell backward onto the landing.

She could see the drainpipe bucking under Bevo's full weight.
As he shimmied to the ground, the upper section of pipe separated
from the wall. With ten feet to go, Bevo let himself drop. He took
the stairs to the second floor this time.

Anna rested on the landing again and let the vibrations of
Bevo's feet jar her body. "You're a show-off," she said when he
stood above her. "You're also paying for that drainpipe."

Bevo offered his hand to Anna. "You should see what you did
to my belt."

Refusing his offer of help, Anna said, "You should see what I've
done to your shop." She fought the urge to grab Bevo's leg as he
stepped over her and went inside. Maybe the spilled paint would
convince him to take over the renovations. She could hand over
a blank check for Jerry White and leave tonight.

The boards on the landing were warm. Anna was beginning to
appreciate the heat when she heard Bevo opening her boxes. "Stay
out of my stuff," she yelled.

Bevo came to the screen door. "Where's Mom's chignon?
Mary Frances said you took it."

A feeling of shame overcame Anna. She saw herself clearly,
dipping Jo's braid into the paint. The action couldn't be undone,
and it shouldn't matter that Bevo wouldn't understand why she
had ruined that last thing of Jo's. Once she had left, they would
never see each other again. It didn't matter what he thought.

Anna made herself go inside. Bevo was lying on the cot, flipping
through a magazine. The fairness of his skin emphasized the
circles under his eyes. "Where have you been?" she asked.

Bevo threw the magazine aside. "Jesus! I don't need you to pick
up where Burgess left off. Why don't you just move out there and
fill Mom's shoes?"

"Why don't you?" He looked so tired that she did want to

mother him; she wanted to smooth his eyes shut and pull the covers over him.

Anna realized she hadn't envisioned the future without postcards from Bevo. The tie with him was her last one to break, and it ran the deepest. She had tried to break it once by leaving for Marfa. Whose house would he run to after she left? What had she thought—that Bevo's ability to come and go would make continued contact safe? That the rootlessness put them on the same side?

Never in a million years would Bevo forgive her for the chignon. "Let's go downstairs. I want to show you what I've done."

Jerry White had had to stop in the middle of Sheetrocking the waiting area to scrape paint and sweep broken glass out of the styling room. Pockmarks and rust streaks from the stapled ivy were still visible around the picture window on the front wall. The shop looked worse in the daylight than Anna had hoped it might.

"Holy shit! What are you *doing* to this place?" Bevo shouted. "Where's Mom's ivy? What did you do with my mother's ivy?"

Anna pointed to a cutting of ivy she'd stuck in an empty strawberry soda bottle. "I saved some. If you wanted the whole wall full, you should have come and gotten it yourself."

"Jesus! You're really pissed off at her, aren't you? You are *really* fucking pissed off at her. Not only because she's dead, not only because you think she wouldn't fight. You're still pissed off because she stole the shop from you."

It had been a bad idea to bring Bevo downstairs. Anna wasn't ready for this final confrontation, but she forced herself to give an answer that would provoke it. "Well, it's mine now. Unless you want to take it back. Your magazine collection's upstairs. I'm sure you'll do fine here. You'll lose the smart women, but it'll take the stupid ones longer to figure out that you're making fun of them."

"Ooh, Anna wants a fight!" Bevo boxed the air with his fists. "Come on. Come on!"

Jerry White stuck his head through the window between the waiting and styling rooms. Sawdust and spackle frosted his hair. "You better go outside and fight. My estimates are screwed up enough already."

"You'll get your money," Anna said. "Keep scraping." Jerry disappeared into the styling room. The crunch of glass underneath his feet sent chills through her.

"Who's he?" Bevo asked. "Are we interested?"

"He's busy until he gets this job done."

"Yeah, well. That could take forever. I don't have that much time." Going to the front door, Bevo traced the backward letters of Jo's name written on the glass. "When's this coming off? Why wait? Let's do it now!" He picked up the soda bottle that held the cutting and lobbed it through the front door.

"What's wrong with you?" Anna demanded. "What am I supposed to do? Turn this place into a shrine? Hope that she'll come back if we leave her ivy on the wall and her name on the door?"

Jerry White ran out of the styling room. "I warned you!" A strong smell of turpentine came from the rag he held.

"I'll pay you extra," Anna said tightly. "The glass had to be replaced anyway. I don't think the door could have taken too many more scrapings."

Bevo was staring at Jerry White. His face had lost more color. "What's that in your hand?"

The braid, pliant and smelling of turpentine, was in Jerry's hand. The thick shell of turquoise had dissolved, but a dull residue of paint remained. It was impossible to tell what color the hair had been.

Anna was devastated by the sight. Jerry's attempt at repair had made things worse; he'd made the hair almost recognizable. How could she have done that to Jo's hair? She couldn't begin to imagine what Bevo was feeling.

"What is that in your hand?" Bevo asked again. He turned on Anna. "What have you done?"

There was no going back now. She had accomplished what she'd set out to do. Turpentine fumes flooded Anna's lungs as she took a deep breath; the smell made her sick. "It's Jo's. I ruined it."

"I can see that!" Bevo shouted. "Why did you do it?"

"She's dead. That won't bring her back."

"I know what dead is. I don't need to learn that lesson from you."

"What difference does it make now? It's the same thing as if Mary Frances and I used it. It's the same as if it was buried with her. It's gone."

"It was my mother's—my *mother's!*"

"What were you going to do with it?" Anna asked mockingly. "Wear it?"

Bevo slapped Anna. The surprise of the blow took her breath away. "You deserved that one," he said. "You deserved it."

"Hey, hey, wait . . ." Jerry protested, but Bevo took possession of the braid.

"Get out of here," Anna said. "Get out of my shop."

"I *hate* this place!" Bevo said. He kicked the remaining shards of glass out of the door and climbed through the door.

Anna watched him cross the street and vanish into the creek. She couldn't believe she still wanted to go after him, to make sure he would be all right.

"Are you all right?" Jerry asked. "I should call somebody . . . do something. . . ."

"Finish your job," she said and climbed through the door. "Lock up when you leave."

"Lock up what?" Jerry yelled.

Bevo's trail was easy to track. He always took the northeast channel and headed for the hills. Rocks had recently been dislodged; and despite the creek's dryness, their exposed beds were damp. Tall weeds that had been uprooted and flung to the side were tangled in old flood debris.

From time to time Anna looked over her shoulder. The day was overcast, and her back felt vulnerable as if a wall of water from the mountains were about to overtake her. She covered half a mile and then rested underneath the bridge that carried traffic north to Fort Davis. The road climbed into dense mountains, twisting through treacherous valleys. Drop-offs there were guarded by three-foot-high stone walls. Rusted truck cabs that the walls hadn't stopped pointed nose up, lodged on the steep slopes by boulders. As a reward for safe passage, the road topped out before

Fort Davis and traveled across highland plains before gearing up for the next set of mountains.

Anna touched her cheek. It was beginning to hurt. Bevo wasn't her responsibility; he would survive. But the urge to follow was too strong. She hurried past the spray-painted bridge supports toward the hills.

Two grade school girls slid down the bridge's concrete skirt. They shrieked and stuffed their coats into their mouths at the sight of Anna and scrambled back up the embankment. The surprise pulled her up short.

She sat on a rock and pressed a finger against her cheek. Provocation or not, Bevo had hit her. He was no better than Ronnie Mauss. The renewal of anger turned Anna toward the shop. The tie was broken. She could leave now.

———

The Valiant was backed up to the outside staircase, its tailgate open and ready to receive Anna's possessions. "Jerry!" she yelled from upstairs. "Jerry White!"

A figure streaked out the back door of the wooden camper parked next door and disappeared into the alley. Jerry White was the next one to pop out of the camper. "Hey!" he shouted as he ran after the departed person. "It's okay! Hey!"

"Job's over," Anna yelled and slammed the window.

Loading the Valiant took twenty minutes. Two boxes in the back seat, a suitcase in the front, and Anna was out of the shop. She taped an envelope with a blank check made payable to Jerry White to the inside of the plywood he'd nailed over the front door. A note reverting the title of the shop back to Burgess was strapped to the deed; both documents were stored in a strongbox, which Anna placed on a sawhorse where Jerry was bound to see it. She poured the half-and-half down the drain and sprang a beer from the soda machine. As her last official act as shop owner, she locked the door and threw the keys into the creek.

A Comanche moon, low and orange, strong enough to hunt and travel by, rested on the mountains. The light charged the atmosphere. Looking both solid and weightless, the moon seemed ready to roll over the face of the earth with no concern to the damage it might leave behind. Anna had a feeling the moon had already started shifting course. Only after strapping herself into the driver's seat did she adjust the rearview mirror to check the new position of the moon. There was no need to rush out of town in a panic, especially when she had one more duty to perform.

A soft-banked back road took Anna to the intersection she wanted. Jo's illness and death had taken away her self-assurance; she hadn't gunned the Valiant in and out of the creek in too long a time. Tonight the steep unpaved road was the only road to take. Anna left her car to check the cross street in both directions. She knelt and put her hand on the pavement to feel for any vibrations. Nobody was coming. Nobody would get in her way.

Confidently, Anna backed halfway down the block. She counted ten and gunned the accelerator. The stop sign flashed past. She steered into the deep ruts that signaled the approach of the drop and fed the Valiant more gas. Her arms were braced to turn the wheel sharply to the left, but the left front tire was hung temporarily. Momentum plunged the Valiant into the creek. The back end fishtailed to the left and sent the car traveling along the creek's rocky side in a path perpendicular to the road. Something caught the chassis; the forward motion of the Valiant was stopped violently, but the back end of the car swung toward the creek bed and the nose pivoted toward the bank. Finally, all motion stopped.

Anna couldn't tell if whatever gripped the Valiant's underpinnings would hold. The contents of the boxes that were stacked in the rear started to shift. She thought that the redistribution of weight would send the car somersaulting end over end to the bottom; the balance was too delicate. Gravity forced her neck against the seat back. Holding her breath, Anna stared through the windshield to focus on a star set in the middle of the sky that was now eye level.

The radio was on. Anna didn't know how many songs came and went. Both feet were involuntarily pressing the brake so hard that her knees had started to shake badly. She couldn't sit there forever and wait for something to happen. Lacing her arms through the steering wheel, she hauled herself forward. Luckily the Valiant didn't react to her body's movements. The car was anchored to the creek wall by no action of hers. With one hand Anna worked the seat belt open. The passenger door wouldn't budge, so she had to crawl through the window. She was unable to gain her footing on the rocky slope and slid four feet to the bottom on her seat and back.

Scared and grateful to be alive, she lay motionless in the creek bed. When her heart slowed and her lungs were able to expand, she tested various parts of her body for damage. Nothing seemed to be broken. There were cuts and scrapes but no major flows of blood.

Anna realized how lucky she'd been. Navigating this road had always been a test of how much she could get away with, not a test of skill. The admission brought a sense of relief. She wasn't like Grace Nettinger and the mountains. There was no accompanying despair within Anna at her own failure to conquer the road. Taking this particular road had never proved what she had wanted it to; all the safe passages to the other side hadn't guaranteed the future and hadn't confirmed that she was capable of staying in one place. Ed Nettinger had been right about one thing—she was a coward. Biting off her relationships in town hadn't made the leaving any easier. If she went now, the people she cared about would haunt her forever.

Bevo had been right, too. She was angry with Jo. For everything. She hadn't been waiting to be released from her anger and sadness by a sign from Jo; she had been trying to haunt Jo, and the shop, like some vengeful ghost. There hadn't been time to hash it out between them. The anger had had no place to go. "I'm sorry," Anna said. "I'm sorry." The blanket apology wasn't strong enough to reach Bevo in his sleep, or Ed Nettinger in his, but she would stay to deliver those. Tonight's message went out to Jo, and Anna believed that it had been received.

The moon had risen and was smaller. Its light glinted off broken beer bottles and made them precious. Anna lay among the rocks and considered the distance between all and nothing and began to see that there were other avenues.

At dawn she stood up. Her legs held and she walked out of the creek by the shop. Peering through the front window, she saw clearly what Jerry White had accomplished. The war between her vision and what had been Mary Frances's was over. It wasn't the fact of Jo's purchase or her death that had destroyed the dream of ownership; those events had altered the situation and made it possible for her to leave the first time. She didn't know if she was capable of adjusting to the change.

The flimsy plywood door gave way against her weight. Breaking through the door was her last act of sabotage. Jerry White would finish the renovations and she would see to the shop for Burgess and Bevo. Anna retrieved the strongbox and the envelope and started to clean up her mess.

Vibrations caused by Jerry White's hammering on the first floor created a small wash of water against the sides of the tub upstairs. As the water cooled, Anna reduced the level and added hot water. She would have liked to stay in the tub until the scratches were healed and the soreness was gone, but the sound of the hammer motivated her. Before going downstairs, she called and left a message for Burgess at the GM used car lot. Nobody had answered at the house. More than a verdict on the Valiant, she wanted Burgess to see the shop as it was. Once it was sold or taken over by Bevo, she thought she might try Nebraska or Kansas, someplace flat, where she could see something coming a long way off.

His back to her, Jerry rubbed the new glass in the door defensively. "You're a fast worker," Anna said.

"We signed a piece of paper," he said. "Your plans might have changed, but that don't mean mine have. I contracted to do a job."

"I'd like you to finish it. I know it's going to cost more and take longer. That's okay."

Jerry turned around and saw Anna's face. "Wow . . . I was here for the bruise, but where'd all those scratches come from?"

"Just clean up the detail work and we'll let somebody else decorate the place. I'll recommend you to whoever buys it. You've done a good job."

Expansion pockets of air blew out his cheeks. "This is the craziest job. . . . I can't take the Formica back. It's been cut. You said I should go ahead and get it. You picked it out and ordered it. You can't do things like this. You can't decide in the middle of everything—"

"Jerry. It's paid for. Keep it. Use it on another job. I don't care. It's yours."

Jerry White's fingers combed his beard in agitation and got stuck. "I don't know, I don't know . . ."

"I made a mistake," Anna said. "I shouldn't have ordered the Formica. All right?"

"I can't deal with this. I'll be back later." He opened the front door and stopped. "This glass—this glass just better be here when I get back."

Anna crossed her heart. "It will be. I promise."

Despite her promise, he looked as if he wanted to lift the door off its hinges and take it with him.

———

Favoring her left side, Anna was stacking Claude's three return cases on the porch when Burgess drove up. He tapped on the new glass and walked in. "Giving away soft drinks, are you, Anna? Trying to drum up a little business?"

"There's cold in the machine if you want one. I don't know how old it is." Anna hadn't seen Burgess since the funeral three weeks before. There was a gap between the shirt's starched collar and his neck, and his pants legs drooped around the work boots. She didn't want to look too closely at him.

Burgess worked a root beer free. "You ought to tell Claude

about this popped locking mechanism here." Bumping the root beer bottle against his leg, he wandered into the styling room. "An old tree stump caught hold of your front axle," he said. "Lucky for you it looks like. Not so lucky for the car. There's a '74 Cutlass on the lot I'll take what's left of your Valiant as down payment for. I've got your boxes and your suitcase out in my car."

He sat on a sawhorse in the styling room. "It kills me to admit it, but credit where credit's due. This place is shaping up."

"Jerry's a good worker." Anna's feet stuck to the black rubber backing that was exposed when the old green linoleum had been pulled up. She looked at the holes in the other room where the bank of dryers had been. The framework for the ceiling tiles was in place. Loops of wiring bellied through the open squares.

Burgess bent to study the paint cans that James Bailey had dropped off while she was in the tub. He read aloud the name handwritten in Magic Marker across a piece of masking tape. "Aquamarine on a Sunny Day." He pried a lid off with fingernail clippers. "Turquoise, is it? Nice. Should look good with that Formica."

"The shop'll be easier to sell without a color scheme. It'll be easier to see the possibilities. Unless you think Bevo would want to go with the turquoise?"

"Your problem is, Anna—one of them—is you don't see. You don't ever see what's right in front of you. You never want to wait around long enough to see the thing through. You ever think that what you do might change the way things turn out for anybody else?"

"Burgess, it's not mine. I didn't do anything to earn it."

"Jo must have thought you did."

"She knew how much I wanted it. And she knew I would always let Bevo have a chair here. Things have changed."

"I don't know what happened between you and Bevo yesterday, but he's gone again."

"Do you know where he went?" Anna asked.

Burgess rubbed his eyes and sighed. "You know better than to ask me that. I can't accept what he's doing with his life. You're the only pipeline I have to him."

"We don't have Jo between us anymore. It wouldn't work. It would make things worse. He wouldn't trust either of us."

"She's still between us," Burgess said. "We have Jo in common. We always will."

"I don't feel her anywhere. I thought I would. Here—especially. I kept waiting. I can't do that anymore. I can't stay here because of that." Anna hesitated and then asked, "What do you do? Do you ever want a drink?"

"I had my drink." Burgess tilted the root beer bottle back and forth. "Not this stuff, the real thing. A brandy. I bought it when she told me, and I put it in a safety-deposit box, that's why you and Bevo didn't find it." A longing filled his face. "That's one liquor I never touched. It was one of Jo's treats—you remember the Christmas suppers? So I went into the bank the day after the funeral, I took a little shot glass in with me, and it was the smoothest stuff I'd ever tasted. I enjoyed that glass. And I felt like she enjoyed it, too. It was our own little send-off. Nobody knows the difference better than me, Anna. I poured out the bottle after that one glass. The next drink wouldn't have been the same. It was a one-time deal.

"Jo beat it. She did the thing in her own way, on her own terms. I'm not saying I agree with what she decided, but she saved herself the only way she knew how, and she had to fight all of us off to do it, too. There were times when I thought you'd do anything to keep her here—and I mean anything. I could have saved you the trouble if I thought you'd listen. I went through that a long time ago, trying to hold on to her, and she got a broken arm out of it."

Anna didn't regret the violence of her will on behalf of Jo. What she regretted was not being able to see the misapplication of force sooner and having the chance to redirect her energy.

"But Jo stayed with you," she said. "I never doubted that you loved her. Sometimes I think you loved her too much." To ward off Burgess's protest, Anna patted his arm. "It doesn't matter. I'm leaving for a lot of reasons. I just don't think I can do it. Maybe all I'm cut out for is sink rights someplace. Women like Mary Frances and Willi are good with the details. I like having somebody like Mary Frances or Willi take the heat. The shop's yours. I'll stick around to handle the details if you want to sell or bring somebody in to manage it until Bevo comes back. It's up to you."

Burgess docked his empty root beer bottle. "Sorry, Anna—my turn to walk. This is your baby. You better see a doctor after that tumble into the creek."

"I'll offer it to Willi then." The thought of adding the shop to Willi's chain gave Anna a twinge. She pressed the bruise on her cheek to remind herself what real pain was. "I'll split the money between Bevo and Marvin."

"That's between you and them." Burgess stood in the doorway to take a last look. "It looks good. Let me know about that Cutlass."

––––––

An artist in residence at Los Olmos scavenged the shampoo couches and paint-washed dryers from the alley. "Don't do anything else without me," he said and handed Anna a receipt.

"That's the last of it."

"Keep my card." He shrugged. "So it's twenty years before you tear it out again. I'll be around."

"Yeah, but I won't." Still, she stuck the card in the strongbox; her redecorating days might be ending, but the next owner might decide to overhaul the shop every other year.

Leo's white van drove slowly through the Los Olmos truck's dust. "Recycling!" Leo was in rapture when he hugged Anna. "Good girl! I dropped Lizzie off in front. I didn't want her and Baby Jo getting bounced around." He scouted the alley and lowered his voice. "Okay, here's the plan. She'll want four half days, give her two and tell her you'll try to work her in more. Also, I need an ironclad guarantee from you that she gets an hour—minimum—rest time when one of the shampoo things is empty. You can break it up into half hour segments if you have to. No chemicals, no permanents, not even cold waves. Deal?"

Anna let Leo's outstretched hand hang in the air. "Save it. You're not talking to the owner."

Leo dropped his head in graduated nods. "Anna, we all know

what the story is. You're blocking, you're transferring, you're projecting, postponing—"

"No, Leo. I am not. The shop is not mine. I will be happy to give Liz a good recommendation. And you. Are you taking a class in negotiating?"

"Anna, Anna, Anna. Anna. Denial. A false sense of well-being. Classic symptoms."

There was no need to challenge Leo. Let him get some mileage out of his college education. "You're right, Leo. I'm running away. I can't face it. You're absolutely right. I'm repressing. So Liz is inside? With all that turpentine and those insulation fibers?"

Leo deserted the alley to go in and rescue Liz. Anna wished she'd held on to one of the mutilated dryer hoods as a reminder of how close she'd come to losing everything.

———

"These don't even look dirty." Delia dropped a fistful of neck towels into the washer. "I'm glad I finally found you. Don't you want your parents to meet Daddy? We can look very presentable all dressed up. Well, we can."

Anna warmed her hands on the glass face of a clothes dryer. Mary Frances's pink bath towels danced behind the glass. She doubted the strips of fabric softener would do much good to plump and soften the weave. But before calling Willi, she wanted the clean towels cleaner and the plugs of hardened shampoo punched out of their plastic caps—despite the fact that Willi would sweep it all aside and bring in her own towels, yellow with a white WILLI woven in reverse pile down the length, and her own specially mixed egg shampoo.

"Pay attention to the wash cycle if you want to help," Anna said. Liquid fabric softener was going in the wash cycle and the cloth strips of softener were in the clothes dryers; she wasn't taking any chances.

"You know what it is," Delia said, "you're in mourning and you act like you don't even know it. It takes a long time, people don't realize. They bring over a casserole dish that's got their name written on the bottom, and as long as they get the dish back, they think that's the end of it. They think everything's fine. They think all you need to do is have a good cry and get it out of your system."

"You can't waste time mourning about something you had no control over. People die."

"You can miss them," Delia insisted, "you can remember they were here, you can honor what they went through. Daddy's still in mourning, so am I—so are you. Only now he's in mourning for you, too, and that's the worst. You're not dead. He could run into you anywhere."

Anna leaned into the dryer and met the hot, confined air. She wished she could hire somebody like Jerry White to renovate her relationship with Ed. She didn't want to leave her mark on Ed like Grace had. "He's a good man. But some things don't work out. He needs somebody who's not . . . grieving."

Delia separated the short neck towels in the cart from the longer ones. She spread a short towel on the large center table and smoothed it. Then she folded it lengthwise precisely into thirds, put her hand halfway across the width and folded it once more.

"You don't have to be so careful," Anna said. The Nettingers needed somebody they could talk comfortably to about death. Somebody who wouldn't keep shoving it in their faces. "At that rate we'll be here all night."

"I always fold towels like this. That's the way my mother taught me," Delia said defensively. "That's the way I do it."

―――――

Jerry White took the plastic laundry basket out of Anna's hands and blocked her entry to the shop. "Shut your eyes," he commanded. She tried to brush past him, but he put his hand over her eyes and bumped her into the styling room. "Tada!"

The counters and each cabinet set as an island between the four chair stumps had been sanded to a satin finish. Each island offered the combination of openness and self-containment that Willi's stations pretended to. The operators would still have to fight for shampoo time at the two sinks in the back room, but they would

have their own cabinet space. Anna was glad she hadn't ordered
the gray sinks and the chairs and couches in a moment of weakness.

It was hard enough to see the Formica glued down. Pink and
turquoise wisps floated on the gray surface. The pink seemed
strongly lit from an outside source like clouds at sunset. From
another angle, the pink was more delicate, like the inside of a
seashell. She wished she'd gotten to Jerry before he put down the
Formica and replaced the mirrors. He had a right to showcase his
work, but the reality of the cabinets and the counter was too much
for Anna. She couldn't let herself be seduced into going ahead
with the shop because Jerry White loved his work. She loved her
work, too, but she had to face her limitations.

"Wait! There's more." Jerry led her to the cul-de-sac of the
second station. "Look at the floor!"

Jerry had tiled the floor at the station. The tiles were a pattern
that Anna had chosen one day at the hospital while she and Jo
were pretending to pick out color schemes.

"Burgess's gift." Jerry beamed. "He wanted to make sure you
hadn't changed your mind about the style before I laid them down
for good."

The tiles and the Formica complemented each other better
than Anna had hoped they would. After flipping through three
chains of tile samples, she had always returned to the same pattern. "I hope the new owners like the colors."

She didn't own the shop. Fitting the tiles into place wouldn't
change that. She had gone as far with her commitment here as
she could. The one thing she'd learned from Jo's death was when
to stop fighting. This was a dead-end alley. The only thing to do
was to back out of it. Carefully.

"Well, too bad—they're staying," Jerry said with determina-
tion. "If the owners don't like them, they can get somebody else
to tear them out."

————

Elidia's shiny tricolored hair radiated from crown to jaw in one
length. A peak down the middle of her neck matched the peak

in her bangs. This new cut emphasized the upward slant of eyes and cheekbones and made her look more Oriental than Indian.

A two-inch space shaved around Susie's right ear had been tinted a rainbow of blue, green, yellow and pink. Earrings climbed higher up her ear than Anna had remembered. Some of the holes must have been drilled through cartilage.

"Valentine—can you believe it? Of all places. She can't do it, she just can't do it," Susie declared. "Let me tell you something —that woman wants to take over the world. She gets women at their weakest, they're down there looking up at her—they're never on her level, they're always tilted back into the sink, and they know she'll snap off their neck if they make one false move. Then they're trapped under some five-hundred-degree dryer—" She lost interest and twisted around suddenly to search the shop. "Don't you have a radio in here or something? It is *so quiet.* How can you stand it? I don't care, I'm not driving over there every day. She tells me and Elidia we can trade off every week between Valentine and Marfa. She's talking about putting a gas pump behind the shop. Let me tell you something else—she's going after your hospital and nursing home contracts, too. She's told Elidia she can manage that, and what does she give her? Two-fifty a head, regard-less—perm, dye job, cut and and blowout. She's supposed to get the administrator to verify the head count, too. Can you believe it? Like somebody croaks and Elidia props them up and keeps pretending to do their hair."

"Get another job," Anna said. She doodled on the December 25, 1986, entry in one of Mary Frances's old appointment books. FOR SALE filled the eight o'clock space. "Beauty salon, recently remodeled. Needs fixtures" filled the slots from ten to noon.

"Well, what the hell do you think we're doing over here right now? Only you're pulling out—you're playing right into her hands. She wouldn't make a move over in this direction if you were sticking around. I could sure stand a little music. Open the door at least. Maybe a little tune'll float by."

Elidia stood at the middle station. She brushed sawdust off the counter and peered into the Formica as if the pink and turquoise swirls had cleared and the future were being forecasted.

"What does your family think of you quitting Willi's?" Anna asked Elidia.

Susie pounced. "Ha! Willi's got her over a barrel—Grandma's in the hospital. 'Don't you think a professional shampoo and set would do more for your grandmother than all the miracle drugs in the world? Yesss.' "

"What's wrong with your grandmother?" Anna hoped the smell of potatoes fried in lard hadn't left her. She hoped the smell spread into other rooms and made people hungry, made them get out of their hospital beds and go home where they could see and hear the thin-sliced potatoes spitting in oil and smell the onion that was grated into the layers.

"Cataracts." Elidia stared into the mirror. "This is a good station for me. It has a good feel. My cousin Rafael is coming up from Guadalajara to do the operation. It's a trick. My aunt wants him closer to her, so my grandmother gave herself cataracts."

Susie rolled her eyes. "Here we go again. I mean, you see what happens when there's nobody around to snap their fingers in front of her face." She passed a hand along the rainbow over her ear. "What do you think? Elidia did it. She did! We did each other's. Don't sell out. There's no place else I want to work. I'll have to go back to being a telephone operator, and I'll have to start getting stoned first thing every day because I hate it so much—"

"Susie," Anna said, "forget it."

"She's right," Elidia said. "She used to walk around in a cloud." She pulled cuticle scissors out of her purse and quickly snipped a piece of Anna's hair. "It's all spells, Anna. We break this one and give you another one that makes you stay. It doesn't hurt you, it doesn't change you, it changes the forces around you. You can't be responsible for the spells that are worked on you."

For a brief moment it made sense to Anna that there were probably five or six different spells working on everybody. She fingered the chunk of hair Elidia's cutting had created. The possibilities seemed endless. "Make me rich. Make me faithful. Give me the power to go back. Give me the power to save. *Make* me stay." She held out her hand for the hair Elidia had cut. "You don't believe in all that stuff."

Elidia expertly rolled the hair into a tissue end paper and wound up with a thin cigarette. "I don't, but you do. You're one of the most superstitious Anglos I've ever seen."

"Hey—it's worth a shot." Susie shrugged. "Sometimes you have to give yourself over to something else for a little while. So somebody else takes some hair or a toenail and takes control over you for little bit—"

"No!" Anna said. "You *never* give yourself over. *Never.* Not to anybody or anything." She was shaken by the force of her own response. Hadn't she learned anything?

"I told you that would get her going," Susie said.

Elidia wet her fingers and twisted the ends of the cigarette she'd rolled. "We can guarantee we'll bring over thirty-three new regulars a week."

"Give me a bid on the shop then," Anna challenged. "Fifty cents. Anything. Just give me a bid and it's yours."

"No way, José." Susie swatted the air. "I don't want to own a shop. Are you crazy? I don't want to live, drink, and breathe it —I have a life."

Susie's rejection of power angered Anna. Elidia's willingness to trick somebody into giving her power angered her, too. The forces of nature weren't arrayed against them. "Then somebody else gets it," she said. "I'm not going out on the limb."

Georgia and Frank arrived for their Thanksgiving visit on Wednesday afternoon. A smoked turkey dangled from Frank's hand. Georgia looked around for a place to put her sack of groceries. "Can't you call and tell them to turn the gas back on?" she asked. She crowded four wig stands to the back of the kitchen counter and set her grocery sacks down.

"It's the holiday already," Anna pointed out. "There's no sense in having it turned on for a day and then shut back off. I had planned on us eating out."

"Frank won the turkey in the Band Booster raffle," Georgia said. "I guess it should go into the refrigerator."

A shiny brown stain had dried on the refrigerator's white porcelain bottom and there was a fishy smell. Anna wished she had taken out the light bulb and unplugged the refrigerator. "Here. I'll take it. The bottom shelf sits funny."

Relieved of responsibility for the turkey, Georgia opened several drawers. "Now what was I looking for?" she murmured. "I can't think when I'm the company."

"I'll tell you anything you want to know," Anna volunteered. "You won't find out anything in there."

In an effort to help, Frank moved the half-and-half to the refrigerator door and blocked Anna's passage. "You got this bird here somehow," she said. "You should be able to carry it back the same way."

"I've never been overly fond of turkey," Georgia said. Wandering by she absentmindedly tested Anna's forehead with her palm.

"We can drop it off at the Community Center then," Anna suggested. The smell of green onions cleared her nose.

"I thought it might be nice to meet some of your friends," Georgia said. "What's that poor Burgess going to do for Thanksgiving? And that man and his daughter that Mary Frances mentioned—"

Anna almost dropped the turkey. "Mary Frances? When did you talk to her?"

"I can't remember. . . . When was it, Frank?" Georgia asked and disappeared into the other room, out of range.

Frank held the refrigerator door open and watched Anna dock the turkey on the bottom shelf. He shut the door and released his breath. The narrow kitchen gave his stomach no turnaround room. "She called day before last," he said.

Anna looked at Frank and raised her voice to snare Georgia. "Which one called and why?"

"Oh . . . I don't know," Georgia answered. Her voice didn't cover the sound of a box being opened. "You know how Mary Frances is. She loves her telephone."

"I know how you are. Who called who?"

Frank eased himself out of the kitchen backward. "We've been worried about you."

Anna wished that his eyes weren't so big and brown and that

she didn't feel as if she had to defend herself against his concern. To even the balance, she concentrated on Frank's sensitive spot, his receding hairline. "Well, that was nice of Mary Frances, but —as you can see—I'm fine."

"Yes ma'am. Except for those bruises," Frank said. "I won't mention the limp."

"Too bad Ronnie Mauss isn't around to pin it on." Anna raised her voice again. "Where is he this week, Mama?"

"She was wrong about that, and she knows it. I hope you have the sense, and the grace, to accept her apology, when it comes," Frank said.

"Not if she ties it to all that bullshit about the Phantom Mechanic, I won't. That's not what makes me her daughter. I don't buy her version of the past. I can't help it. I'm not taking something just because it's offered. Isn't that the point now? Not that we can do everything but that we get to do what we really want to? She's got to settle in her own mind what she wanted Michael Leandros for."

"I know that's between you two, I know," Frank said. "I love you both. I can't help but want to try to fix things between you."

"You can't," Anna said. "I'm sorry I couldn't take your money. I couldn't accept it to make you feel better. You don't have to try to buy my love. You should have more faith in how I feel about you." Frank had come to her; this apology should have been easier to make than it was.

"That wasn't it, Anna. It wasn't a question of faith with me, it was a question of overflow. I invested in a well, and it came in. I got lucky, I wanted to share my luck. Some of it was pride on my part, true, but I thought helping you get a stake was the perfect way for us both to get what we wanted. You don't always have to say no flat-out."

Anna ruffled her hair and then squeezed the ends tight. "Frank, can't we just leave it that if I need something else from you, I'll ask for it?"

"Except that that doesn't give me any room to operate. Tell you what: I'll keep offering, and you do whatever you have to, and I won't take it so hard."

"And we can blame my stubbornness on Michael Leandros," Anna said.

"He was a wonderful man!" Georgia's voice filtered through Frank's body. "He was a giving—"

Anna shielded her ears. "Please!"

"Georgia," Frank warned, "why are we here?"

"Yoo-hoo, Anna!" Mary Frances's voice rose from the alley. "Yoo-hoo! Am I allowed up?" Her heels began to pierce the wooden steps. "Just for a second, I promise."

Georgia beat Anna to the screen door. Mary Frances smiled bravely at them. "Well! Here we all are—one big, happy family." Her voice caved in on itself. "I've left Alfred," she said dramatically. "I had to do it. I had to—I had to do it for love." She commandeered Georgia's arm. "You understand, don't you? You won't think terribly, horribly, badly of me, will you? You'll still welcome me into the fold for Thanksgiving dinner, won't you?" Her voice dropped to a whisper and she glanced over her shoulder. "You don't mind if I bring along a friend, do you—a gentleman friend?"

———

Mary Frances had made reservations for Thanksgiving at the Yucca Flats dining room. Their table overlooked the swimming pool where Anna and the man who mixed her paint had sat. Anna looked sharply at Mary Frances to see if she knew anything about the color turquoise and the failure to turn it into a paint, but Mary Frances was busy presenting her gentleman friend, Walter.

"Last names aren't important," Mary Frances explained as Georgia and Frank waited for the introduction to end. "Walter says they get in the way."

Frank kept staring at Walter's full head of tar-colored hair. He looked wistfully at Walter's dandruff-free shoulders. Anna tried to telegraph the message to Frank that Walter dyed his hair. She could see Mary Frances sneaking smudged pillowcases into the Laundromat by the marina.

Georgia seemed more restless than usual. Her attention vaporized after a few seconds. Mary Frances and Walter were too wrapped up in each other to notice. Frank's hand held Georgia's down on the white tablecloth as if he could anchor her. Anna felt her mother's energy concentrated on her, losing none of its potency by appearing to drift to every table in the crowded dining room. Frank seemed wary of them both, and Anna didn't blame him.

"Why, look who's here!" Mary Frances said brightly. "I believe it's Ed Nettinger with his lovely daughter." She arched an eyebrow significantly in Georgia's direction and tossed her chopstick-skewered topknot at the Nettinger family.

They stood by the cash register and waited for the hostess. Dressed in his gray suit, Ed stared out the restaurant's front window at the experimental livestock pens across the highway. Anna felt like a rancher who'd just seen the first cloud after a year of drought. She was unprepared for the surge of hope that rose so strongly at the sight of Ed. The intensity of the feeling made the hope seem more like desperation.

Delia searched the dining room and finally spotted Anna and Mary Frances. Without waiting for the hostess, she tugged her father's elbow and squeezed between tables in the shortest route across the room. Ed's path followed the outer periphery of tables. The hostess, waving menus, tried unsuccessfully to flag the Nettingers to their table on the other side of the room. Delia stopped short of Anna's table as she realized that her father wasn't right behind her. Breathless and nervous, she hung back and waited for him.

I could do it now, Anna thought. I could leave her standing there. I could cut her dead and that would be the end of the Nettingers in my life once and for all. She reminded herself that they were finished business. This might be the last time she saw them. She could afford to be polite. Trying to undo some of the damage wouldn't delay her departure any. There was no need to keep killing something that was dead, unless you thought it wasn't dead.

"Delia Nettinger." Anna felt her lips press into a smile.

The acknowledgment set Delia into motion. She flew behind Anna's chair. "Look, Dad, it's Anna! What a coincidence! That's a small town for you." Ed remained on the sidelines. He unclasped his hands and opened one palm in greeting.

For once in her life Georgia seemed honestly confused. Mary Frances compounded the confusion by using her eyebrows to telegraph the situation. Walter must have thought Mary Frances's facial movments were involuntary because he kept trying to smooth the skin at her temples.

Sidestepping a waitress armed with four dinners, Ed almost collided with another waitress loaded with empty salad plates. Out of consideration for the harried women, he walked over to the table.

Anna combined greeting and introduction. "Ed Nettinger. This is my mother, Georgia, and her husband, Frank Gebhardt. Ed supplies catfish to the restaurant, Mama. You might like that better than the turkey." She continued the introductions since Mary Frances seemed content to twinkle silently at Walter and Ed. "This is Mary Frances's friend Walter. Last names don't matter."

"I'm the opposite," Ed said gravely. "I'd get rid of first names if I could."

"A man *would* say that." Mary Frances sighed.

Delia punched Anna's spine. Anna felt a laugh rising in her own throat. She concentrated on the glare coming off the swimming pool. The Nettingers were a bad influence.

Ed bowed toward Mary Frances. "I'll make an exception for you."

Mary Frances's powdered cheeks remained the same color, but she gave the appearance of blushing. "Thank you. But if you do it for me, you certainly have to do it for Anna."

"Certainly," Ed agreed. "In fact, I'm not sure what Anna's last name is."

Georgia focused on a spot above Ed's head. "Leandros is on her birth certificate. I have it with me—"

"Walter's right. Last names don't matter." Anna wanted to cram a cornbread stick down Mary Frances's throat.

Frank buttered a roll and positioned Georgia's fingers around it. Walter scratched his head and then checked his palm for any color runoff. Delia punched Anna's back again. "I think the hostess is about to give away your table," Anna said.

"I'll see you before I go back to Fort Worth, won't I?" Delia asked. "I won't be back till Christmas."

Anna shook her head. "I expect Willi to make a bid on the shop early next week."

Mary Frances gasped. She threw Walter's hand off her shoulder. "You can't! You can't possibly give the shop to her! I have a partnership deal to work out with you. I've left Alfred—don't you understand? Where will I go? What will I do? The shop, of course, it's the only thing. You won't even know I'm there. It'll be like it was before."

Walter nursed his rejected hand. "Hey! What about me?"

"Oh, you," Mary Frances complained. "With Alfred it was houseboats, with you it's motorcycles. My skin just will not hold up to the elements. After fifty-six years—yes, fifty-six—why should it? Anna, you can't be serious!"

"Find another partner then. I'll give you till next Thursday to come up with a bid."

"Jo gave my shop to you," Mary Frances insisted. "You can't—"

"She gave it to me because she knew it would be too much for Burgess to deal with. I've done what she wanted. It's in good shape. They'll more than make their money back."

The hostess appeared beside Ed. "Excuse me," she said. The peach blush on her left cheek was higher than the smear on the right. Mary Frances tapped her own left cheek to alert the hostess to the misalignment.

"Excuse me," the hostess repeated, "but the Nettinger party has to be seated or they lose their table." She swept her arm wide to indicate the way.

"Anna . . ." Delia began.

"Good-bye," Anna said steadfastly. She trained her eyes on Frank's congealed salad.

The hostess dropped her arm abruptly. "Anna? Is your last name Bryant?"

"O'Bryan," Mary Frances corrected.

"It *was* Bryan. Why?" Anna asked.

Walter smiled generously at them all. "See?" He tickled Mary Frances's sagging earlobe. "See, sugar?"

"There was some man calling to see if you were here. He finally said he'd better come out and look for you himself. Actually, you look just like he said you'd look."

"What was his name?" Anna asked. She flashed a look at her mother, but for once Georgia didn't look as if she had anything to hide.

The hostess shielded herself with the tasseled menus. "Who knows? I can barely remember Nettinger, party of two."

"It wasn't me!" Georgia swore. "I haven't talked to Ronnie since he called to see what time his girlfriend left."

"It's true, Anna," Frank said.

Accepting his confirmation, Anna relaxed and looked out the window. A tan Chevrolet, like K. O. Browne, Jr.'s, was parked in front of one of the rooms. The Border Patrol might have a dozen unmarked cars in that same shade. K.O.'s wife and children might be visiting from El Paso for the holidays. She turned back to the dining room to see if the patrolman was seated at a table with his family.

As if Anna had summoned him, the hostess and Ed parted to let K. O. Browne, Jr., through. "Mrs. Bryan? Prepare yourself. The news is bad but not serious."

A roaring started in Anna's ears. "What's happened?"

"Thomas Bryan, Burgess Anderson and Jerry White are in jail—"

"*God* damn it!" Anna threw down her napkin. Bryan in jail was one thing, but Burgess and Jerry shouldn't be with him.

"His lawyer seems to be out of town. I thought you might know someone else."

The emergency telephone number that Bryan had asked her to memorize popped immediately into Anna's head. She couldn't believe how automatic her response was.

"The charges are—"

"Don't!" Anna pushed her chair back. "I don't want to know what the charges are." Of course, K.O. had gone out of his way to find her. His response was probably as automatic as hers was. Bryan had drilled them both. He and Bryan must have reached an understanding after playing cat and mouse with each other for so long.

"I'll drive you to the jail," K.O. offered.

Ed Nettinger steadied the chair Anna had vacated. "That's all right, I'll drive her."

"Wait!" The hostess wailed. "What about Nettinger, party of two?"

"Don't worry," Delia said, sliding into Anna's empty chair. "I'm fine right here."

Burgess and Jerry White were sharing a cell. They had been caught nine miles from the Mexican border, part of a caravan that was hauling illegal aliens who had ridden burros or waded across a shallow part of the Rio Grande. Bryan, in the lead car, had been transporting two Afghan men and one Iranian; a Vietnamese family had been found in the back of a van Burgess had borrowed from the GM lot; and Jerry White's camper had been carrying two men from Poland.

Anna leaned against the heavy steel mesh of a cell door across the narrow hall. "Do you have a phone number for Bevo?" she asked Burgess.

In answer Burgess danced a jig that threw the smell of scotch into the air. Jerry White was sitting on the lower bunk, his elbows welded to his knees, and staring at the gray concrete floor.

"Is there anybody you want me to call?" Anna asked, but Burgess wasn't answering any questions. She hoped his drunken performance was for K. O. Browne, Jr.'s benefit. The thought that Burgess might have taken a drink as a ploy to keep Bryan out of trouble infuriated her.

"And what about you?" she asked Jerry. "Am I supposed to pay you for work you haven't even finished so you can bail yourself out of jail?" Without lifting his elbows from his knees, Jerry managed to shrug. "Have you called anybody?" she asked. He wouldn't answer her either.

"Fine. Sit here then. I'll be at the shop if you change your mind."

"Tell the world, Anna," Burgess said.

She knew he didn't mean for her to spread the word and rally people to their cause; he still wanted her to keep her mouth shut. "I don't have anything to hide. It doesn't matter where I go or what I do." Look where all the secrecy had gotten them. She started to walk down the hall toward Bryan's cell.

"Connie needs to be fed, by five-thirty," Burgess called. "She gets the dry food at night."

"Yeah . . . my dogs, too, okay, Anna?" Jerry added.

"You should have thought of these things before." They should have thought of a lot of things. She wished Bryan had been smuggling guns or drugs, objects that could be confiscated and photographed and stashed in a big warehouse somewhere.

Bryan was at the back of his cell, staring through the window. "What's going to happen to all those people? What was the point of bringing them over if they're going to end up in some detention center?" Anna asked.

Momentarily breaking his study of the yard below, Bryan smiled broadly at her and then resumed the watch. "There go the official Border Patrol cars. The taxis in Guanajuato are that color, green and white, maybe a shade more blue. The mountains, too, ah, those mountains—they remind me of Big Bend. The dry air, the hum. I've seen pink lightning there, too. It's a sight, Anna. I thought once we'd go there."

Anna put her fingers through the grid of thick, flat metal that crisscrossed to form diamonds, but Bryan was out of her reach. She didn't know which she wanted more—to shake him for getting so many people into trouble or to embrace him for trying to help so many people. Her grip on the metal slowed her circulation. The tips of her fingers swelled and turned red as the trapped blood was heated. "Do those people understand any of this? Do they know any English? Do they have any idea what's happening to them? What about Burgess? What about Jerry? And what about you? They're going to send you back."

"Ah, Anna, you care." Bryan continued to stare out the second-story window. He rested one foot on the cot's thin pallet, and it shrank from the metal frame. "Is that your Nettinger down there? I believe it is." He looked over his shoulder at her. "Where there's smoke, there's fire."

"Don't try to change the subject. It's too late to pretend like nothing's going on," Anna countered. "Your bail's been set at thirty-five thousand dollars. Bob James tried to get it reduced, but they won't do it. They're going to transfer you to Pecos tomorrow to arraign you. I can come up with twenty thousand tomorrow morning. I think I can get another five from Frank. I'll go to the bank first thing in the morning and put the shop up for collateral. Burgess has to come up with twenty thousand. I can't even guess where Jerry's going to come up with his twenty thousand. What were you thinking, Bryan? Smuggling illegal aliens? And not even wetbacks. You can't wade across the river with a bunch of people like that and expect them to blend right in. Like you're leading some kind of international tour group. Do you know what you've done?"

"The men from Afghanistan," Bryan said, "two of them have Iranian wives in Houston. One is the sister of the Iranian man. A very pretty woman. Thick, beautiful hair. You'd do anything for a chance to work on that hair."

"Well, wouldn't we make a team? You get the men arrested and I fix the women's hair so they won't feel so bad." Anna's fingers began to go numb from being caught in the grid. Diamond-shaped patterns were etched in her palms. "Why are you doing this? What are you trying to prove?"

Bryan came to the door. "Everybody needs a safe place," he said. "A sanctuary. Your ladies in their plastic capes are searching for a sanctuary. We all need it. Look out there—there's plenty of room. What are you afraid of, the competition? If you work hard and do a good job, why should you be afraid? You're afraid because you've gotten soft. You want everything given to you. You *have* everything given to you, and still, it's not enough. Look at all your leisure time, and you still don't know what to do with yourselves.

"And you, Anna. You're not a refugee. Willfully cutting yourself loose from family and friends and always drawing boundaries and keeping everybody on the other side of the mark do not qualify you for status as a refugee. You have no idea what it's like to have had a home and a family and not to be able to go back. *Ever.* We *are* a community," he said fiercely. "We *are* bound to each other, one to the other. Being locked up does not end my responsibility to everyone."

Anger and shame mixed inside Anna. Bryan's definitions, slanted by a past she had no access to, had never reflected her own view of the world, but there was too much truth in what he had just said. "You're not invincible, Bryan. This door isn't going to spring open because you think what you did is right. You broke the law. There had to be other ways. I think you *like* the danger."

"Don't you think I know why you want to sacrifice your shop for me?" Bryan asked. "I could take your money, and you'd really lose it. You would lose the shop. Do you understand me? You would never be able to come back. I am in a position to sacrifice you. I am in a position to enforce your lack of commitment."

Anna understood. There was the possibility that she would never see Bryan on this side of the border again. The chance that the shop might be taken away again jarred her. "Don't do it. Let Bob James try to get you off. There's bound to be some legal technicality. Maybe they screwed up the arrest."

"It was a K. O. Browne, Jr., arrest. Imagine how many times he's played it in his head. Ah, Anna, the man was pleased. It was his life's best work."

"I can't believe it! I can't believe how you men stick together. You're *pleased* for K.O., that he's done such a good job. Burgess —Burgess is climbing the walls, he's so excited. You've got him drinking again—something not even Jo's death could do. Bryan, how could you? He thinks the sun rises and sets with you. Look what he's done for you and you're going to sacrifice him, too. How can you get him into this and then desert him?"

"It's under control, Anna."

"How can you say that?" She wanted to believe that Bryan's certainty came because he was solidly backed by some kind of organization and not from an overpowering sense of the rightness of his cause. She wanted to know what his boundaries were.

The cot creaked under Bryan's full weight as he lay down. "Everything's being handled."

Anna moved her face close to the door so she could see him more clearly. She was free to go. She was free to sacrifice the shop herself under the guise of helping Bryan's cause. But she didn't want to lose the shop. She didn't want leave. "I'll have the money for you first thing tomorrow morning. I want to stay, Bryan. I want to keep the shop."

A slow smile spread over Bryan's face. "This is the first time you've trusted me with anything." He got up and walked to the door. "Hang on to your shop. The money's been taken care of. I'm a romantic, it's true, but not in this case. Nobody and nothing get sacrificed."

"Except you," Anna said.

"If I do, it's by choice. The only option for what we do is thoughtful self-sacrifice. Let's manage a good-bye kiss, quickly, quickly," Bryan urged. He unleashed his huge, kingly voice. "We shan't let mere bars keep us apart!"

Anna tasted metal. Bryan's lips were warm and his tongue almost liquid against the grid. "Look out for a red-headed cab-driver if you're ever in Guanajuato," he whispered.

———

Ed Nettinger sent a green Day-Glo Frisbee across Jerry White's yard while Anna scooped dry dog food into the Irish setters' two bowls. They had already been to Burgess and Jo's to feed Connie. Excited by the ringing telephone and the prospect of company, the poodle had yapped and raced around Anna's feet, tripping her so she couldn't get to the phone in time.

"With Burgess's history," Anna said, "it's not going to make any difference whether he takes the breath test or not." She could see the tops of Mary Frances's, Frank's, Walter's and Delia's heads in the shop's second-floor windows as they played cards. Georgia's shadow was thrown back and forth across the alley from the shampoo room's windows. Still waiting, Anna thought. Always waiting.

"Better driving under the influence than conspiracy to transport," Ed said. "Burgess and Jerry look pretty well protected. It's Bryan who's out in the cold."

"What about the people they brought over?" she asked. "Why didn't they take them all to the detention center in Marfa?"

"If I follow the reasoning correctly, K.O., Jr., doesn't want to risk a midnight raid on Marfa. He seems to think splitting everybody up is safer. Then, too, the detention center in El Paso might have better facilities for the Vietnamese family," Ed said. "Tomorrow they'll figure out if their paperwork's solid, they all had some kind of visas on them. K.O. didn't seem any too convinced that it was solid. I don't know what then, maybe back to Mexico or wherever they came from if they can't get status as political refugees. I know Bob James got hold of one of the Afghans' wives. She's in law school in Houston."

Anna shook the hose impatiently to hurry the flow of water into the dogs' bowls. "That's handy. Bryan's probably got her there under full scholarship."

"That's a strange trio—your ex-husband, Burgess and Jerry White."

"I don't know about Burgess. I don't know whether he really believes in what Bryan's doing or if it's Bryan he believes in and it doesn't matter what he's involved in." Burgess had definitely been intoxicated, but Anna couldn't swear to the cause. It could be alcohol, a delayed reaction to Jo or the thrill of being pursued.

"Does this change your plans any?" Ed asked. "Now that Bryan might need your support."

Anna had been on the verge of discussing creative financing with Ed. Under Burgess's instructions, Bob James had drawn up a power of attorney in Anna's name. Tomorrow morning she was supposed to go to the bank with it and cash in the CD that held Jo's insurance money, but Anna had other plans. She was going to put the shop up as collateral and borrow the twenty thousand for Burgess's bail. As long as Burgess was locked up, she had him over a barrel. Once he took her money, the shop would be hers.

"It changes them," she answered. "I'm staying. For a lot of reasons. Bryan's part of it, but not in the way you think. You're that part of the reason."

Ed smiled and held her face. She thought he was going to roughhouse her ears like he'd done the dogs.

"What about the shop?" he asked.

"Just don't expect me to give you a discount when you come in." She tugged Ed's shirt sleeves and brought his hands to her shoulders.

"What if I can't come in and I need a house call?"

"Stick around," she said, "and find out."

———

Anna was tired but full of purpose. Her mother was up waiting for her, and whatever they managed to say or not say to each other, her mother was up waiting for her. Georgia listened to the update on Bryan and Burgess, but Anna doubted that she could have repeated a word of it.

Paper rustled in Georgia's dress pocket as she paced the reception area. "That Nettinger man looks like he's old enough to be your father. He's got a daughter, too, almost your own age. Maybe this isn't the time. They seem like they're nice enough people." She went straight-backed into the shampoo room to cut the lights as if to remind Anna how expensive trying to change night into day could be. "Frank says as far as I'm concerned, it never will be a good time—you have to believe that I've tried, Anna—I've tried to do what's best. I've tried to make it up to you." She took Anna's hand. "Tell me the truth, baby, this Nettinger man and his daughter—do you want a built-in family, a father and a sister? Is it all my fault?"

Anna sat down on one of the webbed lawn chairs Frank had bought. She heard his own chair creaking overhead. "Mama, can't you let that man go? You don't want him to come back. You never have. You've got Frank. What would you do if Michael Leandros really came walking in here? What we do has nothing to do with him."

Georgia looked startled. "He's your father," she insisted. "I did want him to come back—I do—for your sake. I keep him alive for you. You *need* a father. I can only give you the half of it."

"And you kept me away from your half as much as you could—"

"Because it didn't seem right to have one without the other—"

"You were ashamed. And nobody ever cared about your shame as much as you wanted them to. Even your own mother got tired of hearing about it." Anna snapped her fingers in an imitation of her grandmother, Margaret. 'Take that scarlet letter off your chest, Georgia. It's always been unbecoming, and lately it's wearing thin.' Remember that? And your daughter's sick of it. Look. Can't we drop him? Please? The man doesn't exist—"

"He did." Georgia pulled a yellowed newspaper clipping out of her pocket. "I meant to tell you a long time ago . . . when it happened. I couldn't. I just—I guess I had gotten into the habit." Draped across her palm, the clipping sent tiny particles of newsprint into the glow of the heat lamp that Georgia had turned on for warmth. "You *do* have family. There *are* others. This is the other half. I was afraid you'd go to them. I was afraid I'd lose you."

Anna handled the clipping carefully. Its pinked edges were crumbling. In all the small towns she and Georgia had lived in, they'd never stayed long enough to establish a place for themselves in any of the newspapers. She had no long-tailed clippings to chronicle her life.

The dateline was May 14, 1965. Michael Leandros had been killed trying to beat a freight train across the railroad tracks. His wife, Jill, and his two daughters, Paula and Sofia, survived him. There was no picture.

"I'm sorry," Anna said.

"Don't be sorry for me," Georgia said. "Don't you understand? You have other family in the world."

Anna touched the names of Michael Leandros and his two daughters. She tried to locate a sense of personal loss. What she found was sorrow for his two surviving daughters. There truly was no connection. "It doesn't matter," she said. "It really doesn't matter. When I was five—maybe when I was ten or even fifteen, but now . . . it doesn't matter—"

"It does!" Georgia insisted. "What about your medical history? What about your genes?"

"What about accidents?" Anna asked and displayed the clipping. "I'll take my chances. Mama, I'm sorry he died. I'm sorry his two daughters don't have him anymore. *They* knew him. He was *their* father. He was a man you slept with once or twice."

Anna caught Georgia's face when she flinched. "You better learn to accept that. I don't know what you see when you look at me. If you can't stand the fact that you wanted him, then what about me? Am I your punishment? I may look like him. I don't know. But I can't help that. That doesn't have a thing to do with me.

"You don't have to like me all the time, Mama. I'm responsible for myself. You can judge me, but you have no right to blame yourself anymore for what I do or don't do. It insults me. It says I have no power over my own life. Give that man all the power you want. Let those two nights cloud your life. I won't. I won't do that for you."

Georgia started crying. "Frank says I'm going to lose you if I don't tell you the truth. I tried to be fair, but I was so afraid. . . . He was a sweet boy—he was—that's the truth. He was a sweet, sweet boy. He would have stayed if he'd known. That's what I was afraid of. I was afraid that he would find out and take you away. I was afraid that my mother was going to take you away from me. I was so ashamed . . . and so proud, too, of you. I was afraid if I gave in to . . . that, with him, what would happen the next time? I built him for you *and* me."

When Anna folded the clipping, the edges of the brittle paper crumpled into fragments. She held it to one of the heat lamp's coils until thin orange and black lines ate the paper.

"There. Now it's just between you and me. Two women who happen to be related to each other. The way it's always really been."

———

Frank and Anna stood in the Purple Sage's back parking lot. Georgia, a slow mover in the morning, was in the cabin packing.

A diamond pinkie ring bought during the flash days of the Anadarko Basin teased the sun as Frank weighed his stomach. "So you think Bryan's going to disappear into Mexico?"

"I thought that at first, but now I think he's traded himself for Burgess and Jerry White. If they deport him, he'll go to Mexico, but they might find a way to put him in prison here."

"Well, keep us posted. Let us know if we can do anything."

Anna nodded. "Did she sleep any last night?"

"Yes, ma'am. Some. She's shook up."

"Do you think she'll let him die?"

"She can't wait to get rid of him. She can't quite see yet that that's not being disloyal to you."

"How do you stand it sometimes, Frank?"

"I've had to put up with a lot from the two of you. Right now you owe me." He pulled a white envelope out of his jacket and balanced it in his palm. "The Cutlass or the dryers. I don't know which you need."

Anna eyed the envelope. She had a full staff. The Formica had been cut and glued into place. Once released, Jerry White could finish renovations in a week. She could walk anywhere she wanted to go. "Dryers." She smiled and let Frank put the envelope in her hand.

She hugged Frank hard before they left. Wearing dark glasses and carrying a box of tissues under one arm, Georgia almost let herself be hugged and then thought better of it.

———

Before going to the bank, Anna called the president's wife, who had been one of her regulars for years. She told the woman what it would take to open the shop.

At the bank Anna deposited Frank's check while she waited for the president to get off the phone with his wife. Accepting the shop as collateral, the president reactivated and approved her loan request for one hundred thousand dollars. The power of attorney was filed with the head bookkeeper, and Anna took possession of the promissory note for eighty thousand dollars that Jo and Burgess had taken out to purchase the shop. While her name was being typed in in place of Jo's, Anna signed for a twenty-thousand-dollar cashier's check. This one was staying dry and getting cashed.

"You have no choice," Anna told Burgess before the hearing. "We're even. The shop's mine."

Burgess rattled the mesh to get Bryan's attention. "Do you hear what this scheming woman did? Do you see her footprints on my stomach?"

A deputy encouraged Bryan to keep walking down the hallway, but Bryan stopped to shake handcuffed fists in play at Anna. "Warden," he shouted, "I said to myself upon meeting this woman, 'There's a woman after my own heart; a woman with more aliases than I'!"

Burgess was still much too excited and Bryan was still acting. It wasn't the time to ask either of them how they were doing and expect a straight answer. Anna left them to their brotherhood and found a seat in the courtroom. She hoped Bryan was right and everything was under control.

The final charges filed were driving while intoxicated for Burgess, misdemeanor possession of marijuana for Jerry, and three felony counts of smuggling illegal aliens filed against Bryan. K. O. Browne, Jr., suggested that their three-vehicle caravan had been a setup; the erratic paths of the vehicles driven by Burgess and Jerry hadn't been the work of either alcohol or drugs.

Bryan pleaded not guilty. "Naturally I picked up those people. Standing in the middle of an American nowhere. Anyone could see they were out of their element. Is it any wonder that they accidentally strayed into Mexico? They hurried out when they saw their mistake." He turned to K. O. Browne, Jr. "You wouldn't pass up a stranger on foot in the desert."

"No. I'd radio for backup," K.O. answered.

Burgess and Jerry were released on bail. Bryan was refused bail. Anna had five minutes with him before he was transported ninety miles to federal court in Pecos.

"I've left a going-away present for you," Bryan said.

"My going away or yours?"

"Ah, Anna, you've made Burgess an offer he can't refuse. You're home free."

He looked as if he were about to burst out of his clothes and through the cinder-block walls. She grabbed the chain that held the pair of handcuffs together. "Bryan. Please. Don't do anything stupid—"

"It's all right, love; it's all right. This is a very civilized undertaking. I'm prepared for this contingency. I know where to find you."

"You won't be able to come back here if you do anything stupid."

"They can't stop me, Anna; I don't believe in their barriers. That's the secret. They cannot stop me from going where I want to go."

Whistles and catcalls from the second floor greeted Bryan as he stepped out of the jail. She turned around at the corner for what might be her last look at him on this side of the border. His departure wasn't like Jo's. She would be able to see him again.

———

Perched on a concrete abutment of the bridge, Anna could see her shop's front door a block away. A woman was hand-lettering the glass. When at last she stepped back and seemed satisfied with her work, Anna went to see what Bryan's gift was. She walked on the creek side of the street to gain the widest angle of approach to the shop.

Black angular letters spelled out "A N N A." That much was all right. The woman painting the sign moved in to touch up a stroke and blocked Anna's view of the second line. A foot from the door she saw that "L · M · N · O" was drawn underneath.

"That second line's not right," Anna said.

The woman, a young Oriental woman, slapped her forehead softly. "Oh, no! No more letters!"

"No," Anna said. "No more letters. Too many letters. Did Bryan pay you to do this?" Hoping all the scorpions and rattlesnakes between Alpine and Pecos or between here and the border got to him, she tapped the glass close to the second line. "Who is this?"

The woman's jaw popped as her smile grew. "You know Mr. Bryan? He gave me the Anna name only. The others came to me." She held her paintbrush in her right hand and with her left directed energy from the sky into the brush's tail. "I lost myself. I was overtaken."

"Where did you come up with this last part?"

"Many places. It's very fortunate. See?" She released a piece of brown paper from a clothespin attached to the mailbox. Strings of letters in various combinations decorated the paper. *L, N, G, R, B, O,* and *M* were strung in a circle like a necklace. "There were many to work with, but we decided these four looked best with this lettering. Here is the *L,* and the *M.*"

The renewal from the state of Texas for Anna's cosmetology license had been delivered. Anna Leandros Mauss was typed clearly on the envelope. She couldn't deny the legality of the name; she couldn't even deny that the names had in some sense been hers, but she didn't know how to explain to the woman what little importance the names now carried. It wasn't necessarily the last name that identified and placed a person; a last name might test the strength of the first.

"And the *N* from—this." The woman handed over an envelope containing sweepstakes information. The computer-generated mailing label was made out to Anna Nauss. "Also, a girl came by and verified—"

"Gray eyes?" Anna asked. "Shaggy hair?"

The woman clapped her hands. "Yes! She knows Mr. Bryan, too!"

"Okay," Anna conceded. She was willing to let the first three letters go. She could see how the thing had snowballed. "What about the *O?* Who fed you that?" She turned the sweepstakes offer over when the woman tapped it. "O'BRYAN" curled and looped across the back of the envelope. "This was another woman? Short with a silly walk and frizzy hair?"

"Yes! You know her, too? This is my most beautiful sign," the woman said. "Will you take my picture? I would like a picture to send to my father in Taiwan. He paints signs there. Much bigger than this. Big, bigger, biggest. He paints the biggest signs."

Sighting through the lens, Anna saw that it *was* a beautiful sign. She liked the look of the letters. Their length and width were pleasing, and their weight. They were letters that could be separated from any meaning.

"One more picture, please," the woman requested, "in case the first one doesn't expose properly."

As Anna was about to snap the shutter, there was movement in the shop behind the young woman. The door opened and Bevo stepped outside. Striking a pose for the camera, he said, "We're waiting, Anna."

"Welcome back," she said and snapped the picture. "Now one of him and me. And then one of me and the door."

Bevo crooked his arm and Anna slid her hand through. "You got Budge bailed out?" he asked.

"How did you find out?"

"I have my sources, Anna. *Somebody's* got to keep track of the man."

She and Bevo were the same height. Their feet, hips and shoulders met as if their bodies had agreed to forgive each other. "You were right about me being mad at Jo," Anna said. "I'm sorry that I ruined her chignon."

"When you ruin something, you do a good job, Anna," Bevo said. "I shouldn't have slapped you, but it was the worst thing I could think of to do to you. I really hated what you were doing. I couldn't take any more of seeing what happened to people's things after they were dead." He took a deep breath and slowly released it.

Nudging Anna's side, he said, "So the least you can do is give me honorary chair privileges when I'm in town."

She nodded and held fast to Bevo's arm. "Guaranteed."

The newly painted door opened. Mary Frances tried to sidle between Anna and Bevo, but they refused to separate. "What is taking you so long? We don't have much time to make a new man out of Jerry! We need to emphasize that gray in his hair! We don't want to cover it up! We need the sympathy of the court. I want you to tell Bevo right now that we're using Silver Dawn and not Mocha Creme on Jerry."

"We want him to look young and impressionable," Bevo said. "I'm not using Silver Dawn on his hair. Do you want him to look like a total degenerate?" He pushed Mary Frances through the doorway and followed her into the shop. *"Besides,* Anna knows I'm the best colorist there is."

Anna shut the front door and stood beside it. She could still hear Mary Frances's voice, and Bevo's and Jerry's. The sound of their voices through the glass gave Anna the strongest sense of belonging she'd ever felt. She smiled, and the woman who had painted the sign snapped the shutter.

"I'm happy to change the sign," the woman offered. She stared wistfully at her work. "My next attempt may surpass this one."

"It's a beautiful door," Anna said. She waved good-bye to the woman and entered the shop. The sun slanted through the door and threw the letters to the floor in black bars. Backward or forward, the ANNA was easy to read. She tried to erase the shadowy L · M · N · O with her foot, but the letters surfaced on her ankle. Their durability pleased Anna. L · M · N · O was as good a last name as any.

ABOUT THE AUTHOR

SARAH GLASSCOCK was born and raised in West
Texas and graduated from the University of Texas
at Austin. Since moving to New York she has
graduated from the New York University Creative
Writing Program and enjoyed a residency at the
MacDowell Colony. Her short stories have appeared in *Descant, Sequoiah,* and *Boulevard,* and
an excerpt from this novel was published in *Southern* magazine. A resident of Brooklyn, Sarah
Glasscock is a tutor in the Brooklyn Public Library
literacy program.